A New Requiem

A New Requiem

B. Lance Jenkins

Published by Tablo

Published in 2019 by Tablo Publishing.

Table of Contents

To my love and the one who always inspires me, Courtney.

To the very best Mom and Dad.

In memory of my friend, Dwight Berry.

PART 1: REQUIEM

1: The Guilty Man Shall Be Judged

Requiem. A mass for the dead. A time of mourning. And a fitting concerto for the days ahead.

The calm before an unprecedented storm neared its end. Little did Ben Bailey know, at this moment, just how near that particular end was. The days of normalcy, validated by this typical night at the local concert hall, were numbered.

The stage lights shone so brightly Ben could hardly see into the audience. He stood there alongside his fellow bass and baritone specialists, and realized that for some reason, he always tended to be positioned at the end of the bass section and directly beside the tenor section. He dreaded it; it proved torture for him. He simply had to belt out what he had learned from memorization, all the while battling the sounds of the tenor vocalists standing next to him who so starkly contrasted his part.

On this night, though, Ben sang his part and did it well. His vocal mentor thought he could read music, but Ben knew *nothing* about reading music. He simply listened to those around him, then caught on almost immediately. He was a quick study and a brilliant mind for sure, but if it were required for him to know how to properly read music to be on stage at that moment, he would instead have graced the audience with his presence as a fellow attendee.

A typical concert hall, there was nothing special about its appearance in comparison to other more prestigious venues in the state, yet it was legendary for this small town of about

9,500 people. The fact that a small, rural Southern town even had a successful concert hall still efficiently running was a testament to the people who cared for and nurtured it. Local community theaters were shutting their doors throughout the region, and other cultural spots like non-profit museums were struggling to stay afloat. This concert hall, though, regularly produced performances highlighting some of the greatest works of the finest classical musicians in history.

This was where the arts were on full display in an area that largely seemed to possess no appreciation for them. From the annex where the local arts council held its monthly art shows, to inside the hallowed walls of the concert hall, this venue was holy ground for the more affluent citizens in the nearby region. Every concert since 1988 had sold out.

The hall defied the odds of the arts having no chance for success in a predominately poorer town. It worked here, and it was because of one thing and one thing only: Dwight Kerry.

Few if any people worked harder for the benefit of this community than Dwight Kerry. Dwight was the face of the arts, and was widely-recognized in the community. A music teacher at the local high school, Dwight could be credited with offering a better raising to many of the community's children than their own parents had afforded them. His care for his students was unmatched. He loved teaching and cherished the opportunity to inspire the next generation, but more than anything, he genuinely wanted every student to be a better person when they left his classroom.

Dwight was an accomplished musician; both as an organist/pianist and a director. He did not belong here. He should have been playing in Carnegie Hall on a regular basis, or teaching music at Saint Olaf's, the academic home of some of the most talented musicians. He was *that* good. Yet, here he was, in the little town of Freeden, North Carolina, playing and directing at the local concert hall that was known statewide as *the house Dwight built*.

He had grown up here and elected to come back after college to care for his then ailing mother. After she died, he'd chosen to stay in the community. He loved the town, but sadly, he found that the majority of its members did not have such feelings toward him.

Dwight was gay. In the words of much of the local citizenry, he was queer as a three-dollar bill. His mannerisms were flamboyant and outlandish, and he wasn't accepted with the town's mostly fundamental, ultra-conservative population.

On this night, he directed the orchestra, that in which he could do just as well as he played the organ or piano. He stood in front of the orchestra and the choir, adorned with heavy eye liner on his eyebrows, combed-back, heavily-sprayed white hair, and a face made up with cosmetics and foundation laid on thick. His face was "pretty", but his attire was deemed by locals as something a straight gentleman would wear. He donned a black suit, a crisp white shirt, and a gold-striped tie, and his coat pocket on the chest was accented with a gold handkerchief. His shirt sleeves were pinned together with gold cufflinks, each engraved with his initials, *DK* – a gift from a longtime friend who once sang in the community chorus but had passed, and in Dwight's mind, gone on to be with the Lord.

Other than his hair and face, he looked like a genuine southern gentleman. But no real man, as the good 'ole boys of Freeden would say, had a face that looked that pretty in this town. His mannerisms rarely mimicked his male counterparts in the town's populous.

The wealthy folk in the one-hundred mile radius dominated

the audience that night, as usual, to hear Dwight's chorus and orchestra perform Mozart's *Requiem*. Ben knew this was not the type of event most of the local folks found an interest in, but the few wealthy ones here adored the opportunity to play the part of possessing some culture when attending these local artsy events. Most of the audience, though, usually consisted of "out-of-towners" who came here specifically for the concerts. People from as far as the Triad, Raleigh-Durham, and even the Hampton Roads area of Virginia came to see Dwight's concerts.

The upper echelon folks from Freeden always approached Dwight after his performances, complimenting him and seemingly taking pride in being a part of the arts community in front of their peers from the city. It frustrated Ben. In his mind, as soon as they returned to the normal routine of life, they etched themselves again in a way of life all too familiar in rural America, where those who are different are simply, and often silently, mocked and ridiculed.

No one around Freeden called Dwight names or treated him differently to his face; that wasn't *the way* here. Southerners like the people in Freeden often criticized "Yankees" for being so direct and inappropriately forward, but in many cases they did the same, *just behind one's back*. No one would approach Dwight at a restaurant and say, "You need to stop teaching because you're gay and a bad influence," but they would surely say it in private conversations with their friends.

There were people genuinely worried about Dwight *because* he was gay. They respected him for his talents and his commitment to the community; nonetheless, he was gay, which meant he was different. And Ben knew how things worked in Freeden. If you were different, you were dangerous and threatening.

Dwight, though, never changed his persona to adapt to anyone and was always the same regardless. Ben often wondered if Dwight was even aware of what was said about him in the community. Ben certainly thought he must, at least, suspect the heat directed toward his sexual identity; even still, Dwight remained true to his individuality and proudly maintained it in a silently critical populous.

Ben, on the other hand, wondered how the hell he did it. Ben was a straight man, but he could not fathom the life of a gay man in a town like Freeden. He had witnessed firsthand the mocking of Dwight behind his back. He recalled a time when he was invited to a local bar for drinks with some male acquaintances of his in the area who he was trying to befriend to fit in more, but he left early because he grew disgusted with the chatter about the man they repeatedly referred to that night as "Dwight the gay."

I wonder how many other fudgepackers like Dwight are in this town?

That gay son-of-a-bitch isn't teaching my kid!

He even recalled being asked, "Hey, do you hang around with that gay?"

Ben worried about what others thought of him, so he only elected to be seen with Dwight in professional settings. Nonetheless, Ben privately considered Dwight to be one of his greatest friends. He was ashamed to publicly admit it, worried that people might think he, too, was gay, and hold contempt against him the same way they did Dwight. As silly as it seemed, Ben's experience with the people in Freeden had warranted his concerns.

Ben was born and raised in the town, and he grew up adoring it. He loved living in a town where you could ride your bike to see your friends, where your parents would let you gallivant around the nearby woods and build forts with your friends and never worry about where you were. As he grew older and moved home after law school, he loved how everyone knew everyone and that they seemed to really appreciate him returning and giving back to the community. He adored the small town feel of walking to your favorite lunch spot and seeing several people you knew along the way. He loved Freeden.

That was, until his experiences forced him to realize it wasn't full of great people like he thought. Sure, there were some exceptions, but as a whole, Ben came to know Freeden's populous as a body of people who promised to follow Jesus on Sunday but threw his teachings out the window during the week. If you were different, you weren't welcome here. Not at the workplace, not at the restaurants, not even at church. Ben believed if you were different and became successful here, it was by your own intuition, or stubbornness – or both.

Ben had made a life in Freeden, but had become the guy Freeden wanted him to be: a good 'ole boy just like the rest of them that fit in here. Once he came to know his hometown as a place full of hypocritical, backward-thinking people, he still allowed it to direct him and the way he lived. And he was silently ashamed of it.

Ben respected Dwight, though, as a man who had found success in Freeden and had done it his own way, without regard to the person everyone else probably wanted him to be. Ben saw Dwight as his own man, and revered him for being that way.

There Dwight stood, as postured as ever, directing the orchestra, which to many in the audience may have looked like an endless waving of arms that made absolutely no sense. The orchestra though, was very in tune with whatever his flailing arms were trying to convey, and from the feedback the audience had given thus far, the performance glistened. Ben stared at his fearless leader and could tell he was proud. The eyebrows rising and that unforgettable smile where his grin stretched from ear to ear was the memorandum of understanding Dwight's chorus needed: he was satisfied.

Dwight had the ability to whip practically anybody with a voice into performing shape and get them to do well under his direction, though he did not want you to think he was a proud man for it. He often said, "A man full of pride is a foolish one." But he, too, was human and struggled not to be overly satisfied with his accomplishments. He knew he was a big fish in a small pond, and he was pleased with what he had been able to achieve over the years.

As Ben saw it, Dwight was disciplined, never too immersed with pride, and he was a beacon of wisdom. He may have been oblivious to the behind-the-back criticism of his sexuality, but he was *fully* aware that everyone was not his friend. He could quickly point out if people in his life were acquaintances or if they were real friends, and had no problem telling others which of those he thought they were in his life, either. A few months ago, Ben recalled Dwight telling him, "Ben, I don't tell many people this...but I consider you to be a true friend. One of my best."

In their short friendship that really took off when Dwight started coaching Ben for the *Requiem* performance, Ben had already realized that Dwight's personality was characterized by bold pointedness, and he was quite simply unaffected by anyone else's thoughts and feelings about his opinions and way of life. He was going to do it his way, period. Even those who criticized and mocked him behind his back respected that.

The music behind *Requiem* was beautiful, but the Latin words were deathly. It was believed that Mozart wrote the piece for his own funeral, and the work remained unfinished at the time of his death. But the piece the choir was set to perform next, perhaps the most famous of all pieces from *Requiem* and often played in movies, television, and other media, was titled "Lacrimosa."

Dwight directed the choir to begin singing:

Lacrimosa dies illa,
Qua resurgent ex favilla,
Judicandus homo reus.

Despite Ben's lack of knowledge on how to properly read music, he had studied *Requiem* leading up to this performance and knew the English translation of the classic piece:

Full of tears will be that day,
When from the ashes shall arise
The guilty man shall be judged.

How ominous this would turn out to be.

2: The Final Curtain

Just two days prior to the concert, Ben told his wife, Rachel, he planned to get a divorce. He and Rachel had been married for six years, and everyone in town thought she was the epitome of a Southern belle, a darling of a wife. How incredibly wrong they were.

She had cheated on Ben on multiple occasions. And he knew it. But for the sake of his reputation (and hers, which he for some reason insisted on caring about) in this small town that cast judgment so freely, he dealt with it and continued to take her back as she pleaded each time for forgiveness. Ben recalled a monologue that, unfortunately, like a number one hit on the radio, had been heard far too many times.

Please, baby, I have changed! I was going through such a dark time and I was confused. I love you more than life itself and I would never want to hurt you. God put us together for a reason and I know you are the one for me. Please baby, I love you with all that I am, Ben Bailey, and I am so sorry I hurt you! I know God can and will bring us back to restoration!

Ben had grown tired of her saying that God was going to do something to restore the marriage when she herself made little to no effort to save it. Ben had come to believe that the only time she cared about 'getting right with the Lord' and 'being a good wife' was when the two of them found themselves on the edge of separation, an occurrence that had happened more than once. And just as soon as he forgave her, she resorted back to those same selfish character traits that had habitually led her to another man's bedroom.

Ben often argued, sarcastically of course, that infidelity seeped into the water around Freeden. It was astounding, how many families broke up due to one or both spouses sleeping around with other people, especially in a community where rumors spread like a highly contagious disease.

Infidelity, which at one point was a part of the underbelly of Freeden, now seemed almost mainstream. This immoral behavior was the subject of gossip all over town, including at 3rd Street Café, the town's most famous eatery, where little old ladies and stay-at-home wives would gather for lunch each day and discuss who had cheated on whom most recently. Ben knew it because he heard it almost every day.

Despite the damning behavior, husbands and wives, who willingly and discretely cheated on each other on Saturday nights, would all go to church on Sundays and pray and fellowship and raise their hands to God, all the while sitting next to other husbands and wives they had slept with the night before. One time, Ben drove out of his driveway and saw his neighbor walking out of his house with the City Parks and Recreation director's wife, whose hair looked like it had been pulled at all night long, and two hours later they were all with their own families, reunited for the eleven a.m. service at Freeden Baptist Church where they, along with Ben and the rest of the congregation, partook in holy communion followed by a covered dish potluck with the entire church family.

Deceit, cover up, infidelity, and dishonesty: this small, intimate town was not lacking any of it. And this proved evident in Ben's own wife. He was thirty-seven going on fifty, and Rachel was thirty-four, yet her behavior could have easily been mistaken for twenty-one. Ben lived a straight edge life. He liked to have fun, but he would often be classified by his friends as a workaholic, and he knew it was true. It had gotten better though. The last time he had discovered that Rachel slept with someone else, he had convinced himself it must be his fault since he worked all the time. She even claimed that his working all the time made her feel unloved, and, as a result, it broke his heart to believe that he was the reason for the marital problems they endured. So he stopped working as much to focus more on the marriage and spending quality time with her, but after two years of this, her same antics persisted.

Drug use, parties, constant flirting with other people, and living what Ben referred to as a *double life* persisted. The married Rachel, who took considerable advantage of the stability Ben provided, did what she wanted, when she wanted, without regard to the marriage or her husband's unmatched faithfulness. And it all led to this moment, when Ben had dealt with all he could take.

By this time, his heart truly was broken; he felt helpless. Nothing he could do would change her ways. He wanted to go to counseling, though she never seemed to be interested until he appeared to be ready to give up. Being taken advantage of was gut-wrenching for Ben, and for said advantage to be taken by someone who he thought had loved him… that was even more agonizing.

Knowing of the multiple previous offenses of unfaithfulness, Ben learned in early 2018 that Rachel was cheating again. Nearly everyone in the town had been aware for some time that she was sleeping with Aaron Carroll, but, as usual, the betrayed husband was the last to get in on the news. Aaron was Freeden's city manager, a transplant from northern Virginia. He had what every college girl wants in a guy: jock persona, big-man-on-campus label, a chiseled body, and a decent career with a good-paying job. In Ben's opinion though, he was dumb as a box of rocks, and he began to assume most of the grown women in this area who admired Aaron were too, considering he was what every *college girl* would want, not what every *grown woman* would want.

Aaron was the type of guy who would have you think he knew everything there was to know that was relevant in life, but the reality lay just under the surface of his flat persona. Ben perceived Aaron to be a guy who thought he was the shit. And Ben was right: Aaron was a prideful man who would never stoop so low as to admit he was wrong. When he and Ben crossed paths at local events, he often dropped the jock, most-important-guy-in-the room facade, as if he recognized Ben was not buying it. He rarely talked to Ben, because truth was, he was intimidated by Ben's success and notoriety in the community. Aaron certainly lived a more involved social life in Freeden than Ben did, but Ben had the respect of the community, and that was something Aaron strongly desired. For this reason, Aaron had little to do with Ben, and Ben certainly did not mind.

When it came to being nice and generous to people, you would not find a seemingly better guy. But over time, that too proved to be a result of another motive: he liked to sleep around and show his much-sought-after body to as many women as possible. He could sleep with any woman he wanted in town, and probably would, regardless of the effect it could have in the way of breaking apart families. He simply bet that he would escape each time without being discovered, and that a simple rendezvous would not do any harm. In his eyes, it was just sex.

Ben longed for a relationship built on decent principles, yet Aaron and other community members' perception of *it's just sex* had become the thought of the times –a misconstrued one that seriously conflicted with what Ben thought sex was really supposed to be. Like most people, Ben perceived sex as something he should enjoy, but he viewed it as something he should make exclusive with someone he loved. He didn't feel that way as much earlier in his adult life, but at this point, it made the most sense to him.

Ben wondered if, perhaps, Aaron viewed sex the way he did because he, like Ben, had never actually made love with someone. Ben had tried to make love with Rachel, but she never seemed interested in cherishing a physical relationship beyond that of friends having sex. She often told Ben she only wanted to fuck, and that she was just not interested in making love with him, implying that she too believed there was a difference. And while Ben desired an exclusive relationship, Rachel often told Ben that she wanted to venture out and fuck around with other people, both together and separately. She was not interested in the intimate, loving marriage Ben so desired, and he held onto the hope there was a difference between *just sex* and *making love*, and that perhaps he would one day encounter *real* love. With Rachel, there was nothing of the sort. And much to his dismay, he knew there never would be.

Whether Rachel had sex or made love with Aaron, Ben knew for a fact she was doing one of the two, and both exemplified unfaithfulness that could destroy a marriage. And regardless of whether they viewed it as making love or just sex, Aaron was sticking his cock inside of her, and she was willingly taking it.

A year had passed since Ben had last suspected that Rachel was sleeping around, and at the time he simply dropped the issue and moved on because he didn't want to believe she would do this again, especially after they had committed to showing more love to one another. Now though, he was fully aware that she was sleeping with Aaron on a regular basis.

Concrete evidence of the extramarital affair surfaced as a result of a local woman named Terri Hathaway, a psychiatrist who attended the University of North Carolina in Chapel Hill and returned home to open her own office and serve a community that had a dire need for mental health development and wellness. She, too, performed as a member of the community chorus. A soprano with an angelic voice, she had been selected to be featured as a soloist in *Requiem*.

Terri always had lunch at the same place as Ben each day, but they rarely spoke other than saying, "Hello" and carrying on a minute or two of small-talk. One day though, about a month prior to *Requiem*, Ben noticed that she kept peering at him across the restaurant. Her face was blanketed with anxiety, and even though Ben knew very little about her other than growing up together as children, what she did for a living, and that she was widely known to be a kind-hearted person, he could tell something was gravely wrong. Soon enough she abandoned her half-eaten BLT, signed her receipt for lunch, and instead of walking to the door and exiting, approached his table.

"Afternoon, Ben."

"Terri." He nodded in acknowledgement of her arrival. "How are you?"

"I'm fine." She nervously looked around, then back at Ben. "Mind if I join you for a minute?"

"No, please do!" Ben grew concerned about the way she looked, even more so now that he could see her close up and the anxiety seemed to be growing. More often than not, Terri was a woman who looked calm and poised, and at this moment, she was neither.

She sat down in the booth across from Ben, peered around the restaurant once more to see who might be listening, and said, "I need to tell you something that has really been bothering me. And…umm," she stuttered, "I am not sure anyone else has told you."

Ben raised an eyebrow, leaned back in his chair, alarmed at her approach and what she might tell him. "Well, to be honest, Terri, I have no idea what you are talking about, so it is a good guess to assume no one else has told me anything."

"I didn't think so."

"Well, what's going on?" he asked.

"Ben, I don't know how to say this but to say it direct and straightforward." She stopped, all the while looking down and avoiding eye contact with Ben.

"Go on," Ben nudged.

She looked up, directly into his eyes. "Your wife is cheating on you with Aaron Carroll."

The blankest, most emotionless stare must have come across Ben's face as he looked into Terri's eyes, a gaze that could have drilled a metaphorical hole through her head.

A man constantly worried about the impression he made on others, it killed him to be told this by someone else other than his wife, and it also hurt to think that if Terri knew about it, that it was very possible a large number of others did as well. What made Rachel's past transgressions easier to deal with was that he did not think the folks around town knew, so when she asked for forgiveness and he granted it, Ben thought the hard part was just between the two of them. If a church-going, good girl like Terri knew about his personal problems, he surely believed they had become ingrained into the heart of Freeden's gossip pipeline, and the old adage of *everybody knew but him* was probably applicable.

He did not want her to know, but his heart was breaking again. He could feel the tears welling up, but he fought hard to keep them away. He had tried so hard to be a better husband and had blamed himself entirely on previous occasions for the marital issues. But now, he knew he had given *everything* he could in the last year to be the best husband he could be, and, despite the agony, he felt comfort in knowing that this time it wasn't his fault. He didn't encourage any of this. Rachel just could not resist living her double life.

"Well," he started as he stared down at the table, avoiding eye contact himself now, "I can admit I was not aware of this."

She continued, "I know this is tough, Ben, but I just could not live with myself knowing that I knew this was happening to you and not telling you what was going on. It just isn't right, and–"

"I know," he interrupted, "I know you mean well, Terri." He then looked up, paused for a moment, renewed eye contact with her, and smiled. "I know your heart is good, and I know you mean well."

"I truly do," she said.

Terri was a respectable woman, a wife who encouraged her family to live morally and honorably, and certainly not someone Ben suspected would ever be unfaithful. She was happily married to an equally respectable farmer, so Ben knew her reason for telling him this was not to get close with him and take advantage of the situation. She was a straight-shooter, and she was being truthful about what she knew.

Ben carried on, seeking more details. "How do you know this?"

She gulped, as if she was nervous to tell him. "I had already heard this about four months ago."

"Jesus, that long?"

"I'm sorry, I should have told you before."

"No, no, I'm not upset with you, just a little surprised that, you know, if in fact it's going on, that I wasn't aware *and* that it was going on that long."

"It's *definitely* going on, Ben."

He stopped. "Okay, well how do you know for sure? I mean rumors get around."

She looked around again, then leaned in to talk softer. "I saw them."

Ben's eyes opened wide, both eyebrows raised. "You saw them?"

"Yes, I saw them."

He whispered, "Where? How?"

About that time, Buck Henson walked in. Buck led the Freeden Planning and Development Department as the senior city planner and was one of Aaron's friends, or goons, as Ben saw it. And like Aaron, Buck was an active participant in the town's social arena.

Buck sped right in, headed to his usual lunch table to wait for Aaron and the other city hall folks who hung together. He surprised Terri when he came up quickly behind her and said, "What's up, guys? Are you working hard today or hardly working?"

Terri smiled and said nothing. She was visibly uncomfortable, especially now that her fear of someone listening in may have, in her mind, become a reality. She was unaware that Buck had been too far away when she last mentioned Aaron's name to have heard anything.

"Always working hard," Ben said in his typical jolly way, carrying on as if nothing was wrong.

"Well, that's good," Buck replied. He sped back up and walked on to his table.

Terri gazed at him to ensure he sat down and was far enough away, then said, "Did he hear me?"

"No," Ben assured her. "I saw him come in, you're good."

"You know how people are around here."

"Yes, I know," Ben said while nodding. "So, where did you find them?"

She looked around once more to assure no one was listening. "Well, I had to go into the church the other night to get my sheet music. I had left it at rehearsal Tuesday night, and, because I am chairperson of the social committee, they gave me a key a while back. Well, it was about eleven-thirty, my husband was home with our baby girl, and I had not worked out all week, so I went to the gym. Got done and realized I did not have my sheet music and figured since I was out and about that I would just go ahead and get it. When I got there, I parked out front on the street, but my key would not work for the front door, so I walked to the back since I knew my key would get me in there as it had before. As I turned the corner to the back, I saw what I thought was Aaron's Denali and Rachel's car parked in the alley behind the church. It is not very lit back there, so at first I thought it was them but I still did not know for sure whose cars they were. Then I got closer to them and it became very apparent that these were definitely their vehicles. So I walked up to the cars, trying to see if anyone was in them and if they were okay. As odd as it may seem to you that at first, I still did not realize what was going on, and when I got about twenty feet away from his Denali, I heard her…" She paused.

"Go on," Ben said.

"Well, it's just…."

"Please, Terri, just tell me," he pleaded.

She breathed heavily. She was ashamed to tell Ben for sure.

Ben was embarrassed, too, but at this point he considered the damage done. Whatever she had seen was engrained in her mind, and she already knew all she would know.

"It's okay," he said. "Please."

She continued, "The street light in the alley was pretty bright. I don't think they saw me, but I assure you that it was definitely them, Ben. What I saw was validation of what I've told you today… I'll just leave it at that."

Ben wondered if he looked shocked enough for her. It hurt to know Rachel was doing this again, but it unfortunately did not come as much of a surprise to him. With the news came humiliation and sadness, but in reality all of that was coupled with a great sense of relief. Ben needed to know this. He knew there was no need for this fledgling marriage to go on if it had no chance anyway. And Ben knew Terri would *never* tell of such a thing if she was not certain it was true. For a moment, worrying about what the townspeople thought of him, for once, ceased. He was sure most people probably knew what was going on already. And as he viewed it, not one person, until now, had stepped up and said anything to him. That was more disheartening than the act itself. He grew up here. He lived and worked here. He knew these people. And no one had said a thing.

Nonetheless, Ben knew his life was about to change, as he would not tolerate living in the same house as an unfaithful woman any longer. He had struggled to love her in the past despite her infidelity but had tried desperately in the last year. To him, she had become too hard to love. For so long he thought he could fix her and the marriage. Continued unfaithfulness, though, proved to be the last straw for him. He had had enough. And so he convinced himself, that day at the 3rd Street Café, that despite his desire for this to work because he believed marriage simply should, he would not tolerate living like this anymore.

The decision to end his marriage, if he made it, would not come without objection or ridicule. Rachel's father, Dr. Dan Henson, was the senior pastor of Freedom Baptist Church and the metaphorical mayor of Freeden. He ran this town. There was no chance Rachel Henson Bailey would be accused of cheating in a public Freeden courtroom, or even the social arenas of the surrounding area. Everybody believed every word Dr. Henson said like it came from God Almighty himself.

He would not allow his daughter to be publicly shamed. Every judge in the county attended Freeden Baptist and so did the district attorney and his assistants; there was no way his political buddies would embarrass him or his family if this was pushed so far as to end up in civil court.

Ben knew that Dr. Henson would never accept that his daughter would do such a thing as be unfaithful, especially after a raising that was often touted by the Henson family as being a Christian one. Ben knew better, well before he ever had the most recent information that she was sleeping around on him. Dr. Henson might never admit it, but his daughter was uncontrollably unfaithful, and a liar, and while all signs pointed to her at least keeping it exclusive with Aaron, Ben believed that if "you'll cheat once, you'll cheat again." Rachel had proven that time and time again.

Ben never thought he was better than anyone, but he *knew* he was too good for this. As much as he had longed for the marriage to work despite strong indicators it never would, she wasn't going to make any *real* effort to give up her unfaithful ways. It was time to cut the cord. He did not need her or her family to make it, and he knew that as much as she enjoyed the lavish lifestyle Ben provided her that she would milk this allegorical cow as long as he allowed it. So in that moment as he walked from the 3rd Street Café back to his office along the faded brick sidewalk that lined Main Street in Freeden, he decided that, no matter the scars his reputation or career might take as he broke apart from Rachel and her well-known family, he was going to end this marriage once and for all. Unhappiness was no longer an option for him. Suddenly, he did not love her anymore, and when Terri told him what happened earlier at lunch, the grim hope of love returning simply vanished. As of this moment, he no longer *wanted* to love her.

Ben believed that love was a choice. Dr. Henson once told him that, and whether he believed his own teaching or not, Ben certainly adopted the outlook on one of the world's most mysterious subjects. He recalled Dr. Henson saying when he asked him for Rachel's hand in marriage: "Ben, love is work, and you make a daily choice whether or not to love someone." A true Christian principle that, while true, came from the mouth of an authentic hypocrite.

Sometimes Rachel would get on Ben's nerves, and he had to *choose* to keep loving her and look past certain things. But they were the small quarrels; things like how she never rinsed the dishes before putting them in the dishwasher, and how she never cleaned around the house or picked up after herself. Those things Ben *chose* to get over; they were trivial. Unfaithfulness, on the other hand, which he had chosen to move past before, would not be subjected to such passive handling now. In Ben's mind, this simply could not continue.

That day after returning to his office after lunch, he started taking notes to build a case in his own mind against Rachel. *Is it just to leave her? Has she done enough wrong?* One of the things he learned in the coming weeks was how much she was "going to the gym." She would return home drenched in sweat, presumably from getting a great Insanity or P90X session in with her fitness group. Only problem was that once he checked with the gym she claimed to be attending to see if they were all paid up for the quarter, they had no record of either Ben or Rachel being members for the previous two years.

Time brings all things to light. A favorite line of Ben's from the 2006 film *All the Kings Men* that proved true when all the lies told over the years finally came raining down on Rachel in one night. It was Tuesday, February 12, and Ben told her he had to leave town for three days for a class. He went to the class on that Wednesday, and after one session they had to cancel the rest of the class due to the instructor's illness preventing him from being able to teach. So on that Wednesday night, he returned to Freeden, unbeknownst to her, and when he drove onto the street they lived on, he noticed Aaron's truck parked in his driveway. Ben pulled over, and turned his truck off, and watched.

Sure enough, Aaron eventually exited his truck and walked to the front door, which opened and quickly closed behind him. Ben turned his truck back on and drove forward, leaving the lights off, and then parked at a diagonal view of the house from the street. He looked through the window at the now well-lit living room, and saw the two embrace, then kiss, until she finally realized the blinds were open and rushed over to shut them.

Neither of them saw Ben, he was certain, but he had seen enough for himself. As much as he had cared for her, Rachel was just too ignorant to realize this town was too small for that type of thing to go unnoticed forever. Or perhaps she thought, with the clout Dr. Henson had, that it just didn't matter and no one would ever believe she did anything wrong.

Whatever she thought, on this night the veil was lifted from her lies.

Ben turned the lights on, then drove to the nearby Hampton Inn and checked in for the night.

The next day, Ben felt ready to divorce his wife. He was sat in his favorite spot at his favorite place, 3rd Street Café, and was mulling over these thoughts as he drank his first caffeinated beverage of the day.

There was no need to go inside of his home the night before when he found her and Aaron. Ben's pride had told him to go in and beat the shit out of Aaron. It was so clear to him now that there could only be one reason Rachel stayed with Ben all this time: the money. He knew it to be the case, and that was the part that *did* actually hurt. To think she, who he had considered not only to be his wife but for the longest time his best friend, was shallow enough to use him for his money was a major blow for Ben. Whom could he trust? When he married Rachel, he just knew she was the one for him. Her kind, gentle personality was all he had ever wanted; she was a sweet soul, someone who, for the first time, granted him the feeling that the stresses of life were usually exaggerated, and that life was to be enjoyed to the fullest. She had once made him feel like his money, or money in general, did not matter, and that she was committed for the long haul to a relationship together no matter the trials they might face; but on that night where he finally caught her in her wrongdoing, he began to see clearer the scars on his soul that had worsened over time. From day one of their marriage, literally the day they married, Rachel changed. And to this point, she too, worsened, caring less about Ben and the marriage and more about herself.

Have I tried everything? He wondered if there was anything left he could do, even though his pride was telling him the marriage needed to end.

Will God be disappointed with me? He couldn't determine if this was God's attempted inspiration or if it was the remnant of another long, deep "talking to" from Dr. Henson, who often felt the need to have these narratives with Ben after Sunday lunches and social gatherings, perhaps because deep down he wondered if his daughter was a snake and he wanted to do all he could to ensure Ben stayed around. The idea that he simply wanted to refrain from embarrassment if the two ever split up proved more probable, though. If there is one thing Ben had learned about Dr. Henson over the years, it was that he cared about self and image more than anything and anyone, and that's probably why he had risen to the top in the Freeden pecking order. Ben whole-heartedly believed that Dr. Henson would care more about his own embarrassment than his daughter's well-being if they separated. Ben wondered if the talk from him, which was sure to come, about how God wanted this marriage to stay together would surely be a disguise focused on one thing: saving face for Dr. Henson. Not for Rachel or for his daughter's marriage. Solely for the benefit of Dr. Henson.

Only a sick son of a bitch would feel this way. How did I not know who I was dealing with? Perhaps it was because Ben finally had begun to realize that people weren't so good in Freeden. For the longest time he was engulfed in trying to raise his status in the community he grew up loving that he wondered if he had just been blinded to who Rachel and her family really were.

Sometimes people force something as long as possible, even when it is not for the best. That is what Ben believed he had done in his marriage. If he wanted true happiness, he knew what he had to do.

Before when Rachel and he nearly separated, she would sob and beg him not to say what she referred to as "the D-word." But he knew it: the "D-word" was now the *only* option. And he hoped he had prepared enough for the ramifications that would ensue in this hateful, judgmental town.

There was a clatter in front of him as the waitress put his plate down on the table. The noise cleared his foggy mind and pulled him from the mist he too often got lost in. "Thank you," he said. "I guess I was in my own little dream-world there."

"Don't worry, dear," she said. "Lord knows everyone else in this town is, too."

She was right, and Ben hated her for it. Today that would end though. He wouldn't succumb to this town and its judgmental ways. It was time to live his life the way he wanted to, and damn anyone who frowned on him for that.

He devoured his scrambled eggs, praising the cook for doing a good job with the most key detail of such a dish. Scrambled eggs were way easier to eat in a hurry. He slammed back the rest of his coffee and headed for the door. His office awaited.

"What the hell happened to you?" Brenda Haley, his administrative assistant, who had worked for him since he opened the firm, noticed he looked significantly less put together than normal.

"Rough night," he replied.

"No kidding. You look like shit."

He continued walking past her desk toward the hall to his office. "Try not to flatter me, darling."

She was always very forward with him, but he liked it and encouraged it. The two playfully picked at each other almost every day, and in many ways he believed it kept them both sane. Ben's team, in general, fostered a good, playful relationship.

Ben sat in his office with the door locked and waited. He thought of how he would say it, how to respond if she went on another emotional tirade where she begged for forgiveness or where she fought hard to persuade him she hadn't done anything wrong. He knew it was coming, and even though he shouldn't have worried one bit about how she responded or felt, somehow he still did. He wanted this to be a moment for her where she realized she needed to change her life around and be a better person. He doubted that would happen, but wanted it badly, not only for her own wellbeing and future but also because he wanted her and her family to move on as soon as possible.

He sat at his desk, deep in thought, and waited for night. Then he returned home.

He walked in the front door, and Rachel was sitting on the couch. The house reeked of pot; she had clearly intended to light incense, but must have grown too tired to light it as it remained unlit on the coffee table with the lighter set right next to it.

She was not expecting him home until the next night, so she had her tablet laying out still with a video of two guys fucking a girl in a gym locker room. She didn't know Ben saw it, as she hurriedly pushed the button to put the tablet to sleep.

"Hey baby," she said. "I didn't expect you home."

"My training ended early," Ben replied as he went to sit on the love seat next to her. "Got home yesterday evening, actually."

She looked confused, and slightly worried. "Yesterday? Why didn't you come home? I wish you would have."

"Rachel, I saw Aaron come into our house last night. I know what's going on."

"Oh," she paused, trying to figure out how to respond to his abruptly calling her out. "Baby, he was just dropping by something I left at the gym. Why would you think–"

"Cut the shit, Rachel. I saw you kiss him, and I've heard a lot worse. No telling what else went down here last night… in my house."

"No, no, no, baby," she said as she began to cry. "Please understand."

"We are getting a divorce, Rachel."

"No, no, no," she said, "he made me do it! I would never choose to hurt you."

"It's finished, Rachel, I can't take this heartache any longer."

"He raped me! I swear he made me let him in!"

He chuckled in a disgusted manner, and got up from his seat. "Oh, please – Rachel, I saw for myself. You've done this before. I'm not putting up with this anymore."

"Baby," she pleaded, "I need you."

"We're finished, Rachel," he said as he walked out of the room.

She sobbed, cried out for him, then literally screamed as loud as she could. "Ben what is the matter!? I want you but you work all the time and don't act like you love me anymore. I feel so unloved and now you're blaming it all on me!"

"Rachel, you are a pathological liar and you're convinced that this must not be your fault. I've done everything I can to help build a stronger marriage. This divorce will be on your hands."

She grabbed him. "Please don't say that word! Daddy won't let that happen."

"Daddy doesn't give a shit about anyone but himself!" Ben shouted. "And your Daddy doesn't have anything to do with me or my choices anymore. And you can tell him I said that when you move back in with him."

Ben started walking to his home office, which was upstairs. It was where he planned to sleep that night. He was halfway up the stairs when she said calmly, "God wants us to be together. He shared this vision with me. I am a better person from within because of us going to church and getting involved in the marriage classes. You've been with me through the dark times. I'm coming out of them! Can't you stand with me now through the good?"

Ben had his back to her the whole time. He just stood there, looking up the stairs and listening. It was symbolic in many ways; he was facing up finally and realizing there was something higher and better than what he had and where he had been in life, but the simple reality was that Rachel was still trying to drag him back down into a pit of unfaithfulness and misery in which she was deeply rooted. In many ways, he felt sorry for her.

"Tomorrow, you will pack your things and go somewhere," Ben said, still refusing to look at her. "And you will not be welcome back in this house. We are done, Rachel."

"No, no, no," she said as she began to cry again. "I don't have anywhere to go."

"Go to your parents'."

"I can't," she said, still whimpering and sobbing. "I don't want to go there... I want to be at home with you, like I should be."

"This is not your home anymore," he said. "This will never be your home again."

She was an emotional wreck. He peeked back, and she had

fallen on the floor. She was propped against the wall and crying hysterically. Emotions always got the best of Ben; he hated to see even his enemies in this type of pitiful display. This time, though, he felt nothing. No remorse and no sympathy. He had given in so many times because he did not want to see her hurt, even when she had pained him. It would go on no longer.

She cried and wailed, now laying in the fetal position. Instead of walking down to comfort her as he always did, he just walked upstairs, never looking back.

3: And Silent He Was

Quia pi-us es!

Translated to: *Thou art merciful*. The last line of *Requiem*.

The audience erupted in applause. Dwight turned to them, bowing to recognize their appreciation for yet another work of art he had just displayed in this rural, cultureless town, all the while embracing the implied notion that he was, in fact, a big fish in this small pond. He then moved over, pointing with his entire hand toward the choir, which drew more applause. Ben stood there, enjoying the moment, but realizing that this six-month preparation process had just culminated with a production that lasted slightly less than one hour. He always dealt with depression once something like this ended.

In college he acted in both stage productions and film, so he stood there recalling the feeling of life slowing down when a project like that ended. For him, it was never a good feeling; he missed the hustle and bustle of going non-stop to achieve a goal, so the thought of summer approaching with nothing to keep him busy except for work proved deflating. And now that Rachel was out of the picture, he expected to have more time on his hands. At least he could finally spend the time focusing on how to make himself happy.

The house lights turned on and the audience began moving to the lobby. An announcement played over the speakers: "Ladies and gentlemen, we thank you for attending tonight's Freeden Community Chorus performance of Wolfgang Amadeus Mozart's *Requiem*. We invite all of you to join us now for a reception in the lobby."

Dwight had already worked his way into the audience, taking compliments that blew his head up like a hot air balloon. He loved every minute of the attention he was getting.

Ben walked to the backstage area to grab his phone and keys from a bench in the dressing room. Dr. Colin Johnson, a fellow bassist and well-respected seventy-two-year-old local doctor who was nearing retirement, approached him. "We did well, I'd say!"

Ben nodded in affirmation while grabbing his things from the bench. "We did indeed."

"You almost sounded like you knew what you were doing," he said.

Ben laughed. "And we all know that's only because you're standing right next to me practically telling me what to do."

"Now, now, give yourself some credit," he said. "You've come a long way since the beginning."

"Again, I have you to thank for the guidance."

He patted Ben on the back. "Hopefully we can do it again in the fall. You were a good addition to our bass section, my friend."

"Well I've always wanted to be a part of the community chorus, just finally made the time for it after Dwight asked me about fifteen times."

He chuckled while he, too, grabbed his belongings. "Well, you better sing with us while you can," he said. "Rumor has it Dwight may be retiring from the school and the community chorus, too."

"What?" Ben asked, surprised. "Dwight didn't tell me, I would have remembered if he had."

"Yes, he's been teaching for thirty years and directing this choir for almost the same amount of time, maybe more. And of course, as you know, he serves as music director and organist at Freeden Baptist. From what I've heard, he plans to give that more attention in the days ahead."

"I had not heard that."

Selfishly, Ben did not want Dwight to retire. They were, of course, friends, but in addition to their companionship, his musical mentorship proved great for Ben and he had extended his range considerably since working with him. But his retirement would be an even bigger loss for this chorus -- and for this town, for that matter. They could surely find someone to fill the role, but it was hard to believe that anyone would give the effort to this thriving yet small, local chorus like Dwight did. He and Ben had bonded quickly once they began working together, but he had not mentioned anything about retiring. He wondered if it were simply a rumor that perhaps sparked about this time every year when the concert was over and summer was approaching.

"You staying for the reception, Dr. Johnson?"

He walked toward the door, and turned back to Ben before exiting. "No, sir, early start tomorrow." He winked. "Take care of yourself."

Most choir members had already left the dressing room to socialize at the reception, so Ben walked to the lobby to join them.

Dwight continued to work the crowd and take in all compliments that attendees sent his way. Ben wanted to talk to him, pay him his own respects for another tremendous production, but all the old ladies in town were so enamored by him that Ben recognized he would simply have to wait. Ben walked closely by him and heard a bit of it. Kathy Thompson, chair of the Freeden Town Beautification Committee, said,

"Dwight, I think you just make 'em sound better every time!"

Julie Patterson, chair of the Freeden Baptist Finance Committee said just after Ms. Thompson spoke, "Well, Kathy, *we* get to hear him every Sunday!"

It amazed Ben how many people loved him for his music and ability, but if the man ran for political office in the local elections, he would be slaughtered. One time over lunch, Ben heard an elderly lady say, "Elton John might be going to hell for being gay, but I still love his music!" Likewise, people just could not get over Dwight's sexuality. He was gay, and that was *different*. It hurt Ben to know how people felt about Dwight, because the little old ladies and others that often paid him compliments for his work at the concert hall and church would be the first to drag him through the mud behind his back.

Ben went over for a glass of wine at the bar, and saw Terri standing there with her husband, Shawn.

"Terri," Ben said, smiling as he approached them.

"Ben!"

He shook her husband's hand. "Shawn, so good to see you."

"And you too," Shawn replied in his subtle, soft-spoken way.

"How's the baby girl?"

Shawn picked her up and held her as she sat on his left arm. "Oh, she's doing good, aren't you, Anslee?"

Anslee chuckled.

"How are you holding up?" Terri asked.

The joy of watching Shawn and his baby girl bond left Ben's face as he pondered over how his marriage had failed and hopes of having a child would have to be delayed, but he still smiled, hopeful that his decision to leave Rachel would still prove to be good for his happiness. And sanity. "I am doing well." Then he leaned in and spoke softly, "We separated a few days ago."

"Oh Ben, I am sorry."

"Don't be," he exclaimed, then nodded in affirmation. "It had to be done, and I am doing okay."

She sighed. "Well, we will be praying for you."

"Yes, yes, I know you will."

Shawn walked away with Anslee in an obligatory manner, understanding that the subject matter was really between Ben and Terri. They both watched them walk away.

Terri restarted. "If there is anything we can do for you, please let me know."

"I will, but seriously… I'll be fine. I'm relieved more than anything."

"I can imagine it's a load off, with all that was going on."

"You are correct." They both shared a laugh.

"Take care of yourself."

"I will. See ya."

Ben began to walk away when he overheard someone say, "Terri!"

"Kate!" Terri replied.

"You did so great tonight."

Ben turned his head as he gradually walked away and noticed a woman, dressed in a classy, semi-formal dress, approaching Terri. They hugged, and then restarted the conversation. Then suddenly, Terri yelled toward him. "Ben!"

He turned back and looked at her, but not for long.

The woman next to Terri was gorgeous. Stunning. His attention was naturally drawn to her.

"Ben, please come meet my friend," Terri said.

Ben stepped back toward Terri and her friend. He had

never believed in love at first sight; in fact, his experience with love had long been so dismal and disappointing that he believed it was the most ridiculous notion. But he felt something at this moment that he could not explain.

"And who is your friend?" Ben asked.

"Ben, this is Kate Gregory, she is the new assistant district attorney and her office is right here in Freeden. We went to Chapel Hill together. She just moved here from Charlotte."

Ben shook her hand, and they made eye contact. "I see. Well, Freeden is quite a different place from Charlotte."

"Yes, you could say, that," she replied, smiling.

"Ben Bailey," he said. "It's nice to meet you, Ms. Gregory."

"Wow," she replied, "you're quite the gentleman to be calling someone your own age Miss anything." The two shared a laugh. "Call me Kate."

"Well, it's nice to meet you, Kate," he said.

Terri jumped in. "Ben is a local attorney. He has his own firm here in Freeden."

"What kind of law do you practice?" Kate asked.

"Criminal law."

"Then we will likely see quite a bit of each other, I would imagine?"

"Perhaps we will. I practice more cases outside the county than here though."

"Wait, didn't you perform tonight too?"

"Yes, he is an extraordinary baritone," said Terri.

"Is that right?" Kate asked.

He chuckled. "I would not say that. But thank you for the compliment, nonetheless."

Kate noticed him, and that excited Ben. He was awed by her beauty and kindness. For once, it did not seem forced or awkward for Ben to encounter small-talk.

"He is very good, don't let him fool you," Terri said.

"A man of many talents," Kate said. "I'm impressed."

Ben smirked. "Well, when you practice criminal law in a small town, you have to do something that'll make people like you."

Kate and Terri both laughed at the comment.

He looked at Kate, wondering if he'd be rejected. *What the hell, go for it.* Then he said, "Perhaps I could show you around town sometime?" Ben thought Kate looked shy suddenly, though she had not looked this way the entire conversation.

"That would be great, Kate," Terri spoke for her. "Ben knows so much about the area. This is his hometown, too."

"Well," Kate said as she smiled, still appearing a bit nervous, "I suppose that would be nice."

Ben could not tell if she felt obligated because Terri had forced the notion on her, or if she truly wanted to, but he really did not care. She had agreed to it. There was something about Kate he instantly admired. Sure, she exemplified beauty and seemed to have a nice, approachable personality, but something about her seemed down-to-earth and genuine. It felt unlike anything he had ever felt before.

"Let's do it soon," Ben said.

"Yes," Kate said, appearing less anxious now. "Let's do that."

Ben, who worried he would not shine in small-talk situations, figured he had better leave while he was ahead. Despite the fact that so many people thought he possessed an incredible ability to talk to anyone and comfort them from the beginning, he did not have the same confidence in himself.

"Well, I'll let you guys go," he said. "Terri, you did an amazing job tonight on your solo. Kate, it was nice to meet you and I'll look forward to seeing you again soon."

"Take care," Terri said genuinely.

"Nice to meet you, too." Kate followed. "Bye."

Kate's smile spoke to Ben. He could not put his finger on it, but there was something very special about her. He hoped to get to know her. She, like Terri, seemed to be a breath of fresh air amid the toxic environment that was Freeden.

As Ben walked away, Dwight peeled from a nearby conversation with out-of-town regulars at the concert hall.

"My good friend, Ben." Dwight exclaimed.

"Did it again, Mr. Kerry." Ben replied.

They hugged. Dwight did his usual kiss on the cheek. Most men in this area were so homophobic that they would not be able to live with themselves if they allowed him to do that, though he never did it to show romantic affection; he simply did that with his friends. Ben was always weirded out a bit by it, mainly because he feared what others might think if they saw it, but he appreciated it as a gesture of kindness from a dear friend.

"Congratulations, Dwight, on another success."

"Well, I am just so glad you finally agreed this time to participate in the chorus. You did great!"

Ben chuckled. "I successfully filled a void, we'll say that."

"Oh please." He laughed. "You've come a long way."

"Yes I have," he acknowledged, "thanks to you."

"Well, you have been just a pleasure to work with."

"Please let me pay you for the private vocal lessons you provided me, Dwight."

He looked around the room to see if anyone had heard the conversation, then he placed his hand on Ben's right arm. "You already paid last week, remember? You wrote me a check for the whole spring season."

Ben looked confused. Then Dwight leaned in and

whispered, "You're not paying me for anything and don't speak about this too loudly. I've got about five old ladies I am charging out the ass for their grandchildren's lessons within twenty feet of us right now."

"Ah, yes," Ben whispered, "my apologies."

Dwight stepped back and started laughing and smirking again. "Shall we continue on Tuesdays in preparation for the next performance?"

"Nice try," Ben said. "I'm not committing to anything quite yet."

"Oh please, you're hooked now. I can tell it."

"We'll see. Seriously though, thank you for mentoring me. I really have gotten a lot out of it."

"I know you have. Everybody gets something out of a lesson with me."

Ben laughed. "Tone it down. I'd hate for you to come off as humble."

"Well, you know me, I'd hate for anybody to notice my work," he said sarcastically.

"Look, you're a great friend, Dwight. Seriously, thank you for everything."

"Jesus, please tone down the emotions here! Let's have a good night. Say, why don't you join me tonight for dinner at David's?"

"Well, it's going to be late probably and–"

"Oh please, you don't have anything to do."

Ben sighed. "Okay, okay but I will not stay too late. And I am not drinking wine with you tonight."

"See you there at nine-thirty."

Dwight immediately walked away as soon as the time and place were set and continued his politicking with the little old ladies and wealthy folk, taking in every compliment he could find. Ben made his way to the exit, and on to David's Restaurant. David's was the only fine dining in Freeden, and Dwight's favorite place in town. He ate there every night except for Monday, and only because David's was closed on Mondays.

Ben arrived at David's around nine-thirty-five. He thought he was late, but Dwight was not there yet. *Go figure.* Dwight was sharp and on-time for serious things, but often in social settings preferred to show up fashionably late. Since they had become friends, Ben had regularly reminded Dwight he could be quite the diva – and Dwight never disagreed.

Finally, about fifteen minutes later, Dwight walked in the front glass door of the restaurant, and everyone in the building heard him talking on his phone as he belted out a recap of the concert to whoever was listening on the other end. Ben was already seated at Dwight's table, the table that was reserved for him by restaurant owner David Ball for his every-night-other-than-Monday dinner. Ben sat in the seat that was usually left open at his table, as he knew better than to sit in Dwight's seat.

Dwight walked to the table and joined him.

"Well, let me let you go, I've carried on long enough and I'm having dinner with a friend," he said. "Why, yes," he paused, "I'm at David's, where else would I be for dinner?" He looked at Ben, smiling. This was one of Dwight's happiest moments. Ben was happy for him. The night belonged to Dwight.

"Okay, yes, take care… okay… bye bye…yes." He put his phone face down on the table. "My goodness, I'm finally here." He looked down at his watch. "And shit, I'm late!"

"Sixteen minutes late to be exact," Ben said.

"Well, damn, what did you expect? You know I've got to

shake hands and kiss babies."

"You did enough of it tonight to last a year."

"Well, you know, I've got to kiss ass long enough for these people to think I like them," he said.

Ben laughed. "Well, you really did a good job."

"Thank you" he said hurriedly, then he raised his right hand, looked toward the bar and said loudly, "David, can I get a glass of that sauvignon blanc I like?"

David crept out of his chair next to the bar without uttering a word, and made his way to the wine shelf to pour Dwight a glass.

"So, did you enjoy it?" Dwight asked. "You know, performing?"

"I did. I really did. Kind of depressing to think it's over."

"For me, it's on to the next one," he said. "I do concerts nearly every other week. It's just another concert to me. Though I will say, this is one of the bigger ones. So, will you be back for the fall chorus?"

"Eh, I believe I will."

"Well, you should be. You did very well and you look like you had fun."

"I did have fun."

"Then you should do it again, no questions asked. Enough about that. That sounds like a commitment to me."

Ben smirked and playfully rolled his eyes back.

"David, make that two glasses, will you?"

"No, no, no, I'm not a huge fan of wine anyway."

"Well, you haven't had *this* sauvignon blanc yet, so you really don't know. And we all know you don't know unless you've tried."

Dwight was the kind of guy that should have been in sales; you could not tell him no. He wouldn't let you turn him down, at least for long.

David brought two glasses to the table. "How'd the concert go?" he asked in his monotone, emotionless voice.

"Well, damn, David, I thought you'd never ask," Dwight said. "Wonderful as always, though you weren't there per usual."

"How am I supposed to have dinner ready for you if I show up at your concert?" he asked.

"Good point. Let's start with some fried cheese please."

Every time Ben had dinner with Dwight, they started with the fried cheese.

"How are you doing, Ben?" Dwight asked. "You just don't look yourself."

"I'm okay."

"Lies, lies, lies! I was not born yesterday. What is going on? We're friends, I know something is up."

"A lot of stress lately."

"And why?"

"Dwight, let's just celebrate."

"I've done enough of that, what is going on with you?"

Ben sighed. "Well, if you insist. I asked Rachel to leave."

"What?"

"Yes. She's having an affair."

"Not surprising."

Ben chuckled. "Why would you say that?"

"There was no connection between you two. I could tell it. Didn't want to disrespect you or your marriage, but I knew you weren't happy."

"Really?"

"Oh God, you had to be dead not to realize it. Look, I've seen how she looks at you. She doesn't gaze at you with wonderment. With stars in her eyes. It just wasn't there."

"Fair observation, but why didn't you tell me you noticed this before?"

"Did I have to?" he asked. "You knew you were miserable. Regardless, I'm glad you are relieved and moving on, if that's what makes you happy. You deserve that."

"I guess I'm worried about the fallout and what people may think of me."

"When will you stop worrying about what other people think and start worrying about what Ben thinks? I mean, damn! You've got a great career and life, why worry so much about what everyone else thinks?"

In all fairness, no one had the right to say that more than Dwight. He could likely guess what people around Freeden *really* thought of him, but it never seemed to faze him.

"You know I'm going to take heat for leaving her," Ben said. "I'm surprised Big Daddy Dan hasn't already led a protest of my decision in the streets of downtown. Her father is a handful."

"Oh, please," Dwight paused to take a sip of wine, "it's none of his damn business."

"Well, I agree – but you work for him."

"Stop right there." He paused to take another sip. "I do not work for Dr. Henson. I don't care if he's the senior pastor, as far as I am concerned we are in different departments. Only thing I work for is the holy mother church of Freeden Baptist and Jesus Christ. And it does not matter what he thinks anyway. It's bad advice to tell you that anything matters more than you doing what makes you happy."

"Well, I appreciate that," Ben said.

Ben took a sip of the wine.

"How is it?" Dwight asked.

"Not a big fan of sauvignon blanc, but probably the best

I've had."

"Of course it is," he replied. "When it comes to wine and wisdom, listen to me. Look, you will find someone who loves you one day. Someone *you* can love."

"I believe so."

"You will," he said. "And perhaps one day you will find a wine you love as well. Listen, let me tell you a story about how I found the one that had stars in his eyes for me."

Ben discretely looked around the restaurant, nervous about who might notice Dwight telling what he expected to be a gay love story. He felt overwhelmed with guilt, though, that he was worried about who might be listening. Dwight was a *real* friend, and despite the overwhelming anti-gay sentiment that persisted in this area, he knew deep down that he should not be ashamed or nervous.

Dwight began. "Twenty years ago, I experienced a one-week rendezvous with a man named Rafael. He was a PhD candidate studying in Madrid, and we met on a cruise I took as a relaxing getaway along the Mediterranean coastline. I was having dinner one night and was seated with Rafael, and immediately thought he was the most gorgeous man I had ever cast my eyes upon. A lucid image of our first meeting with one another remains embedded in my memory; he wore slim-fit green pants with a predominately navy blue shirt, unbuttoned almost to below his mid-chest, with his hair neatly styled in a seemingly modern, gentleman's cut and a hard part. I certainly expected he was gay."

Ben always enjoyed Dwight's stories, and as far as he could tell, no one was listening in, so his anxiety retreated. "Do you consider yourself able to detect that sort of thing – that he was gay?" Ben asked.

"Yes, you could say my 'gaydar' was going off."

Ben burst into laughter. Dwight was not offended; after all, his intention was to make Ben laugh and enjoy the night, too. And this wasn't the first time Dwight had referred to his 'gaydar'.

"Is that right?" Ben asked, still laughing.

"Yes, yes," Dwight said while chuckling himself, "but in all honesty, I didn't want to jump to conclusions about Rafael's identity, so I chose not to do so concerning Rafael despite my preliminary sentiments. I recall our first conversation. He was shy at first, but the more we talked the more I realized just how laid back and enticing he really was. At this point I had never told anyone other than my mother that I was gay, but the longer the night went on, the more I wanted to confess to him my sexuality. I desired so badly to unveil who I really was, to pleasure myself in relief that someone else other than my understanding and loving mother recognized my true sexual identity and accepted me for it."

Ben was in a trance. He'd never thought about such things so deeply.

"So on that week-long cruise in the Mediterranean, my desire to unearth the man I truly am reached a climactic point. While having drinks soon after we met at the bar, I recall explicitly interrupting Rafael mid-conversation and saying, 'I want you.' He gazed at me with the most surprised look on his face. I was frightened at the thought of rejection, most notably because I had just made the boldest move of my life. He left me very little time to fear being denied, though, as I soon found myself in his room making intimate love with a man for the first time."

"Well, the story you just told me sounds more like a glorified one-night stand with a fuck buddy."

"Oh, you're so silly," Dwight said as they laughed together.

"Not hardly, though. I woke up the next morning nestled against Rafael's body, my head on his chest and my left arm draped over him, holding him. It was undoubtedly the single most liberating feeling I had ever experienced, far better than the sexual endeavors of the night before. It felt right to be embraced by a man. It did, in fact, feel natural. And I remember looking up at him as he gazed down at me. We loved one another from that point on."

"Well, I can honestly say I have never had the privilege of meeting a woman and experiencing anything quite like that."

"You just know when someone is right for you, Ben. We spent the next several years, visiting occasionally, each time growing stronger in our relationship. I loved him, and he loved me. We had stars in our eyes for one another. Rachel never had that for you."

"Do you think I had that for her?"

"No. She was a prize, not a lover."

"A prize?"

"Oh please, Ben, you have spent the last ten years worrying about what everyone else thinks of you. The idea of marrying the daughter of the pastor of the holy mother church's very own Dr. Dan Henson and building a reputation here in that kind of power family… that was golden to you once before."

"I would not have married for a prize. That's ridiculous, Dwight."

"Look, I know you're an intellectual and an accomplished attorney, okay? But you've got about as much common sense when it comes to women as this wall behind me."

"Oh, go to hell, Dwight," he said. The comment made Dwight laugh.

"I've had too much to drink tonight, three glasses of wine at the reception and I'm on my second glass here, so I'll just let that little dig slide." Dwight then looked toward the bar and saw David sitting in his chair behind it. "David, when is the fried cheese coming? I mean, damn, we would like to eat today," he said, continuing to laugh and carry on.

"You haven't gotten the fried cheese *yet*?"

"No," Dwight said.

David blew air with disgust, then rose from his chair. Both Ben and Dwight knew what was about to happen. Dwight's remark was made in jest, but David could be an ill-spirited man and was clearly irritated that he had to get up from his chair to whip his staff into shape. He walked to the kitchen door, opened it, and yelled, "Where is the goddamned fried cheese?" Seconds later, the waitress came from the kitchen with the appetizer dish and walked it over to Dwight and Ben.

"I'm so sorry, gentlemen," she said.

Ben felt sorry for her. Dwight shared the sentiment, and he worried that he should not have made the joke and subjected the young lady to David's wrath.

"It's quite all right, don't worry about it at all," Ben said to the server before she turned and walked away.

Ben focused his attention back on Dwight.

Dwight took another sip of wine, then leaned in toward Ben and whispered, "David can be a real asshole."

"You think?"

Dwight started eating the dish.

"Look, I want to know what you meant by what you said?"

"Oh, about Rachel? Yeah, I don't think you really loved her."

"I think I did at one point, some kind of love that is. I surely wasn't 'in love', I'll admit that. But looking back at it... well, the reality is that I think we were just great friends for a while, you know? That was the extent of it. But I don't really believe she ever loved me either. I mean, she claims she did, and still does for that matter, but I… I just don't buy it anymore. Nor will I again."

"So you're really done with Rachel this time?" he asked.

"Don't say that too loud, Dwight," Ben replied. "I don't want people to hear you. Folks are either going to judge me for ditching the daughter of the great Dr. Dan Henson, or they will judge me for putting up with her shit for this long. They'll think poorly of me either way."

Dwight stared at Ben, an expression of disbelief on his face. "Ben, the only reason I'd think poorly of you is if you continued to put up with that shit," he said. "To be a criminal defense attorney, a profession that really is subjected to ridicule merely for defending people who society pre-determines as guilty regardless of whether they are or not – how have you made it this far being so concerned about what people think of you?"

"My entire reputation has hinged on what I have done in this community and the career I have built," he replied sharply, "and if it will be torn down, I want it to be torn down by something I have done, not something I have been a victim of."

"Your reputation is not at risk just because your soon-to-be ex-wife is a slut," he said in that typically bold, Dwight-like way. "Stop worrying about it and started living your life how you want it to be, not how everyone else wants it to be."

Ben knew Dwight was right. Anytime anyone suggested to Ben, in some variation, this same advice, Ben always recognized it as true but ultimately refuted it in favor of his old, worrisome ways.

"Hear you loud and clear," Ben said.

"I do love you, my good friend."

"Yeah, yeah. I reckon I love you, too."

It was a big step for Ben to say that aloud, particularly in a public place, but he truly did love Dwight like a brother. Dwight was a good friend to Ben, and despite his pointedness and honesty, Ben cared for him. The bond, nonetheless, was in Ben's mind tarnished by his unwillingness to be comfortable spending time in the public with a man who identified as gay. He was fine now, but that's because no one he knew was watching.

Ben wondered what kind of friend he could truly be to Dwight if he was so wrapped up in protecting his own image that he was ashamed to spend time with Dwight in public, to be seen with a gay man in public, or to talk about his personal problems with a friend in fear that others would judge him. He knew it was a ridiculous to feel the way he did, but his nearly unblemished image as a professional with few personal problems had built the reputation of all-American guy that he held onto today. He constantly feared losing his reputation and career, which he felt was the only thing he really possessed anymore that held worth.

But like Dwight's cruise ship experience, something felt liberating to Ben about telling this gay man, who was a dear friend, that he loved him. It certainly had nothing to do with Ben's sexuality; he was undeniably a straight man, but the feeling of voicing admiration for a man who regularly received nothing shy of ugly stares and judgement from people who didn't know him proved redemptive. Dwight meant the world to him, and as sharp as he could be, Ben still knew the man truly cared about him.

"You know, I could be home alone right now," Ben said. "But I'm not. Thanks for keeping me busy during this time."

"Keeping you busy? Hell, I figured you were here because

you felt sorry for me."

Ben laughed again.

"Hey, thank you for celebrating with me," Dwight said.

They both enjoyed the fried cheese until it was all gone. Then they shared stories and reflected on each other's past, garnering interest from both sides. Dwight had an incredible curiosity about Ben; he possessed an incredible work ethic, showed focus in everything he did, and was perhaps more driven and ambitious than anyone Dwight had ever met. Dwight admired this about Ben since there were so few people in the area who believed they could make themselves better like Ben did. Ben believed that if he wanted to make more money and have a better career, he would have to earn it and work for it, a trait that so few people in Freeden seemed to share.

Dwight worried about Ben, though. Practically nothing in Ben's personal life ever strayed along a narrow, routine path. His life was constantly in turmoil with spousal infidelity, extended family in and out of jail, parents who had died at an early age, and a sister who had died from a drug overdose after years of abuse. Dwight did not befriend Ben because he felt sorry for him, but he often did, in fact, feel pained for the sorrows he had endured. While he joked about Ben's love and passion for his career, he recognized it was a real situation and that one day Ben would likely regret spending so much time working and not building relationships and friendships with people.

Ben, too, worried about his lack of relationships, though he would often cast it off, only for the same grave concerns of being alone at an old age to resurface later. This, Ben thought, was what Dwight and he had most in common: separated from one another, they were very alone. People admired the both of them for their talents, but for various reasons resented them as people. In Dwight's case, his sexual identity was not welcome in this rural Southern town, and in Ben's case, his financial success, all a result of his established legal career, was viewed with distaste by his local peers who barely made ends meet while watching him enjoy the successes of never worrying about when the next paycheck would come. Ben believed this was why he and Dwight connected, that he and Dwight both *needed* real friendship. In this moment, as he sipped on his sauvignon blanc which he didn't like, Ben realized that Dwight was truly a breath of fresh air in his life.

Ben took another sip of his wine, and suddenly, a loud noise captured his and Dwight's attention at the entrance to the restaurant.

The glass front door swung open as Freeden police officers barged into the dining room as if they were diffusing a hostage situation. The police officers made their way into the building, ten of them, marching toward Dwight and Ben's table. The one in the front, who was Chief Gary McDowell, walked up to their table, his officers behind him. "Dwight Kerry?"

"Yes?" Dwight answered.

"You are under arrest for the rape and murder of Braxton Jones. You have the right to remain silent."

And silent he was.

4: The Gay

"Excuse me?" Dwight sat there with a surprised smile on his face that soon turned to a frown when he realized this was serious. "What the hell are you talking about?"

One officer, whose name neither Ben nor Dwight knew, approached Dwight and pulled him from his seat like a rag doll. Dwight snatched away.

"Do not touch me like that, young man!" he yelled.

"Dwight, we are going to need you to calm down," said Chief McDowell.

"This is ludicrous!" he yelled again. "I haven't done a thing and I don't even know what you are talking about."

Ben, confused, interrupted to advise Dwight in the only way he knew how in situations such as these. "Dwight, stop talking."

"I'm serious. I didn't do anything. This is absurd!"

"Stop talking, Dwight," Ben restated. "Let them do what they have to do, we will figure it out. This has got to be a mistake."

Dwight attempted to calm himself. He blew and blew breaths of air in an attempt to lower his stress level. As one of the area's cultural dignitaries stood there humiliated in front of his peers and fellow guests at the restaurant, he began to practice the art of mindfulness, trying to remain calm in the embarrassing moment of being handcuffed, and arrested, at *his* place. The assurance that Ben recognized what and what not to do in a situation like this certainly helped the matter.

The officer handcuffed Dwight, his arms secured behind him like nothing more than a meth-head, which of course was the usual arrestee in Freeden. Nothing as serious as murder ever happened in this town.

The police began walking Dwight out of the restaurant. Dwight turned his head back toward Ben, and shouted, "I'm going to need your help."

"Yeah," Ben said, slightly above normal tone but not too loud. Ben then looked around the restaurant. People gazed at him. *What the hell has Dwight done? Did he actually do something wrong?* There was no way, but the sad reality was that a local boy was apparently dead.

Braxton Jones, who had, according to the policy, been murdered, was the seventeen-year-old son of Dale and Lucy Jones, a prominent family in the community. Braxton was an academically gifted senior at Freeden High School, and though not very socially involved outside his music circle, was admired by people throughout the community as a young man with a promising future. He was the offspring of his father, for sure; he was set to be the valedictorian of his graduating class, a feat his father had achieved at the same high school back in his senior year.

Dale was an accomplished certified public accountant. In fact, he was *the* certified public accountant in town. *Everyone* used Dale as their CPA. Dale had been here his whole life. Every major operation farmer used him, every businessperson used him; he lacked nothing so far as respectability was concerned.

This would not bode well for Dwight. And even though Ben could not fathom Dwight committing such an awful act, it was apparently a certainty that a boy born in this community was dead, and that evidence against Dwight existed.

To imagine that a young, well-raised boy could be murdered in Freeden was simply unthinkable. Something like this just did not happen here. A fact that was quickly emphasized. As soon as Dwight was dragged out of the restaurant, the scuttlebutt began. Ben got up from his table.

"Can you believe that?" one woman said to her husband.

"I have to call Joanna... Lord, she will never believe what just happened," another woman said. "I always knew that man was up to something."

Ben threw a one-hundred-dollar bill on the table, assuming that would cover the tab and more. He had no desire to stick around to finish dinner or the typical *it's-been-a-pleasure-serving-you* small talk with the server at the end of the meal.

Soon enough David's did not even feel like a restaurant to Ben. Instead, it looked like a church fellowship hall, as people began getting out of their booths and walking away from their tables to others, gossiping about what they had just seen. Folks started getting on their cell phones, calling their friends and neighbors and telling them what had happened. Ben walked to the entrance, still hearing all the loud chatter, and turned back to them. The way they spoke of all this disgusted him. A young boy found dead and a pillar of the community arrested should have *saddened* everyone. Though it did not seem that way. It seemed to Ben as if this all was just a made-for-TV occurrence that presented these higher-end citizens with something meaningful to chat about over their late-night dinner and drinks.

Ben wondered what this might do to him and his reputation. Guilt overcame him again for worrying about this type of thing. He knew he should not care. Dwight was a friend. But a murderer? He just could not come to believe it. He knew Dwight could not have done this. Or could he? He suddenly doubted everything. Ben wondered if, perhaps, like so many others in his life, he did not know Dwight as well as he thought. No matter the case, the police had enough evidence to arrest him. Or enough of something.

Ben turned back toward the door and walked out onto the sidewalk that ran parallel to Main Street, realizing that this would likely shake this town to its core by morning.

Little did he know.

Ben arrived at the Freeden police station, which was just about a half mile down the road from David's. He parked his truck alongside the road, and sat there, waiting for the call. He knew Dwight would reach out to him.

About two hours later, his phone finally rang.

919-537-0911.

He knew the number. It was the police station for sure.

"Hello," he answered.

"Any secret as to why I'd be calling?" Dwight asked. Ben could tell he had been crying.

"I'm going to come in and see you. Do not say a word to them if they question you."

"Ben, I swear to you, I did not do this," he said as the bawling picked up.

"Regardless of if you did anything or not, do not say a word to them. You know how this works."

"I have no idea how this works!"

"Well, we are in the rural South and you know how things work here. You're guilty until proven innocent and you know it."

"But I didn't do it," he yelled, weeping more and more as

the conversation went on.

"I hear you, Dwight, but it doesn't fucking matter, so don't say anything until we are face to face, okay?"

Dwight breathed heavily, trying to reduce his emotional outburst. "Okay," he sighed, "I-I-I… hear you."

"I'm coming inside." Then Ben hung up.

He got out of the truck and walked across the street and into the police station. A woman with the nametag *Pam* was sitting at the front desk, dressed in a pair of jeans and a *Freeden Police 5K* t-shirt from the annual event that took place each March.

"Can I help you?" she asked.

"Here to see Dwight."

She frowned, visibly convicting him in her own mind. "He doesn't get visitors yet."

"Pam, I'm an attorney."

"Well, are you going to be *his* attorney?"

"Yes," he said boldly as he cut her off. Ben worried about his reputation, but in this moment felt a greater sense of duty. He needed to talk to Dwight. He needed to get the facts.

She sighed in a disappointing manner, as if she was surprised Ben would be here to help him. Ben knew what this meant. This was just a small, subtle sign of what was likely to come.

"Just a moment, Mr. Bailey." She got up from her seat and walked out of sight. Ben often harbored sarcastic thoughts about most everything, and rarely conveyed them into words unless around his closest friends. But still he thought, *I bet her lazy ass has not gotten up from that chair all day.*

He immediately felt guilty for thinking this; it was a product of the disdain he had developed over time for many of those in local public service – particularly leadership. Ben had once worked as an assistant district attorney but then left to start his own firm, Bailey and Associates. He had grown aggravated with the politics of the local justice system and government. He found himself to be considerably more entrepreneurial than his colleagues, too, and he wanted to work for himself. In addition, Dr. Henson and Rachel's family, who all were very intertwined in local politics, had added to his frustration by working to influence the local justice system. He had wanted out and bought a building downtown that became the home of his law firm.

So here he was, likely to represent a man who surely would be convicted in the court of public opinion by morning. This case would be different from any Ben had tried before. If in fact Dwight did not do it, it would be the most difficult trial in his career. And a difficult uphill battle to fight.

Ben took a seat in the lobby. It had now been ten minutes or more since Pam had walked to the back. He wondered what would happen to his firm. Dwight was very successful in his career, but Ben knew he did not have the money to pay for a trial attorney. He looked down, sighed, and covered his face with his hands.

He knew his worries were selfish. He did not get in the business to *only* make money and gain notoriety, but he was very worried that this case would ruin his career and firm, at least in Freeden and the surrounding area. If it became public (and he knew it would) that his firm was defending Dwight, he worried that no one would *ever* hire them again. Defending a gay man accused of rape and murder in this town would be career suicide. And it did not matter if Dwight was guilty or not.

Ben had always been worried about the opinions of others regarding his association with a gay man. Now, he could not hide it. The town he had grown up in, if he defended Dwight, would see him standing by this gay man's side. Freeden would exile him just as fast as he could blink when they found out he was defending Dwight Kerry.

"Mr. Bailey?"

Ben looked up and saw a police officer he did not recognize at the door leading to the back. He nodded his head to the officer to affirm that he was the man he was looking for.

"Come with me," the officer said.

Ben picked up his briefcase and followed the deputy through the winding hallway of the cut-up building. The deputy stopped at an old, steel door with padlocks on it. He opened the door to a depressive sight: a dark room barely lit by one fluorescent light bulb, intended to be lit by eight, with Dwight crouched over in a chair, leaning awkwardly on the table in front him. He sobbed uncontrollably.

Ben walked in, and the door shut behind him and locked. Dwight looked up at Ben, lowered his head again, and continued sobbing. It seemed to Ben that Dwight's depressive state was growing even worse, likely because Dwight *knew* no one had ever seen him like this. Ben had no clue how to comfort Dwight. He cared deeply about people, but he just did not do well with helping others cope in times of strife.

He sat down across from Dwight, setting his briefcase on the floor against the table leg. Ben looked up at Dwight and then looked away. Regardless of whether or not he did it, this was miserable to see.

They both sat across from one another, with not one word spoken for nearly ten minutes.

The sobbing stopped, and Dwight just breathed heavily for another two or three minutes. Finally, he spoke.

"I imagine..." he wiped away tears and tried to get himself

together. "I imagine this is sad to watch."

Ben, who had spent the last several minutes simply looking down to avoid the awkwardness of Dwight making eye contact, replied, "It is."

"Well, damn," Dwight wiped away the last of his tears, "try not to be too sensitive."

"You know I'm not too good with stuff like this."

"That's why you became a defense attorney I imagine. Damn near emotionless, I see."

"I have emotions," Ben replied. "I just don't know how to show them sometimes."

"You're risking a lot being in here with me, you know?"

Ben responded, "And what do you mean?"

He wiped at his face, trying to get it back to normal. "You know what I mean."

Ben sighed. "Dwight, I have to set aside our friendship for just a moment and be totally objective, okay?"

Dwight looked down at the floor, chuckled in disgust, and said, "I know what you're going to ask me."

"I have to ask you, Dwight. Did you do it?"

"No."

They both paused. The room was silent.

"Okay, any idea why they think you did?"

"I don't know."

"How did you know Braxton? Surely you knew him."

"Of course I knew him! He was a student of mine."

"What classes?"

"Music. He played the piano for the school choir, too."

"Were you friends?"

Dwight teared up again. "He was one of my best students. An avid learner for sure. Intelligent, quiet, but so loving. He understood how to be loving and kind well beyond his years."

"What else did you know about him?"

"He was a troubled young man. It was tough for him to grow up here."

"What does that mean?"

"He reached out to me once this past semester," he paused, "explained that he was gay and had loved a boy, a fellow classmate, for years, and that he had come out to him and wanted my advice on what to do moving forward."

"Did he tell you all this?"

"Yes, he had no one else to talk to."

"Is it protocol for a teacher to counsel a student in this capacity?"

"He was a student *and* a friend, Ben. I was his mentor. And he had *no one* to talk to. Take it from me, there are not a lot of people around here to talk to talk to about things like that. At least not that I know of."

"Does anyone know about this? That he confessed this to you?"

"No, I never told anyone! I have always believed it was up to an individual as to when they elected to 'come out' to the public. This was not my decision to make, and I would never have told anyone this."

"Would he have told anyone that he spoke to you?"

"I don't know," he paused, "I cannot tell you for sure if that happened or not."

"When he confessed this to you, what did you say?"

"I told him the same thing I've told other students who have come out to me."

"And that is?"

"That they may be judged just for being different and that they had to come to terms with whether or not that was okay with them. That it's a constant struggle in a town like this, but that I have found happiness in being my true self, and that they can too."

"Is such authorization given anywhere?"

"Not particularly, but–"

"Do you see, though, how this might not work well for you?" Ben asked.

Dwight grew defensive. "Ben, I have never been one to do only what I was *authorized* to do. I believe in doing what is best for the students as learners and as young people trying to find a way in this often cruel world." His voice was rising. "I mean, damn!" He leaned back in his seat and shouted. "What would you have expected me to do?"

"I am not saying what you did is wrong, Dwight. Truth be told, what you said… it's the right thing to say, okay? But this is not going to help you here. Let's just hope no one knows about this."

"And if they do?" he asked.

Ben sighed again. "Dwight," he started, "you're a gay man in the fucking Bible belt of America." He paused again, leaned forward, and continued, "And you have just been accused of raping and murdering a boy who no one else likely knew was gay. Now I don't know all the facts yet, and you can bet your bottom dollar I will find them out, but your sexuality alone is going to hurt you. When the story hits tomorrow morning's paper that the legendary chorus director Dwight Kerry has been arrested for the rape and murder of a local boy whose parents happen to be elites in this area, you will be glad your ass is in jail, because you likely won't want to see the reaction from all this."

"And how do you think you'll fare out there, defending the community faggot?" Dwight asked.

Ben looked bewildered. He was surprised he asked the

question the way he did. Ben was *very worried* about how this would work out for him. He was, however, embarrassed to admit it.

"I don't know," he said. "I really don't know."

The room fell silent. Dwight needed Ben's help, but he worried about putting Ben in this situation. "Ben, if you can't do this, I understand. It will likely ruin you and your career."

For a brief moment, it satisfied Ben to hear Dwight recognize the impact this would have on his life and career. But in that same instant, Ben had *never* felt so ashamed. Here was a man whose life was on the line for something he claimed, determinedly, he did not do. And this was the same man who had befriended Ben and been someone to turn to during all his personal strife, and now all Ben could do was think about himself. He was ashamed.

Dwight interrupted Ben's deep thought. "Seriously, Ben, I understand. Just please, I beg you... put me in contact with someone who can save me. I swear to you, Ben, I had nothing to do with this."

Ben realized what he had to do. Dwight was perhaps the most unorthodox teacher that had ever taught – certainly in Freeden. He always went above and beyond the call of duty; in many cases, he had become the only father-figure some of the local children had in their lives. And while it was not ideal to counsel students in the ultra-sensitive climate of the modern day, particularly on issues of sexuality, he knew Dwight did it only because he wanted what was best for his students. And it was time show Dwight the same kind of love he showed so many others.

"Dwight, you have always been good to me. And to so many others."

"Well, thank you, but–"

"Let me finish," Ben interrupted. Dwight's eyes widened. Ben continued, "When this God-awful town and its backward, selfish people brought me down, you always found a way to bring me up. And as simple as I can put it: when I was struggling with my marriage, you found a way to bring me up from my lowest points and keep me going. I owe you, and I am going to help you. But not because I owe you. I'm going to do it because I believe you."

"Thank you, Ben. That means so much to me. I want you to know upfront I don't have much saved and–"

"Your money is no good with me."

Dwight began to tear up again. "Oh my… you can't be serious."

"I am."

"Ben, I cannot thank you enough." Dwight rose from his seat, and walked over to give Ben a hug. He stayed seated, and Dwight wrapped his arms around him and held on as if Ben was his only hope.

Then Ben rose from his seat, and wrapped his arms around Dwight. Once the two finally dropped the embrace, Ben stood about two feet from Dwight, looked him directly in the eyes, and said, "Now, it only gets tougher from here."

Ben still worried how this would look, but knew this was the right thing to do. If Dwight truly did not do it, he deserved Ben's help. No one else here would defend him, other than a public defender who was forced to, and Ben knew it. And with the public defenders they had in this area and the influence the wrong people had over them, Ben believed Dwight had just as well tie his own noose.

Ben patted Dwight on the back and picked up his briefcase to leave. Dwight walked over to his chair and leaned against it with his arms straight and his hands grasping the back of it firmly. Ben knocked and the officer immediately opened the door, joined by five other officers standing outside the door. Next to them stood the *Freeden Tribune* editor Preston Hall, a representative from the local television station, and three reporters from newspapers in the surrounding area, all decked out in their company attire, their necks adorned with lanyards featuring their press badges. Ben did not believe the press was usually allowed in this part of the police department, but, sure enough, all of them were present, waiting for anything newsworthy that might come their way.

Dwight could not see the reporters from where he was standing, nor could they see him. Ben looked at them, hesitant to walk out for concern of what they may ask him. He had committed to defending Dwight, but he suddenly felt unready for the stigma that would accompany his defending an accused murderer. *This* accused murderer.

When Ben took a step forward, Dwight yelled, "Before you go, tell me you truly believe me, Ben."

Ben had his back to Dwight, and once Dwight asked the question, he stood there in front of the officers, four of whom he knew personally, and the media representatives, realizing he had to say something.

He turned back to Dwight who now sat alone in the dark room. A man who had built his entire career in this community would, as Ben expected, now be shunned by it because of an accusation that would label him guilty no matter what. Ben realized that if he was going to truly give everything in defending Dwight, it had to start now.

Ben turned his head back to Dwight, cameras and recorders now rolling from the reporters, and said to Dwight, "I most certainly do."

One officer walked forward, shut the door, and the

reporters flocked around Ben like vultures on a piece of road kill. Ben avoided them, and continued to walk as they came after him down the hall and ultimately out of the building. The reporters followed him right up to his truck, yelling questions, and he hopped in, locked the door, and drove off, answering none of them.

As he drove home in the early hours of the morning, he realized that life would never be the same again. For Ben, the days of taking a stroll down the sidewalk to 3rd Street Cafe for lunch were likely over. Drinks at David's were a thing of the past. He feared that he would no longer be welcomed here in Freeden.

Ben had once really loved his hometown, but with the realization that the town was full of people who could not move past old practices and discriminatory ways of life, he knew by morning that Freeden would have already convicted Dwight in the court of public opinion. Dwight was the only openly gay man in Freeden, and Ben believed that most people in town would likely think he was the only person sick enough to do something like this.

He knew the townspeople. He knew Freeden. And he knew they would think the only person who would do something like this was "a gay."

Freeden would believe it was Dwight.

Dwight the gay.

PART 2: DIES IRAE

5: Day of Wrath

Day of wrath
That day will dissolve the Earth in ashes.

The sun rose just as it always had. Saturday mornings were Ben's favorite. Usually.

He woke up after only a few hours of sleep. Ready and dressed in no more than fifteen minutes, he grabbed his briefcase and headed out the door of his empty house. He needed breakfast before a busy day. He drove to his office, then walked to 3rd Street Café on his usual stroll there for a weekend brunch. On Saturday mornings, no one was ever out unless they were at 3rd Street Café, and this morning proved no exception.

A few cars passed by Ben as he walked along the sidewalk, but they came in spurts and usually one at a time. Some of those who drove by stuck their hand out the window to wave at him, which in the South was almost a more obligatory act than anything else. He didn't feel like anyone recognized him; they just waved as if they were indebted as genuine Southerners to do so.

Morning birds chirped in harmony on the cool late spring morning that welcomed comfortable temperatures, bringing a peace over Ben that he feared he might not enjoy for long.

Ben walked in the front door of 3rd Street Café to a packed eatery. Outside, Freeden looked like a ghost town. Inside, the café emulated Wall Street. There was a seat at the lunch counter, though, and that's where Ben went.

"Coffee?" the server asked as he ran around behind the counter, scrambled and disoriented due to piling responsibilities from waiting tables at a traditionally short-staffed venue.

"Black, please," Ben replied.

The place was loud, but Ben could hear the conversation the three men next to him at the counter were having, and it was clear that they had heard about Dwight.

"They say they found him at the school early yesterday evening," one said.

"Do they know who did it?"

"That Dwight Kerry, teacher over there at the school."

"Isn't he a gay?"

"Yes, sir."

"I'll be damned, that's what you get for letting queers teach the school children."

The third of them took a sip of his coffee. "They ought to let a firing squad shoot him dead at the front of the school building."

"No, no that would be too quick – what they ought to do is have somebody do him the same way he did Dale's boy."

"The faggot would like that too much," the other said.

"It's a damn shame our police can't walk into the jailhouse and torture and kill that son of a bitch. What has our world come to, letting these freaks walk around, rapin' and killin'? What has it come to?"

Indeed, Ben wondered, *what has the world come to? What has Freeden come to? It's a damn shame. How has this place I loved turned into such a hateful, scummy place? Why are people out here letting hearsay rule their opinions before even considering the development of their own?* The way he viewed it, the town had become a judgement-spouting megaphone, and hate had its finger on the operating button.

About that time, Aaron walked in.

"What you say, Johnny?" he said to one of them as he walked over, standing behind the three men.

"Me and the boys just talking about what happened last night."

"Can you believe that?" he replied. "It's all over the paper this morning."

"Waiter!" Johnny shouted playfully at the server working the counter. "Why ain't y'all got the paper yet this morning?"

"They haven't delivered it."

"Well, you just wait until you see it," Aaron said. Then he looked over and noticed Ben. "I'll be, there he is right there."

Ben looked forward and did not even glance at Aaron. He was not eager to engage in conversation.

"He who?" one of them next to Johnny asked.

"Ben Bailey," Aaron said as he pointed at Ben. "Do y'all know this man?"

Ben hung his head down, trying to remain calm. He knew Aaron was up to no good.

"I'm afraid I do not," Johnny said.

"'Fraid not," one said.

"Looks familiar," the other said.

"Oh yeah?" Aaron paused, and started walking toward Ben. "Looks familiar, you say?"

Ben now stared directly ahead at the mirror across from the counter. He saw Aaron walking toward him.

"He does look a bit familiar," Johnny said.

"Oh I'm sure you've seen him in here," Aaron continued. "But when that paper gets here, you'll recognize him there, too. He's on the front page of it today." Aaron was about six feet away, continuing to walk slowly toward Ben. "This man is the Ben Bailey in today's headline, you see." He finally arrived and stood right next to Ben. Ben continued to look forward. "He's Dwight Kerry's attorney."

"The queer we were just talking about?"

Aaron leaned over and whispered in Ben's ear. "You're fucking done here."

Then he backed away from Ben – slowly.

"This boy right here is defending that faggot?" one asked.

"Oh yes," Aaron replied, "and he's from here, too!"

"Momma didn't raise you real well did she?" Johnny said.

"It's amazing what money will get people to do," the other said. "Damn shame."

"Money has nothing to do with it, and you don't know what you're talking about," Ben finally spoke.

"If you can sleep at night knowing you're defending that murderer – fine!" Johnny said. "But you'll have to answer to the good Lord for this."

"Hey, Bob, this man over here is that Dwight Kerry's attorney," one of them said as he pointed to Ben.

Bob was the owner of 3rd Street Café, and he usually only showed up for breakfast and was gone by ten a.m. each day. Since Ben rarely graced 3rd Street Café with his presence on weekday mornings, Bob did not know how much of a lunch regular he was. It likely would not have mattered in this moment, though, as an angry Bob got up from the table he was sitting at with friends and walked over to the counter.

"Are you kidding me?" Bob asked as he made his way over. Capturing the attention of all restaurant guests, he yelled, "Dale's a friend of mine!"

The restaurant suddenly grew quiet as Bob, an overweight and irritable staple of Freeden, towered over a seated Ben at the lunch counter.

"Dale's a good guy, and I know this is a terrible situation," Ben said.

"Terrible situation?" he yelled. "His boy is dead!"

"I am aware of that, and–"

"If you're defending that fag, you're not welcomed here."

"Bob, please… with all due respect I'm a regular and I live here and–"

"I don't care who you are and where you live," he said. "You're not welcomed at my restaurant."

Ben sighed, staring into Bob's eyes. "What happened to Dale's boy is awful, I understand and sympathize with that–"

"I don't think you understand a damn thing!" Bob yelled. "Get out of my restaurant!"

Ben recognized that the situation was not going to improve and wanted to be sensitive to emotions, but still felt incredibly wronged by this. He looked around the restaurant, and *everyone* was looking at him. Some of them may not have even known what was going on, but it was obvious he was being kicked out of the place. He looked over at Aaron, who had retreated to a corner booth and was shamelessly grinning. As Ben saw it, Aaron stirred the pot, and knew how to do it well. *No wonder that wife fucker fits in so well here.*

Ben nodded to affirm that he was leaving. The place was silent. He walked over to the cashier at the far end of the counter.

"I need to pay," he said to the cashier.

"We don't need that blood money," Bob yelled. "I'm not taking money from someone who profits from defending murderers and rapists!"

Ben turned his head in astonishment. This kept getting worse. People were starting to chatter.

"What's going on?" one woman asked her husband.

"Is that Ben Bailey? The man who is defending Dwight?" another woman asked.

"You should have heard what he did to Dr. Henson's daughter," another woman said to her husband. "He's a bastard of a man."

"I heard Dwight killed a kid," another man said at a table of men.

The place was full of chatter and gossip, even before Ben had the chance to get out the door. Ben knew gossip was embedded in the heart of this town, and the majority of those sitting in 3rd Street Café relished in the opportunity to indulge themselves.

Ben walked away from the counter, and as he walked toward the door, the place grew silent once more.

Ben was nearly at the door when Bob said, "And don't come back ever again."

Ben kept walking.

"Keep eating folks, all is good here," Bob shouted as the door closed behind Ben.

Ben left the building and started walking to his office. His heart was racing at what had just happened, only two miles from his old home-place. This was his hometown, and he had just been kicked out of the most famous place to eat in the tri-county area.

Word had gotten out that he was defending Dwight, and his suspicions about how the town would react were already coming true. The most worrisome thing was that, as a whole, the majority of the town likely still didn't know he was going to defend Dwight. And the response so far was already ugly.

He reminded himself as he walked away from the restaurant that he committed the previous night to doing the right thing for Dwight no matter what, and while there was still much to be done to determine Dwight's innocence, it was not the time to sentence him just yet. Although, the court of public opinion seemed to already be voting in favor of a conviction. And from the sound of the 3rd Street Café patron's rhetoric, an execution.

As he walked along the sidewalk back toward his office, a truck pulled up next to him, driving in parking area that ran parallel between the street and the sidewalk. It was Aaron. He rolled his window down.

"You know you're done here, right?" he asked as he continued to drive slowly forward to keep up with Ben.

"Please," Ben replied, "I have no reason to talk to you."

"And Rachel wanted to leave anyway you know?"

Ben kept walking. "Well, that makes two of us that are happier then, doesn't it?"

"There is no way you'll be able to stay here after all this."

"Wouldn't you be pleased?"

"Oh I would. I want you gone."

"Yeah, dick measuring with me never really worked well for you, did it?"

"Got jokes, huh?"

"Aaron, I do not have time for this."

"I just want you to remember that your wife sucked my big fat cock more in the last week alone than she ever did yours."

Ben sped up the walking. "Aaron, I don't have time for this. Go to hell."

"Oh buddy, that's where you're going when they get done with you here."

He drove off. Ben stopped once he sped off in his big Chevrolet Silverado 2500. *When they get done with me here? What does that mean*? Were Aaron and the good ole boys he hung with going to try to hurt him? He did not know what to expect after this chaotic morning.

He kept walking and finally got back to the office, went inside, and locked the door. He picked up his cell phone and scrolled through his contacts.

BRENDA HALEY.

He clicked her name and it began to ring.

She picked up. "Is it true?"

"Yes ma'am."

"Jesus, Ben, you know this ain't good?"

"I know."

"Why didn't you call us? Like usual?"

"There's nothing usual about this. It was late. I knew it could wait until morning."

"It's all over the front page of the *Freeden Tribune*. Have you seen it?"

"Not yet, but I've heard about it in a, let's say, contentious environment at 3rd Street this morning."

"You gotta see it. It isn't good for us."

"I need you and the team down here as soon as possible. Bring it with you please."

"I'll call around."

"Be safe."

"Yes sir."

Brenda knew when not to be funny and keep it together. And she was the best employee Ben had ever hired. She would always do what he asked, so long as it was right and ethical. And Ben could always count on her to do what was best for the firm.

An hour later, most of the team had arrived.

Brenda walked into Ben's office. "We're ready."

"Yeah? Everybody here?"

She shook her head. "Negative."

"Who isn't?"

"Kelly and Dana."

"Hmm," he replied, "what was their reason?"

She stood there with her clipboard, reading her notes. "Well, Kelly's husband wouldn't let her."

"Was he scared for her or embarrassed?"

"If I had to guess, I'd say embarrassed. The way she sounded implied her husband would have fit in with the crowd you saw at 3rd Street this morning," she said, as she dropped the Saturday morning *Freeden Tribune* on his desk.

"Figures." He looked at the paper. He unfolded it and shook out the wrinkles so it would stand tall as he read it. "And Dana?"

"Yeah, you'll need to let her go after this one I'm afraid."

"What now?"

"She said she, and I quote, wouldn't be a part of this money-driven team if we were going to stand for this faggot."

"Well, she won't have to I guess," Ben said as he stood up. "Meet you in the conference room in five minutes."

Ben read the article, and then moved on the meeting in the conference room.

All five other members of his team were there: Ken Hughes, the in-house private investigator, Liz Webster and Kristen Growe, the two attorneys Ben had hired with the firm, and Tracey Daughtry and Deb Matics, his two paralegals.

Ben walked into the room. "Thank you all for coming, particularly under these circumstances."

No one said a word. Ben sat down, took his reading glasses off, placed his hand on his forehead, and propped himself up on his elbow. "Everyone knows what has happened here," Ben started. "And I want to thank you for still being here. We have two team members that you likely won't see again."

"Where are they?" Kristen asked.

"Not coming back I'm afraid," Ben replied. "Look, I appreciate all of you being here. You don't have to be, I get that." He sighed, and leaned back in his chair, now resting his arms on the rests. "We have got work to do."

"Are we intending to enter a not-guilty plea?" Liz asked.

"Yes, unless something has drastically changed since last night when I met with Dwight, we will enter a not-guilty plea."

"Did he do it, Ben? Do you think he did it?" Ken asked.

"No, I do not believe he did it," Ben said.

"You know I'm good friends with Dale?" Ken asked. "We play golf together from time to time."

"Look, I get it if you don't want to do this, Ken. I know this is hitting home pretty hard."

"Yeah, it is," Ken said. "But listen here, I have worked with you for how long now?"

Ben grinned. "A long time. We've had some good years."

"Exactly. If you tell me you think the man is not guilty, I believe you, and that's where I'll start."

"Thank you for the vote of confidence, Ken. I do appreciate it."

"But let me tell you this," he quickly spoke again, "I want justice for Dale and his family. And I'm going to make damn sure I do my part to sort through the facts."

"We are going to need you in order for us to do that," Ben said. "I need all of you. But that's why we are here, and that's what we need to talk about."

Everyone was paying close attention to what Ben had to

say. "I need all of you to realize that this is going to alter your life, potentially forever. You saw the paper this morning, right? Kelly and Dana aren't here because they are ashamed to be associated with this. And there are a large number of people in town, I'm sure, that won't look favorably at any of us for defending Dwight. Your peers, friends, family... they *will* associate you with this case. This case is going to get attention, and you'll be right in the middle of it. And so will I. But I need you to know all that before we go into this, because I don't need anyone backing out mid-stream. I know we haven't tried cases like this before. The risk of public criticism has never been so great, and I expect it to be personal, too. Freeden will be at the heart of a case that is in the spotlight, and you're going to be smack dab in the middle of it."

He leaned forward, arms rested on the table. "So, if you're going to back out, or you don't want to be a part of this, I need to know today. You don't have to tell me in this meeting, but I need to know today. Because when we enter a not-guilty plea at the arraignment, it's going to get even crazier. Can I count on all of you to be on board?"

The team members looked around, moving their eyes from person to person to see what the others would say. Finally, Deb spoke up.

"Ben, I have always trusted you. And yes, I know it is going to tear this town apart. But if you believe the man is innocent, then I do, too. And no matter what, it isn't right to send that man to jail, not if he didn't do it."

"Ben, I'm with you," Tracey said. "I owe you. You saved my family during our darkest financial strife. Let us stay in your rental house for two years rent free when we didn't have the money." She stopped and looked around at the others. "You all know this happened. I'm not telling you anything you don't already know. So yeah, I'm here with you. Until the end. You've always been good to me, and I trust you."

"Thank you guys," Ben replied. "Thank you… this means a lot."

"Let me ask this, Ben," Kristen said. "I'm grateful for the opportunity you gave me, too, but let's be reasonable here, okay? You are very good friends with Dwight and we all know that. How can we be so sure that your friendship isn't clouding your judgement?"

He leaned back again. "Well, that's a good question, Kristen. Truth be told, I have no proof that the man is innocent. But I've been doing this a while," he paused, "and I know a guilty man when I see him. We have to research, fact-check, and trust me, we will, and if what we find is damning evidence against Dwight then we need to advise him to plead guilty, or change his plea if by that point we have already entered a not-guilty plea. But like I said, I know a guilty man when I see him. And the man I saw last night at the jail," he paused again, shaking his head, "that man did not look guilty."

"That's a very emotional remark," Kristen said. "I'd be careful of your emotions getting in the way."

"I know, and frankly, you're right," he replied. "But sometimes, going with your gut is best."

"I'm trusting you," Kristen said, still appearing to be skeptical, "you know I am. But I'm not sure I agree that going with your gut is best in our profession."

"Just promise me this, Kristen," he said. "Give him the benefit of the doubt until we know otherwise. I'm not sold on anything yet, either, I'm just telling you what I know and how I feel."

"Fair enough," Kristen said. "You know I'll do everything I can regardless.

"I understand if you need time to think about whether or not you want to continue to be a part of this team moving forward," Ben said. "Please let me know by the end of today."

"I'm in," Ken said.

"Me too," Liz replied.

"Me as well," Deb followed.

"And me," said Tracey.

"You know I'm in," Kristen added in her usual monotone manner.

Ben looked at Brenda. "And you?"

"Sure, what the hell. They don't like me around here anyway."

He smirked. "Okay, well we have work to do. I plan to touch base with Dwight today, and meet him tomorrow to get the entire story. Brenda, I need you, Deb, and Tracey to man the office and begin gathering the police report and documents that are already available. Get in touch with the district attorney's office and get what they already have in place, too. We're working around the clock until this is done."

"Are we safe?" Liz asked abruptly.

The place fell silent again, and all eyes turned to Ben. After a long pause, Ben said, "I think we are, but do be aware that this case will trigger emotions of all kind, and that these are tense times."

"Reason I ask," she said as she looked down at her Samsung phone, "is that my husband just texted me and told me to turn on the news."

Brenda got out of her chair to turn on the television that was mounted on the wall at the far side of the conference room. "What channel?"

"Texting him now." She waited for seconds, and already had a reply. "He said…WYTG twenty-five Freeden News."

She switched it to WYTG. Most of the team was surprised it had hit television news already, but Ben wasn't. He had seen the reporters at the jail the previous night. Now they were broadcasting live from in front of city hall in downtown Freeden.

"Dwight Kerry stands accused of first-degree murder and statutory rape of seventeen-year-old Braxton Jones, a local boy who was a long-time student of Kerry's in his music and choir classes. There is already a considerable amount of anger in the community. We spoke to several community members earlier today at the local landmark eatery, 3rd Street Café."

The picture cut to an earlier recording. "Death row at a minimum," said a local interviewee.

Another standing beside her added, "He deserves to die, sooner than later."

The live feed returned and the reporter continued, "Now the arraignment is coming up this week and it remains to be seen whether or not Kerry will plead guilty. Local firm Bailey and Associates is leading the defense, and the community is not taking too kindly to one if its own, Ben Bailey, defending Kerry for such a heinous crime."

"If ole' Ben Bailey and his team can feel good about it, then that's on them," another interviewee said. "But they will answer for it, I assure you of that."

The team looked around at each other.

"Answer for it?" Liz asked.

"Yeah, I heard that," Ben replied. Then he stood up, placed his hands on the table, leaned against it, and looked up at the team. "Be safe folks. When you come here, you lock the door. When you go home, you lock the door. Take all necessary precautions. Please."

"Can we pray? As a team?" Deb asked.

Ben didn't feel like praying. Thinking of God made him think of one person: Dr. Dan Henson, a man he knew would be a major problem moving forward. He knew Dr. Henson would lead the movement; if people got out to protest against Dwight and his defense, it would be because Dr. Henson rallied the troops. In the last year, when Ben thought of God, he thought of Dr. Henson, and he didn't like how awful it made him feel.

Sympathetic, though only halfway willing, Ben replied, "Sure, Deb. Let's pray."

They all bowed their heads. Ben looked around the room at his staff, all of whom seemed to be taking the prayer a lot more serious than he. He bowed his head, and silently prayed for about thirty seconds.

Lord, I know you're good. I know deep down you're not Dan Henson. But it's so hard for me to turn your way when all I see is him. Grant me freedom from this, oh Lord. Please. I need you to show me you are different than him and the people here.

Suddenly, all Ben could think of was the second piece from *Requiem,* entitled "Kyrie." After praying to himself, he felt compelled to share the translation aloud.

"Lord have mercy, Christ have mercy, Lord have mercy."

6: Rex Tremendae, King of Tremendous Majesty

Dwight sat alone in his jail cell, wondering how he had never had so much time to think. Life had always been busy for Dwight, yet now he had so little to do it brought on a persistent headache he could not shake. He gazed up at the ceiling, leaned back in his chair with his arms crossed, tapping his right foot on the floor, wishing he could experience once more the feeling he enjoyed the night of the *Requiem*. He was quite certain, no matter the outcome of his current predicament, that he would never enjoy that sensation again.

He had never minded being alone, though now it felt miserable. Some of his most enjoyable moments over the years had been spent alone, preparing for his concerts and practicing in his study at the concert hall. Still peering toward the ceiling of his cell, he recalled staying late one Wednesday night after church choir rehearsals, reviewing a piece the community chorus was having a difficult time with in preparation for the *Requiem*. He began to sing:

Rex tremendae majestatis,
Qui salvandos savas gratis,
Salve me, fons pietatis.

The English translation:

King of tremendous majesty,

who freely saves those worthy ones
save us, oh source of mercy.

To Ben, Sunday mornings always looked different than any other day of the week. The same sun shone every day, but something about dawn always looked different on Sundays.

Ben contemplated not going to church. Given the incident he had dealt with the day before at 3rd Street Café, it was a safe bet that more of the same would follow. *I shouldn't show my face anywhere right now.* The thought was simple enough, but he realized living in his house and office, stowed away for the rest of his life, would also not work. If he was going to continue to live in Freeden, he knew it was best to face the music head-on.

He believed Dwight was innocent, but the mounting concerns of being exiled from his hometown still bothered him. He knew nothing else; Freeden was his life. Perhaps, had he not returned to Freeden after college, his life would have been noticeably different, and potentially better. This though… this was his life now, and knew he had to make the best of it. But after the previous morning's events, he could not fathom recovering from the embarrassment.

Ben sat, drinking his coffee in the sunroom of his custom home, and wondered if he should go. He checked the church website; it said Dr. and Mrs. Henson would be out of town this Sunday and there would be a guest speaker. *Perfect.* For some reason, he knew he needed to go, and while he didn't feel a call to go and receive the Lord's guidance, he did want to see firsthand how the church was responding to all of this. He already assumed how Dr. Henson would respond, but perhaps the church would take a stand this time for letting this play out and not turn against Dwight. If the church-people were going to be like the rest of Freeden, he wanted to see it for himself.

A coward, he thought, would avoid going to church because of what he may face. He was not sure if that something telling him to go was God, or his own mind fooling him, but he was immersed with a feeling that inclined him to go regardless.

One thing would surely be missing: Dwight Kerry. For the first time in decades, Dwight would not be present at a Sunday morning worship service for Freeden Baptist Church. *How would the congregation react?* He longed to know. *Perhaps the church will see this differently than the greater community.* He held church folks to a high standard, and sought validation that the church-people at Freeden Baptist would be different than what he'd encountered at 3rd Street.

But *these* people were followers of Dr. Dan Henson, and that concerned him tremendously. A pastor who, when he spoke, was listened to and obeyed, regardless of whether he was right or wrong. Ben had seen firsthand, over time, Dr. Henson as a man who ran this town, who directed his minions to do anything he told them to do. One way or another, he had a power that was unmatched in this town. His parents did not have the same weight in the community, though. They had both passed on in 1990, and while Dr. Henson was born in poverty, he had risen through the ranks of the community and had become perhaps the wealthiest and most prominent, respected man in town. He made the family name of Henson one of the biggest pillars of the community. And Ben recognized that it made him tremendously proud.

Christians are not supposed to engulf themselves with pride, and while Dr. Henson often preached on that message,

Ben knew better than to think Dan Henson was not a proud man. Dr. Henson believed he was better than others, and Ben had seen proof of this on many occasions. On several Sunday lunches where friends and family were invited to the Henson home, Ben had sat and listened to him and his guests talk about the way some of the poorer members of the congregation dressed when they came to church and how unfitting it was, and how some people in the community, for whatever reason they came up with during each of these gossip sessions, didn't belong at Freeden Baptist Church.

He often preached about the evils of gossip and how a true follower of Christ should leave the room in silent opposition when their peers gossiped, yet, he was the one leading the gossip train on Sunday afternoons when the upper-echelon church folk came over for afternoon tea.

This was the same man who claimed to represent God Almighty himself. A man who, on the day the birth of Jesus is celebrated, invited his sister and his niece to their home for Christmas dinner, only to shout at them and force them to leave after being there for a mere three minutes because his niece brought her lesbian girlfriend along with her into his *Christian home*. This was the man who metaphorically led this town and possessed a base of followers concerningly large in numbers. And Ben worried that his followers were blind to his ways.

Nonetheless, Ben still wanted to believe that his hometown had some good in it, and if he could not find it at the church, perhaps that would be all he'd need to know. If the town's increasing evil had somehow spread into the Lord's house, allowing premature judgements and allegations to be passed from lip to lip, then Ben hoped to see the smoke of a fast-approaching hellfire.

He dressed, readied himself, and left for the church.

The sky was more radiant now somehow, as if it was calling on Ben, urging him not to give up hope. The sun's rays beamed down on the towering church steeple, as if God expected his people to be the beacon the town needed. The parking lot looked fuller than usual. Ben walked to the front door, and bolted for the balcony stairs, hoping not to be seen.

He took his seat in the back pew of the upstairs balcony, and some people who could not find seating in the bottom level of the sanctuary joined him. He didn't know any of them well, and thought they likely did not know him. The folks in the balcony were not forced to sit there, but were the type of people Dr. Henson referred to as the common folk. No well-known, highly regarded families sat in the balcony. Dr. Henson ensured those people had seats in the pews downstairs that were practically reserved, and while there was no literal assigned seating, people understood that you did not sit where the regulars sat. If you did (and Ben had seen it firsthand) it would afford you scorn, hard stares, and an uncomfortable atmosphere.

The organ, usually played by Dwight for the ten minutes prior to the start of the eleven o'clock service, was not played at all. People chatted loudly in the church, so much so that it was deafening. Finally, the church tower bell rang.

People took their seats. The congregation grew quieter.

Complete silence took over. No talking. No organ. No choir. Nothing but silence. The side door next to the piano opened, and much to Ben's surprise, Dr. Dan Henson entered. Tall, lean, and dressed prominently in a suit and bow tie, covered with his black robe and adorned with a purple and gold stole, he walked directly to the pulpit.

No one said a word. All eyes were on their leader. Ben suddenly did not want to be there. The awkwardness of seeing his father-in-law after leaving Rachel was not something he wanted to experience, and this was exactly that. Plus, his vision of the church withholding judgement against Dwight until legal proceedings played out was much less likely now that Dr. Henson was present.

In his commanding, deep voice that was unique to a person as imposing as he was, he spoke: "King of tremendous majesty, who freely saves those worthy ones... save us, oh source of mercy, from the wrath you will bestow on those who do not truly know you as the Lord God Almighty!"

The congregation remained silent.

"Today is a different day at Freeden Baptist Church. Something is missing." He walked away from the podium, pacing along the stage. "The first thing that is missing is a boy. A young man who was very active in the church, he was a part of the youth group and youth missions, was the son of a great Christian family in Dale and Lucy Jones, also prominent members of our church, and he has now gone on to be with the Lord. Yet his family, they question many things now I am sure." He turned back in the other direction, staying on stage. "'My God, my God why have you forsaken me?' The verse from Psalms 22:1 that Jesus repeated on the cross is the very thing Dale said to me when I met with the family early yesterday morning at their home. I reminded him of another passage from the book of Revelation. 'He will wipe away every tear from their eyes, and death shall be no more, neither shall there be mourning, nor crying, nor pain anymore, for the former things have passed away.'"

The congregation stayed attentive.

"We cannot harbor anger with God for the world's

transgressions. This is not of God, this act was a horrible, sinful act from the world and of the world! A world that is torn and broken more and more each day by people, as they go on living their lives without the regular and everlasting presence of Christ who loves us."

Ben sat and listened. He knew Dr. Henson, and he knew much worse was coming.

"But for our church, we haven't just lost young Braxton. We've lost quite a bit in these last few days. Someone who our church revered with high regard has betrayed you, the church, and subsequently, he's betrayed Jesus Christ."

He continued to slowly pace on the pulpit platform. "Ideally, we would have already lined someone up today to play the organ. Have someone direct the choir. Show the church and the community that we won't skip a beat." He looked down, arms behind him, still pacing. "Yes, that is what most churches would do. That is the decision most pastors would make." He looked back up at the congregation. "But not I. No… I want you to see what it looks like when there is a gaping hole in the body of Christ." He pointed his finger at the congregation, moving his hand up and down. "I want you to see what it looks like when a man who claimed to be such a follower of Jesus's teachings abandons the body of Christ for self-interest. It leaves a hole in God's heart. In the church. One that often remains for some time. Yes, Dwight Kerry thought so much of himself that he was more willing to satisfy his own sinful and evil pleasures than to continue his *supposed* calling to nurture the body of Christ through music and song." He paused. "Dwight Kerry has served us well, especially on this Sunday. He has reminded us how ugly it is when we turn our backs on God Almighty."

Ben leaned back in the pew and rolled his eyes. He was not

surprised at Dr. Henson's monologue, just disappointed at the number of people nodding their heads in affirmation. This was bullshit. He suspected it all along, but he just could not understand how people *already* believed Dwight was undoubtedly guilty. Nothing proved it yet, and already they had turned their backs on him.

Dr. Henson nodded slowly. "But hasn't Dwight always reminded us of what it looks like to defy God? We all know Dwight practiced homosexuality for years. He was, and clearly still is, a troubled sexual deviant who took advantage of his stature and murdered and raped a child when he couldn't get what he wanted from the boy. We truly may never know all the sinful acts he committed, right here in the confines of our church, or on the grounds of the school he taught in!" He paused again. "Just like the drug addict, the sex addict often wants to take things a step further; see how much they can get away with. And that's exactly what he did, which led to this heinous crime of committing an abomination and ultimately taking the life of Dale Jones's son, Braxton. A young man who was taken way too soon. But we can be proud of Braxton. He's a young Christian man, raised by a Christian family, who loved the Lord and took a stand against evil in his final act, fighting valiantly when Dwight assaulted him."

He stepped back to the podium in his pulpit. "Dwight Kerry will get justice when the wrath of God rains down on him and he is sentenced to an eternity of fire in hell. But he'll get justice on this Earth, too." He sighed. "My heart goes out to the friends and family of Braxton, as they try to cope during this terrible time. May they know that their church family supports them, that we love them, and that we are here for them." A final pause commenced. "Will you bow your heads with me as we pray?"

The congregation bowed their heads. Ben couldn't stop looking at Dr. Henson. As a man of God, he should have delivered a much different message. He knew Dr. Henson never liked Dwight, anyway; he was as radically fundamental as they came and had long opposed Dwight's service as music director at Freeden Baptist. He never let it be known in the public, but in conversations Ben had overheard in the past, Dr. Henson had made it very clear that he wished Dwight would resign and leave. This was his opportunity to forever stain the legacy of Dwight Kerry, and he was taking a full swing at it.

Ben thought for sure that with such a damning message, the choir members who knew Dwight might speak up. People who knew the real Dwight and worked with him every week knew him better, and he thought they would at least speak up and err on the side of caution that, possibly, a terrible mistake had been made in his arrest. No dissent came. No one said a word. They just listened to what Dr. Henson had to say, and nodded as if they agreed. Ben felt an obligation to stop this madness, but considered that it would likely not be in the best interest of his client or the case to speak about the matter openly – and emotionally. Even so, he wanted to say something badly. This was wrong.

"Heavenly Father," Dr. Henson started praying, "we are not worthy to serve you. God of mercy and grace, forgive us for our sins. King of tremendous majesty, who freely saves those worthy ones, save me, source of mercy, save me, source of mercy! For you are God Almighty, the only one who can save us from eternal damnation. Show us your way. Teach us to be your servants, oh holy one."

Ben kept staring at him, and suddenly, Dr. Henson opened his eyes and looked Ben straight in his eyes. He was about forty feet away, but Ben did not doubt, in the least bit, that Dr.

Henson was staring directly at him.

He continued to pray aloud as the two stared at one another. "Father, I know there are people here today that are lost. They are in a storm like they've never been before." He paused, continuing to stare straight into Ben's eyes. "And they have no idea what life is about to throw their way." He paused again, then slowly said, "No idea."

Ben felt his heart racing. Clearly Dr. Henson's message was intended for him.

With his eyes wide open and still staring at Ben, Dr. Henson continued, "Lord, be with them. Show them that they are wrong to think their way is just. Show them, oh Lord, that they are making a grave mistake. And Lord, we know that for our sins, we shall pay dearly."

Ben started to get up to walk out, but fought the urge and remained seated. Enough was enough – he wasn't going to sit here and listen to this anymore. Was Dr. Henson threatening him? At the very least, he was clearly using his platform and God's house to target him.

"Guide us, oh Lord, to repentance," he said, as he reached his hand out toward Ben, "and our sins will be forgiven." He meant no good will toward Ben, and that was clear in the wicked smile he revealed as he stood there looking directly at him. "Amen."

The congregation followed. "Amen."

Dr. Henson took a seat in the plush, royalty-like chair behind the podium. Julie Patterson, a longtime member, deacon, and chair of the Freeden Baptist Finance Committee who had praised Dwight to his face just two nights before for his masterpiece choral rendition of *Requiem*, stood up from her front row pew. She walked to the podium with her New International Version Bible in hand, and approached the microphone.

"Today's New Testament reading comes from 2 Corinthians 11:12-15. Listen now to the word of God as I read. 'And I will keep on doing what I am doing in order to cut the ground from under those who want an opportunity to be considered equal with us in the things they boast about. For such people are false apostles, deceitful workers, masquerading as apostles of Christ. And no wonder, for Satan himself masquerades as an angel of light. It is not surprising, then, if his servants also masquerade as servants of righteousness. Their end will be what their actions deserve.'" She took her glasses off, set them on the podium, and looked up at the congregation.

"Dwight was not the man we thought he was. He masqueraded as a servant of righteousness for years, every Sunday, right here in God's house." She began to tear up. "What he did to that boy, to my friend Lucy's son," she paused and cried harder, "is unspeakable."

She held her hand to her forehead to cover her face, and Dr. Henson stood up and walked over, putting his arm around her to comfort her. Members of the congregation were now sobbing in a sad and unfortunate display. It was heartbreaking for Ben to see people hurt like this, but it bothered him immensely that in their sadness they had deemed Dwight as automatically guilty. It was unfair.

Dr. Henson looked up at her and nodded. She continued, "Ashamedly, many of us ignored Dwight's immoral behavior over the years. Dwight chose to be gay and live that lifestyle. Dwight made the choice to rape and murder a child. And our church must move on in the days ahead and learn a valuable lesson: we must take a stand for what is just in God's eyes and shun away the immorality of the world. The kind that Dwight

Kerry endorsed."

The statement led to several hand claps from the congregation. Julie Patterson stepped away from the podium and walked back to her seat. Dr. Henson re-approached the podium.

"No," Dr. Henson said, "Dwight was not the man we thought he was. My people, we must move forward and show love to our church family, particularly Dale and Lucy Jones, in their time of grief. We must recognize that unifying this church and community against the unholy and the immoral is the only hope we have of creating a society of people who strive to live like Christ in every way." He raised his voice. "But I want you to know upfront that when Christians mount up, the world tries to strike us down. This could get ugly. Liberals may bring in groups from the outside to come in to our town and take a stand for gay rights, all the while forgetting that a faggot raped and murdered a child in our own community. We have to stand up and fight this filth, as God would desire us to. And anyone," he said as he looked at Ben, "in this church who is not committed to serving Christ by standing for our faith should leave now."

Everyone stayed in their seats, hushed. Ben didn't budge because he didn't want to be noticed, but he obviously wanted no part of this misguided crusade. There was no sign of opposition to Dr. Henson's message. The congregation's demeanor seemed to be indicative that they would continue to follow Dr. Henson blindly, and believe whatever he said.

After a spell of silence, Dr. Henson looked back toward Ben and leaned into the microphone. "And how about you, Ben?"

Did he just call me out in church?

"How about you, Ben?" Dr. Henson asked. "What will you do in this moment of truth?"

Ben could not believe this was happening. The congregation turned and saw him in the balcony. The revelation of his presence was followed by a large number of gasps from people who obviously had read that he would be defending Dwight in the previous day's edition of the *Freeden Tribune*.

Dr. Henson eyed him. "Your church is calling you to do the right thing. God is calling you to do the right thing. Put Christ first! Will you, Ben, put your faith before your Earthly desires? For once?"

Ben stood up, having little to no choice now but to do something. His fellow church members in the balcony, who did not know him personally, began recognizing him from the front page of the *Freeden Tribune* the day before, as noted by their gasps that seemed to echo those down below. He walked toward the stairs, then down to the main level. At the bottom of stairs he stood still, now completely visible to all those on the main floor of the sanctuary. *Walk out. Don't do anything emotional.*

He looked down the aisle at Dr. Henson as the two of them stared into one another's eyes. Deep stares. Deathly stares. Ben had long wanted to *be* this man. A man with unmatched authority. But now, he detested his very being. He hated this man. In his mind, Dr. Henson was the exact embodiment of the passage Julie Patterson read from 2 Corinthians: a masquerading servant of righteousness. To Ben, Dr. Henson was the worst kind of person; the kind who makes you believe they love you and have your best interest at heart, but truly care about themselves only, and will metaphorically slit your throat if necessary. To Ben, he was the epitome of the type of person that turned people away from the Christian faith.

Ben stood there, continuing to stare at Dr. Henson. The

congregation, all of them, peered at Ben. Ben felt like a whore in church. They looked at him bitterly, with scorn in their eyes. Ben would remember this scene forever.

He looked around to take in all of the acrimonious gazing from people he had known his entire life. Then he fixed his eyes once more on Dr. Henson. Still, no one said a word. Dr. Henson wanted Ben to respond, but he would not do it. Ben turned toward the door, and exited without a sound.

Fast-walking toward his car, Ben was perhaps more disappointed than ever in his life. The people he had grown up with in the church had turned their backs on him. But he had done nothing for that church compared to the likes of Dwight, who had given his entire being to his church and community. And they had surely turned their backs on Dwight Kerry.

Suddenly, Ben felt a renewed and worsened distaste for church and the faith. He had struggled as of late to read his Bible, mainly because every time he read it, he associated it with Dr. Henson, a man he knew to be a hypocrite. After what he had just witnessed at his home church, he convinced himself as he got into his car that he wanted nothing to do with the ideology and faith Freeden Baptist adopted. In this Sunday morning worship service, Dwight had been called gay in a derogatory manner, a murderer, and a faggot by the senior pastor. This was unreal. He could not believe that after all Dwight had done for the church and community, that they would abandon him so quickly in such a bold, outrageous manner.

Aaron was right about what he had said the day before: Ben was finished here. But that didn't matter anymore. He was done with this town and its judgmental bullshit; done with all those who had turned their backs without second thought. Ben had spent way too long caring about the opinions of these people. It was time now to dwell not on the evil masquerading as good – that's all those people were, after all – but on the good that was helplessly entrapped, regarded as a criminal for no other reason than his sexual identity.

The way Ben saw it, there were only two things of importance left in this hellish situation: helping his good friend Dwight Kerry, and not giving a single fuck about what any of the pretentious, pseudo-Christian halfwits thought about it.

7: Kate Gregory

Kate Gregory sat on the floor in front of her full-body mirror, finishing her makeup as she prepared for a night out and to see her friend perform in the community chorus' rendition of Mozart's *Requiem*. The small town of Freeden had charmed her since her arrival, but it was starkly different from her life of old. The requiem for her prior life had long been sung – or so it seemed. She set her eye liner down, staring blankly into the mirror, and reflected on what brought her to this point.

After a long and laborious two years, Kate graduated from law school with her J.D. from the University of North Carolina at Chapel Hill in the summer of 2012. She worked as a paralegal when she left undergrad school in an effort to simply make ends meet, and saved enough money from working to pay her own way through law school.

Having grown up in poverty and with a physically abusive father, she was determined to make her own way in life and believed whole-heartedly that one's destiny is what they make of it. And this education was not the first time she had paid her way for something. Not even the second.

She had bought her first car as a high schooler with money she earned working at a grocery store as a cashier, just so she could interview for the job she really wanted and be able to drive there daily. When she attended Wake Forest University for undergrad, she had worked three jobs: delivering pizzas, lifeguarding, and as a fitness assistant at the local gym. A wide array of duties, but they all had one thing in common: they allowed her to pay her way through college and leave undergrad school debt-free.

Her goal the entire time was to go to law school, so instead of settling and taking higher-paying job offers elsewhere, she worked as a paralegal for ten years so she could continue to be involved in the field she wanted, all the while saving for her dream education.

She graduated law school, also with no student loan debt, and took a position as a criminal defense attorney for Boone, Boone, and Martin, an established firm in Charlotte. The job was the only thing she hadn't earned entirely herself. Her husband knew partner Josh Martin, and the connection had helped her land the opportunity.

She had married Patrick White, a native of Charlotte, two years prior. The two met as undergrad students at Wake Forest and began dating during their junior years, but Patrick made it clear he wanted to move back home to Charlotte once college was over. Kate, with little to no family in the state anyway, really didn't have a problem with that, and agreed to the move.

Kate and Patrick were good friends and loved each other, but their personalities didn't nurture one another and the relationship soured over time. They were never *in love*. Patrick was nowhere near as motivated as Kate, and he resented her for her desire to grow in her career. He had no intention of developing in his and just wanted to get by, but since he was a child of a family who had prospered financially, Kate often wondered if he fully understood her ambition. She knew he had never known what it was like to *need*. He had gotten everything he ever needed in life on a silver platter from his parents, who he knew would watch out for him if he ever faced dire straits. She had never enjoyed the same luxury.

On July 2, 2017, Kate walked into their uptown Charlotte apartment during lunch and found Patrick having sex on the sofa with another woman; her long-time best friend, actually, who she did not know was in town. Kate never came home during the day, which likely was the reason they were caught off guard. She ran out, back to the parking deck, and got in her car to drive off. She had never been more humiliated in her entire life. For once she felt she had lost control of her life, and it pained her.

She stayed at the Hyatt Place adjacent to her office building for about a week, never going back to the apartment for clothes or anything. For days, Patrick pleaded for her to come home. Her phone dinged from text messages nearly ever twenty minutes.

I made a mistake babe. Please come home.

We make a great team. Let's please stay together.

Babe, please talk to me.

Why won't you at least text me back? I'm worried about you.

I need you in my life. I'm so sorry. It was a one-time mistake I'll never make again. Please forgive me and come home.

Unfortunately, it was not a one-time mistake. Her best friend, who he had slept with and was ridden with guilt since the discovery, called her and told her they had been having an affair for months. The work trips he frequently had to leave town for around the weekends were not work trips at all. He had been driving on a regular basis to Roanoke, Virginia, where she lived, to spend long weekends with her.

This had been calculated, and was certainly no *one-time mistake*.

She showed up at the apartment one night, and he acted so relieved to see her. "I'm so glad you came back."

"I'm not coming back," she said.

"What do you mean?"

"I'm leaving you."

"Are you for real?"

"Yes."

"Seriously? You won't even hear me out?"

"It wasn't one time. You're having an affair."

"That's not true!"

"Yes, it is."

"What makes you think that?"

"She told me."

"Who's she?"

"Shouldn't it be obvious?"

"Oh, *her*? She's a liar! How can you trust her anyway? I'm telling you, she is lying."

"Patrick, please just quit. You're lying. I checked. You stayed at the same hotel every weekend in Roanoke. I verified it."

"That was work-related, I'm telling you."

"What is work-related for you in Roanoke?"

"I had thought about starting a side business."

She rolled her eyes and shook her head. "Patrick, I want a divorce."

He sighed in disbelief. "Well, it's not happening."

"Yes, it is."

"You can't make it without me. You would have never

gotten that job at the firm without me!"

"I'm grabbing a few things, and then I'm leaving." She walked into the bedroom to get some of her keepsake jewelry and sentimental items.

He followed her, crying. "I haven't done anything to deserve this. You should give me a chance."

Just as her previous experiences had shown, Patrick believed he was entitled. His behavior now was indicative of that. From Kate's perspective, he believed, for some reason, that he was *owed*. And despite his true wrongdoings, he simply could not own up to them. It wasn't natural for him to admit he was wrong.

Kate left that night and went to stay with a friend she had met a few months back named Samantha, who worked as a paralegal at the firm. After months of trying, it was clear that working at the firm was going to be too awkward. Everyone there was fully aware of what was going on in her personal life: that she had left her husband. Josh, the partner, had likely been the one who told everyone, and she grew uncomfortable and contemplated a change. Nothing tied her to Charlotte; she could go anywhere she wanted, and with her ambition, start a new life not contingent on a repaired relationship with her unfaithful, self-serving husband.

She started looking online for jobs and noticed a considerably higher number of state legal jobs outside of the metro areas, but one caught her attention particularly: an assistant district attorney position in a rural NC district, Freeden County.

Kate had met a brilliant young woman while in law school who was going to school to be a psychologist. She became a great friend. Her name, prior to being married, was Terri Marks. Terri was born and raised in Freeden and had moved back home after school to open her own practice and marry her long-time sweetheart, Shawn Hathaway.

Kate checked into the town of Freeden. At face value, she liked what she saw: small town (which she had never experienced), simple living, and an opportunity to truly focus on her career and gain some excellent experience in a role she might not land in a more populous area at this point in her young career.

She wanted to go somewhere and start a new life, but the thought of being close to her grad school friend Terri was also appealing. Kate submitted her documents online to apply for the vacant assistant district attorney position in Freeden, and never dreamed of looking back.

About five days later, she received a call to interview for the position. She drove to town, and felt very comfortable with what she saw and the feeling that came over her when she explored the area. Unfortunately, though, she would only spend about three hours there outside of the interview, but liked what she saw: the town was charming and it looked as if it had never left the 1960s. If you hadn't known better and the streets hadn't been lined with modern cars and trucks, she would *never* have known it was 2018. Plus, it was relatively quiet, quaint, and simple. And she envied a simple life.

Freeden, on the surface, looked like an excellent fit; the perfect place to start her new life.

A day after her interview, Scott Stevens, the District Attorney for the Freeden County District, called her.

"Hello, this is Ms. Gregory, right?"

"Yes, sir?" She knew who it was already.

"Ms. Gregory, this is Scott Stevens, DA in the Freeden County District."

"Hello Mr. Stevens, how are you today?"

"I'm fine, thank you. Ms. Gregory, I would like for you to join our team, and would like to extend the offer to you to serve as an assistant district attorney here. Would you like to accept the position?"

Her mind was made, and frankly, it had been made earlier in the day. She knew if she got the call with an offer that she would accept it. She found something very appealing about Freeden. She almost felt as if something was calling her there. Unsure of what it was, she was intrigued. For once, she felt adventurous, like she was taking a step into something she had never experienced. The leap to something entirely new and foreign to her was so attractive, and moving from a bustling Charlotte to slow-moving Freeden was just the change she desired.

"Yes, I would like to accept. Thank you so much for the opportunity, Mr. Stevens."

"You were raised well," he chuckled. "Call me Scott, though. We are a team, so we'll be on a first name basis."

She chuckled from sheer excitement. "Okay, Scott, thank you so much. I'm so excited to join the team. When will I start?"

"That's exactly what I was about to get to," he said. "Can you start April 2nd? I know that's only three weeks away, but–"

"Absolutely!" she politely interrupted. "I can start then."

"Great. That will work perfectly. Now look, I do want you to know that this is a lot different than Charlotte, and I want to make sure you are okay with that. We don't have a lot of serious criminal trials here, just petty offenses. Which is a good thing, really, just not a ton of excitement in that regard and I wanted to make sure you knew that?"

"I have always worked hard at everything I've done and

this will be no exception, no matter what comes our way."

"Good, that's good to hear. I figured as much, you seem like a person of dignity and a hard-worker, and that's exactly what I'm looking for."

"You got the right person then, sir!"

"There you go again with that sir mess," he responded, chuckling as he said it.

"Ahh, sorry Scott."

"No worries," he said. "I'm kidding."

"Well thank you so much for the opportunity, and I can't wait to join you."

"We are very excited to bring on someone of your caliber. One quick thing though..."

"Okay?"

"Nothing is more important to me than loyalty. Can I count on you to be a loyal, team player?"

She spoke confidently. "I have always been loyal and committed to my superiors, and I'll do the same for you."

"Good to know! Okay, that's all for today. Congratulations again, and I'll see you soon."

"Thank you!"

She tapped the end button on her iPhone. She could not wait to tell Terri she was moving to town.

And that's what she did. Kate moved into a small, nine-hundred-square foot house in Freeden on Jefferson Street, a four-block walk from her office and less than a half mile from the downtown eateries and shops. She had not met anyone yet, but absolutely loved the simplicity the town offered. Short work commutes, no people screaming at each other as a result of road rage – everything was easy to get to and she absolutely loved it.

The cases she worked in her first month were mostly drug-related crimes. Nothing too serious, just as Scott had forecasted. Perhaps the most serious case was where a man stole his mother's coin collection to pay for the opioids he was buying, and now she was ticked off that her favorite rare silver dollar was missing.

Scott said it right — nothing serious.

She spent the first few weeks becoming acquainted with the town in her own way, eating breakfast at the famed 3rd Street Café, enjoying the small but pleasant local library, the parks and nearby trails that seemed rarely used by the locals yet captivating to her, and trying to embrace the overall local scene as much as possible. She had yet to meet many locals, though, and wondered if she should look to participate in things that would force her to meet more people. She had encountered a ton of people around town in small-talk situations, and though everyone was extremely nice, she just didn't feel she had truly *met* anyone.

She called Terri one night and chatted with her about this.

"I feel bad we haven't been able to do much together, yet," Terri said.

"It's okay! I know you have a family."

"I mean I know we've gone shopping and out for lunch, but you've been here three weeks and I feel like I haven't done enough."

"Terri, please! You've done a plenty, you have to live your life, too."

"I know, I know."

"I just want to meet people. Dive into the culture here."

"Well, I would love if you'd be my guest at something I have coming up this Friday."

"What is it?"

"I'm performing with the community chorus and it's going

to be great. Plus, a reception will follow and a lot of people will be there. You should totally come. I would love to introduce you to people."

"I'd love that. That sounds like a lot of fun. Just want to do things where I'll meet people, you know? I'm just not one to go to the bar or club to meet people."

"Oh Lord, yes, we are too old for that." They both laughed at the comment. "So it's a date then?"

"Yes, it's a date!"

"This will be great, Kate. I'm so glad you're here, I really hope you're going to like it in Freeden."

"I already do! It's so peaceful."

"It is! And hey, maybe after the concert we can grab dinner and drinks at a restaurant downtown called David's. Have you been yet?"

"No, but I've heard it's good."

"Make that a part of the plan too, then!"

Kate came out of her dream-like state, and realized she was running short on time. She scrambled to finish her makeup, gathered her things, then hurried out the door.

When she arrived, she walked inside the concert hall lobby, and much to her pleasant surprise, a packed lobby of attendees. It was clearly a major thing in town. Terri walked in from the auditorium, dressed in full choir regalia.

"Hey, Kate," she said, waving to get her attention.

"Hey." She waved back.

"Look, Shawn and Anslee are already inside, you can sit with them if you'd like and I'll introduce you to everyone after the concert."

Kate smiled. "That'll be great, good luck tonight!"

"Thank you, I have a solo so I'm a bit nervous.'

"You'll do fine, I know you will."

Terri said goodbye for then, and left for backstage. Kate took her seat about ten rows from the stage.

The choir came out to the applause of the audience. Kate joined in. Then, the director, who the program identified as Dwight Kerry, entered to equal praise. Kate had heard Dwight Kerry's name since she had moved to town, but had yet to meet him. She had already heard how talented of a musician and director he was. To her, this was so exciting. Small-town feel with a splash of culture. She continued to love this even more.

The orchestra began to play. She loved the violins the most, and they were prevalent in this prelude to *Requiem*. Then, the emphatic horns dominated, and the chorus began to sing:

Requiem aeternam dona eis, Domine,
et lux perpetua luceat eis.

She couldn't believe what she was hearing. For a community chorus in a small town like Freeden, this amazed her. Terri's solo part came in the first piece titled "Requiem Aeternam":

Te decet hymnus, Deus, in Sion,
et tibi reddetur votum in Jerusalem!

She had never heard Terri sing and wondered how she could have known Terri this long and never known this about her. But amidst all the astonishment surrounding this stellar concert in such a delightful town, she noticed a man standing in the back row in what she knew was the bass section. He was handsome, well-groomed, and for some reason, he stood out to her. She couldn't take her eyes off him.

After the concert, Kate began socializing with attendees and meeting people she had not seen before. This was exactly what she wanted to achieve; delving more into the Freeden community. Minutes later, Kate noticed that Terri was talking to the man she had seen on stage. *She must introduce me to this man.*

Kate rushed over, but the man was already walking away.

"Terri!" she shouted, hoping it would get the man's attention.

"Kate," Terri replied.

She walked over to Terri. "You did so great tonight."

The man turned his head toward them. The two women hugged, then Kate said, "I wish you could have introduced me to the man you were just talking to."

Terri smiled. "Well just hold on a second… Ben!"

He turned back and looked at her.

"Ben, please come meet my friend," Terri said.

He re-approached Terri, now joined by Kate. "And who is your friend?" Ben asked.

"Ben, this is Kate Gregory. She is the new assistant district attorney and her office is right here in Freeden. We went to Chapel Hill together. She just moved here from Charlotte."

Ben shook her hand, and they both made eye contact. "I see. Well, Freeden is quite the different place from Charlotte."

"Yes, you could say that," she replied, smiling. She tried to make an effort to see if he had a wedding ring on his finger, but couldn't catch a glimpse without being too obvious before he put his hand back in his pocket.

"Ben Bailey," he said. "It's nice to meet you Ms. Gregory."

"Wow," she replied, "you're quite the gentleman to be calling someone your own age Miss anything."

The two shared a laugh. She said, "Call me Kate."

"Well, it's nice to meet you, Kate."

There was something about him. She absolutely did not believe in love at first sight, but she was so intrigued by this man.

Terri jumped in. "Ben is a local attorney. He has his own firm here in Freeden."

"What kind of law do you practice?" Kate asked.

"Criminal law."

"Then we will likely see quite a bit of each other, I would imagine?"

"Perhaps we will. I practice more cases outside the county than here, though."

"Wait, didn't you perform tonight too?" she asked as if she didn't know.

"Yes, he is an extraordinary baritone," said Terri.

"Is that right?" Kate asked.

He chuckled. "I would not say that. But thank you for the compliment, nonetheless."

She hoped he felt just as intrigued by her. This man was handsome and came off as extremely intelligent and kind. She wondered if she was dreaming or if this was real.

"He is very good, don't let him fool you," Terri said.

"A man of many talents," Kate said. "I'm impressed."

Ben smirked. "Well, when you practice criminal law in a small town, you have to do something that'll make people like you."

Kate and Terri both laughed at the comment. Kate didn't necessarily find the comment funny, she just wanted to impress this man.

"Perhaps I could show you around town sometime?" Ben asked.

Yes, please do. Kate froze at the prospect of this man asking her if he could take her around town. She *never* did anything like that. All the sadness and misfortune in her social life seemed to suddenly fade away. There was something about this man she really liked.

Terri realized Kate was deep in thought and had yet to respond, so she elected to do it for her. "That would be great, Kate." Terri said. "Ben knows so much about the area. This is his hometown, too."

"Well," Kate said, "I suppose that would be nice." Kate mentally kicked herself for not being able to come up with a better response.

"Let's do it soon," Ben said.

"Yes," Kate said with more confidence this time, "let's do that."

"Well, I'll let you guys go," he said. "Terri, you did an amazing job tonight on your solo. Kate, it was nice to meet you and I'll look forward to seeing you again soon."

"Take care," Terri said.

"Nice to meet you, too." Kate said, smiling. "Bye."

Ben walked away. Kate kept her eyes on him.

"I take it you liked him?" Terri asked once she felt Ben was far enough away.

"I'm not sure what that was, but it was something I haven't felt in a long time, perhaps ever before," she answered.

"Careful girlie, he's recently separated."

"Maybe that's why I felt drawn to him, since I've dealt with the same. I don't know."

"Hey, don't get me wrong," Terri said as she took a sip of

wine, "you should certainly get to know him, he's a great guy."

"I can tell, seemed genuine, really."

"He is, but there's some baggage there, I will say."

"And what's that? I could handle a crazy ex-wife, because he'd have to deal with me. And let's be honest, I've had one failed marriage, too, you know?

"Get to know him. Just be careful. It's not his ex-wife I'm talking about."

"What are you talking about?"

"Can't say much here, but," she leaned in to whisper, "his ex-father-in-law."

"What about him?"

"We'll have to talk later, this is not the place."

"Okay," Kate said nervously.

"But hey, thank you so much for coming tonight. I really appreciate it."

"I was so glad to come. This was amazing, and you did so well."

"Thank you. So, can we still go get drinks and some food? I'm so hungry. Didn't eat before the concert."

"Definitely, whenever you're ready is fine with me."

Kate's phone rang and she looked at the screen.

SCOTT STEVENS.

Why in the world would my boss be calling me right now, at nine at night? She picked up.

"Hello?"

"Kate, it's Scott. We need to talk."

"Okay, what's up?" she asked, then signaled to Terri that she had to step away for a minute.

Terri nodded. Kate walked away, pacing as she talked to

her new boss. Terri sensed something was wrong; Kate's face was adorned with concern.

A few minutes later, Kate walked back over to Terri, then ended the call.

"Everything okay?" Terri asked.

"Terri, I'm afraid I'm going to have to cancel dinner and drinks tonight."

"Is everything okay?"

"No, not at all. A seventeen-year-old boy named Braxton Jones was raped and murdered at the school tonight. I have to go."

Kate bolted for the door. She didn't feel like she was in charming little Freeden anymore.

8: Braxton Jones

Prior to the *Requiem*

The bell rang. The bell at Freeden High had stood the test of time; it was installed when the school was built in 1913. It had become just as much a centerpiece of the school as the building's fascinating architecture. It was no ordinary high school.

To Braxton Jones, most of the students were ordinary, however, in the sense that they were just like other high school kids their age. There were the cliques that rode their trucks to school, revving them up as they passed by as loud as they possibly could to impress the girls and make sure everyone knew they had arrived. There were the typical nerds and band geeks, the jocks who played every sport the school offered, and then the usually small sector of students, outcasts, who focused on social justice. These were the ones who dressed differently and were the anti-norm for Freeden and rural North Carolina. They got picked on, mocked, and made fun of. Although small in number, their presence was noticeable because they were *that* different.

Braxton knew many students wanted to be them. Cool, the way the world described it in 2018, but far too different for other Freeden High students who wanted to be a somebody while in school. To be somebody in *this* school, you had to play sports (and be good), have a big truck, wear a hat everywhere, go mudding on Friday nights and attend the cotton field drug parties on Saturday nights. Braxton believed there was only one way to be cool in Freeden: be normal, the way it was here. He recognized, even at his young age, that the culture of compliance with the social norms of the rural South had infiltrated the youth just like it had the adults.

Braxton, the son of Dale and Lucy Jones, was seventeen years old, stood about five-seven, and weighed around one-hundred-and-twenty-five pounds soaking wet. He was not an athlete. He had a brilliant mind and played for the school choir that had declined in popularity due to the serious lack of interest in the arts among students at Freeden. He scored a 1590 on the SAT, and had received offers to attend any Ivy League school he desired. He had a 5.0 weighted GPA, loved reading classic literature like *The Great* Gatsby, and could play the piano unlike anyone his age. His parents were extremely proud of him.

Braxton, though, struggled with his social life. He knew he did not fit in and had no desire to integrate himself into the social arena Freeden High presented. He had friends, but they were just as introverted as he and rarely came out of their shells. He viewed his closest friends to be those he studied with, his choir mates, and those he played music with. Other than that, he associated with very few people.

From the October of his freshman year to now, Braxton had held onto a secret that embodied the central focus of his private life, unearthed to no one until just weeks before the *Requiem*. Braxton had a crush on someone he had met just weeks after moving from Jesse Helms Middle School to Freeden High. He had met his crush in his choir class that year and had practically been on the same class schedule as that person since the first semester of high school.

His name was Ian Christopher. Ian did play sports and was

a standout basketball power forward who had already received an offer to play for North Carolina State and the famed Duke Blue Devils. The only reason he had even joined the school choir, though, is because his mother, who was the director of the North Carolina All-State Choir, had forced him into it back at the start of his freshman year. He possessed an incredible talent to sing, perhaps passed on in his genes from his talented mother, and had come to enjoy the choir. He accepted his role with the choir more over time, realizing that people with his diverse abilities and talents can often control the way people see them. He became more comfortable being himself, even if it sometimes violated social norms he had grown accustomed to.

Braxton loved this about him. When he first saw him, Braxton was immediately attracted to him; he loved his brown hair that grew thick on the top but close-cut on the sides and adored his physically-fit, chiseled body. But his true feelings of wonderment came on when Braxton finally mustered up the courage to talk to him for the first time and they became friends. Braxton felt empowered by having such a popular friend, but Ian simply enjoyed being around Braxton because he was unique, different from so many others at Freeden High. Ian's willingness to go outside his usual sports clique bridged the gap between Freeden High normalcy and something different. And he was able to get away with it and still be liked by the 'normal' kids.

The two became very close, studying and spending time together, but Braxton did not suspect anything more than friendship from Ian and tried to make it appear that the same came from him. Over time, he developed a love for Ian and wanted to take their relationship to a new level, but worried how it might affect them moving forward. He preferred having

Ian around as a friend, rather than not having him around at all. The thought of him revealing his feelings to Ian, and those feelings causing a rift between the two of them, was something Braxton could not bear.

One day, in early March, the two decided to buy tickets to a late night showing of *Black Panther*, about thirty days after its debut. Not a single attendee joined them; it was as if the two had rented the entire theater out for themselves on the eight bucks they spent for their tickets. They had become best friends by this point, and Braxton longed for the opportunity to tell Ian how he really felt about him. As the movie went on, he tried to convince himself that he would lose everything if he did it. *I just can't fathom losing him. I love him. I need him in my life. He brings out the best in me.*

He needed to tell Ian. His feelings were at a boiling point. He had never revealed to anyone, including his parents who he was extremely close to, the truth about his sexual identity. He was dying to tell Ian, and he believed he might understand more than anyone else would. And as close as he was to his parents, he was not mentally prepared to tell them just yet. He worried they would kill him. Literally.

If Ian doesn't love me back, he has proven reasonable enough to at least support me for who I am, right? Of all the people in the world, he was certain that Ian would, at the very least, not cast him out.

So he did it. Right there, in the Freeden Independence Theater with no one in the room except him and the boy he had fallen for. He reached across the armrest and grabbed Ian's hand. In less than a second, the two of them had interlocked fingers, holding onto one another. Ian never even looked at Braxton, nor did Braxton eye Ian. They both felt, deep down, that this was right.

As Braxton held onto the hand of the boy he loved, he realized he had never felt more at peace. His most well-guarded secret had been unveiled to someone without even speaking a word, and he was overcome with an unparalleled joy.

When the movie was over, Braxton and Ian walked out of the theater and into the nearby empty parking lot where they had left Ian's Jeep Wrangler. They both got in the car, then Ian locked the doors.

"Are we okay?" Braxton asked.

"Why wouldn't we be?" said Ian.

"You know, what just happened."

"I have feelings for you," Ian said. "I've really grown lately, but it's been hard for me to express that, still. I'm really happy you held my hand. It gave me the courage to show you the same feelings."

Braxton, a traditionally introverted young man, felt extremely endowed by Ian's statement. In the same way Ian had made him come out of his shell, Braxton had apparently done the same for him.

"Well, I think it's obvious I have feelings for you, too," Braxton said.

"Can I kiss you?" Ian asked nervously. There was no reason to be anxious as the two had already shared their mutual feelings, but everything was still so new and frightening to Braxton, who had never experienced the feeling of allowing his sexual identity to be revealed to someone else until now. Braxton moved toward Ian and the two kissed in a moment neither of them would ever forget.

At the end of the night, Ian brought Braxton home, and even walked into the house with him. That's when the two found Dale sitting in his recliner in the living room.

"What's up, boys?"

"Hey, Mr. Jones," Ian said.

"Hey, Dad."

"You boys catch a movie tonight?"

"Yes sir, *Black Panther,*" Ian said.

"How you boys looking in the third round of the state playoffs next week?" he asked Ian.

"I think we are going to be okay. We get at least one more home game if we win this one," Ian said.

"You got a bright future playing ball, son," he said to Ian.

"Thank you sir," he said. "Well, I better get home before it gets too late. Goodnight, Mr. Jones."

"Goodnight, boy."

Ian then looked at Braxton and winked. They did their usual, unique handshake, and Ian left.

"Hey, Braxton, your momma left something in the kitchen for you to eat if you are hungry."

"Thanks, Dad," he said as he walked out of the room and down the hall toward the kitchen.

Braxton had come alive. He had never felt more energetic and excited for his life. He believed he had truly fallen in love. He had been attracted to boys before, but never like this. The bond he and Ian shared was love and he knew it. And he wanted more of it.

After revealing to Ian how he felt, he felt like the true Braxton was coming out and he wanted to tell someone else. He thought it would be a good idea, perhaps, to chat with someone who could make him either feel more comfortable with that choice, or realize that it was a poor decision and that he would regret it. He needed to talk to someone who, if necessary, would level with him and bring him back to reality, irrespective of what he wanted to hear.

For so many reasons, he had one person in mind. This man had a reasonable understanding of life that spanned far outside the confines of Freeden, yet he had found a way to be successful and enjoy life in what Braxton saw as a terribly judgmental place. The best person to talk to was someone who had likely been in the same situation before, and although long removed from it, would probably remember the impact coming out had on his life. His school choir director, who had counseled him on other less serious matters before, was the perfect choice.

The following Monday, Braxton had been waiting impatiently for the school day to end when the loud, old bell at Freeden High signaled to dismiss his music theory class. He had approached his teacher's desk while the other students fled out the classroom for their three minutes of socializing in the hallways. It had been a number of hours ago, but the conversation was still fresh in his mind.

"Mr. Kerry?" he asked.

"Yes, Braxton? What might I do for you today?"

"I'd like to talk with you after school, if that would be okay?"

"Sure. Of course, you know we have choir rehearsals immediately after school... you'll be there, yes?"

"Yes, yes. I mean, after that?"

"Why sure," he responded. "I imagine that will work just fine for me. I do have a dinner date tonight with an old colleague of mine visiting town, meeting at David's at six. Would permitting an hour for this work for you?"

"Yes sir, that should more than do it."

"Great! We'll chat after choir then."

Later, the final school bell rang. Most students jumped out of their seats immediately, but Braxton sat there in a blank stare as the bell continued to ring. Finally, the loud, extended sounds of the bell brought Braxton out of his extended daydream.

He hurried to Dwight's choir room for rehearsal. Rushing to ready himself, he set his sheet music in place and fell into a comfortable position on the piano bench. He peered up the risers at Ian, who stood on the back row, and smiled. The expression was reciprocated.

"Okay, let's start from the beginning, shall we?" Dwight said. "I really want to hear the sopranos, you guys were lacking last week."

"Mr. Kerry!" one junior soprano said.

"I'm just saying you guys need to turn it up. We got a lot of Whitney Houstons singing like Aaron Nevilles. You all sounded like this last week – 'look at this face, I know the years are showing,'" he sang in a near perfect Aaron Neville imitation that exhibited from little opening of the mouth. The class erupted in laughter.

"Okay, okay, okay, settle down. Let's take it from the top, shall we? And open your mouths, sopranos!"

The students silenced. Dwight looked over at Braxton. "Braxton," he said while nodding and signaling to begin.

Braxton began to play the prelude to his favorite piece, a piece the choir would perform at the end of their spring concert come April. It was one of Dwight's favorite pieces, too; a piece that ended the spring school chorus concert every year. The four-part choir joined in:

If music be the food of love, sing on, sing on

Sing on 'til I am filled with joy!

Dwight directed the choir flawlessly. The room was full of love. The students loved Dwight. Dwight loved his students. They cared about what they were doing. And they all cherished this song that embodied how what they all cared about – music – was a symbol of the most powerful thing in the world: love.

For then my listening soul you move,
For then my listening soul you move,
To pleasures, to pleasures that can never cloy.
To pleasures that can never cloy.
Your eyes, your eyes, your mean, your mean…

Braxton looked away from his sheet music and up at Ian as he played by memory, the two gazing into one another's eyes.

Your tongue declare that you are music, everywhere.
Your eyes, your mean
Your tongue declare that you are music, that you are music everywhere!

Pleasures invade both eye and ear,
So fierce, so fierce the transports are they wound
They wound, they wound
And all my senses feasted are…

Braxton continued to play in the most angelic way. This was, in Ian's eyes, perhaps the best he had ever heard Braxton play. His fingers rolled across the piano in a way Ian had never seen. Suddenly, it looked more natural for Braxton than it had looked all these years before. He truly looked alive.

Though yet, though yet the treat is only sound,
Sure I must, sure I must perish by your charm,
Unless you save me in your arms.

Silence overcame the room amidst this impenetrable rehearsal, moments before the choir picked back up and finished this powerful song. Nothing ugly could interfere with what was going in the choir room. While the small pond of Freeden ran amuck with gossip, hatred, and disdainful misunderstanding, in this room, there was freedom for all. The gay, the straight, the black, the white – in this room, there was love.

Braxton began to play again, the prelude repeated, in a slower manner as the song neared its end. The choir joined in, following his lead:

If music be the food of love, sing on, sing on
Sing on 'til I am filled with joy
Sing on, sing on, sing on!

"Excellent work!" Dwight exclaimed.

"I love that song, Mr. Kerry," said a young female student from the alto section.

"Yes, it's one of my favorites for sure," he said. "Okay, let's dismiss early today, I liked what I heard and once you have it right, you have it right. See you all tomorrow."

The choir students hurried along, out the door. Ian walked over to Braxton. "Can I call you tonight?"

"Sure," Braxton replied with a grin.

Ian smiled, and turned to walk out the door.

"So, Mr. Jones," Dwight said as he sat in a chair on the front row of the risers, "what is on your mind?"

Braxton ensured no one else had lingered around.

"Well, Mr. Kerry," he said as he sat a couple of seats down from him, " I want to tell you something that I trust you will not tell anyone. Can I be confident you will keep this private?"

"Anything you say stays between us, sure."

"Do I have your word?"

"Yes, you have my word," he reassured.

"Mr. Kerry… I… well, I need you to know something only one other person knows about me, and I trust that you will be honest with how I should channel these feelings."

"Okay," he said, smiling, still very unaware of what Braxton would say.

"I am in love."

"Well," Dwight said while he smiled, resting easy now that the subject did not seem to be anything out of the ordinary for a high school student. "That's a very common thing for someone your age and despite your very uncommon abilities and talents, it's perfectly normal to feel the way you do."

"I'm in love with Ian, Mr. Kerry."

Dwight stopped, realizing now why Braxton wanted to talk to *him*. "Ah, I see," he said as he leaned back in his chair.

"Please don't judge me, Mr. Kerry, I–"

"Judge you?" Dwight interrupted. "Oh, please Braxton. I'm the queerest thing that ever hit town. You know that and so does everyone else, okay? This here," he pointed around the room, "is Planet Fitness, my dear friend… a judgment free zone. So you just sit there and tell me whatever you need to say and stop worrying about being hung on the courthouse square for just being yourself, okay?"

Braxton laughed at Dwight's implication that it was absurd

for him to worry about this. It was quite relieving to hear Dwight make light of what Braxton considered to be such a serious issue. "Okay, sir."

"So how does it feel to say it out loud?" Dwight asked.

He chuckled. "Really good!"

"Of course it does, feels good to be *you,* doesn't it?"

Braxton smiled. "Yes, yes it does."

"Listen, Braxton, I want to tell you something. If you are gay then it is okay. This town and its people might not make you feel that it's okay, but the world is changing for the better, even if this town isn't, understand?"

"Yes, sir."

"And it's not just here, but many places in the world – they still lack tolerance for people simply being who they are, you get me?"

"Yes, sir."

"And that part of the world, they'll judge you because you're different, but you've got to come to terms with whether or not you're okay with that."

"I'm trying."

"It'll take time, trust me, I know!"

Braxton and Dwight shared a laugh.

"You have a bright future, young man," Dwight said. "You're going places. For me," he leaned back in his seat, arms crossed, "I was called to come back here, though I'm not sure why yet. I always thought it was to take care of my mother before she passed and that I had just gotten stuck here long after that moment in my life had come and gone, but I am still trying to believe there's something else."

"Perhaps there will be," Braxton said. "You've certainly done a lot of good for this place. For me, too."

"Why thank you, young man," he said. "For a guy like me,

even though you think I'm doing okay around here, it's a constant struggle, and it'll be the same for you too if you end up being open to others about who you are. And I'm not going to tell you that you need to come out, or that it will solve everything if you do. But I will tell you that even here, in a town like this, I have found happiness being my true self. And despite the fact that some people probably don't like it all that much, well, I like me very much."

Braxton giggled. "That's funny, Mr. Kerry."

"I do like me. Hey, somebody has to!"

"Thank you for making me comfortable."

"You do it on your own time, okay? You've got your whole future ahead of you, and a great one at that. Take care of yourself."

Braxton grabbed his book bag. "Thank you Mr. Kerry," he said as he bolted for the door and exited the room.

About a week later, Braxton was feeling more confident than ever before. His parents had even noticed it. He was considerably more enthusiastic about life, much-less reserved in social settings, and had blossomed into a young man that had found more balance between his studies and simply enjoying life. Both Dale and Lucy loved seeing it, too, as they had longed for their boy to stop being so serious and find a way to enjoy relationships with other people – including them. They talked with him more than they ever had, and they relished it.

"Perhaps he's about to pick a school and is just thinking of how he will miss us when he's gone?" Lucy asked of Dale one night while Braxton was out with Ian.

"Perhaps," Dale responded. "Better late than never, I

presume."

All was good in the Jones household until that night. May 5th, 2018. A day that Dale and Lucy Jones would never forget.

It was a Saturday, and Braxton had just come home from a night out with Ian and their friends. The two didn't act like they were in a relationship when they were with people, as Braxton wanted to tell his family himself before they found out from someone else. Once he did, and assuming all went well, he planned to come out to his friends, and Ian planned to join him, despite still being a bit nervous about it. Braxton imagined how liberated he would feel if that happened. He decided the time was now – this was the night to tell his family. He showered and then came downstairs to find his mother and father sitting around the breakfast nook in the kitchen, sipping on their nighttime tea.

"Mom, Dad, can I talk to you?"

"Sure you can, honey," Lucy replied. "You can talk to us about anything."

He was still anxious, worried that the notion of 'he could talk to them about anything' may not be entirely true. Nonetheless, he proceeded, envisioning how good it would feel to get this off his chest to the people who cared for him the most.

"It's life-altering, really, and I want you to love me no matter what."

Dale perked up from his relatively non-attentive state to now listening keenly. "What is it, son?"

He paused for nearly twenty seconds of silence. "I'm gay."

Lucy immediately gasped. Shock and awe blanketed her face.

"Do what?" Dale asked harshly.

Braxton felt vulnerable; this suddenly didn't seem like the

right time. They were not going to take this well and it was all over their faces. But he couldn't stop now, as much as he felt he should. He needed to do this.

"Please don't hate me. I can't help who I am."

Dale stood up. "Did you just tell your mother and me that you are gay?"

"Dad, please, this is who I am."

"Are you shitting me?" He stood up and backhanded his son across the face, who fell on the floor, hitting his head on the door frame that led into the living room.

"Dale!" Lucy screamed.

"No son of mine is going to be a little ole' queer, Lucy!"

Braxton lay on the floor, crying. "Dad, just hear me out," he pleaded.

Dale grabbed him by his shirt and yanked him off the floor, snapping his neck back uncomfortably. Then, he pinned Braxton against the wall.

"Dale, stop!" Lucy screamed again. "He's our son."

"Shut up!" he angrily yelled at her, then turned his attention back to Braxton, keeping him pinned against the wall. "You will go to hell if you're gay, you know this, yes?"

"Please, Dad, stop!"

"Take it back," Dale said. "And don't ever say that again in my house." He was sweating now. "You're confused, that's all."

Braxton cried. "No, Dad, I'm not."

"Oh, my boy," Lucy said, seemingly ashamed of him.

"No boy acts like this. My son will not be a fudge packer! Tell me, right now, that you will not be this way."

"It's a not a choice Dad–"

"Tell me right now!" he shouted, interrupting Braxton. Then, in a softer tone, trying to calm himself down, he said,

"Tell me, right now."

"Dad," Braxton said while tearing up again, "I can't tell you that."

Dale hung his head and shook it. "God, what have I done to deserve this?" he asked as he sobbed.

"Dale, try to calm down, I'm sure we can talk this over," Lucy said.

"No," he said, continuing to sob.

"Dad, I talked to you because I love you. I didn't make this choice. It's who I am, and it's who I've always been!"

"No, it's not!" Dale said.

"Oh honey, please, now that's not true," Lucy said.

"Yes, Mom, it is!"

"Is Ian gay?" Dale asked. "You've been spending a lot of time with him."

Braxton knew he could not admit that right now. He could not fathom bringing Ian into this situation. "No. No!"

"Are you trying to turn Lawrence's son into a fag, too?"

"No, Dad. I swear Ian doesn't even know this about me."

"This is not you, son. You're possessed by demons, don't you get it?"

"Perhaps he is just confused, Dale?" Lucy asked, indirectly pleading for Dale to stop.

"You'll go to hell for this," Dale said.

"God still loves me Dad, why won't you?"

Braxton realized his Dad was not going to budge on his harsh stance. It hurt him to think, even when it involved his own son, that his father's feelings toward his sexual identity could be so cruel.

"I want to fix this… fix you! God doesn't approve of this demonic behavior."

"I don't need to be fixed, Dad. I need to be loved. This is

who I am," he shouted.

Dale began murmuring to himself crazily, still holding Braxton against the wall.

"Dale, I think we all need to take a break and try to figure out how we can stop Braxton from having these feelings, okay?"

"Mom, it's not a feeling, please! I'm trying to be honest with you all."

Honesty was a virtue his mother and father had preached to him for years, but in this moment, Braxton knew they would have preferred he lie about who he was rather than accept his identity, which so strongly contrasted with the Jones' family ideals.

"You can't do this to our family," Dale murmured.

"I'm not doing anything but trying to tell you who I am."

"I'll tell you what you are." Dale grabbed him by his hair, pulled back, and forced him to walk with him as he hurried toward the basement door.

"Dad, you're hurting me!"

"God will hurt you if you don't repent and fix yourself," he yelled.

Dale still held onto Braxton's hair, and dragged him down the steps of the basement. The automatic light came on, and he threw him onto the floor. Braxton cried uncontrollably.

"Stop your crying," Dale shouted.

Braxton lay on the floor, looking up at his father.

"You will stay here until you're fixed, you understand?"

"Dad, please–"

Dale kicked him hard in his side. "Do you understand?" he yelled.

"Yes!" Braxton responded, whimpering in pain.

Dale wiped the tears flowing from his face, then he looked

up. "Lord… have mercy," Dale said. "Have mercy on my son." Then he glanced back at Braxton. "Pray for healing, son."

He walked out, then shut and dead-bolted the door.

After four days with no sign of Braxton, Dwight had asked the headmaster if he had heard anything about him. All he would tell him is that his father had called in each day to let the school know he would be out sick. Dale and the headmaster were good friends, and golfing buddies, too.

Dwight knew Dale and Lucy from church so his suspicion about Braxton's absence ended there, but about mid-way through the second week of Braxton being away, Dwight grew very concerned that his absence may have something to do with what he had revealed to him in their post-rehearsal conversation.

Dwight had called Dale. The phone rang. No answer. Finally, Dale called him back.

"Hello?"

"Yes, Dale this is Dwight Kerry over at the school," he said, as he paced around the front of his classroom. "Just wanted to check and see if Braxton was okay, I know he has been sick for going on two weeks now–"

"Oh, he's fine!" Dale interrupted. "The boy's contracted mono, you know how that is."

"Yes, that can be terrible I've heard." Dwight replied, still uneasy about the explanation.

"Of course, but he will be fine. They have him on medicine and bed rest, but he'll be back in no time."

"Well, I sure hope so. We do miss him. He's a personality everyone just loves, and they miss it when he's gone, you know?"

"Oh yes, he'll be getting better soon enough to come on back. Thanks for checking in on him."

"Yeah, Dale, no problem."

"Okay, talk to you soon."

"Okay."

"Bye."

"Bye, bye."

At first, Dwight didn't feel good about this. Dale was a respectable man, but Dwight felt suspicious and wondered why Dale might be dishonest. He and Lucy adored their child, and that was clear to everyone in the community. There was no reason for Dale to lie; so Dwight quickly dismissed his suspicion, realizing he may be overreacting.

Ian, on the other hand, *knew* something was wrong. He had heard the sick story passing around school, but did not buy it for a second. Before, he had regularly texted Braxton and vice versa, yet he had not received a single text since Saturday night, May 5th; it had been nearly two weeks. When he rode by the Jones's house at night, he didn't see any lights on through the window of Braxton's upstairs room. Ian had grown to be very concerned.

Finally, on Thursday evening, May 24th, after no response to his calls, texts, or Snaps in days, he dropped by the Jones family residence.

He rang the doorbell. Lucy answered.

"Hello, Ian," she said.

"Hello ma'am, is Braxton okay? I haven't seen him at school in a few weeks."

"Oh yes, he's fine. Just sick, trying to get over some things."

"What's wrong with him?"

"Mono, I'm afraid," she said while trying to rush the conversation, "but he will get over it and be fine eventually I'm sure."

"Oh, well he didn't seem all that sick the last time I saw him, must have come up quickly."

Dale appeared behind the door, opening it wider so he could be seen.

"Hello young man, how are you?"

"I'm good sir, thank you."

"Ready to go play ball at Duke?"

"Yes sir."

"I bet your parents are mighty proud of you," he said.

"Yes sir, I think they are."

"Say, you wouldn't want to change that would you?"

"What do you mean?"

"Well you know," he said as a he leaned against the doorframe as Lucy peeled away from the conversation and out of sight. "Lawrence and your mother are respectable folks. Say, you wouldn't want anything to get out that, you know, may hurt you, would you?"

"I don't understand...."

"No... I think you do," Dale harshly replied. "Run along, my boy will be just fine and he'll see you when he returns to school. Okay?"

"Okay sir, but–"

"Goodbye," he said, as he shut the door gently and locked it behind him.

Ian knew right then and there what was going on. Who could he tell? He wondered if he should tell Mr. Kerry. Braxton told him he had talked to Mr. Kerry, and Mr. Kerry had proven to be understanding of his sexual identity and the associated struggle. Surely he could speak with him.

He planned to chat with him the next day after school.

For twenty days, Braxton remained locked in the basement of the Jones's household. His father, like many of the higher-ups at Freeden Baptist Church, was well-to-do, yet still very fundamental. He, like many of his colleagues and peers in Freeden, were staunch conservatives, intolerant toward anything outside the literal norms of the most fundamental variation of the Christian faith; yet, nothing seemed very Christian-like to Braxton in relation to how his father was handling this. Braxton was a prisoner, allowed to shower only in the basement bathroom, and waited each day for his mother to bring fresh clothes and food to him.

His dad wanted to make Braxton regret his 'choice', but he couldn't come to terms with giving up on who he was. He loved Ian, but more importantly, he loved the person he had become. Giving up would be taking a major step backward. One he could not accept. Dale Jones wanted to make his son *fear* what would happen if he didn't retract his statement and feelings, but the only thing Braxton truly feared was to revert back to living a life that forbid him to be true to his identity. In his darkest moments of sitting and lying in the cool, damp basement, he debated taking it back and pretending he had just been confused about himself, but he eventually committed that no matter what, he would not give in.

He knew his father, who possessed just as firm a stance, would not give in either. He had heard his father yell to Lucy one night in the previous week, "That boy will not come out of that basement until he promises to not be a gay."

His mother came down to the basement every day, and each time she would say to him, "Do you have something to tell me?" – a question Dale mandated she ask. And every morning since the night he was thrown into the basement,

Braxton answered the question, "I'm gay." Without fail, she would shed a few tears and leave his clothes placed neatly on a bar stool that sat next to the stairs, then retreat back up the stairs, dead-bolting the door on her way out. She believed homosexuality to be an abomination, but it still pained her to see her son treated like this.

Day of the *Requiem*

Ian left his last class once the final bell rang and bolted to Mr. Kerry's classroom. When he got there, Dwight was gone but a student was cleaning his whiteboard.

"Where's Mr. Kerry?" Ian asked.

"He left early today," the student said. "Has the *Requiem* concert tonight at the concert hall he had to prepare for."

Ian never spoke to Dwight about his concerns. He was too late.

That morning, Lucy came down the stairs around ten a.m. with breakfast. Braxton knew this because they had a clock in the basement with the loudest ticks he had ever heard, intended to practically torture him and drive him mad. He knew his father was likely at work, as he worked at least twelve hours every day.

She walked to the bottom of the stairs and set his breakfast on the bar stool. Then she stood upright, and asked her daily question, "Do you have something to tell me?"

Braxton began to cry. "Yes."

She perked up. For the first time, he had said something new. "What is that, honey?"

He walked over to her, standing about a foot in front of

her. "I'm sorry."

He embraced her, and she wrapped her arms around him, holding him for a minute. Then, he threw her on the floor with all the strength he could muster, ran up the stairs, and dead-bolted the door. She was only feet behind him, but had not made it up the stairs in time to prevent him from shutting the door. He hated to do this. He believed his mother, too, was a victim of oppression, but this was his only chance of getting help and he knew it.

She banged on the door and screamed. "Braxton, please don't leave me!"

"I'm sorry," he whispered under his breath.

He looked around for his phone, but could not find it. He knew time was running out. He had to get out of the house before his father came home unexpectedly while he was still there, or his mother got out somehow. He wanted to see Ian so badly, but Ian would not be able to help him right now. He had to find the one adult he could trust and that could truly help. He had to talk to Mr. Kerry.

He found the keys to his mother's Land Rover LR4, and drove it out of the driveway and away from the house. He began crying, mostly from the trauma of what had just transpired, but also from the reality that his father would be insatiably pissed. He needed help. Fast.

He drove to the river about ten miles outside of town and parked the SUV down a path he and Ian often hung out at. He stayed there until the school day was scheduled to end.

Then he drove back toward the school, in hopes of finding Mr. Kerry after school when no other school personnel would be there. He waited in the parking lot until about four, recognizing that he needed the school to be practically empty before he went in so no one could say they saw him. It was likely, since his father was probably still at work, that his mother had still not gotten out of the basement. If she had, time was rapidly running out.

He ran inside the building, and there were no signs of anyone there. Mr. Kerry, however, always stayed on Fridays until about six-thirty, so he knew he would be in his classroom. Much to his surprise, though, he rushed into Mr. Kerry's room to find no sign of him. A student was walking out the door.

"Have you seen Mr. Kerry?" Braxton asked. "It's important."

"You're the second person to come by in the last thirty minutes and ask for him," the student said. "He has a concert tonight at the concert hall."

Shit. I forgot all about the community chorus tonight. This isn't good. I'll have to go there.

The student left the room. In a panic, Braxton went and hid inside the closet of Dwight's classroom until he could figure out what to do.

What am I going to do? Braxton had to get help fast and worried he would not make it to the concert hall before being discovered. He wondered if a phone was close-by; Mr. Kerry's contact information was certainly somewhere in the room or on his desk. He scrambled around, knocking things over without regard. For the life of him, though, he could not locate Mr. Kerry's contact info. *I'm going to have to take my chances and go to the concert hall.*

Braxton ran for the door, cut into the hall, and noticed a school custodian go in one of the classrooms about twenty feet down. He backed up into Mr. Kerry's room, and peeked around the corner.

The custodian was talking on the phone. No one else seemed to be on the same floor of the building as them. "I think I heard someone up here," the man said to whoever he was talking to on the phone.

Braxton panicked, wondering if this man was looking for him. *I'm being paranoid.* He had every reason to be, though. He bolted back to the closet, shut the door gently behind him as to not make any noise, and remained silent.

He listened. The silence deafened. This being the music classroom, the insulation was thick: hardly no noise came in, and none went out. Then, he heard what he assumed was the same man come into the room, still talking to someone on the phone.

"I will find him, I assure you," the man said as he walked inside the room and shut and locked the door. "I know what to do." Then he closed what sounded like a flip phone, and said, "Braxton? I know you're in here."

Braxton began breathing heavily. The charade was finished. He was found. *What am I going to do?* He cried without making a sound, the tears now flowing, realizing he was in major trouble.

"Come on out, Braxton, I'm here to help you. Ian sent me."

Braxton was sweating. He was terrified. He didn't know if this was real or not. *What choice do I have though? I've got to come out.*

He knew he had to take the risk. So he opened the closet door.

"Hey, Braxton," the man said once he saw him.

The man appeared to be in his late twenties, physically-fit, and stood at about six-two. His baby-face was clean-shaven and he had blond hair brushed back. Braxton had never seen him working at the school before.

"You're here to help me?" Braxton asked.

"Yes, Ian sent me."

"Why would he do that? He doesn't know I'm here."

"He saw you run into the building and told me you were in danger."

"How would he know that?"

"He came by your house last night. At least that's what he told me."

"I don't know anything about that."

"Do you want to call him? He gave me his number. Here." He slid the phone over to Braxton along the floor. Braxton reluctantly bent over to pick up the phone, and when he looked up, the man punched him in the face, knocking him over a student's desk and onto his back on the floor.

The man got on his knees above of Braxton, and grabbed his throat, choking him. Gasping for air, Braxton grabbed his oppressor's hands, trying to yank them off his throat, but he could not overpower this unknown man. He was choking to death.

The man leaned in. "Listen to me, the best chance you've got of staying alive is to do what I say, you hear me?"

Braxton nodded in affirmation, desperately needing him to stop with the choking. He couldn't breathe. He needed the man to stop or he would die. The man let off of his throat, and Braxton let out a big gasp, holding his throat and trying desperately to relieve the pain caused from the man's attempt to strangle him.

Then, the man slid his pants down.

"Might as well get something out of this," he said. Then he grabbed his penis with his right hand and shoved it into Braxton's face.

"Please, no!" Braxton yelled.

The man slapped Braxton as hard as he could and said, "Do what I say or I swear to God I'll kill you!"

"Please," Braxton pleaded as he sobbed.

"Do it!"

The man thrusted violently forward at Braxton's face as he continued to cry.

Braxton bawled as the man forced him to participate in oral sex for what seemed like an eternity. The trauma he had endured for the past three weeks did not come close to what he was experiencing now.

Once the man finished he stood toweringly over the top of him. Braxton whimpered on the floor and balled himself into the fetal position. He hit Braxton across the face again. And again, and again, until his face was bloodied all over.

"Stop, please!" Braxton begged. "Help!" he screamed desperately.

"Nobody can hear you in here. Nobody is here but you and me," the man said, holding him down.

"Please stop!" he shouted. "Please!"

"Oh you want more?" he asked.

"No."

The man grabbed him by his hair, picked him up, and threw him at Dwight's desk, forcing him to bend over it. He brought out his knife and ripped Braxton's pants off with it, cutting him in the process. Then, he pulled out handcuffs from his pocket and handcuffed Braxton's arms behind him.

"Please, stop," Braxton yelled, wailing uncontrollably.

"Shut up!"

The man raped Braxton while he screamed in pain and terror.

"This is what you wanted, right?"

Braxton's cries and screams continued.

After a few minutes, the man finally stopped.

The man pulled his pants back up and walked away, but

Braxton did not move. With his hands still handcuffed behind him, he just leaned against the desk and whimpered.

The man said, "You want more?"

"No, please don't," Braxton said under his breath, barely able to speak from the pain he had endured.

The man put rubber gloves on, adjusted his clothes back to normal, and then walked over to Braxton. He leaned in and whispered in Braxton's ear, "Now I'm going to do what Daddy sent me here to do."

"What?" Braxton asked. "Daddy?"

The man pulled a large kitchen knife from his belt, and stabbed Braxton endlessly in the back. Braxton kicked and fought, but the man's strength overpowered him. Stab after stab, the knife punctured the young boy's body, each scream becoming fainter and fainter as the blood flowed.

After thirty-six stab wounds, Braxton was dead. A promising young man, a brilliant mind, and a genuinely decent person – murdered.

This room was special. It was the room in which Braxton had first encountered his true love. It was the only place where he felt at home and truly accepted. And now, his raped, violated body lay lifeless on the ground in a pool of his own blood, in the classroom of the only other man in town known to be openly gay. The accused perpetrator: Dwight Kerry.

PART 3: CONFUTATIS

9: How Can I Keep from Singing?

Dwight sat in his jail cell, alone. He had so much time to think now. For once in his life, silence dominated most of his day. He recalled the hectic school days he now longed for, and thought of a moment from the previous semester:

"Where is Braxton?" Dwight asked. "Is he coming today?"

Right then, Ian and Braxton entered the classroom together.

"Where have you two been? You're never late for rehearsal!"

"Sorry, Mr. Kerry," Braxton said.

"You should *never* be late for rehearsal."

"Sorry, Mr. Kerry," Ian said.

"Sorry," Braxton followed.

"Well, I suppose I'll let it slide this time. But when you're late, Braxton, the whole thing is put behind."

"I know, sir."

Dwight sighed. "Well, forgive me, perhaps I'm being too hard on a first-time offender." He turned back to the choir. "Okay, today we are going to work on an old traditional hymn that I do love very much. It'll start a cappella, Braxton will come in when I cue him. Okay? Let's start from the top."

The sopranos began, and the choir followed Dwight's direction:

My life flows on in endless song;

Above earth's lamentation,
I hear the sweet, tho' far-off hymn
That hails a new creation;

Thro' all the tumult and the strife
I hear the music ringing;
It finds an echo in my soul —
How can I keep from singing?

Dwight remembered this song so well, and couldn't get it out of his mind as he sat helplessly in his cell. It was a song that had been a traditional part of at least one concert each year since he began directing the school's chorus. Now, he was experiencing his own tumultuous period of strife. The song of his life felt as if it were fading.

Present

Ben arrived at the jail on Monday morning, only to be greeted at the front desk by Pam, the same, unpleasant woman who greeted him the night of Dwight's arrest. The only reason he knew her name the first night, and again now, was because she wore an old department name tag that seemingly no one else wore anymore.

"Can I help you?"

"Hey, Pam. Yes, I'm here to meet with Dwight."

"He ain't here right now, he's at his arraignment."

Ben slightly rolled his eyes, then realized he was doing it in front of her and cut it quickly. "That's tomorrow."

"I don't think so, sir–"

"I'm his attorney, I can assure you it's tomorrow."

"Oh, okay," she said clumsily. "Wait just a minute."

She rose from her seat, which must have been the first time that day, and left for the back to see if he was, in fact, not at the arraignment. "He's here," she said.

A frustrated Ben rolled his eyes. "Thank you, can I go back?"

"No."

"Okay, well when can I go back?"

"I'll let you know," she said.

"Lovely," he said sarcastically, as he walked back to his seat. Once he had sat for about three seconds, the door opened, and an officer walked into the lobby.

"Come on back, Mr. Bailey."

He followed the officer down the hallway and to the room where he would meet Dwight.

Just like the previous meeting, Ben walked inside, and the officer locked the door. He sat in his chair, alone for a while, until the door opened once more. Dwight was ushered in and relieved of his handcuffs.

"Please tell me you brought some real food," Dwight said. "My dog wouldn't eat this shit."

"I can't do that."

"Well, I'm going to need you to step up your game, my friend."

"You're in a better mood today, I see."

"I'm trying," Dwight said, shrugging his shoulders. "I really am. I've done nothing but cry the entire weekend. I'm tired of sobbing."

"I can only imagine what this has been like. I'm so sorry."

Dwight sighed, and remained silent for a long time. "Braxton was such a good boy. I cannot believe someone would do this. It's awful. He may have been my very best student."

"Well, you–"

"And I cannot fathom why they think I would have done this. But above all else, Ben, I'm still here. Perhaps I'm locked up and a slave to an obviously discombobulated justice system, but I'm still alive. There's still a chance for me. Braxton," Dwight began to tear up, "he is gone."

Ben looked down to the floor in a daze, realizing that despite the dire situation Dwight faced, in this moment he still put others before himself.

"Dwight, most people wouldn't be thinking of anything other than saving their own ass right now, you know that?"

"Not trying to be pompous, but I know I'm not most people. I care about others, even those who don't care much for me. I am fully aware most people out there right now hope I rot in hell, okay? But I don't have to feel that way about them. And I don't have to lose compassion for Braxton just because I've been wronged, either."

"You're a good man, Dwight."

"Isn't that sad?"

"What do you mean?"

"All I've done is be decent to people, and you think that's *good*. Hell, lots of people think that's good. It should be the norm if you ask me."

"The world's a rough, bitter place, Dwight."

"That's where you're wrong."

"How so?"

"Freeden is a bitter place. The world is not."

One thing was certain to Ben: bitterness had surely overridden Freeden. The begrudging assault on Dwight and Ben was indicative of that. The experience Ben had endured at 3rd Street Café indicated a more public, staunch stance against him and Dwight and what they stood for, but it paled in comparison to how the church, Dwight's own church, had so rapidly turned against him.

Ben steered the conversation toward a formal discussion of the events on the day of the *Requiem* concert. "Let's get to it." He pulled out his phone, set it on the table, and started recording. "Dwight, I need you to answer everything I ask to the best of your ability and answer everything honestly, do you understand?"

"Yes."

"Okay, let's talk about Friday, May 25th."

"Okay."

"What time did you arrive at the school that morning?"

"Seven-fifteen, as always."

"And did you leave the school at any point that day?"

"Not until I left for the concert hall, if I remember correctly."

"Take me through the whole day from that morning."

"Well," he said as he gestured with his hands as he so often did, "I'll do the best I can. Up until the *Requiem* and my subsequent arrest, I don't recall much about the day other than it being a typical Friday at Freeden High."

Ben was pleased to hear this. Dwight's lack of a concise recollection of the day's events continued to affirm his feelings that he was innocent. In his opinion, a guilty man would recall *much* more about what happened that day because he would have a reason to remember it.

"I had four classes that day, per usual. My early morning Music Theory class at eight-fifteen, Band at ten, Music History at eleven-thirty, lunch around one – or whenever I got to the cafeteria soon thereafter, and then Chorus at one-thirty. Usually we have rehearsals for the Freeden High Choir after school, but that day I had the *Requiem* concert, as you know."

"Yes."

"And so I left early, probably about three-twenty-five that afternoon, and headed over to the concert hall, where I stayed until I had dinner," he paused to correct himself, "or tried to have dinner – at David's, with you."

Ben still did not have a copy of the police report, but he had conducted some interviews with the police over the weekend. He pulled his notes from his bag. "From what I know so far, the police say they found Braxton dead at the school right around eight p.m., and that investigators believe he was murdered at or around four to four-thirty. Where were you at that time?"

"At the concert hall."

"Was anyone there with you?"

"No one showed until later. I'd say probably around five-thirty."

Ben made a clicking noise with his tongue as if something had become clear to him.

"What?" Dwight asked.

"Are you sure no one was at the concert hall until five-thirty?"

"I'm fairly certain. I'm sure I would have known if they were."

"Who was the first to arrive?"

"Dr. Colin Johnson. He's always the first to arrive."

Dr. Johnson was the bassist who Ben had run into backstage after the concert that night. And Dwight spoke correctly; Dr. Johnson was *always* the first of the choir members to arrive. No one was as pointed, or eloquent, as Dr. Johnson. And everyone respected him.

"And he was the first person you noticed come in, around five-thirty you say?"

"Yes."

"Okay, so it doesn't help that no one can corroborate your story that you were at the concert hall as early as you say you were, but perhaps we can achieve something on the other end."

"What do you mean?"

"Well, if we can prove that you were *not* at the school close to that time, then that may be an equally beneficial alibi."

"Where did it happen?" Dwight asked. "I know at the school, but where?"

Ben paused. "In your classroom."

Dwight's mouth gaped open in shock. "My God," he said. "Is that why–"

"It's not the only reason they think you did it, no," Ben interrupted. "According to the police, preliminary testing that was carried out over the weekend shows your DNA on the murder weapon. It was a knife."

"How is that possible?"

"If you didn't do it and I trust that you didn't, I don't really know how to answer that yet."

"I don't even own a knife aside from my kitchen knives."

"It was a kitchen knife, the murder weapon, I mean."

"Well, go in my house and see if they are all there."

"Did you ever take one to school?"

"Never."

"And you're certain of that?"

"Yes. One-hundred percent positive. Would never have brought something like that to school."

"Okay," Ben said, then paused. He took notes of some key things Dwight said, and assumed the recording would suffice for anything else he did not take down. "Was anybody supposed to be in your classroom that afternoon?"

"Yes, one of my students typically cleaned my boards and such for me on Fridays."

"What was that student's name?"

"Ashlee Peterlynn."

"What time did she usually leave the room?"

Dwight looked confused.

"Scratch that," Ben said. "Let me rephrase, how long did it usually take her to complete the task you hired her to do?"

Dwight nodded. "I'd say it usually takes her about forty minutes." Dwight shook his head, then leaned back in his chair. "I'm not supposed to hire a student like that in the first place, but the school janitors never really did a good job of cleaning, so I hired her every Friday to clean my classroom and wash my white boards."

"Did she know Braxton?" Ben nearly interrupted.

"I believe they probably knew one another, but they were not in any of the same classes and did not hang out together to the best of my knowledge," Dwight said. "Braxton was a very quiet gentleman, only in the last several weeks did I really see him come alive and start spending time with others. He was special friends with Ian Christopher."

"Special friends?"

"Gay lovers. I'm trying to be sensitive to your virgin ears."

Ben looked puzzled. "How did you know this?"

Dwight leaned forward again, still upright and postured. "It's an assumption based off what Braxton had told me when he *came out* to me. He told me he had a crush on Ian. I think the two had a relationship of some sort prior to him telling me about it. I know they were friends, but I believe there was something more going on even before he talked to me."

Ben began to speak, but Dwight interrupted, "I will tell you neither one of them ever came out publicly to their school mates to the best of my knowledge."

"How would you know that?" Ben asked.

"It's Freeden High School. If somebody came out as gay, everyone would know and gossip about it. And as unfortunate as that may sound, it's true."

"Did anyone know about this relationship other than you?"

"Well, I'm not one-hundred percent sure it was a relationship, but I do think it was. I know Braxton told me he was into Ian and that the two had shared their feelings with one another. As to what happened after that... I'm clueless."

"Let me–"

"Wait a second," Dwight said. "I will say that Braxton expressed concern about coming out. It could have been the same concern everyone has, but I felt you needed to know that because I could tell it worried him."

Ben leaned back in his chair, arms now crossed. "That's interesting. Do you recall what he said?"

"Nothing more than the concern anyone else has when they're coming out," Dwight replied. "What people may think, what friends and family may think."

"Did he tell you he was going to come out? Publicly, I mean?"

"No, but he did leave fairly excited about the prospect. I think it made him feel good that I accepted him so much. He had clearly been worried when we first started talking, but seemed very positive about things when he left."

Ben could not help but wonder if Braxton's murder and sexual identity were related in some way. "So, when did he come out to you?"

"A few weeks before his death."

"Hmm," Ben said as he took notes, then set his pen down, leaned back, and crossed his arms once more. "Did he have anyone he would have talked to about this other than you?"

"I do not know, really," Dwight answered. "I never knew him to be close to anyone until he mentioned Ian to me. He was always a mama's boy, though."

Ben's gazed at Dwight with a blank stare. The mama's boy comment made Ben wonder if he may have come out to his parents. It made him wonder what their reaction might have been like if he had.

"Let me ask you this," Ben restarted. "When's the last time you saw Braxton?"

"Not too terribly long after that, though I don't recall the exact date. I could look at my attendance chart in class. That would help pinpoint the exact date."

"Was he not at school the day this happened?

"No," Dwight said. "He had been out sick."

"Out sick? How long?"

"About two weeks or so if I remember correctly," Dwight said. "In fact, after a while I got worried, and administration wouldn't tell me anything. So I called his father directly. Dale said he had been sick."

"Did he give any details?"

"Mono is what he said Braxton was dealing with. I found it all to be a strange coincidence."

"Did anyone tell you to call? Was it against protocol to call?"

"No and no. Braxton was my pianist for the school chorus. It wasn't like him to be sick like this, but more importantly, he is and always was an integral piece of the choir, so I called to check on him and make sure he was okay out of genuine concern. Dale told me he was sick and would be back in no time."

"And I just want to confirm that he was not in attendance

on Friday, May 25th, is that right?"

"That's correct. He was still marked as sick that day by administration. I never saw him that day – that I can tell you for sure."

Ben thought this seemed very strange. Being out over two weeks from school and suddenly raped and murdered *at the school.* And Dale Jones had verified to Dwight that Braxton was, in fact, sick. He couldn't help but wonder why he would be at the school that Friday afternoon if he had been out sick with mono for the previous two weeks, including that day.

"When you called Dale and spoke to him directly, was that the last time you contacted anyone about Braxton being absent?" Ben asked.

"Yes."

Ben paused, thinking about what to ask next. He gathered his thoughts and restarted. "Let's talk about Braxton a little more," Ben said. "Other than this conversation you had with him when he came out to you, did you notice anything strange about him in the last days you saw him?"

"Nothing at all. In fact, he seemed very chipper in the last days I spent around him. I assumed it was because of a burgeoning love life. I don't know, but I can say with certainty that nothing seemed wrong with Braxton the last time I was around him."

"Okay," Ben replied. He started writing on his pad again, then sat upright from his note-taking position and set his pen back down. "I'm going to want to talk to Ian Christopher. Did you ever talk to him about his and Braxton's supposed relationship?"

"No, he and I never spoke about the matter, but I do know him because he is also in my choir – a baritone to be exact."

"Alright," Ben said, "so my early assessment is that even in these few short minutes there is quite a bit of uncertainty in the charges you are facing and a lot of uncertainty in the last couple weeks of Braxton's life." He paused, stroked his short beard with his right hand. "Let me ask you this, do you have any idea why he would have been in your classroom that afternoon? Because if there's one thing we know for sure, it's that they found him dead lying next to your desk, so he was definitely in the–"

"Oh my," Dwight said.

Ben noticed that this troubled Dwight. "I'm… sorry for the boldness. I didn't mean to be insensitive."

Dwight held his hand out, trying to stop Ben from saying anything further that would expand on this terrible vision. Once he composed himself, he said, "I'm fine. Sorry."

Ben waited for a moment, then spoke in a softer tone. "Do you know why he may have been in your classroom that afternoon?

"Ben, I truly do not know," he said, followed by a deep sigh. "I had told my students I wouldn't be there that afternoon and had canceled afternoon rehearsals. He likely didn't know that since he hadn't been to school in a while, but I truly have no idea why he was there or how he got there."

Ben took his glasses off, set them on the table, and leaned back in his chair. "Okay, Dwight, I have to ask you this. Do you know why they believe you did this?"

"I'm afraid I do."

"Yeah," Ben replied.

The room fell completely silent for the first time in their meeting.

"This would never happen if it wasn't a place like Freeden," Dwight said.

"What do you mean?"

"They think it because I'm gay, don't they? They think I'm a freak."

Ben sighed. "Forgive me for the graphic detail," Ben said, "but Braxton was raped by a man, that is for certain. You're the only person around here that people think would get pleasure out of something like this. You're the only person they think could logically do something like this."

"That's a fool's ideology."

"Of course it is. But Dale Jones seemed pretty adamant that he believes you did this in his interview over the weekend with police, and subsequently, the police support the notion that *you* did this. And you can bet your bottom dollar that Dale's status in this community is having a major effect on your charges, too. He's respected here, and for some reason, he believes you did it. Now I've got to look into this, because I do believe his son's recently unveiled sexual identity has something to do with the whole situation. It's very strange that he came out to you and weeks later, he's out sick for two weeks, and then is suddenly found dead."

"It's very odd," Dwight replied. The two paused again for an extended period of time. Dwight interrupted the silence. "Why would someone want to frame me for this?"

Ben put his glasses back on, gazing at his notes as he answered the question. "Not sure that they would want to frame you. You could instead be a mere scapegoat for the real perpetrator. It may not be as malicious toward you as it is simply using you for them to get off. But I think we have identified a few things: one, that your own sexuality isn't helping you. In fact, it's pretty obvious that it's hurting you. Your openness with your students seems to be hurting you, too. I mean no harm by this, but I maintain what I said the first night, that your willingness to counsel and be open with students about subjects the school system would not typically permit teachers to discuss with students has been damaging for you in this case so far."

"But how can I stop, Ben?" Dwight said. "How could I quit being the mentor they needed me to be? You have no idea how many students have come to me and expressed fear for simply being *different*. Not just gay, but *different*! You have no idea how many young people growing up in the same town you and I did have wanted to kill themselves because they're different from everyone else here, and made to feel like that's a bad thing. You have no idea whatsoever, and I'm not going to let them be alone," he said as he wildly shook his head, then stood up from his seat and paced. "I don't give a damn what the school system says, or what the norm is. I will never let my students feel like they're alone. And you have no idea how many of them would if it wasn't for me being there for them!"

An officer opened the door. "What's going on in here, counsel?"

"It's fine, officer," Ben replied.

Dwight had clearly grown upset, and the officer noticed. He still looked suspicious, despite Ben saying things were okay.

"Seriously, officer," Ben reiterated. "All is fine."

The officer, still concerned, backed out and left the room, again locking the door behind him.

Dwight almost immediately continued, now in a softer tone, "I will never compromise and comply with the administration's status quo if it jeopardizes my students' well-being. And while I know I'll likely never teach again, I wouldn't change a damn thing I did." He began raising his voice again, "And I will never regret telling Braxton Jones that it's okay to be himself!"

Ben interrupted, "Dwight, calm down."

"That it's okay to be different than everyone else here," he yelled, growing more frustrated. "He's not alone, you know? Listen to me, I will never regret telling him it's okay to be gay. Because it *is* okay to love Jesus and be gay, all at the same time. I have followed Christ my whole life, and I know my heart is in a good place. But I'm attracted to the same sex, and damnit, that's okay. And it was okay for him too." Dwight's angry monologue brought tears to his eyes as he continued pacing around the table. "He was scared to death for being who he was born to be, and I'll be damned if I was going to contribute to that fear. So, I don't care how damaging it was to my case or whatever is going on here. At least the boy learned in his final days that being himself was okay. And if my punishment for that is getting locked up, then it was fucking worth it."

"Dwight," Ben said as he got up to calm him. He walked over to him, and Dwight fell into his arms, now sobbing again.

"How can I keep from singing?" he asked while resting his head on Ben's shoulder. "It's all I know to do."

Dwight's selflessness astounded Ben yet again. He wondered what, if anything, had happened in his life to trigger Dwight being so caring toward others. For as long as he had known Dwight, he had *always* been this way, putting others first and spending as much time as needed to help those who sought it from him. Truthfully, Dwight could not keep from singing. His passion was to help others no matter what, and no rules or guidelines would prevent him from doing what was best for his students. His students were his family; caring for them was his passion.

He truly epitomized the person Ben desired to be. Ben stood there, holding a broken, weeping man in his arms, now recognizing even more the ridiculousness of having spent his whole life trying to please the people of Freeden. He recognized he must raise his standards. These were not the people Ben cared to associate with. But Dwight had long known how the people were here, and despite it, he still longed to serve them.

Dwight wasn't guilty, and Ben knew it. But someone was, and he had to figure out who. And why. And fast. Or the wrong guy would certainly go down.

That night, Ben worked at the office preparing for the arraignment and trial that would likely follow. The police had finally sent the official report. The others on the team, having worked all day and since the report was received, had just left. It was ten minutes to eleven. Ben had no desire to go home yet.

The streets were already adorned with barricades separating the sidewalk from the road, as the city were operating under the assumption that protesters would line the streets in the morning as the police brought Dwight to the courthouse. Local news stations had positioned their trucks by the courthouse and jail so they would get the best angle for every potential rating-building segment they could find. It all disgusted Ben. He sat there, sipping on a Crown on the rocks, wondering if the worst of the community response was yet to come. He assumed so.

Thinking everyone had already left for the night, Brenda walked into his office, almost unnoticed, and alarmed him. "You still working?"

"Something like that. Just gathering my final thoughts on the arraignment and what will follow. I didn't know you were still here."

"I know. Are you ready?"

"Pretty simple what we plan to do. I'm nervous about the

way it goes after."

"Me too, Ben. Have you heard?"

"Heard what?"

"It's going to be a packed house in the courtroom tomorrow, and I'm quite certain from what I'm hearing that the group there won't see eye to eye with you."

"Figured."

"Keep your head up, Ben. You've always done the right thing."

Ben took another sip of his Crown. "Yeah, well, has it always been for the right reasons?"

"What do you mean?"

He sighed. "Eh, sorry... been doing a bit of self-evaluation lately."

"Well, you've always had a good heart. Stop beating yourself up."

"Yeah."

"How long you plan to be here tonight?"

"Not sure."

"Do I need to pick up dinner for you? I know you haven't eaten. You didn't eat any of the pizza I brought earlier."

"I'm fine, thank you though, Brenda. That's very nice of you."

She took a deep breath. "Ben?"

He looked up from his desk. "Yeah?"

"Get some rest. I'm worried about you."

He chuckled, but then realized she was serious and cut it. "Thanks, Brenda, you've always been good to me."

"Oh, don't get all mushy on me now," she said, laughing. "See you tomorrow, sugar."

"Bye," he said, smiling as she walked out.

He heard the back door shut behind her and continued

reading the police report. Ben was baffled at the events he had discussed with Dwight earlier in the day. Something just was not right. He read the police report again.

CHIEF MCDOWELL RECEIVED A CALL AT SEVEN-FIFTEEN P.M. FROM SCHOOL SYSTEM EMPLOYEE, PEGGY POWELL. SHE TOLD HIM THAT A DOOR HAD BEEN LEFT UNLOCKED AND CRACKED OPEN TO THE MAIN BUILDING. OFFICERS JON VAUGHAN AND RICKY MARKS ARRIVED ON THE SCENE AND NOTICED THE OPEN DOOR, AND DID A CHECK THROUGH THE BUILDING TO ENSURE NO ISSUES REMAINED BEFORE LEAVING. ON THE THIRD FLOOR, OFFICERS VAUGHAN AND MARKS CHECKED A ROOM IDENTIFIED TO BE MR. DWIGHT KERRY'S MUSIC CLASSROOM AND FOUND THE BODY OF BRAXTON JONES, THE VICTIM, ON THE FLOOR NEXT TO MR. KERRY'S DESK. A NOTE WAS LEFT BEHIND ABOUT TWO FEET FROM HIS HAND THAT READ 'DWIGHT KERRY'. NOTE WAS IDENTIFIED BY DALE JONES, THE FATHER, AS THE BOY'S HANDWRITING. THE PEN USED WAS ONE FROM MR. KERRY'S DESK, INDICATED BY THE LABEL "D. KERRY" TAPED TO IT. FULL DNA TESTING BEING COMPLETED, ORDERED BY CHIEF MCDOWELL. MURDER WEAPON WAS RECOVERED IN THE BUILDING, PRELIMINARY TESTING SHOWS MR. KERRY'S FINGER PRINT ON THE MURDER WEAPON: A LARGE KITCHEN KNIFE.

RAPE KIT WAS CONDUCTED; VICTIM APPEARS TO HAVE BEEN VIOLENTLY RAPED IN THE ANAL CAVITY. NO BODILY FLUIDS WERE FOUND IN THE RAPE KIT, PROTECTION LIKELY USED SINCE NO DNA FOUND.

VICTIM WAS STABBED TO DEATH. THIRTY-SIX PUNCTURES TO THE BODY; THE WOUNDS MATCH THE SIZE AND SHAPE OF THE APPARENT MURDER WEAPON.

Ben knew nothing about the handwritten note until his team received the police report that evening. *How in the hell would someone be stabbed thirty-six times and write a note clear enough that someone could identify the handwriting?* This all seemed so strange – and ridiculous. He also wondered who would be foolish enough to ditch the murder weapon on campus? If Dwight was, in fact, innocent, he knew someone must have planted the note to make it look like Dwight committed the act, and the police were buying the absurdity – or selling it.

If this was done deliberately, who would have such a vendetta against Dwight? Ben thought about the conversation earlier at the jail, and remembered telling Dwight that it could simply be someone trying to get off from being charged with the crime and using him as an easy target. That was still a possibility, too.

Another point of concern for Ben was the two weeks leading up to the murder. Braxton was absent from school for two weeks and suddenly found murdered at the school. *Have the police even investigated this?* Whatever the case may be, all of this was not adding up for Ben.

By the time Ben began packing his things to leave, it was nearly midnight. He grabbed a few things, set the alarm, and walked out the back door to his truck, which he always parked in the farthest spot from the door to make room for his employees to park closer. He could still hear the alarm, which chimed loudly every five seconds for a minute until it finally set.

He got to his car, pushed unlock on the key fob, and opened his door.

"You ready for tomorrow, Ben?" a voice asked from behind him.

Ben turned around quickly, a bit startled. There stood Buck Henson, the city planning director and Aaron's close friend, and two city police officers he recognized by face but not by name, who were not dressed in uniform.

"What can I do for you gentlemen?" Ben asked.

"You're going to do the right thing tomorrow, right?" Buck asked.

"I always do, pal," Ben replied.

"I'm not sure about that."

"Well you can bet your bottom dollar on it," Ben said sarcastically.

"Look, buddy, this is a courtesy I'm affording you. You know he did it, and it's not going to be good if this thing drags out."

"Yeah, well to be honest," he paused briefly, "things just don't seem to be adding up for me." Ben started getting in his truck.

"Well, they need to start adding up," Buck said sharply.

Ben turned his head and looked directly at Buck. "Is that a threat?"

"No," Buck replied, "you just need to make sense of all this before it gets bad."

"That most certainly is a threat." Then he pointed at the officers and said, "And I can certainly get you two fired for threatening me."

"Can you?" one asked.

"It seems you don't have the say in this town you had as recently as a week ago," Buck said.

"What the hell is going on here?" Ben asked.

Buck and the officers started to back away. "Just be smart and do the right thing," he said, "and this will all be over."

Ben stared at them, then proceeded to get into his truck and shut the door, watching them the entire time. He put the key in the ignition, started the truck, and shifted to drive.

"Do the right thing, Ben," Buck yelled. Ben could hear him through the windows as he drove off.

The threats. The absurdity of the police report. Dwight's interview. Everything confused. *Why would Buck be threatening him?* Ben knew for sure now that this *would* get worse. Driving home, he worried what might await him there. He wondered what, if anything, he should expect when he got home, or anymore, for that matter. One thing he knew for certain: he was going to do the right thing. Not for the purpose of personal gain, or for the purpose of conforming to this hateful town's norms; he would simply do the right thing because it was just.

He recalled lyrics from a *Requiem* movement which were most applicable:

Confutatis maledictis
Flammis acribus addictis,
Voca me cum benedictis.

The English translation:

When the accursed have been condemned
And doomed to the searing flames,
Summon me with the saved.

Ben began praying that Dwight might, indeed, be

summoned with the saved. Because he would surely need saving from the hell that lay ahead.

10: The Worst of Sins

Dark, cloudy skies loomed over Freeden. Just days removed from Dwight's arrest, the arraignment was scheduled to take place in just under an hour at the Freeden Courthouse. Police officers readied Dwight to leave the jail and transport him to the courthouse.

"Let's move," one officer said as he opened the door to Dwight's cell.

Dwight, who sat in an upright, postured position, stood up, never breaking his stiff stance. The officer walked over to him and reached for Dwight's arms, but a cooperative Dwight put his own hands behind his back as to avoid being shoved and tugged on in an abusive manner like he had been in the previous few days. The officer noticed, pulled his hand away from Dwight's arm, and proceeded to handcuff him gently. The officer tapped Dwight's shoulder, signaling him to move forward, and they walked out of the cell.

After leaving the building through the back exit, Dwight noticed they were putting him in the back of a large truck, a maximum security vehicle that carried only the most heinous of criminals.

"What is this? "Dwight asked while laughing disgustingly. "I could understand if Hannibal Lecter were to be carried around in something like this, but Jesus Christ, I'm just a teacher and a choir director."

"For security reasons," the officer responded.

"What do you mean?"

"You'll see."

Other officers opened the back of the truck. Dwight stepped in and they closed the door behind him. He hurried over to the single bucket chair in the back, facing forward, and the truck began moving within seconds without regard to whether he had found his seat.

The truck, with an escort of police vehicles in the front and back, turned out of the lot and onto the street next to the jail that led to Main Street. Dwight had a decent view of the street out of the front window from his seat, and it became apparent when they turned onto Main Street why he was being carried in a maximum security vehicle.

The street was lined with protesters, a several hundred people on that block alone, pushed back by barricades to allow the vehicles to pass. Protesters hurled items at the truck, and the sound of them hitting the sides grew deafening. He could hear the chanting and the hollering, and he could see many of the signs people were holding:

FAGS WILL BURN!

GAY IS WRONG!

GAYS = FREAKS

Television station trucks were parked on the road, likely filming all of this. All the stations appeared to be local from what Dwight could tell.

"Oh my God," Dwight said aloud.

He couldn't believe what he was seeing. For a world in 2018 that was so progressive, it was unimaginable how backward life still was in Freeden.

He recognized some people he saw through the front window but did not know most of them. The hatred they exhibited paralleled nothing he had seen in his hometown before. He knew he had done nothing wrong, but the people screaming, yelling, and throwing objects at the truck surely thought differently. It was clear that they already believed he was guilty of this crime. *How will this town ever know the truth?* For him, this was the first time he had witnessed a public reaction to what he was accused of, and the protesting made it clear that convincing the masses he was innocent would be an uphill battle.

The driver, another Freeden police officer who was separated from Dwight by a metal cage barrier, spoke to him, "Well, Mr. Kerry, there's one thing I can say for sure."

Dwight could hardly hear him over the loud truck motor and the chanting outside. "What did you say?"

The officer spoke louder. "There's one thing I can say for sure, Mr. Kerry."

"And that is?"

"You done brought this town together," he said, as he chuckled clumsily.

Dwight thought this was an incredibly disturbing way of looking at the chaos that ensued on Main Street. He wondered how many other people might view what was going on this way. Would the townspeople consider this to be a rallying cry for fundamentalism? He certainly hoped not, not only because he vehemently disagreed with some of the many principles of the most radically-conservative sector of the faith, but also because he didn't want to be the catalyst for further institutionalizing an ideology he so strongly opposed. The bottom line, though, is that he knew he didn't do it, but the thousands of people that stood along the street wholeheartedly believed he did. And it was disappointing to think that this false allegation may ultimately be his downfall.

Would someone... anyone... watch this on the news and believe that this is wrong? The thing Dwight knew he had going against him was not *just* that he was a gay man in a small, rural town, but also that he was an accused murderer and rapist. The two combined, he believed, created something this town *really* hated.

There is nothing I can do to change this. Dwight knew he would have to rely on Ben and his team to help him, but worried there may be nothing he, or anyone for that matter, could do either. If the authoritarians of the town harbored the same ill will as the thousands of people that protested on Main Street, he was doomed.

The truck arrived at the courthouse, and another near thousand protesters stood there at the back entrance where Dwight was expected to enter. He looked out the window and asked, "What do you plan to do to keep me safe?"

The officer, about to get out of the driver's seat, replied, "Hope for the best." Then he got out and shut the driver-side door.

"Great strategy," Dwight said. "What a brilliant mind."

The back doors swung open and about five officers rushed him out and guarded him the best they could for the short walk to the courthouse entrance. People were visibly angry. They chastised him, pointed at him, and mocked him as he walked by in a degrading display.

"Go to hell you child killer!" one protester yelled.

"Death row! Death row! Death row!" others chanted.

The crowd started throwing small objects at him; something actually hit Dwight in the face.

The officers finally got Dwight inside, and the doors locked behind them. The protesters continued to beat on the door, not hard enough to break the glass but forceful enough to make Dwight uncomfortable. He wiped his face on the shoulder of his grey jumpsuit, and was marched into the courtroom.

Dwight immediately noticed Ben at the defense table with his two attorneys Liz and Kristen. Ken Hughes sat on the row behind them. Ben rose to greet him, and an officer removed the handcuffs from Dwight's hands.

"Hello, my friend," Dwight said, trying to calm down.

"Dwight," he responded as the two embraced. "You doing okay?"

"Yeah, I guess so."

"Don't let what's going on out there get to you," Ben replied. "They don't know anything about this… or you."

"And that's what bothers me the most."

"Well, are you surprised? You know you shouldn't be."

"No. Disappointed, though. Helpless, you might say."

"Well your disappointment may not get much better after this. I'm worried, Dwight."

It was just before nine a.m., and not one seat remained empty in the courtroom. The gallery was packed with a few local reporters, citizens, and members of the Jones family, highlighted mostly by Dale and Lucy Jones, who sat front row behind the prosecution.

District attorney Scott Stevens walked in with his recently hired assistant district attorney, Kate Gregory. Ben noticed her as soon as she walked in, and the two made eye contact as they approached the prosecution's desk. She didn't smile, as the moment simply didn't call for it. But she was stunning, just like the first time he saw her.

About two minutes later, the bailiff stood to begin the

arraignment.

"All rise," he exclaimed.

Everyone complied and stood.

"Oh yes, oh yes, oh yes, the Freeden County Superior Court is now in session," he said in a thick, Southern accent. "The Honorable Judge Phillip Freeman is presiding."

Judge Freeman, a towering figure with a close haircut and a clean-shaven, long face, entered the room from a small door adjacent to his bench and proceeded to take his seat.

"Thank you, bailiff," Judge Freeman said. "You all may be seated."

Everyone followed suit and took their seats. Judge Freeman shuffled papers in front of him for over a minute, and finally looked up toward the defense. "This is an arraignment for you, Mr. Kerry. I'm going to read the indictment aloud, so please, pay attention. Count one: the grand jury charges you with murder in the first degree alleged to have occurred on the evening of Friday, May 25th, 2018. Count two: statutory rape in the first degree, also occurring on the evening of Friday, May 25th, 2018. The defendant, Dwight Kerry, knowingly and intentionally committed an act of non-consensual sexual relations with Braxton Jones, the victim, and in an apparent moment of frustration with his victim not complying with his demands of the sexual nature, murdered the victim by stabbing him thirty-six times in the back until the victim bled to death. Mr. Bailey, have you discussed the charges set forth in counts one and two of the indictment with your client?"

Ben took his glasses off, laid them on the table, and stood. "Yes sir, I have."

"Does your client wish to enter a plea at this time as to the charges in the indictment?"

"Yes, sir."

"And how does your client plead?"

With no hesitation, Ben said, "Mr. Kerry pleads not guilty to each count."

"Blasphemy!" Dale Jones stood. Most of the attendees began to applaud.

"Light him up!" another attendee yelled to increased applause.

"Order," Judge Freeman said in a light-hearted tone. Most judges Ben had worked with in other counties would *never* have tolerated this outburst from the gallery, even if it came from the father of a murder victim. This worried him, tremendously. He grew concerned that Judge Freeman would not be fair and honest in this case. He already suspected it would be a problem since Dr. Henson was good friends with Judge Freeman, but until there was an evident issue of unfairness, he didn't have a case for removing the judge.

"All right, all right," Judge Freeman said. "Are you sure this is the desire of your client, Mr. Bailey? These are very serious charges."

Ben looked over at the prosecution, wondering if they too, as respectable attorneys, recognized how ludicrous it was for a judge to essentially ask the defense counsel if he was sure this was the desire of his client. "Your Honor, my client enters a not guilty plea on both counts and that's final!"

"Don't raise your voice at me, Mr. Bailey. Not ever. You understand me?"

"Yes, your honor. I understand."

"All right." He paused as if he was waiting for Ben to say something differently. Then he stared at Ben for about fifteen seconds, and finally looked down,. "A plea of not guilty is entered as to both counts of the indictment. Is there discovery?"

Scott Stevens stood to represent the prosecution. "Yes, your Honor, there is discovery and it will be released to the defense no later than tomorrow. The prosecution expects to engage in plea discussions with the defense in the coming days. We would like, perhaps, to conduct a status conference with your supervision this Friday morning, if that works for your schedule?"

"That'll do," Judge Freeman replied.

Ben stood again, with a perplexed look on his face. "Your Honor, I have no problem sitting down and discussing the possibility of a plea agreement with the State under your guidance after review of discovery, but I'm not sure two days is enough time for preparation, since the State has said we will not receive discovery until, perhaps, tomorrow."

"I think you'll have more than enough time," Judge Freeman replied.

"You're kidding?" Ben asked.

"What did you say to me?" he fired back sharply.

"I said you're kidding, right? There's no way forty-eight hours is enough time to work with discovery, and it's absurd to hold a status conference this early in the first place."

"Mr. Bailey, I'm asking that you sit down, now."

"I'm asking for more time, your Honor, which I think is very fair."

"Sit down, Mr. Bailey!"

"No. There's not a case I've ever tried where the prosecution and the defense didn't agree on a time for a plea discussion, and you're forcing us to prepare in two days based only on the little we have already been given by the State?"

"Mr. Bailey, I'm warning you–"

"Your Honor, if the State is already prepared for a plea discussion this Friday, then you can bet your ass that somebody was prepared for this long before last Friday's arrest, and you must understand what that looks like to me and my client."

"Enough!" he shouted. The chatter in the gallery heightened.

One person yelled, "The gay's trying to find a hole!" The comment was received with laughter and applause from the gallery. Dwight turned around in his chair, looking back at the gallery in disgust.

"Order!" the judge shouted in a much bitterer, harsher tone than the last time. The gallery silenced at his command. "What are you implying, Mr. Bailey? That the State is acting wrongfully?"

"I'm implying that Dwight Kerry deserves fair, due process, and giving us two days to prepare for plea discussions after receiving the State's evidence a day *after* the arraignment is a fucking joke."

"Mr. Bailey, one more word like that, or at all, and I'm holding you in contempt!"

Ben knew it was time to stop, so he sat down. *I'll be damned if they're going to push Dwight to death row without a fucking fight.* There was no reason to rush this plea discussion, and certainly no reason the two sides could not agree on when that would be. A rushed process was being forced on the defense. Ben did not like the way this was looking. Not one bit.

Silence again filled the courtroom. Judge Freeman said, "A status conference will be held in my office this Friday morning at eight-thirty. Mr. Bailey, you better come with a much different attitude on Friday than the one you've brought with you here today, you understand me?"

Ben did not reply.

"Mr. Bailey," he yelled, "do you understand me?"

Ben rose from his seat. "Yes, your Honor."

Judge Freeman was none too pleased with the dialogue he and Ben were engaging in, so he leaned back in his seat with a look of repulsion on his face. "Now, it seems to me the charges are pretty cut and dry. How soon, if no plea agreement is made, could the State be ready for trial?"

Scott stood again and said confidently, "Your Honor, the State can be ready as early as next week if no agreement is reached Friday."

"And the Defense?" Judge Freeman asked.

"I would prefer at least a month to prepare for trial," Ben said. "The State never moves this quickly on a first-degree murder case, so I'm not sure why there is a need to rush the Defense on the matter in this case."

"Mr. Bailey and Mr. Stevens," Judge Freeman started, "I expect each of you to have a fair opportunity to gather evidence in support of your case; however, I will not tolerate dragging this out. I have a major desire, given the seriousness of these charges and how it is affecting this community, to complete this trial, if there even is a trial, as expeditiously as possible. Now we will discuss this more at the status conference, but understand that I want all witnesses to be ready in a very timely manner and I expect that if this does, in fact, go to trial, then it will do so very soon so this community can be relieved of this ongoing heartache and we can go ahead and find some resolution in this matter. Is that understood?"

"Yes, your Honor," Scott said.

Ben nodded, though he truly resented this decision. "Understood."

"Anything else we need to address?" Judge Freeman asked.

"No, sir," Scott said.

"No, your Honor," Ben said.

"I will see you on Friday. Thank you, we're adjourned." Judge Freeman rose from his seat.

"All rise as the Honorable Judge Freeman exits the courtroom," the bailiff yelled.

Dwight leaned in. "What just happened, Ben?"

"I'll tell you what happened," Ben said. "They're trying to make sure you get locked up for life. Either that or death row… one or the other. And they're trying to make it happen fast. And I don't know why."

"How are we going to prepare for the status conference in two days?" Kristen leaned in and asked. "There is no way that can happen."

"Kristen, I think it's fair to say we don't have much of a choice," Ben replied. "You know as well as I do what's going on here."

"It's corrupt," Ken said as he walked up to them. "And Dwight, my friend," he turned to face Dwight directly, "we're going to have to prove much more than not guilty."

"We'll have to prove he's completely innocent," said Liz. "That's the only way."

Dwight turned to Ben, looking to see if he agreed. Ben nodded, affirming his fears. This would be a long, uphill battle to exonerate Dwight.

The officer came over to take Dwight back to the jail.

"What's the plan?" Dwight asked as he was being handcuffed.

"I'm coming to see you in just a bit."

The officer pulled Dwight away forcefully.

"Hey, can you lighten up with my client?" Ben asked the officer as he guided Dwight away.

"No need," Dwight answered as he was escorted out of the room. "Already tried. Not the brightest bulb in the chandelier.

Never had a Mr. Kerry lesson in courtesy and respect, I can promise you that."

Even with all the tragedy that had consumed his life, Dwight still found a way to be humorous. *How could he still be such a pleasant person with all the anguish he was enduring?*

Liz stepped over to talk to Ben privately, and leaned in to whisper, but was forced to speak louder due to all the noise from the gallery. "I'm genuinely concerned about what just happened."

"Yeah, I know," Ben responded. "I'm going to meet with Dwight. I need you to find a way to get discovery evidence from the prosecution sooner than later. We don't have much time."

"I'm on it."

Liz and Kristen grabbed their briefcases and left through the middle aisle and out the main entrance toward the back of the courtroom. Ben packed his briefcase, and Kate was standing close to the prosecution's table, seemingly waiting for him to notice. He turned toward her.

"Ms. Gregory."

"Ben."

"Ah, yes. You told me to call you Kate."

"I did."

"We met in the courtroom sooner than I had anticipated."

"Yes, so it seems. Look, I'd like to get together soon? I'd like to chat. Perhaps Friday night would do?"

"Depending on where this case stands at that point, but yes I'd love that. Have to eat, right?" *Have to eat? Is that the best you could come up with, Ben?*

"David's, perhaps? I've been wanting to go," she said.

"Deal. Eight p.m.?"

"Sounds great, looking forward to it," she said.

Ben smiled, then proceeded to walk down the aisle to the back. Kate stood behind for a moment.

As Ben walked away, someone yelled at him, "I hope you feel good about this, you bastard!"

The gallery went silent. It was Dale Jones. He was being held back by two of his friends who were there to support the family. Ben looked at him. Realizing it was best not to interact with an angry, obviously emotional Dale Jones, he then turned back, looking at an astounded Kate. Ben nodded at her, and started walking again to the exit.

"You won't even say anything to me you coward," Dale screamed, still being held back.

"You aren't one of us Ben Bailey!" another citizen in attendance yelled. Cheers followed the remark as Ben walked down the aisle. The gallery booed Ben as he walked out, screaming profanities and calling him names. He looked up toward the main courtroom entrance at the end of the aisle he was walking down, and just next to the door stood Dr. Dan Henson.

Ben made eye contact with Dr. Henson, who stood there with the most sinister grin on his face. The contrast was incredible; as the gallery booed and shouted at Ben while he walked out the room, Dr. Henson did the exact opposite, grinning in apparent satisfaction. Ben stopped just feet in front of Dr. Henson, and stared at him. The tension was unmatched, but despite Ben's visible anger, Dr. Henson never budged from his cunning smile.

Amidst all the chaos in the courtroom that went unaddressed by the bailiff or any court official, for that matter, Ben stood there, still staring at Dr. Henson, and said, "How can these people not see you for who you really are?"

Dr. Henson never said a word. He simply continued to

grin. Ben turned back toward the door and walked out the courtroom. In the hallway, Scott Stevens stood near the courthouse entrance on his cell phone.

"Yes, I'll have a chicken parmesan sub please. No, just half, just a half sandwich. And can you make sure they have a pickle on the side?"

Ben stood next to him, waiting for him to end the call. Scott made no rushed attempt to get off his phone.

"Okay, I'll be back in a bit. Oh, and can I get a Diet Mountain Dew, too, please? Okay, thank you. Yes, bye."

He ended the call and slid the phone in his pocket.

"You see anything wrong in there?" Ben asked him.

"Well, let's see. We had an arraignment, your client entered a plea, and we established the procedure moving forward," Scott said. "No, I really didn't see anything wrong, other than you doing Dwight an incredible disservice by entering a not guilty plea. But we'll discuss that on Friday, I'm sure."

"What's going on here, Scott? I thought you were a decent attorney."

"Oh, hurling insults, I see? That'll get you places."

"Why is this being rushed?" Ben asked.

"The judge said it, Ben. This is going to rip apart our community if we don't put it to bed soon."

"Put it to bed? Trust me, I want to end this as soon as possible too, but not at the expense of an innocent man."

"Oh, the song sung by so many," Scott said. "Innocent man? Not hardly."

"You read that police report and honestly think it makes sense?"

"Discovery surely does."

"Well, if we don't get it by tomorrow, then we won't be at

a status conference on Friday."

"Oh, I'll see to it that you get it by then. After that, this will surely end with a plea agreement on Friday morning. And it likely won't be anything better than life without parole, if that."

Scott's phone rang. He picked it up and started talking. "Hello? Yes, Chief how are you?" He nodded at Ben, then walked away. Ben shook his head at the ignorance, but didn't dwell on it for much longer than a second. He had to get to the jail.

As he drove, he noticed the considerably large number of protesters that seemed to be growing on the streets. No one recognized him in his truck, at least the protesters didn't, so they weren't hurling objects toward him like they had the vehicle hauling Dwight to the arraignment. Local television cameras were rolling, capturing all of this. He wondered how long it would take for someone to look at this circus and say, *What the hell is wrong with these people?* So far, no one in the media had.

He arrived at the jail, and Pam was yet again at the front desk.

"Here to meet Mr. Kerry?"

"Yes, ma'am."

An officer walked in the lobby. "Right this way, sir." This was the same officer who had led Dwight out of the courtroom.

As the two walked back through the hallway to the room he would meet Dwight, Ben said, "Hey, why don't you take it easy on my client, okay?"

"I don't answer to you," he said.

"What a prick."

"What did you say?"

Ben realized all of this was getting the best of him. "Nothing, sorry."

The officer opened the door to the questioning room, and Ben walked in and set up shop. The morning had underwhelmed, and he knew he had a terrible attitude. In a way it was warranted, though, as he had grown angry over the arraignment proceedings and the reaction of the gallery as he walked out. He continued to believe he was doing the right thing. His job, for one, and standing by a helpless Dwight for the other, but it still hurt to see his hometown treat him and Dwight this way. The protesters and gallery attendees treated Dwight as if they knew, without question, that he was guilty, but they also directed that same hatred and fury to Ben for defending him. Ben's frustration mounted, but he knew that in order to give Dwight a fair trial he needed to reign in his emotions and rely on his talent and reputation as a respected lawyer. He hoped that would be enough.

The door opened again, and Dwight was brought into the room. "Miss me?" Dwight asked as they relieved him of his handcuffs.

"You bet," Ben said.

The door locked behind him. "So tell me, how did this morning *really* go?"

"To be honest, not good," Ben replied. "I was already suspicious of whether or not you'd get a fair trial with Judge Freeman at the helm."

"He's good friends with Dr. Henson, yes?"

"He most certainly is. And Dr. Henson was there."

"I didn't see him."

"Well, he was certainly there. And to think it was for no reason would be naïve."

"Why would Dr. Henson be so against me? I know we

haven't always gotten along, but you'd think a man who claims to be of the faith would be more tolerant and understanding… at least about things like this."

"Are you kidding? You know how he feels about you."

"Threatened, maybe?"

"Maybe, but not as much as he simply despises the fact that you are who you are. You're not a fundamental Christian like he *expects* of his staff and congregation. You are the anti-Daniel Henson. You are gay, you're in church leadership, and you were there for many years before he became senior pastor there. You have an influence here, and you're doing it the way he does not agree with. And the judges here are fundamentalists, too, just like he expects them to be. Radicals. Conservatives. And I mean extreme social conservatives. His massive influence on the people in this town and nearly every element of it cannot be good for you. I mean, you saw what the judge did. He's giving us no time to prepare for this. That shit does not happen in the real world."

"So, is it a lost cause?"

"Well, no, not exactly," Ben said. "Look, we're going to prepare to win this. I don't expect a plea agreement – this is going to trial for sure. Hell, I'm sure we would want it to at this point, because they want to put you away and I doubt any plea agreement would not include significant time in prison. But if we go to trial and it's not fair, then we appeal. One way or another, I plan to clear your name, Dwight."

"Is that possible?"

Ben stopped, not realizing how best to answer his simple question. His words sounded as if he were quite confident, but truth be told, he was not so sure it was possible. Simply put, the exact notion of clearing Dwight's name was all but impossible. Thousands of people stood alongside the streets that morning just to protest the man who had lived his life loving others and showing it to them each day. Ben knew they detested him simply for who he was: a gay man. There had been a few murders in the one-hundred year history of Freeden, but none of the previous instances involved a gay man as the accused culprit. The streets had never been filled with rioters for any case before. Just this one.

The protesters were not targeting Dwight as a killer or rapist, but rather, a *gay killer*. Therefore, the outrage ensued. *Gay* was something this radically-conservative citizenry could rally against. It was clear to Ben that being gay was something people here didn't understand or choose to understand. Freeden citizens, from Ben's perspective, were a body of people who never seemed to understand how one could love God and be attracted to the same sex. It was against the teachings of nearly every pastor, most certainly Dr. Henson, in the area. As a result, gay was evil. Gay represented what Dr. Henson often referred to as *the enemy*.

Being gay was something Ben believed the people of Freeden could not justify in their minds. It didn't make sense to them, because they had been told for so long it was *wrong*. By the church, by their families, by their teachers, and by their friends. To them, it was one of the worst of sins and they hated it. There was something different about that hatred now though, in the sense that it was no longer kept behind the veil of put-on righteousness.

Grown adults had stood on the side of the road that morning, screaming for Dwight to be executed, shouting profanities at him, and holding signs that called for gay people to burn in hell. Ben believed they had felt this way all along. Now, though, they had seized the chance to legitimately and publicly convey it. And as Ben saw it, they were taking full advantage of the opportunity.

"The silence isn't exactly convincing, Ben." Dwight looked more concerned than he had all week. "Go ahead, break my heart. But please, do it gently." He sat further upright and leaned across the table. "Is clearing my name possible?"

Ben thought about it, and then stopped, because thinking about it hurt. "I really don't know, Dwight." He closed his notebook. "I really don't know."

11: In Mercy Spare Him

A representative from Scott Stevens' office arrived at four-fifty-nine p.m. on Wednesday, the last minute of the government work day on which the prosecution had promised to provide discovery to the defense. Fortunately for Ben, Bailey and Associates was not affixed to the government work schedule, and would work tirelessly that night, and the next day, to best prepare for the status conference come Friday.

"What's in discovery?" Liz asked, as the team met around the conference table.

"It appears the prosecution did, in fact, obtain the murder weapon from the premises," said Deb. "They also have the handwritten note with Dwight's name on it."

"What else?" Kristen asked.

"The DNA report," Tracey said.

"So, what does it say?" Kristen asked. "It is unusual for a DNA report to be returned so quickly."

"It reads that Dwight Kerry was a match on the knife and the handwritten note."

"Anyone else's DNA found?" Kristen asked. "I mean, it was his classroom. His DNA is all over everything in that room.."

"No other matches outlined here," Tracey replied.

"How does that make any sense?" Deb asked.

"It doesn't," Ben said. "Dwight was not there. His DNA on the murder weapon makes no sense."

"Why would the DNA report say as much, then? Liz asked.

"Not sure," Ben replied. "Let me ask you, does it make

sense to any of you that someone stabbed in the back thirty-six times could write a name on a piece of paper, or anything for that matter, as easy to read as this handwritten note is?"

"It does not make any sense," Liz said.

"But why would the DNA report implicate Dwight?"

"Tampering?" Deb asked.

"Look, I know this appears to be very suspicious, but are we taking it too far here to say the DNA test was tampered with?" Kristen asked. "I mean, I want to believe Dwight is innocent, too, but it's pretty farfetched to think this is all a set up, *and* the justice system and state medical examiner's office were involved, too. That type of thing would require a lot of planning."

"Are you ruling that out?" Ben asked her.

"Not entirely, but there's a lot else going against Dwight here. Whether you think the handwritten note with Dwight's name on it is hard to believe, the evidence still exists and will likely be admitted in trial."

"But let's take a look at something else, Kristen," Ben responded. "The rape kit in discovery reveals nothing. Are you kidding me? The boy was raped in the anal cavity, and the rape kit shows nothing? Can you admit that is farfetched, too?"

"Could it be possible that, whoever was supposed to kill Braxton, was not supposed to rape him?" Liz asked. "Perhaps the kit was not handled properly, and they're trying to cover up their incompetence by simply stating the rape kit unveiled nothing. Or, perhaps someone involved in conducting the rape kit is covering up something?"

"Very possible, but that is assuming there was some sort of set up with more than one person involved, and we simply do not know that," Ben said. "Nothing is pointing in that direction for sure just yet, but there is a lot that seems strange enough to make me wonder."

"But why Dwight?" Kristen asked. "Why frame a high school teacher?"

"Because he's gay, Kristen," Ben replied. "You're from here, you know how people are here. Whether more than one person was involved or not, how easy is it to pin it on Dwight and get people to believe it?" Ben shrugged his shoulders. "Very easy."

"Do you think more than one person was involved here?" Deb asked.

"I don't know yet. But if they were, we are going to find out."

Ken Hughes had been tasked by Ben to do two things: find Ashlee Peterlynn and Ian Christopher. Ashlee could offer Dwight an alibi since she knew he was not at the school on that Friday afternoon, but she was a minor, and getting her to talk would require parental consent.

Ken stopped by the Peterlynn house on Lee Street the night of the arraingment to see if her, and her parents, were home.

He rang the doorbell, and Mr. Peterlynn opened the door.

"Can I help you?" he asked in a befuddled manner.

"Yes sir, I'm Ken Hughes, I don't believe we've met?"

"I don't believe so either," he said, then rushed the conversation along. "What can I do for you?"

"Yes, Mr. Peterlynn, I'm wondering if I might speak to your daughter, Ashlee?"

"Why do you need to speak to my daughter?" he asked, now suspicious of Ken.

"Your daughter seems to be the only person that knew Dwight Kerry was not at the school the day they allege he murdered Braxton Jones, and–"

Mr. Peterlynn started shaking his head. "No sir, you can leave right now."

"Please, sir, a man's life is at stake."

"A man who deserves his life to be taken from him, too." Then, Mr. Peterlynn slammed the door, and dead-bolted it shut.

Ken was never able to convince Mr. Peterlynn to allow him to speak to his daughter. Several voicemails and random stops by the house over the next forty-eight hours resulted in no further contact. Mr. Peterlynn would certainly have cooperated with the police, Ken thought, but he knew the police would *never* reach out to her because it conflicted with their narrative. Ashlee was not added to the witness list for the defense, and Ken was never able to reach her as a result of the impasse with her father. He turned his attention to Ian Christopher.

He knew Lawrence Christopher and figured this may be a bit easier than trying to convince Mr. Peterlynn, who he did not know, to assist him. The day after the arraignment, he phoned Lawrence.

"Hello?"

"Lawrence, it's Ken, buddy. How you been?"

"I'm okay, Ken, how are you?" Lawrence sounded as if he knew why Ken might be calling.

"Doing pretty good, you hittin' em good, lately?" he asked.

"Haven't even played golf recently, really. Wish I had, though."

"We'll have to get out there sometime and hit some together."

"That would be nice," Lawrence agreed.

He still sounded hesitant, but Ken decided to cut the small-talk and get down to business. "Lawrence, you know why I'm calling?"

"To ask me to play golf? I hope that's all."

"I wish it was, my friend. We've been friends a long time, you and I. Your son is eighteen, and I don't have to call you, but I respect you and wanted to before I–"

"You're not talking to my son about Braxton Jones."

"Lawrence, they're going to try to execute Dwight. We just want to make sure we know the facts."

"Good," Lawrence said. "I hope they do kill him."

"Buddy, I can't believe you're saying that."

"Well that's how I feel. He's fucked up a lot of lives."

"Look, Lawrence, I'm not going to tell anybody anything about Ian, okay?"

"There's nothing to tell," he said, clearly attempting to move on from the subject and end the conversation.

"Come on, you know what I mean."

"Ken, my son is about to go to Duke University to play basketball on a division one scholarship. Duke fucking University, are you hearing me? I've already had to talk to him about not screwing that up, do I need to have that same talk with you, too?"

"You know I would never want to screw up anything for you or your family."

"Well, this has already screwed up my family, more than you know."

"I know this is a contentious subject, okay? I'm not trying to embarrass anyone – you or your son."

"I'm already embarrassed, and no one really knows except me and his mother. I'd rather keep it that way."

"At what cost, though, Lawrence? Dwight Kerry is innocent."

"See, that's where you're wrong, Ken. Whether he killed Braxton or not, Dwight Kerry is not innocent. Anybody who is openly gay and condones young men being like that, too, is most definitely not innocent."

"I'm not here to engage in conversation about whether being gay is right or wrong, I'm here because your boy *knows* Dwight didn't do this."

"I think the court will decide that, but as for me and my family, we want no part of this. Don't call about this again, Ken. I'm serious." He hung up.

Ken had no choice but to defy his friend's wishes. He believed Dwight was innocent, and had to talk to Ian Christopher. Ken followed Ian the two days that followed the arraignment. Ian went into the local coffee shop each of those mornings, sat down and read the news, scrolled through some sort of social media on his phone, wrote in a small journal, and left after about an hour. The routine was repeated each of the three days Ken followed him. Finally, Ken approached him on the Thursday after the arraignment, and sat down at his table.

Ian peered up at him. "Can I help you?"

"Do you know who I am?"

"I've seen you."

"I'm Ken Hughes. I know your father, Lawrence, real well. You have a minute?"

Ian looked perplexed. "Sure."

"I work for a man named Ben Bailey."

Ian's face turned white. "Mister, I can't talk about this."

"Ian, you are literally the only hope Dwight Kerry has."

"My Dad said it would ruin my scholarship."

"Your Dad and I have been friends for a long time, but you're a man as the state sees it and can make your own decisions. Please, Braxton needs you to do this."

Ian grabbed his things in a hurry. "I can't, sir, sorry." He bolted for the front door of the coffee shop, and ran out the building.

Ken understood the mounting pressure Ian must feel, but he worried that unless either Ashlee or Ian testified, Dwight may not stand a chance.

The same day Ken tried to talk to Ian, Ben and Kristen both called the state medical examiner's office. Every time they called, the staff would put them on hold for nearly a half hour, only to come back and tell them they would have to take a message. Both of them complied; they left messages throughout the day, but by day's end no one had called them back.

The two of them were the last ones at the office that day, and to stay awake, they both were partaking in another round of java. "Is it odd that no one called us back today?" Kristen asked as she took a sip of her coffee.

"Yes, very," Ben answered. "I'm worried, Kristen."

"Worried about what?"

"Dwight. There's a lot going against him, and we can't seem to drum up anything in his favor. And we're getting no help from anyone, it seems."

"The more I look at the evidence, the more suspicious this all seems to be."

"You were right, what you said this past weekend about my emotions potentially getting in the way. This is going to be so hard, especially since I care so much for him. I can't imagine how I will feel if he is convicted. What if we don't find a way to exonerate him? Ken hasn't been able to reach Ashlee Peterlynn, who clearly knows Dwight wasn't at the school.

Her father won't let us talk to her. That was Dwight's only chance at a real alibi."

"I know. And did Ken mention if he had had any luck with Ian?"

"None. Lawrence doesn't want him to talk. Ken tried to anyway, but Ian ran away and refused to talk when he brought it up. I'm sure Lawrence had scared the shit out of him over all this. All in all, we've got very little, other than the fact that this all doesn't make sense."

"It really doesn't. The DNA tests, no explanation from the state medical examiner's office because we cannot get a call back, our knowledge that he most certainly was not at the school during that time of day, and the ludicrous idea that Braxton was stabbed thirty-six times and wrote a note, with clear handwriting, that identified his killer."

"It doesn't add up."

"Exactly, it does not add up. What are we going to do at tomorrow morning's status conference?"

"I don't know, they will likely offer a plea agreement for prison time, though I'm surprised they haven't made an offer yet. Regardless, if they do offer prison time, I guess that is better than the death penalty."

Kristen looked down, appearing to be nervous. "You know, maybe the best thing is for this to go to trial."

"Most likely. I'm just worried that if we go to trial and it doesn't go his way they'll kill him, too."

"They?"

"The State. By execution. If it goes to trial, you can almost certainly bet on Scott to seek the death penalty."

"But what if they offer life in prison? That's not something worth taking if we don't believe he did it, right?"

"I don't know, Kristen. My gut says no, but I worry my

friend is being framed beyond our control. Either by an individual, or a group of individuals. And that scares the hell out of me. I want to fight, but I'm scared to for concern we might lose him all together. Does that make sense?"

"None of this makes sense."

Ben sighed and leaned back in his chair. He felt helpless. "Oh, God," he said, "in mercy spare him."

12: The Mouth of the Lion

Night of the *Requiem*

Dwight stood there, poised as ever, following an astounding rendition of 'Lacrimosa.' He conducted the chorus as they began singing the next piece in Mozart's classic masterwork:

Domine Jesu Christe, rex gloriae
Libera animas omnium fidelium
Defunctorum de ponenis inferni
Et de profundo lacu
Libera eas de ore leonis.

Lord Jesus Christ, King of Glory,
deliver the souls of the faithful dead from punishment of Hell
and from the bottomless pit;
deliver them from the mouth of the lion.

Present

Protesters continued to line the streets, still limited mostly to local extremists who, in Ben's mind, sought after opportunities to shout their beliefs at others and cause a stir. The media presence on the streets consisted of mostly regional stations, as the news had not hit national airwaves. Local stations were too afraid to do anything that would hurt their ratings, and ultimately advertising and income, so Ben suspected they had no plans to take a stand against the outrage directed toward Dwight.

The status conference, required under federal law, is the meeting where plea agreements are heard and agreed upon. Ben hadn't heard a word from the prosecution, but surely expected district attorney Scott Stevens to levy a hefty price in any plea agreement he proposed. Ben had no intention of settling, though. In his mind, there was no question that a reasonable doubt existed, perhaps more than he had ever witnessed in any murder case. He knew Scott Stevens, though, and he was a man of little compromise.

Ben sat in the room with Liz and Kristen, across the table from where the prosecution would sit when they arrived. Minutes later, Scott Stevens and Kate Gregory walked into the room.

"Greetings," Scott said.

"Morning," Ben replied.

Ben looked directly at Kate. The two held eye contact for a moment. He tried to maintain a professional demeanor, but wondered if she felt a spark as well. He had to look away before betraying his feelings to others in the room. Ben wondered how she could not see the hypocrisy in all of this. He imagined she would be reserved about the case at their get together later that night, and understandably so. It was her job to prosecute, but he wanted to know how she viewed all this. Ben envisioned Kate as someone who would see past all this and be better than Scott, and better than Freeden. He held onto hope that she would rise above.

"I hope we can make some progress, today," Scott said.

"We do as well," Ben noted.

Judge Freeman walked into the room. "Ladies and gentlemen."

"Good morning," all said, nearly in unison.

Judge Freeman took his seat at the head of the table. "Of course, this is just a status conference, but I do want to know if we will avoid trial before we leave today," Judge Freeman said. "Have the two sides discussed any plea agreements?"

"Your Honor, we have made an offer of life without parole, to avoid the death penalty."

"To who?" Ben asked. "We've been made no such offer."

"That's not correct, your Honor," Scott continued, "it was personally delivered to the office of Bailey and Associates."

Ben looked confused. "Your Honor, I am telling you, our office has received no such offer."

"Regardless of whether or not it has been received," Judge Freeman interrupted, "does the defense intend to accept such plea agreement?"

"No," Ben replied sharply.

"That's our only offer, Ben," Scott said. "The evidence is overwhelming, and we are prepared to go to trial, but we will seek the death penalty if we go there."

Ben paused. The thought of Dwight being sentenced to death was something he could hardly bear. In that moment, he could not imagine defending Dwight on trial and watching him be sentenced to die.

"Mr. Bailey, do you intend to accept this plea agreement?"

Ben looked up from his daydream, which lasted twenty seconds or more. "No, your Honor. We do not accept."

"Well, I'll only ask you to counteroffer once," Scott said. "I don't typically negotiate."

"Good," Ben replied, "then no need to waste our time. We aren't accepting a plea unless it features a dismissal of all charges. My client is innocent."

Something was wrong with Kate, and Ben could tell it. He

didn't know what, but she grew visibly troubled. Scott, on the other hand, began shuffling his papers around, his usual, arrogant body language beaming from him. "Well then," he paused briefly, "I suppose we shall go to trial. It is a real shame, Ben, that you continue to drag this good town into the mud to waddle around with you."

Ben ignored the comment. "Your Honor, we would like to request to begin trial no earlier than Monday, July 8th. This is still quick but will give us much more sufficient time to prepare."

"Your Honor," Scott interjected, "there is no need to drag this out and further subject our town to the turmoil pouring out on the streets."

"You sure it isn't our own people from this town encouraging the chaos?" Ben replied.

"Enough," Judge Freeman said.

"What exactly does that mean?" Scott asked.

"Over half of the people on the streets are from the local churches, including Freeden Baptist," Ben said.

"And that should tell you something right there."

"Oh it does, Scott, it tells me that the churches here seem to be the worst of it."

"Enough!" Judge Freeman shouted. "If the prosecution and the defense cannot agree on a time for trial, you will comply with my order on the matter. Trial will begin on Monday, June 10th at 9:00am. Mr. Bailey," he looked at him when he spoke, "I'm giving you an extra week to prepare for this trial and gather your witnesses, but don't you dare ask me for more time when this trial begins. You understand?"

Ben sighed. "Yes, your Honor. I understand."

"Good," he replied. "Mr. Stevens, the same goes for you."

"Yes, sir."

"Be ready. And Mr. Bailey?"

"Yes sir?"

"I will not tolerate another out-of-line outburst from you. Not one."

Ben nodded.

"Good day," Judge Freeman said. He rose from his seat, pushed back his chair with the back of his legs, and left the room.

The prosecution and defense stayed seated.

"You're making a huge mistake, Ben Bailey," Scott said.

Ben eyed him. "For some reason, you want this over fast, Scott. I'm not going to let you push this man onto death row without resistance."

"It's a shame, really. The fall from grace. Ben, you were respected here." He scratched his forehead, then said, "Why are you defending a murderer like this with overwhelming evidence of guilt? It was him! DNA shows Dwight Kerry, and only Dwight Kerry, all over it. There's a note written by a boy in his final moments of life, pleading for justice. Handwriting identified as the boy's by his father and by examining Braxton's other written work. Why are you being so stubborn here? I mean, I know you want to do the right thing, but by trying to do that you're doing the wrong thing. Can't you see?"

"Yes, I can see," Ben responded quickly. "I see just fine. I know for a fact that Dwight was at the concert hall at the time of the murder. I know the rape kit on file revealed no evidence incriminating Dwight Kerry, it wasn't even conducted properly, I suppose, because it showed nothing at all. And I also know that mysteriously, no one from the medical examiner's office will contact me back about the DNA tests. Not to mention, I've been threatened multiple times by leaders in this town to stop this and essentially lock this man up, and I also know that you and Judge Freeman ironically would prefer this trial be over with and have the man executed by next week, so to be frank, all this isn't adding up, Scott."

"What's your point? Are you an attorney, Ben, or a conspiracy theorist?"

"I've got a team of attorneys who know what the hell they're doing," Ben said, pointing to Liz and Kristen, "and we don't like what we're seeing."

"Very well," Scott answered. "If this is what you want, we will seek nothing less than the death penalty. I didn't come to negotiate, and I won't now. So we will see you at trial."

Scott grabbed his items and harshly shoved them in his briefcase before storming out of the room. Kate, slow to pack her things, looked up at Ben. Ben was already looking at her, and the two locked eyes again. Ben wondered if she felt any conviction from being on the side of what seemed like a shady prosecution. This wasn't right, and he hoped Kate knew it. She grabbed her bag after packing everything and turned toward the door to leave.

"Eight," Ben said.

She nodded, then left the room.

"What was that?" Liz asked.

"She knows," Ben replied.

Ben and the team left the courthouse and exited the building to go to the parking lot. Once they got in Ben's truck, Liz in the passenger seat and Kristen in the back, he locked the door, and took a deep breath.

"I want to know right now," he said. "Which one of you kept their offer from me?"

Neither Liz or Kristen said a word.

"I know one of you did it," Ben said. "But if we're going to be a team, somebody needs to give me an explanation."

"Why do you think we would do that?" Liz asked. "We're on your team, Ben."

"I trust that, but I just want to know why it happened? The prosecution usually offers a plea for the first time prior to a status conference, you know this. Negotiations are also typically held before the status conference. I did assume they may bring an offer since we hadn't heard one, but only as a stunt. He said the district attorney's office made a formal offer and delivered it to us."

"Is he lying?" Liz asked.

"I'm suspicious of all this and think there's more to it than what we know, but no, I don't think he would lie about that."

"I did it."

Ben turned around, gazing at Kristen. He stared at her, trying to compose his frustration before he spoke. "Why?"

"I'm sorry, Ben, but I felt I had to," Kristen said.

"Why would you hide something like that from me? I told you that we must work together as a team to do this."

"Because I thought you'd give in if you had time to think about it," she said.

Ben appeared surprised, his mouth gaped open in shock. "Wh-why do you think I would have given in?"

"I saw you think about it, in that meeting just now. And last night at the office."

"Think about what?"

"I think for a moment you considered whether the plea deal might be Dwight's only hope," she replied. "And I think you're wrong."

As astonished as he was at her rogue move, Ben knew she was right: he had thought about it. He wanted to save his friend, no matter what, and he was genuinely worried that the trial was not going to go his way, no matter what evidence existed in his favor. For some reason, everything was going against the defense so far, and if only for a fleeting moment, he *had* wondered if a plea agreement would be best.

"Dwight is a friend of yours, and even though you're a great lawyer and you know what you're doing, you love that man. I can tell it. And I wanted to prevent you from making a move based on emotion. I didn't know what to believe at first, but now I believe Dwight is innocent. And he deserves a fight."

Ben looked down, his right arm resting on his steering wheel as he looked out the driver-side window. He took a deep breath. "Kristen," he sighed, "you're right. I do love that man. And yes, he deserves us to fight for him. He's got nothing else." Ben began to tear up. "I don't want to lose him. This town *can't* lose him. People like him are the only hope this town has."

Liz started to cry, and in a rare moment, so did the usually impassive Kristen Growe.

"And you're right," Ben said. "He deserves a fight, and I'd like to think I would never have given in. But you have definitely brought to light one of my biggest weaknesses," he paused, "and strengths at times," he said while chuckling over the tears. "I do show emotion. And I believe Dwight is innocent, and we're going to do the right thing for him, okay?"

"Okay," Liz and Kristen said almost simultaneously.

He started the truck. "But Kristen...."

"Yeah?"

He soaked up his tears as best he could. "Don't do that again."

They drove off to go back to the office. It was time to prepare for trial.

The clear night sky, filled with stars visible if you were outside of downtown and far enough away from the bright, yellow street lights that adorned Main Street, highlighted the perfect relaxing summer evening on the outside patio at David's Restaurant. David offered exquisite tastings on Friday nights – it was known to be his menu's most experimental evening of the week. You could always get the David's classics every night except for Monday (since they were closed, of course), but Friday's specials always offered something unique for the most proficient food connoisseurs.

Ben was a classic man but possessed an exploratory taste. The good news was that Kate was largely the same way, having traveled quite a bit on her own dime during the summers of both undergrad and grad school. She loved trying new things, and on this night, she would enjoy her first ever fine dining experience in Freeden, the only one of its kind in town.

Ben walked into the restaurant a bit early and noticed a large party in the back where most people there were attending. He was quite happy to see most of the people in the restaurant occupying the back party room for a private gathering, as he had been worried about interactions similar to the one he had experienced at 3rd Street Café – something he did not want to endure in Kate's presence.

He wasn't sure how to dress, so he wore his typical Southern gentleman night-out-on-the-town attire: a pair of dress khakis, brown shoes, a Joseph A. Bank button-up long-sleeve, supplemented with a slim-fit, navy blue jacket.

"Good evening, Mr. Bailey." David greeted him as he walked by the bar of the nearly empty main restaurant area.

"Well good evening, David."

"Didn't know if I'd see you back in here."

"Well I hope it's alright that I'm here?" Ben asked.

"Your money is the same as anyone else's."

Ben looked startled at the unglamorous response.

David smiled. "You're *always* welcomed here."

Ben grinned in return. "Thank you, David."

"How's Dwight?"

"Good as he can be."

"Tell him I miss him, will you?"

"I will, David."

Ben was done talking, but David didn't realize he was finished. "Hold... hold on, Ben." He walked to the kitchen door where a loud, piercing sound rang from. He pushed the swinging door into the kitchen and poked his head in. "Will somebody shut that goddamn alarm off?" he yelled.

While David was doing his best impression of a pissed-off wasp, Kate walked in the front door. Ben looked at her, and she noticed him as he waved. She was gorgeous; drop-dead gorgeous, actually. She wore a black dress that rested slightly above her knees, and she made it look so unbelievably becoming. Her face was beautiful, adorned with very little makeup – her natural beauty beamed. He couldn't help but stare.

"Good evening, Ms. Gregory," Ben said.

She raised an eyebrow. "I thought I told you not to–"

"Call you Ms. Gregory, yes," he interrupted, "but you warrant it tonight. You look wonderful."

She smiled, blushing a bit. "Well, thank you."

"David, can we have a drink?" Ben asked.

"We got all kinds," he said as he attempted to escape his grumpy tantrum and return to the likes of the kind exchange he and Ben engaged in moments before.

"I'll have a sauvignon blanc," she said.

David focused back on Ben and smiled. He recalled Ben saying before that he hated sauvignon blanc.

"And Ben, you'll have the same, right?" he said, while grinning ear-to-ear.

Ben rolled his eyes so only David could see. "Sure."

David chuckled as he walked away to fetch two glasses and the bottle.

Ben turned his attention back to Kate. "So how do you like this town so far?"

"It's… nice," she replied, a bit half-heartedly.

"You sound a lot less excited than you did last time we spoke?"

"Well, a lot has happened since the last time we spoke."

"Yeah," he replied. David walked over with two glasses of wine and set them in front of the two. Ben eyed his drink. "So tell me, how did you get to Freeden?"

Kate took a sip of her wine. "That's so good," she said.

Ben took a sip of his. "Shew," he said as he came up from the glass, "I'll need an IV from being dehydrated after drinking this. That is very dry."

Kate laughed, then took another drink of her wine. David laughed at Ben, then kept working behind the bar, inattentive to their conversation.

"I'm sorry," Ben said while laughing, "we were talking about what brought you to Freeden?"

"Yes," she restarted, "well, I guess you could say I needed a fresh start."

"Sometimes I think that's exactly what I need," Ben said. "A fresh start from this town, that is."

Kate giggled. "Yes, sometimes a fresh start is exactly what you need."

"If you don't mind my asking, what did you need a fresh start from? I mean–"

"A failed marriage. I needed to get away from the place I was in."

"Oh, I'm sorry if I was too forward, Kate."

"No, no, you're fine," she said as she smiled. "My husband was unfaithful, let's just say that."

"Ah, I see. Well, I'm sure it won't make you feel any better, nor is it intended to, but I've experienced the same thing recently."

"I have to admit," she replied, "Terri told me as much."

"Well, thanks for not letting that scare you away from me," Ben said.

"Why would it scare me away?" She took another sip of wine.

"Well I don't know. I just feel like it's a burden on–"

"So what do you think of me? I'm bringing the same thing to the table."

"No, I mean…."

"I'm kidding." She smiled. "I understand what you mean."

"I'm sorry, I didn't mean to–"

"Look, I gotta get you to stop a few things," she said. "One is calling me Ms. Gregory, and the other is saying you're sorry as often as you do."

"I know, I know," he said, then took another sip of wine, almost as if he were enjoying it. "I'm sor–"

"You almost said it again!"

"My goodness." He took another drink of the sauvignon blanc, swallowed, then laughed while setting his glass back down on the bar. "Let's restart this whole thing, shall we?"

She smiled. "We don't have to. I think it's going just fine." She continued smiling at him in a cute, lightly flirtatious manner. "You're very kind and you have a good heart. I can tell that for sure."

He returned the smile to her, happy to know she wasn't displeased. Ben was always hard on himself, largely because of the failures he had endured from previous relationships, most notably his failed marriage with Rachel. He always worried, as far as relationships were concerned, that he was a screw-up and was to blame for most things that went wrong, so he didn't want it to pour over too much into his first experience with Kate. He worried Kate would eventually be turned off by his apparent lack of confidence and move on.

"May I ask what happened to you and your ex-wife?" she asked.

"Yeah, sure," he replied. "Not much to say though. I imagine it's just that I wasn't good enough for what she really wanted. I've found peace with that now, but when you first find out who you are is not sufficient for someone you care about, it's heart-breaking."

"Seems like we've both been through hardships like that."

"It does, and yet, we made it here."

"We did."

"Cheers to us," he said.

She laughed. "Cheers to us."

The two toasted and took another drink from their glasses.

"So, what do you like to do?" Ben asked.

"Well," she paused, "I love adventure. Trying new things, exploring, traveling, and I love to read."

"I love to travel, too. You have to leave this place behind from time to time if you want to remain sane."

"I'm learning that," she said while giggling.

"Yes, and there's one gem I truly love that I must share with you. I absolutely love to go to the Homestead in the mountains of Virginia. It's an escape for me."

"I've been there, went one summer during law school," she said. "Absolutely love the spa there."

"That deep tissue massage." Ben closed his eyes and exhaled at the thought.

"Oh my God."

"You know what I'm talking about?"

"I do! I love that place."

"And the hot spring in the Garden there?" he asked.

"The best," she said.

"How neat." He smiled. "It's one of my favorite places to go, like you said, to escape."

"It's one of mine," she said.

"How ironic."

"Indeed."

The two took another sip of their wine, then looked at each other. Kate smiled; Ben snickered. Kate joined in the laughter.

"What?" Kate asked, continuing to smile.

Ben laughed some more, then stopped and simply smiled. "You're just so easy to talk to."

Kate blushed and looked away from Ben, trying to hide it from him. "I feel the same about you."

Ben had wondered if this get-together was a date or not, but this exchange left no question: she was just as intrigued by him as he was her.

David reemerged and interrupted. "You two lovebirds need another glass?"

"David!" Ben fired back.

"What?"

Ben looked over at Kate, and she had taken a sip of her wine when David made his remark, so she was struggling not to laugh and spew it everywhere. She finally swallowed and started laughing aloud.

"Would you like another glass?" Ben asked her.

"Sure," she replied. Then David walked away again to fetch more wine.

"So how do you like this town, Ben?" she asked. "You're the one who has lived here your whole life, you know how it is… deep down. Tell me, how do you like it here?"

Ben didn't know what to say without sounding negative. "Well," he paused for a moment longer, took another drink of wine, set his glass down and turned directly toward Kate. "I worry I won't make it here much longer."

"How so?"

"For starters, the outpouring of hatred toward Dwight and my team," he said. "It's going to make it very difficult now… to be happy here long-term. Assuming this never blows over, and I don't think it ever truly will. I grew up loving this town, but I don't know how to feel about it anymore. Seeing this place respond the way it has to Dwight… it makes me bitter, really."

"I know that's tough for you."

"It is, but if they're going to run me out of town when this is all said and done, I'm going to do something good before I go."

"Earlier today, you said you had been threatened." She looked uneasy. "Were you serious?"

"Of course I was," Ben said.

"Why?"

"I don't know. It's obviously to intimidate me. But why? I don't know. Perhaps because they fundamentally disagree with who Dwight's character and that I'm supporting him, or perhaps–"

"They would call his character a lifestyle, you know?"

"And notice I refrain from calling it a lifestyle because a lifestyle, I believe, is something you choose. I do not believe Dwight chose to be gay and I'll never believe it. I mean, think about it... why in God's name would anyone elect to live in this hateful town and *choose* to be gay?"

"I must agree."

"That's just my opinion, Kate. Sorry for the forwardness."

"What did I say about the sorry word?"

"Yes, I know," he chuckled.

"Look, I need to know something, Ben." Kate paused, appearing to be nervous. "I'm worried."

"Worried about what?" Ben asked.

"I have to know. Your rhetoric in our meetings make it seem as though you are suspicious of wrongdoing. Do you think that there may be a cover-up going on here?"

"A cover-up?" Ben asked. "I don't really know. But I will say that I find it very alarming that both your boss and Judge Freeman seem to be rushing this."

She was looking down, now appearing very concerned.

"I will say that I do not believe Dwight did this, and it's very clear that someone went through great lengths to free themselves of the punishment this crime warrants."

The look on her face grew even more worried as she looked toward the back of the restaurant. She noticed Scott and his wife, chatting with other restaurant patrons at the entrance to the back party room. She knew he couldn't see her, but she worried she didn't have much time before he did. "Ben, hurry... do you believe it's a cover-up?"

He paused, seemingly confused. "Well, I don't know yet, I–"

"You need to know," she said. "I am certain, now. This is a cover-up of the worst kind."

He stopped talking. He didn't know what to say.

"I can't say anything else here, and I don't have much time because Scott is in the building, but I need you to trust me," she said.

He leaned back on his bar stool, still stunned at the revelation. "Kate, you realize what this means?"

"Yeah, it's an ethical concern for sure, my giving you information and essentially switching sides. But this whole case is an ethical concern, beyond that really. We must talk, but not here. I want you to call me," she said, as she left her card in front of him. "Tonight." She got up, grabbed her purse, and hurriedly walked out the restaurant, unseen by anyone other than Ben and David.

13: Let Your Light So Shine Before Men

Hired by the *Freeden Tribune* about four years prior, Preston Hall came on as a reporter, but after high turnover from writers using the *Tribune* as a platform simply to move up in the journalistic ranks and on to bigger publications elsewhere, Preston quickly found himself as the *Tribune*'s editor.

He was not a Freeden native, but he wanted to stay put long enough to achieve something here. His dream was to one day return to his hometown of Charlotte and become the editor of the *Charlotte Observer*, but two attempts to apply for the position already had resulted in zero callbacks. In time, though, he believed if he continued to grow his CV that one day he would be afforded the opportunity. Until then, he would serve the *Tribune*.

To him, journalism was much different here, and he worried about how it impacted his ability to do his job ethically. The publisher, Peter Hefner, and the company who owned the paper out of Ohio, often pushed the newsroom into certain angles on stories for the sake of protecting advertising income. One time, a used car dealer and a prominent figure in town was accused of insurance fraud and found guilty, and he was forced to pay a tremendous price in restitution. The story never hit the front page, though, or any page for that matter, as his dealership was a major client for the Advertising Department. Preston hated the control administration hammered down onto the newsroom, as he felt it inhibited him and his very small staff from doing their jobs as journalists.

In addition, the townspeople knew they possessed influence over what went into the paper. Or at least some of them. Preston knew not to write in a way that cast a bad light upon the city, as Aaron Carroll was not one to tolerate it. Several local business owners were the same way, but he recalled his hiring as editor and being told, at his first meeting with Hefner upon accepting the position, never to cross the metaphorical mayor of Freeden, Dr. Daniel G. Henson.

No one ever offered any detail, but he was strictly told to *never* irritate him. And so he didn't. A young man, trying to keep his job and move up in the ranks, did as he was instructed. And as a result, he had served as one of the longest-tenured editors in *Tribune* history at an unimpressive length of two-and-a-half years.

Night of the *Requiem*

Preston sat in the living room of his eight hundred square foot apartment, eating a Lean Cuisine ready-made dinner he had retrieved from his extensive collection of such meals in his freezer. He was watching an episode of *The Big Bang Theory*. It was a typical, lonely night for Preston; he was incredibly introverted and hardly spent time with friends.

His phone rang, and he looked at the screen.

FREEDEN CHIEF

He answered. "Chief McDowell?"

"Preston, got something you're going to want to know."

"Okay?" he said, as he rose from his old, stained couch.

"There's been a murder at the high school, wanted you to

have the heads up before any of the out-of-town news folk try to come in."

"Thank you, yes. Who is it?"

"It's Dale Jones's boy, Braxton. Found him upstairs in a classroom at the school."

"My God. Do you know who it is? Who did it, I mean?"

"We believe we do, but hope to be sure very soon."

"You at liberty to say?"

"Not yet, but I will let you know. You can come down to the school anytime. I'll meet you outside. We're not allowing anybody inside right now."

Preston rushed to gather his tablet and bag, and hurried out the door. Once he arrived at the school, police cars and an ambulance were parked at the side entrance to the main building, but there were no other vehicles there. People drove by slowly on the street in front of the school, as they wanted to see if they could catch a glimpse of what was going on. Preston walked up to the tape barricade around the side entrance, and saw Chief McDowell standing there.

"Chief!"

"Hold on," Chief said to an officer. "Hello, Preston."

"Can I turn my recorder on?"

He hesitated and looked around. "Off the record for now, just take notes, son."

"What can you tell me about the victim?"

"The victim has been positively identified as Braxton Jones, son of Dale and Lucy Jones, and was found dead upon arrival."

"How was he…"

"The victim was found with thirty-six incisions, apparently caused by the blade of a large knife."

"And?"

"And we have also confirmed that the boy was raped prior

to death."

Preston could not believe it. Nothing like this *ever* happened in Freeden.

"Are you at liberty to say who you think it is, now?"

Chief McDowell looked around, then leaned in closer and spoke softly. "Yes, but again, this is off the record until we make an arrest. We believe the perp to be Dwight Kerry."

Preston gasped. "The teacher? Choir director Dwight Kerry?"

"I'm afraid so," he answered.

"Based on what evidence?"

"Well, we'll release that soon, okay? Just wanted to give you the heads up on all this."

"Are you arresting him tonight?"

"We plan to bring him in tonight, yes."

"He's at the concert right now, I wrote a story about the concert just yesterday."

"Yes, we know. We plan to apprehend the suspect tonight, but nothing about this until we do, okay?"

"Yes, sir," Preston replied.

"Want to make sure we get our ducks in a row, first, if you know what I mean."

Truth be told, Preston didn't know what he meant. *Get our ducks in a row?* What was that implying? Regardless, Preston was speechless. He had never covered anything like this in Freeden, and had never expected to, either.

Preston left for the jail, and upon arrival, simply waited in the lobby. Within about an hour or so, a few other local newspaper and television reporters from outside the immediate town started trickling in, likely having heard what was going on via their scanners. An officer came into the lobby and said, "You all are welcome to come back now."

Dwight Kerry was being ushered in through the back door. They brought him to the magistrate's office and he stayed there for what seemed to Preston like an eternity. Finally, they led Dwight out and into another room so he could make his phone call. Preston couldn't hear what was going on, but Dwight was clearly upset and emotional.

He still couldn't believe it. He was never friends with Dwight per se, but the two had connected through his coverage of his concerts, initiatives he launched for students at the school, and other community events Dwight was involved in. His experience with Dwight had always been a pleasant one, and the fact that he now stood accused of rape and murder was shocking to Preston. It was almost unbelievable.

"Didn't you know this guy, Preston?" an out-of-town reporter whose name he could not remember asked.

"Yeah, well I guess you don't know them until you do."

Dwight finally came out of the room, vividly emotional, assuredly struggling with the notion that he had been arrested and the humility that came with it. He looked up and saw Preston and the other reporters, and just sobbed even more. Finally, they carried him into the interrogation room next to where they were standing, and the door shut behind them. The officers did not stay in there long, assuming Dwight didn't have much to say, and about fifteen minutes later, Preston saw Ben Bailey come into the hallway from the lobby.

Preston tried to add up how strange all this seemed to be. Dwight was the choir director and organist at Freeden Baptist Church, Dr. Henson was the senior pastor there, Dale Jones was a deacon and member there, Ben was married to Dr. Henson's daughter, Rachel (as far as he knew) and now Ben was presumably here to represent Dwight. The first thought that came to Preston: stark divisions are coming at that church

– and in this town. The connection all of them had to the church, and each other, forced him to wonder how catastrophic it may be for the town as a whole, which he *knew* was heavily influenced by the church.

Ben Bailey and Dwight Kerry met for a while, but finally the door opened, and Ben exited the room. Out of habit, Preston started his recorder. When he did, Preston heard Dwight say, "Before you go, tell me you truly believe me, Ben."

Preston's eyes were solely on Ben, who stood in front of him and the reporters along with five officers, waiting for him to respond. Preston realized this was a pivotal moment. Ben turned his head back to Dwight and said, "I most certainly do."

In that moment, Preston realized how critically damaging this whole situation would be to the community he served. Ben, who was well-known in the community, clearly had aligned himself with Dwight. Preston grew uncomfortable, realizing how this would inevitably involve Freeden Baptist Church, and subsequently, Dr. Dan Henson. He had been put on notice only once before, but he remembered it to this day: do not cross Dr. Dan Henson. He still didn't know why, and in that moment, he didn't care to know. It was a warning he had not forgotten.

Ben started walking out toward the front lobby, and all of Preston's fellow journalists, television and newspaper, started following him. Preston came out of the daze he found himself in and hurried to catch up. Ben said nothing to him or the others as he left the building, but in many ways he said everything he needed to say when he left the room: he believed Dwight's story.

Preston walked back inside the station, and met Pam at the front desk.

"Can I help you sir?" she asked.

"Pam, yes, I need to see Chief McDowell."

"Hang on and let me see if he is still here," she said as she picked the phone up to dial him. She paused, then said, "Chief, can you see Mr. Hall from the *Tribune*?" A few seconds later, she hung up.

"Go on back, Mr. Hall. You know where his office is."

Preston nodded and headed for the hallway. "Thanks." The door clicked open and he followed the hallway to his office. "Chief," he said as he walked in.

"Come on in, Preston." Chief McDowell was sitting at his desk eating what appeared to be a not-so-fresh Subway turkey and ham sandwich.

He took a seat, pulled out his notepad and pen, and began interviewing him. "Chief, just have a few questions and I'll get out of your way."

"Okay. Go on."

"What evidence helped you identify Dwight as the alleged murderer?"

"The boy was not dead when Dwight fled the room," he said quickly. "He wrote a note to tell us Dwight did it, just before he died."

"And you know the note was written by Braxton?"

"Yes, his father positively identified his handwriting."

"What else?"

"The murder weapon was left on campus."

"You have the murder weapon?"

"Yes sir, we do," Chief McDowell reiterated. "The knife belonged to Dwight Kerry, we have identified that as well."

"How do you know this?"

"Preliminary testing shows a match to Dwight."

Preston leaned back, wanting to clarify a few things. "Chief, all this just happened tonight. I'm a bit confused on how you found the boy dead, identified his handwriting in the note, arrested the alleged murderer, and assumedly identified his DNA in such a short time?"

"Well, you need to get unconfused," Chief McDowell responded sharply.

Preston's eyes opened wide, shocked at the dissent he seemed to be facing from the Chief. "Sir, I was just–"

"Remember your place in this community, Preston," Chief said. "Details like that are irrelevant. We found the assailant and he will be prosecuted at the fullest extent of the law. Now, we called you first for a reason… because we trust you."

Perplexed and offended by the Chief's implication that he would print whatever they instructed him to write, Preston pretended to be taking notes, all the while looking down at his paper wondering why Chief McDowell would not give him more details and had grown so defensive. He realized it was his duty as a reporter to ask questions, so he continued, "Sir, I don't mean to push, but I'm just trying to make sense of it all."

"It makes sense," he shouted. "The boy was raped and murdered by Dwight Kerry. We have sufficient evidence for the arrest and the prosecution will show that to be true, too. That's all the questions for now."

Preston was in awe. He gathered his things and proceeded to leave.

As he left the room, Chief McDowell said, "Now, make sure that story is accurate, son."

Preston nodded, and walked out.

Preston was just about to leave the newsroom after a restless night of writing this dreadful story when he decided to enjoy a cup of coffee brewed by support staff before he left. It may be a necessity, he thought, just to make it home. He was exhausted.

He set his piping hot beverage on his desk and picked up his copy of the weekend edition of the *Tribune*. After taking a sip that nearly burned his lips, he leaned back and started to read his story:

DWIGHT KERRY ARRESTED
Charged With the Rape and Murder of Local Boy

FREEDEN – Local high school teacher and choir director Dwight Kerry was arrested last night, facing charges of first-degree murder and rape of local boy Braxton Jones.

The body of Braxton Jones was found inside Kerry's classroom at Freeden High School late Friday evening. Jones was apparently raped, then stabbed to death. A call reporting an open, unlocked door at the school prompted police to search the building and ultimately find the body. Jones was found dead upon arrival.

Braxton Jones was a 17-year-old student of Freeden High and the son of Dale and Lucy Jones. An honor student, Braxton was actively involved in his church, Freeden Baptist, and was a member of the Freeden High Chorus as well as the Freeden Baptist Youth Choir. It was in the choir program where the victim met and worked with the suspect on a daily basis.

A note, written by the boy in his dying moments, was found lying on the floor close to his body. The note simply read: DWIGHT KERRY.

Chief McDowell says the handwriting on the note was positively identified by the father as the boy's handwriting.

"We believe Mr. Kerry desired an intimate relationship with the boy, and when the boy did not succumb, Mr. Kerry raped and murdered him violently in a rage," said Chief Gary McDowell, head of the Freeden Police Department. "The evidence is there to support it."

The evidence, along with the note, includes the murder weapon, a large kitchen knife, which was left on the campus following the crime. Preliminary testing completed overnight on the murder weapon does implicate Kerry, as no other prints were found on the knife.

Local senior pastor of Freeden Baptist Church, Dr. Daniel Henson, spoke out about Kerry, who had previously served as the music minister for over three decades before being relieved of his duties following the arrest. "We are absolutely devastated that one of our own would do something like this," Henson said. "Rest assured, our church, as a whole, loves God, and is not a representation of Dwight's heinous acts. We, as a body of Christ, will grow stronger than ever to support Dale and Lucy and all those affected by this terrible situation, and work to combat the immoral behavior that led Dwight to take these actions."

Ben Bailey of Bailey and Associates will represent Dwight in the pre-trial process and if the case goes to trial. When asked Friday night if he believed Dwight was innocent, he said, "I most certainly do."

Kerry is being held on a $1,000,000 bond at the Freeden City Jail. His arraignment is scheduled for Tuesday.

Preston sat at his desk, reading the article in disbelief. He set the paper down and rubbed his eyes. He wondered: *Was he reading this right?* This was not the way he had written it.

Preston marched angrily down the long hall to Hefner's office.

"What the hell is this?" he asked Hefner.

Hefner calmly took a sip of his coffee, never looking at Preston. "It's the Saturday morning paper."

"This is not my article. I didn't know a thing about DNA evidence or prints, and as far as I know there has been no completed testing, just speculation. And I did not get that quote from Chief McDowell, and I never spoke to Dr. Henson. Not to mention the fact that Ben Bailey never offered me that quote for print in this story. Did you get that quote from him from my recorder?"

"I did."

"Why am I even the editor if you're going to go behind my back and rewrite my stories?"

"Preston, calm down. Really. We have a duty to serve this town."

"And I'm trying to do it *ethically.*"

"But we can't serve this town if we're not in business, Preston!" Hefner finally made eye contact with him.

Preston fumed but didn't say anything in reply.

"Now, I don't see a thing wrong with the story, so proceed with your daily activities, please."

Preston stood there, stunned and ashamed at the response, or lack thereof, and the evident unethical behavior from his own publisher. He walked out. He understood not attacking certain pillars of the community in a small-town paper, but something seemed wrong here. Very wrong.

He needed this job, there was no doubt about that. He

could barely make ends meet now; he struggled to pay his apartment rent, ate TV dinners every night, and had already had his lights cut off twice for a two or three-day period when bills were due before payday. He was struggling to survive. He knew he had to comply with company standards and simply move past it.

Present

Preston's phone rang around eleven-thirty p.m.. For a Friday night in Freeden, that seemed strange. He had been sitting in front of his television, like usual, wide-awake, and binge watching Netflix shows. He looked at his phone and didn't immediately recognize the number, but the area code was 704, a number from the western part of the state. He wondered if it were the job opportunity with the *Charlotte Observer* he had recently applied for again, but surely no one would be calling him this late to offer a job. He could wish, though.

"Hello?"

"Mr. Hall?" The person on the other end of the line sounded like a woman.

"Yes?"

"I need to see you. Can you meet me down by the river landing at midnight?"

Preston seemed very confused. "Who is this?"

"I can't say over the phone, but I need you to trust me."

He shook his head. "Why in the world would I meet someone who's calling me at eleven-thirty at night down at the river landing? I don't even know you."

"It's about the Dwight Kerry case. We need you, Preston. We've got a smoking gun and if you don't help us, no one will."

Preston began pacing around the room. "Okay, okay," he said, "I'll be there."

"Don't tell anyone you're coming here, you understand?"

"Yes, sure."

The call disconnected. Preston scrambled around his messy apartment to find his bag and the documents he had related to the case. He worried this may be a trap and grew fearful. *What am I doing?* He couldn't believe he was going out at this time to meet someone down by the river, a place that usually no one went at night due to safety concerns. Nonetheless, he walked out the front door, hopped in his Toyota Prius, and proceeded to drive to the river.

When he arrived, no one was there. No cars were in the parking lot, or in sight, for that matter. He got out of his car and looked around, terrified at what may soon greet him. His phone, which he had turned on vibrate only, rang again. It was the same 704 number.

"Are you here?" he answered.

"Yes, but we're not meeting in the lit parking lot. Walk to the landing."

"How do I know this isn't a trap?"

"Trust me." She hung up.

The hell with it. Here we go. He hoped whatever came of this would be good for him, but realized he had to take the chance to find out. He walked to the landing and didn't see anyone. It was dark. And unnerving.

"Hello?" he said softly.

"Thank you for coming," the woman said.

"Who are you?" he asked.

As his eyes adjusted, he could see there were two people. He couldn't make out who they were, but one was clearly built like a woman, the other a man.

"My name is Kate Gregory," the woman said. "I think you know the gentleman with me, Ben Bailey?"

Preston knew instantly that something would come of this. He knew Ben was defending Dwight, and he recognized the name Kate Gregory from the arraignment transcript. She was an assistant district attorney. And they were here together.

"What is going on?" Preston asked.

"We didn't know where else to meet so that no one would find us, at least not around here and in the current climate," Ben said. "Kate just told me all this after we met tonight at David's. You have to hear what she has to say."

"Why are you here anyway?" Preston asked. "The two of you... a prosecutor and a defense attorney working the same case… together?"

"I know what this looks like," Kate said. "Let me be clear, I am not playing both sides. I am going to step down from my position as assistant district attorney."

"Why?"

"Because I can't stand by this, what's actually going on," she replied.

"Okay," he paused, "so what's actually going on?"

"We've asked you to come, Preston," Ben said, "because you're the only hope we have of getting this story out."

"What story?"

"A cover up," Kate said. "A massive cover up."

"What do you mean?"

"Dwight was not involved," Ben said. "He had nothing to do with this."

"Of course you'd say that," Preston responded. "I'm not putting myself out on a limb without something substantial here."

"We don't expect you to," Kate said. "But you have to

believe us once we tell you, and you have to get the word out."

They likely couldn't see his expression, but Preston's face featured one of grave concern. "I'm listening."

"The preliminary DNA test," Kate said, "is not the one the defense actually received in discovery. The test on record that will be admitted as evidence in the trial is a hoax. A complete bogus test, not properly completed on either the knife or the note."

"Wait, how do you know this?"

"Because I saw the original test. The initial test showed no one's DNA on the knife and only one man's DNA on the handwritten note: the DNA of Dale Jones."

"Oh wow. Please guys, this is ridiculous," Preston said.

"Wait," Ben said. "You need to hear the rest."

"You can't possibly believe his father murdered him?" Preston whispered loudly. "Or had something to do with it?"

"That's not what we are saying," Kate said. "But I saw the original report. Scott thinks he is the only one who saw it, but I saw it too, and that's what it unveiled. But Scott never said anything about it, so I didn't either just to see what he would do. Then, on Tuesday night, I was running through town at around one a.m., it was the earliest chance I had had to exercise that day. I ran by the DA's office and noticed Scott's car parked behind the building, which was odd because Scott *never* works after hours, no matter what. I've learned that about him in a short time. So I didn't feel good about it. The arraignment–"

"Was a complete joke," Ben said.

"Yes," Kate continued, "I've never seen anything like it. Everyone, including the judge, was trying to rush this thing. I worried something was being hidden from me. Plus, the DA's office was holding discovery until the day after arraignment, which I thought was odd since everything we had could have been given to the defense that day. So, since I was very suspicious of all that, I snuck into the back of the building, and overheard a conversation happening in Scott's office."

Preston raised an eyebrow. "What kind of conversation?"

"Preston," Kate said, "Scott was in his office talking to Dale Jones."

"And your point?"

"I heard all of this verbatim. Scott told him the DNA test showed only *his* DNA on the handwritten note," Kate said. "He was outraged, yelling about how 'ridiculous' this investigation was and how he wasn't even at the scene when it happened. Scott said he knew it wasn't him, and then something slammed up against the wall. It sounded like someone had thrown a glass or something – I'm assuming it was Dale. Then, Dale yelled to Scott and told him to 'squash the preliminary test' and to 'figure something else out' – I kid you not."

Preston was listening so intently that he realized he was hardly breathing. He could not believe what he was hearing. Even though his first exchange with Chief McDowell seemed odd and almost as if something was being hidden, he still wondered if all this was too farfetched to believe. "So, what are you saying?"

"That's not all," Kate restarted. "The next day in our two p.m. office meeting following the arraignment, Scott handed us all a DNA test report showing only one match: Dwight Kerry. Excluding me, this was the first report our team had laid eyes on. No one else knew any better, but I did."

"So, they could have made a mistake, that's possible I'm sure."

"I checked into it, contacted the examiner who had completed the testing."

"Yeah?"

"She or the office had not been contacted to re-evaluate the report."

Preston didn't know what to say. "Okay, so–."

"Let her finish," Ben said.

"I confronted Scott and told him I had seen a different report than the one he presented us, and then he closed the door to his office. He reminded me what he said in my initial job interview, that 'loyalty' was important and that he didn't want me snooping around. He reminded me to trust him."

"The next day, the examiner's office staffer had been relieved of her duties," Ben said. "Nowhere to be found. You want to tell me that this is a coincidence?"

Well," he said, hands in his pockets, "it certainly doesn't sound like it. But what are you implying?"

"There's even more. I found the examiner," Kate said. "She was literally leaving town. I went to her house in the middle of the night last night and saw she was packing her things into her car. It must have been almost midnight. I asked her where she was going, and she told me she was moving. I asked if moving in the middle of night had anything to do with her losing her job, and she rushed back toward the house from her car, saying she couldn't talk about it. I promised I'd keep her safe, and after much quarreling, she eventually told me the truth."

"And that is?" Preston asked.

"That she was threatened to squash the original report, and told to leave town immediately and not talk to anyone else. That she was offered payment from a private source to keep quiet."

"Is that all?"

"No," Kate said. "She also confirmed that the handwritten note revealed only one positive DNA match as well: Dale Jones."

"Oh my God," Preston said. "Oh my God, oh my God.."

"Listen, Preston, you are our only hope in setting this straight," Ben said as he grabbed him with both hands by his shoulders, trying to calm him down. "Something is happening under the table here, and if somebody doesn't show the people of this town what's truly going down, an innocent man is going to die."

"Do you think," Preston said nervously, steadying himself. "Do you think Dale Jones murdered his son?"

"We don't know for sure," Ben said. "But what I do know is that his son revealed to Dwight that he was gay just a few weeks before his death. I know he had a love interest in the class who I intend to call as a key witness. And I know he was mysteriously held out of school by his father just days before his death. In my opinion, he came out to his father, and the rest is history."

"Why would that be a problem?"

"Don't know for sure that it would be," Ben said, "but I certainly suspect it would. Dale and Lucy are devout Christians, fundamentalists to be exact, intolerant of 'immoral' behavior, as I've heard Dale call it before in church."

Preston appeared confused.

"Homosexuality," Ben said. "That make it clearer?"

"Preston, we believe his father had something to do with this," Kate followed.

"Jesus," Preston said, "even if I could publish a story like this, they'll have my head at the paper. Dale's a major player here in town, big supporter of the paper, on the Board of Directors for the *Tribune*. His companies advertise big dollars.

Why would I want to do this?"

"Our lives are done here," Ben said. "If it means so much to you to be a *somebody* here that you'll let an innocent man die when you know you can do something to change this, then so be it. But I'll be damned if we are going to let this happen without a fight."

"I need something tangible before I run a story like this," Preston said reluctantly. "I'm not going on hearsay alone."

"Here," Kate handed Preston a file. "Here are the original DNA reports, unveiling no connection to Dwight whatsoever, and a positive match to Dale on the report regarding the handwritten note."

"How in God's name did you–"

"Before I safely escorted the examiner out of town and to a remote location, she provided them to me," Kate said. "They're official, you'll see that."

"I'm going to have to think about this, I just don't know."

"Look at the reports, then think about it," Ben said. "But not for too long. Someone's life is at stake."

It was 3:45am, and Preston still hadn't fallen asleep after returning home. A once Mayberry-like town where he had taken a barely-above minimum wage reporting/editorial job, Freeden was now home to a major murder case with unimaginable twists that, he suspected, would forever alter the course of the town. He was torn, undecided on what to do.

The report files, lying on his couch still unopened, would likely push him over the edge to publish the story. He knew he would be risking everything; his livelihood, potential advancement to other papers owned by the Ohio-based company, or any potential advancement in his journalism career for that matter. He knew the right thing to do was to tell the truth, no matter what that was; it was journalistic creed to report the truth, regardless of the outcome. Perhaps major news outlets would applaud his efforts, but he may go entirely unnoticed, suppressed by the company and put away for good, never to work in journalism again. Publishing this story would likely be subject to one of two things: critical acclaim or career suicide.

He walked to his refrigerator, grabbed a cold Milwaukee's Best, and paced around the apartment. He could literally feel his blood pressure rising. *What the hell do I do?*

In what seemed like an instant, it became clear. His eyes fixed on one of the only decorative pieces in the apartment, that for four years had collected dust on top of his particle-board end table in his simplistic living room; a curved, fake stone with a painted lighthouse on it featuring engraved lettering that comprised the verse from Matthew 5:16: "Let your light so shine before men."

Preston didn't consider himself to be a religious person. He grew up in a Christian home, but had witnessed so much stark hypocrisy from fellow Christians over the years that he had turned away from the faith some time ago. He would never tell anyone in Freeden this, though, as it would have surely exiled him in a town which, under Dr. Dan Henson's direction, had become an epicenter for Christian conservative thought.

This decorative piece spoke to him in more ways than one. It reminded him of the importance of telling the truth, no matter the consequences. And if it cost him his job, then so be it. He decided, in that moment, to be a beacon of light for the truth.

He opened the report file, and subsequently stayed awake through the remainder of the night. Words flowed from his racing mind to the tips of his fingers as he typed the story for the weekend edition.

Peter Hefner was vacationing for the weekend in Charleston, South Carolina. He had just gotten in from his morning walk with his small pooch of a dog named Wylie, and his wife had his coffee ready as he generally expected. He loved to read the weekend edition of *The Washington Post*, as he had always found himself intrigued by the grimy politics running amuck in the nation's capital.

As he sat down to drink his coffee in their suite at the Francis Marion Hotel on King Street, his phone rang. It was Dr. Dan Henson.

Puzzled and nervous as to why he would be getting a call from Dr. Henson, he considered not answering, but then realized how big of a mistake that would be and picked up. "Hello?"

"Good morning, Mr. Hefner. I believe you know who this is."

"Yes sir, good morning."

"I need you to help me understand what I'm reading on the front page of your paper this morning."

Embarrassingly, he had not looked since he was on vacation. He fumbled around, trying to find his tablet to open the website. "Well, sir, I must admit I am on vacation."

"No excuses for this junk that I would equate to tabloid fare, Mr. Hefner. Fix this right away, and don't disappoint me." The phone call ended.

His heart raced ninety miles a minute as he clicked on the *Freeden Tribune* app on his smartphone. It nearly exploded when he saw the headline:

REAL DNA TEST SQUASHED, REPLACED WITH HOAX IN JONES MURDER CASE
No Sign of Dwight Kerry's DNA in Original Test

Hefner looked up. "Holy shit."

PART 4: LACRIMOSA

14: Man Must Prepare for Judgment

It was the night before the trial, and Ben's foot was just as hot on the gas in his truck as it was figuratively in his mind. There was a town forum, set to be held at the concert hall, and he was late. He turned his satellite radio up a couple notches so he could hear the latest.

"Good evening, I'm Anderson Cooper reporting live for CNN from Freeden, North Carolina, where the trial of local high school teacher and church choir director Dwight Kerry is set to begin tomorrow morning right behind me here in the Freeden Courthouse. The case has taken a tremendous turn from when Dwight Kerry was arrested just a few weeks ago. Not only have accusations been hurled at the prosecution for tampering with evidence, but lead defense attorney Ben Bailey has promised even more suspicious activity to be unveiled in the trial that will 'expose this whole thing as a cover up' – and on that I quote him directly."

Once Preston Hall's story hit, the spotlight shone on Freeden. And the view could be seen clearly throughout the nation.

In one sense, it afforded the defense a hope in which it had not enjoyed before. In the other sense, it lit a fire under the Freeden majority who unequivocally believed Dwight was guilty, and stubbornly would not change their minds despite the *Tribune*'s big reveal. And even after Preston's story called out the district attorney's office for proven tampering with evidence, as far as Ben could tell, the majority of the town still believed Dwight was guilty and that the defense was simply throwing false accusations at local boy and upstanding citizen Scott Stevens, just to get their client off the hook.

Preston had lifted the veil on all of it, even publishing the actual original report *and* its falsified counterpart in full. But Preston wasn't from around these parts, and so despite this damning evidence against the prosecution, people in Freeden were inclined to believe what they were told by their own. Even still, the floodgates were open. As much as Dr. Henson and his followers detested the thought, a national audience was now captivated by the trial, a case that legal commentator Nancy Grace had termed *unjust at best*.

Negative consideration from the media lured in Dwight supporters from out-of-town; they began pouring into Freeden daily to peacefully protest what they deemed an unmerited trial. The out-of-towners were met, though, with fire and fury from Freeden citizens, who in no way wanted the *foreigners*, as Aaron Carrol so affectionately coined them on live television, to be causing trouble in their 'peaceful town.'

"We need the foreigners to realize that they are not welcome in our town just to stir up trouble," Aaron Carroll had said on Fox News. "Our town is a peaceful town, and we're just looking for this to all be over and for the Jones family to get the justice they deserve."

Harsh criticisms rained down on the prosecution's case. And there was no turning back now. The kingdom of Freeden was under siege. Dale Jones was so outraged at the story's release that he called the head of the Ohio-based company who owned the *Tribune* and asked for Hefner and Preston to be fired, but out of concern for what it may look like now that the national news had picked up the story, they declined to fire either of them. For the first time ever, the old guard were losing control of *their* town. Things were unfolding. And fast.

Ben pulled his car into the crammed parking lot. He'd arrived at the town forum. Other than the churches, there really was nowhere else to hold such an event in Freeden without the madness of finding seating, arranging for sound equipment, and so on. Plus, the concert hall was relatively removed from downtown and the protests that ensued, so the venue proved ideal for a town gathering.

It was limited to only people who lived in and owned property in Freeden, and town officials worked diligently to ensure only the town's citizens attended by checking IDs before people came into the event. Ben had heard about the event, and against the advice of his team, attended anyway. He was by himself, and he waited until just before the start of the forum when they had stopped checking IDs to slip into the balcony area and stand in the back so no one would see him.

The chatter from the crowd deafened as everyone gossiped about the latest developments in the case and all the drama that was playing out in the streets with the national media and social rights groups rolling into town.

Just before six p.m., Aaron Carroll walked onto the stage to speak. The choir risers and music stands were still on stage from the *Requiem*, as if the concert had ended the night before.

"Ladies and gentlemen, let's get started," Aaron said, as he grabbed the wireless mic from the mic stand positioned center stage. "For those of you who may not know me, I'm Aaron Carroll, your city manager, and I want to welcome you to this town forum. There's obviously a lot going on in our town right now, and I wanted to clear up a few things and answer your questions."

"What do you plan to do about all these liberals coming to our town?" one citizen asked.

"Yeah, I'm tired of these socialist left-wing freaks being in our town and trying to push their liberal agenda," another yelled, to overwhelming applause in the gallery.

"Just like you," Aaron said, "I don't want any trouble in our town. And we're going to do everything we can to limit their impact."

"I can't even go to the grocery store without seeing a bunch of hippies hollering at the entrance," one lady said. "We can't even go to church without seeing this madness."

"People are literally fighting in front of our church," said another elderly, feeble woman. "I saw a group of men, who I know are from around here, beat a young man, college age I'd say, who simply sat in front of the church with a cardboard sign this morning. Is anyone here concerned about what we are coming to – our own townspeople beating a boy on the church grounds?"

"Ma'am, that is not the whole story," said a man who had actually participated in the beating. "That man sat on church grounds next to the sidewalk, repeatedly saying, 'Gays are God's children, too.' He kept repeating that, over and over, in front of my children! We asked him to leave, and he didn't. He just kept saying it. So I had to do something, ma'am, we can't allow our families," his voice rose, "and our children, to hear that kind of nonsense."

Ben, still standing in the back of the balcony to take it all in, shook his head. He was ashamed of what he was hearing.

"Yeah!" members of the crowd chanted.

Ben grew even more embarrassed when the majority of attendees applauded the man's remarks.

"What's nonsensical is beating a man anywhere, much less the church grounds, for what he believes in," the woman replied.

"If you think I'm going to let my kids hear that filth at the church I raised them in, you can forget it."

"Yeah!" said a large group of attendees, who supplemented their chants with applause.

"Tell the truth!" yelled another to more applause.

"Well, if you've convinced yourself that beating a man for speaking his mind is a just solution in God eye's, then I don't want to know the God you worship," the woman said.

The comment garnered loud boos from the audience, and more shouting at the elderly woman who stood alone.

"Now, let's calm down, folks," said Chief Gary McDowell, who stood up from the front row since Aaron Carroll was seemingly losing control over the forum. "It's important during these times that we stick together."

"We want justice, Chief," shouted one citizen. "The world is turning into an ugly place, and they're trying to bring that filth into our town. Why don't you lock them up?"

"We can't lock someone up for peaceful protest," he replied. "That isn't how it works. You have to have just cause to arrest someone under the laws of our state."

"Is that really true, Chief?" a man asked, who had been standing against the back wall the entire time.

"Yes, yes it is," he replied.

"That's odd," the man said as he came forward, walking down the aisle and finally into the light where he could be seen. "Because it doesn't seem very just, what's really happening here."

The man was Dr. Colin Johnson. Ben recognized his voice as soon as he spoke, and leaned over to try and see him from the balcony. He recalled his conversation with Dr. Johnson backstage the night of the *Requiem*, and while he didn't know Dr. Johnson all that well, he had known of him his entire life and most certainly knew him to be a well-respected man. Just about everyone in Freeden was a patient at his doctor's office.

"What do you mean?" Chief McDowell asked, as he covered his eyes from the spotlights to try and see who was speaking. "Is that you, Dr. Johnson?"

"It is," he said, as he came down the aisle alongside the left side of the hall. "Good evening, Chief." He approached the floor in front of the stage. Aaron Carroll stood on stage, still, but was effectively no longer even trying to moderate the forum. Once he got to the front, Dr. Johnson turned to the audience and spoke loudly so he could be heard. "Ladies and gentlemen, this whole thing spawned from the arrest of Dwight Kerry."

"Doctor," Chief said.

"No, let me finish, Chief," he said, as he pointed at the Chief. Chief McDowell looked shocked that he would be spoken to in public in such blunt, pointed fashion. "The whole town needs to know this."

Ben was shocked. To date, no one as widely recognized as Dr. Johnson had come forward to question Freeden's authority.

"Doctor," Chief McDowell said.

"I called your office, Chief McDowell, and I told you about what I knew. But you failed to call me back. And then I called again."

"Doctor."

"And you wouldn't be trying to stop me right now if you didn't know what I was going to say, Chief! I called your office, spoke to your deputy chief, and told him the truth. He told me I was mistaken and hung up on me. I've called three times since, and stopped by your office, only to be told that no one was available. Your staff and your department have failed this town."

"Watch yourself, Dr. Johnson."

"What's going on here?" Lucy Jones stood up from her seat near the front of the audience. "What's going on, Dr. Johnson?"

"Doctor," Chief shouted.

"Lucy, I'm so sorry for what you've gone through, I really am," Dr. Johnson said. "But Dwight did not kill your son."

"Wait now," Chief McDowell said, "I think the trial will show that's not true, if it isn't clear already."

"Dwight is not a murderer! He was at the concert hall all afternoon that Friday. I was there. I saw him arrive just after school let out that day."

"Wait," Lucy said, "that can't be true. The note my son wrote… it said Dwight did it!"

"What I'm saying is true, Lucy."

"That's impossible," Chief McDowell said.

"It is a fact," Dr. Johnson shouted. "I saw him myself. I saw him walk into the concert hall that Friday afternoon. He didn't see me, but I was sitting in the balcony, reading. I had been there for nearly thirty minutes, and after he arrived, he never left the concert hall until at least after the concert. I watched him play the entire time from the balcony, but he did not know I was there."

"That can't be proven, Dr. Johnson, now sit down!" said Chief McDowell who now spoke in an angrier tone.

"Did you make this story up to help the gay?" one citizen stood up and asked.

"I'm not making this up," Dr. Johnson said. "And our own police department wouldn't give me the time of day."

"You're a gay lover!" one citizen yelled.

"Call me what you want," Dr. Johnson shouted. "But I

won't stand here and watch this innocent man be convicted of something I *know* he did not do."

"Dr. Johnson, I think it's time you sat down," Chief McDowell said.

"Is it true, Chief?" the elderly woman asked as she stood up again. "Had Dr. Johnson called your office and told you this?"

"I can't recall–"

"Yes or no, Chief?" the woman said.

"I think he did, yes," he said, "but our office has overwhelming evidence that Dwight did this, and hearsay won't trump that."

"So you refuse to take into account my story, a potential alibi, for a man I know is innocent?"

"You're a fag lover!" one attendee yelled.

"You're going to hell!" another shouted.

"Now, now, now," someone said, coming onto the stage from the backstage area. "Perhaps Dr. Johnson was just... confused."

An uncomfortable silence suffocated the room as a familiar and commanding voice interrupted the debate. Ben knew exactly who it was. Even Dr. Johnson, a powerful man in his own right, felt a tightening in his throat.

"I am not confused, Dr. Henson," Dr. Johnson answered, as beads of sweat began to form on his forehead.

"But Dr. Johnson, how can you sit here, in front of Lucy, and say these things? Lucy has been through so much."

The ladies sitting with Lucy began to console her as she wept, wrapping their arms around her.

"Dale won't even come out of the house," Dr. Henson said. "His child has been murdered, taken from him by an immoral, sadistic man, and–"

"I know this has been hard on Dale."

"No you do not know!" Dr. Henson yelled. If possible, the room fell even more silent. "You do not know what it's like to lose a child. So don't you sit there and tell the people who've made you wealthy that you understand how that feels." He took a deep breath. "How dare you make a mockery of your community's own! Dale, Lucy, and our church are hurting, and you come here to try and embarrass them and our family."

"I want justice for Dale and Lucy, too," Dr. Johnson said, "so don't use this as a platform to defame me for speaking a truth that doesn't match your fabricated version of what really happened. I'm not going to succumb to you like everyone else does, Dan. I am telling you it wasn't Dwight! I'm telling all of you that it wasn't him."

Lucy sobbed. People crowded around her to calm her down.

"Ladies and gentlemen," Dr. Henson said in a much calmer voice, "is it not clear that we are under attack? Attacked by those who would succumb to the anti-Christ himself if he walked into this town and asked them to follow – a liberal world with a radical agenda that wants us to conform to what they call the new normal, and accept gay and lesbian, and everything else under the sun. We will not accept sin in our lives!"

"Yeah!" the crowd chanted.

"We will not conform to the sins of the world here in *our* town!"

"Yeah!" the crowd chanted once more.

"Romans says that men began to harbor lustful feelings toward other men, and so God deprived them of salvation," Dr. Henson exclaimed.

"Yes!" the crowd chanted.

Lucy continued to weep, raising her shaking hands high in a

show of worship.

"We have allowed this in our community and look what has happened now. This filth has resulted in the death of a child, a wonderful child, and now the liberal media has marched into our town and, on account of a fraudulent story written by a second-tier news editor, wants us to change our ways. I'll tell you now, as a follower of Christ you can love your neighbor, but remember that God does not accept this sin, nor will He ever accept this type of behavior!"

"Yeah!"

Dr. Henson pounded his fist down in the air, a show of strength to his followers. "We won't allow these people to be a part of our community and hurt our children any longer."

"Yeah!"

"We will not tolerate something we don't believe in. For the world may die from sin, but Freeden will be a beacon of light for God the Father, the Son, and the Holy Spirit, forever and ever!"

The statement garnered significant applause. Lucy stood to show her support, which in itself was incredibly telling, and most of the audience followed. Dr. Johnson stood there, in front of the stage, his head raised high, though his spirit sinking low. Ben watched him, a defiant supporter of Dwight's, as nearly everyone in the crowd looked at him with scorn, applauding Dr. Henson and his impromptu sermon.

Ben knew he had just witnessed the fall of Dr. Colin Johnson, and that Dr. Henson would ensure that anyone he could talk to would *never* step foot in his doctor's office again. Despite Dr. Johnson's good intentions, Ben knew Dr. Henson would make absolute certain his medical practice of over four decades in Freeden folded, all a result of defying him in the public. That's one of the clearer reasons people feared Dr.

Henson. If you crossed him, you were finished.

Ben stood as the crowd continued cheering in a forum that had now become a rally for Freeden radical conservatives. He had seen quite enough. He walked outside toward the lobby to call Kate.

"Hey Kate, where are you?"

"I'm at your office. Liz, Kristen, and I are working. Are you okay?"

"Yes, just stepped outside the concert hall."

"How is it?"

"About what I expected. Look, we need to put Dr. Colin Johnson on the witness list."

A young man approached him in the dimly lit corridor leading from the balcony to the lobby. No one was there but the two of them.

"Sir?" he asked Ben.

"Yes, young man. Hold on one moment. Kate, I need you to–"

"I need to talk to you sir," the boy said.

"Yes, just a moment."

"I think you probably know me. I'm Ian Christopher."

Ben stopped, his mouth gaped open in surprise. "Uh, Kate… let me call you back."

Ben hung up and couldn't stop staring at him. Better late than never – it was a phrase he had been brought up believing in, and on the eve of the trial, they had been blessed with their best chance at saving Dwight yet.

15: Tuba Mirum

It was the first day of the trial. Ben arrived with his team at the courthouse that morning on just a few hours of sleep, having spent most of the night at the office speaking with Ian. After days of Ben's office trying to get him to come forward, he had told them everything he knew.

For ethical reasons, Kate could not be employed by Bailey and Associates for the remainder of the trial due to her beginning the case as a member of the prosecution team, but she helped in any way she could away from the courtroom, living off her savings in the meantime. She felt a tremendous calling to help Ben in this case, and despite the fact that the two had really connected on their first date at David's, they kept it professional while working to build a case. They both believed in this cause. Dwight was innocent, and they were determined to set him free.

In Ben's interview with Ian, Ian admitted that Kate had convinced him to talk to the defense. Ben had no idea she was working on it so diligently; Ben's own private investigator Ken had had no luck, being shunned away by Ian's father and refuted by Ian himself, who was too frightened to talk at the time. Kate, though, followed the now eighteen-year-old from high school each day to a local coffee shop just off of Main Street, handing him a note and not saying a word. Finally, on the Friday before the trial, Ian had walked over to Kate's table and wanted to talk.

"My parents will disown me if they know I talked," Ian said.

Kate set her coffee down and leaned forward. "You are a brave young man, even to talk to me now. But if you don't come forward publicly, Mr. Kerry will likely stand no chance."

"I know Mr. Kerry didn't do this."

"I know that, too," Kate replied, "but you are the missing piece to the puzzle. You're the only chance he has."

Ian told Ben in their late Sunday night interview following the town forum that Kate's comments to him at the coffee shop were what ultimately led him to come forward.

Ben sat back, looked around the room, and admired what Kate had done. He knew she was not doing this for him. She was helping because she knew Dwight was innocent and felt a conviction to do anything she could to exonerate him. As much as he already respected her in this short time he had known her, she continued to amaze even more as time progressed. Ben knew Freeden had its share of deceitful, vindictive, and dishonest people, but Kate was showing Ben that there was hope after all.

Some of Freeden's own had inspired Ben, too. In the previous week, there had been no sign of doubt from anyone in the community that Dwight was guilty, but Dr. Colin Johnson and the elderly woman he did not recognize from the night before had taken a stand in the forum: at the very least, Dwight was being judged too quickly. Dr. Johnson claimed to have seen Dwight at the concert hall all afternoon, a match to Dwight's story about that same day. Unfortunately, no one wanted to hear Dr. Johnson's story because it did not fit the narrative that Dwight, the gay teacher, had committed a lewd act against his male student and ultimately killed him. The elderly woman, on a similar note, acknowledged her suspicion that he was being treated unfairly *just* because he was gay. And in Ben's mind, both of them were exactly right.

Ben had reached out to Dr. Johnson after the forum, and Dr. Johnson had agreed to serve as a witness for the defense. He could not have respected Dr. Johnson more, either; in their conversation, Dr. Johnson admitted that it would likely put an end to his practice but that it would be for good reason, if it saved a man he had known and cared about for so long.

Ben wondered if the tide was finally changing; if people were beginning to see the prejudice targeting Dwight and people who were simply different from the Freeden norm. Despite there still being a very small number of people who had publicly called out the ridiculousness of the case, Ben hoped the veil would continue to be lifted on this irrational accusation against Dwight.

Ben and his team sat patiently at the defense table, awaiting Dwight's arrival. Scott Stevens, sitting next to another assistant district attorney who had presumably taken Kate's place, leaned back in his chair, his legs crossed, chewing on his pen and eyeing the door that Dwight would soon enter through. Ben stared at him. Scott looked resentful, almost as if he, at this point, was simply trying to stick it to Dwight. The embarrassment he had endured on national television, called out by the major media players for being biased and on a mysterious, personal mission to destroy Dwight – it was reason enough for him to harbor resentment. He was determined to get his way, and prosecuting Dwight to a guilty verdict would be the only way he would be satisfied.

The gallery was full, again, but this time not just by staunchly fundamental Freeden citizens. Dwight supporters, a few locals and mostly *foreigners*, as coined by Freeden's esteemed city manager, also filled the seats of the gallery. All media outlets, both local and national, had a seat, and Scott and the prosecution's supporters despised this. But there was no way to avoid it, the prosecution was already facing mounting pressure from the media over evidence tampering and a number of other irregularities in the pre-trial process, so Judge Freeman simply had to allow it to prevent further criticism of the local justice system which had, too, been accused of being partial, biased, and down-right discriminatory.

Just moments before nine a.m. and the beginning of the opening statements, Dwight was ushered into the courtroom. Dale Jones, who had come outside of his home for the first time in a week, embraced his wife Lucy on the front row behind the prosecution, as she wept at the sight of her son's alleged killer. Dwight looked particularly worn down. His hair wasn't combed back as elegantly and straight as usual – it appeared a bit frizzled, and he wore no makeup at all. To Ben, Dwight actually looked older than he was, and the craziness that had taken over his life seemed to be taking a toll on his health.

He sat down after being escorted to his chair next to Ben, and said, "Good morning, Ben."

"How are you?"

"I'm okay, tired really. I hope to talk to you today, after all of this, if possible?"

"Sure, is there something I should know now?"

"No, no… just want the opportunity to chat today if at all possible. Need someone to talk to."

"Sure, Dwight, you know I'll do that."

The bailiff began introducing Judge Freeman. "All rise for the Honorable Judge Phillip Freeman," he said in his usual thick Southern accent. "Oh yes, oh yes, oh yes, the Freeden County Superior Court is now in session."

Judge Freeman entered the room from the door just next to his bench and took his seat. "Thank you, bailiff." He sat, and the rest of the courtroom, including the gallery, followed suit.

Judge Freeman looked a bit more reserved than usual, likely because he realized that Freeden locals were not the only ones occupying his courtroom. "Okay, this is the State of North Carolina v. Dwight Kerry, first-degree murder and first-degree statutory rape, is the State ready to proceed?"

Scott rose from his seat. "The State is ready to proceed, your Honor."

"Okay. At this time, I'll allow time for opening statements. The State will go first, followed by the defense. I do want to note, though, that nothing they say in their opening statements is to be used as evidence, it can however be used as a way to understand evidence that will be presented during this trial, including but not limited to witness testimony, cross-examination, and evidence admitted to the court. Is that understood by the jury?"

The jurors collectively nodded in affirmation.

"Very well. Mr. Stevens, you may proceed with your opening statement."

Scott again rose from his seat. "Thank you, your Honor." He put on his glasses, and approached the jury box and rested his right hand on the railing in front of them as if he were simply engaging in casual conversation. Then, in his charismatic manner, he turned on his typical charm. "A warm, early summer night. Like always, kids played on the streets, shooting basketball with their friends, riding bikes around town. Parents hired babysitters for their young ones so they could go out for dinner at one of the town's eateries and take part in the wonders of small-town living. Neighbors held early Memorial Day barbecues in their backyards, all while children ran about all over town, just like you and I did when we were young." He chuckled, but then rapidly transitioned to a serious tone. "But suddenly on that same warm, summer night, our darkest fears became a reality. A stark realization that we can no longer live like old times, that the days of simplicity and worry-free living are a thing of the past and now cease to exist – it struck us like a ton of bricks. It was a realization that the immoralities of the world had infiltrated even our small town of Freeden. Yes, a deviant who we allowed to teach in our schools, and direct our children in both the school and church choirs, forced his unnatural behaviors on one of the brightest, most disciplined children in our community, and murdered him when he didn't accept his demonic behaviors."

He paused for effect, eyeing the jury, then turned and pointed to Dale and Lucy Jones. "Look at them," he said as Lucy continued to weep, Dale holding onto her, embracing her with his right arm. "Their only child was taken from them by the man on trial here. And it could have been your child! And if we, as a community, do not take a stand against Dwight Kerry, then more stories like Braxton Jones's will surely be told over time. And that would be a travesty that could have been prevented in this trial by you, the jurors."

He started pacing, his hand dragging along the railing. "The State intends to prove that Dwight Kerry, without a shadow of a doubt, committed this crime, and deserves nothing less than the death penalty. The State intends to prove, with undeniable DNA evidence and a note left by the victim in his dying moments, that Dwight Kerry is unquestionably the perpetrator. Now, the Defense has already accused us of tampering with evidence and falsifying documents to ensure a conviction, you've heard it on the news. But I ask you, why would we do that? Why would we allow this man to serve our community for decades, only to wage war against him now for no just reason? I tell you, my record as a district attorney speaks for itself. These unfounded claims made by the defense will go unaddressed by the prosecution from this point forward, as we see them for what they are: typical propaganda from a defense attorney designed to fool you, the jurors, into believing your justice system is corrupt. I'm from here and my team is from here, just like you. We want what's best for this community. But Ben Bailey… he wants what's best for *him*, and that's why he's defending a rapist and a murderer and making big dollars in the process. That's why he and his team put out a false story in the *Tribune* to make the national media show up in our town and get him even more attention and fame."

Judge Freeman had allowed Scott, in Ben's opinion, to rant well beyond the normal scope of an opening statement. Scott refocused. "The State intends to show you, unequivocally, that Dwight Kerry, who kept his demonic sexual desires behind closed doors for so long, acted in such a horrendous manner that it took a young boy's life. If you let him go, rest assured, there will be more Dwight Kerrys that follow." He paused, staring at the jurors with a stern look on his face. "Thank you, your Honor."

Scott slowly turned back toward the prosecution table and began walking in that direction. The sound of his shoes on the floor was as commanding as his opening statement, a strong click-clack every time he took a step.

"Counsel?" Judge Freeman pointed to Ben. "Your opening statement."

Ben felt a rush of nervousness come over him in a way he never had. In the hundreds of cases he had tried before, he never felt this way, because he had never had an emotional attachment to his client like this. And he never truly believed anyone he had defended before was unquestionably innocent.

Until now.

Ben tried to hide the deep breath he took just before he rose from the table, realizing that from this point forward, everything he did or said would be looked at closely. His body language, the way he talked, everything would either be scrutinized or well-received. He desperately hoped what he saw the night before at the town forum was indicative of a changing tide and a new wave of thought that, perhaps, Dwight was indeed falsely accused. He needed that wave to be evident in this jury by the time they deliberated.

Ben walked over, and stood in front of the jury in about the same place Scott had. "A warm, early summer night. Like always, kids played on the streets, shooting basketball with their friends, riding bikes around town. Parents hired babysitters for their young ones so they could go out for dinner at one of the town's eateries and take part in the wonders of small-town living. Neighbors held early Memorial Day barbecues in their backyards, all while children ran about all over town."

Disgust blanketed Scott's face, as he realized Ben was repeating the first part of *his* opening statement.

"And one man did what he has always done on that night: serve our community. Dwight Kerry went to school that morning at seven-fifteen a.m. like he always does, he taught class like he always does, and left right after school to go to the Freeden concert hall to prepare for yet another non-paid role as director of Mozart's *Requiem* in yet another concert he put on for the townspeople and out-of-towners alike to enjoy. He was there from around three-thirty p.m., all the way to when the concert and reception ended shortly after nine-thirty. Yes, it was indeed a normal day for Freeden, and yes it was indeed a normal day for Dwight Kerry." He shook his head. "Now, make no mistake about it, I do sympathize with Braxton Jones's family–"

"Lies!" Dale shouted. Murmuring and a few hand claps came from the gallery.

"Order!" Judge Freeman said. "I will not have outbursts during this trial, and I need everyone in the gallery to understand me. Am I clear?"

The gallery silenced. Ben believed that Judge Freeman had hardened his tone in an effort to appear fair in front of a challenging national media.

"Continue counsel," Judge Freeman instructed.

Ben nodded and continued in a soft tone. "I really do sympathize with the family. Now, I'm not going to sit here and tell you I know what it's like to lose a child, because I don't. And it's obvious that someone committed this terrible act… but that man was not Dwight Kerry. Dwight cares for his students, in many cases more than their own family does." He paused. "We intend to show you that the prosecution's case is full of holes and corrupt behavior that targets Dwight Kerry because of one thing: the fact that he is gay."

Ben took notice of how the jurors reacted to this. Most of them sat there with stone-like, blank faces, and offered no indication on whether or not that fact would have any influence over them like it, from Ben's perspective, had had on the people of Freeden.

"There is overwhelming reason to believe that the prosecution tampered with the evidence in this case to connect Dwight to a crime I believe he didn't commit. We plan to show you through witness testimony and concrete evidence that the prosecution tampered with evidence, and we plan to show you why they did it, too."

A few of the jurors perked up and raised eyebrows at Ben's

notion that Dwight was deceptively implicated.

"There is more than a reasonable doubt here." Ben paused. He wanted them to hear and remember this. "Dwight Kerry was framed."

Ben turned to walk back to the defense table. He looked in the back of the gallery and caught a glimpse of Kate. She gave him a reassuring smile, and he returned the gesture. He wished she could be sitting next to him. She deserved this, but more notably, he simply wanted to be near her.

"Mr. Stevens," Judge Freeman acknowledged, "would you like to call your first witness?"

"Yes, your honor," Scott answered. "The State would like to call Mr. Dale Jones."

Gasps were heard throughout the gallery. No one knew Dale, the father of the slain boy, intended to testify in open court. Dale slowly walked to the witness stand, and was administered the oath by an officer of the court.

"Mr. Jones, raise your right hand toward Heaven and lay your left hand on God's Holy word, please," the officer said.

Dale complied and tilted his head back, raising his chin.

"Mr. Jones, do you swear to tell the truth, the whole truth, and nothing but the truth, so help you God?"

"I do."

"Thank you."

Dale took his seat, and Scott approached the stand.

"Mr. Jones, before I begin, I'm so terribly sorry for your loss," Scott said.

"Thank you, Mr. Stevens."

"Mr. Jones, how long have you lived in this community?"

"Other than while I was off at college, I've lived here my entire life."

"And how long have you run your accounting business

here?"

"For about thirty-two years."

"And where did you attend church all those years?"

"I've been a lifelong member of Freeden Baptist Church, and I've served as a deacon on three different occasions."

"Is that where you first met Mr. Kerry?"

"Yes, sir."

"And how long did your son attend Freeden Baptist?"

"His entire life."

"Was he involved there in any capacity other than just attending?"

"He sang in the youth choir."

"Under the direction of Mr. Kerry, I presume?"

"Yes."

"He also served in the school choir under Mr. Kerry's direction, did he not?"

"He did."

"How long would you say Mr. Kerry worked with Braxton – in total years?"

"I'd say about ten years."

"Were you ever concerned about Braxton playing and singing in Mr. Kerry's choirs before?"

"No, Lucy and I trusted him."

"Let's talk about the night of Friday, May 25th."

Dale's bottom lip began to quiver. A tear fell from his left eye.

Scott paused. "I know this can be hard, just take your time."

"Thank you," Dale said as he choked back the tears. "Okay," he said while composing himself, "I'm ready."

To Ben, the jury seemed sympathetic for Dale. He eyed them, realizing the emotional effect this must be taking on them to hear testimony from the victim's father.

"Mr. Jones, one of our deputies came by your home after eight p.m. that night, is that correct?"

"Yes, sir."

"And you proceeded to come with us to the high school, is that right?"

"Yes."

"Just before nine o'clock, we showed you a handwritten note, found inches from the victim's body upon our arrival," he said, as he walked back to the prosecution table. He then reached into a box on the table and pulled out a sealed plastic bag with the note flattened and completely unraveled inside. "We showed you this note that night, will you look at this and confirm that it is the same handwritten note we showed you that evening?"

He examined it, visibly fighting back the tears. "It is."

"Can you confirm, like you did that evening, whose handwriting this is?"

"It is my son's handwriting. Braxton's handwriting."

Scott turned to face the jury, but still held out the plastic bag to face Dale and spoke directly to him. "And can you tell me what your son wrote down in his dying moments?"

"It says 'Dwight Kerry'."

"In his last breath," Scott said as most of the jurors looked down to take notes after this information was unveiled, "he wrote down the name of his killer so justice would be served. Braxton was always a courageous boy, as Dale has told me and this community has seen, but nothing was braver than what he did in his dying moments." Scott turned back toward the prosecution table to get another piece of evidence from the box, this time a document. "Mr. Jones, can you do the court a favor and tell me what this is?" He re-approached the witness stand and handed Dale the document.

"It appears to be the DNA report."

"And can you read the last sentence of the summary for the court, please?"

"Yes, sir," he said as reached for his glasses from his shirt pocket and put them on to read. "The State Medical Examiner's office finds the only DNA match to be that of Mr. Dwight Kerry."

"An official DNA report from the State Medical Examiner's office," Scott said, "reveals there only to be one match. And can you tell me if that document you are reading is signed by anyone?"

"Signed by the State Medical Examiner," Dale said.

Scott had begun pacing around the area in front of the jury, but he started to work his way back to the witness stand. "Mr. Jones, the State is deeply sorry for your loss. To us, it appears plain and simple: Dwight Kerry committed a dastardly act that Braxton tried to fend off, and ultimately killed your son in retaliation. We have a note from your boy, which was written in his dying moments, and we have a DNA report, compiled from samples taken from the boy's clothing he was wearing that night and the murder weapon, that conclude that Dwight Kerry was the perpetrator."

Dale began to cry, not making any loud noises to interrupt, but quietly weeping as he heard Scott outline the details from that night.

Ben peered over at the jury once more. Their body language clearly showed their sympathy for Dale. Ben wondered how his cross-examination might be perceived.

Dale continued to sob. Lucy and other family members wept in the gallery, too.

"Take your time," Scott said.

"I just want my boy back," Dale said as he bawled.

"Take your time," Judge Freeman said.

Dale tried to compose himself, and finally did after a couple of minutes.

"Mr. Jones," Scott asked, while trying to see if Dale was ready to continue, "do you believe Dwight Kerry is the man who murdered your son?"

"Yes."

Scott looked at Judge Freeman. "No further questions, your Honor."

Dale started to cry again, now loudly, as Judge Freeman called on Ben. "Counsel?"

Ben looked over at Liz and Kristen, and they nodded. Ben had told his team everything he and Ian had discussed the previous night, so they knew he was prepared to cross-examine Dale. Ben worried, though, about how the jury might take his inevitable, sharp approach to the victim's father.

Ben moved toward the witness stand slowly, trying to give Dale time to compose himself. When he got to the stand, Dale continued to cry.

"Take your time, Dale," Ben said.

Dale held his head high, working to lessen the tears. Ben perceived his now postured and upright stance to be defensive. He could see his expressions change; a frown now occupied his face.

"Mr. Jones, let's talk about the days leading up to Friday, May 25th. Your boy wasn't in school for a couple weeks at least prior to that evening. Why was that?"

"He was sick."

"What was he dealing with to keep him out of school for that long?" Ben asked.

"Mono."

"Oh, well mono can certainly keep you down and out for a

while," Ben said as he smiled. "I've always heard that was the kissing disease."

"Yeah, I've heard the same."

"Did Braxton have a girlfriend?"

"No," Dale chuckled, "but he was so smart and charming, I'm sure he was sought after by his lady classmates."

Several members of the gallery laughed at the comment, including Lucy and the family.

"Oh, I'm sure," Ben said. "Smart guy, very talented musician, had a lot going for him. Let me ask you though, are you sure he didn't have a girlfriend?"

Dale looked confused. "I am pretty sure he did not have a girlfriend. He told us everything, I would have known."

Ben stared into Dale's eyes. He did not smile, or frown, just a blank stare. "Is that right? He told you everything?"

"Yes."

"Well tell me, Mr. Jones," he said as he looked toward the jury, "if your son told you everything, surely he told he was gay?"

Gasps filled the courtroom again, followed by an eruption of chatter, name-calling, and shouting from the gallery.

"Objection!" Scott yelled. "Relevance?" In this shocking moment, Scott didn't know what else to say.

Slurs were hurled at Ben, a few applauded, and the courtroom was in complete disarray. Ben just kept looking at the jurors throughout. A couple of them appeared stunned, but the rest appeared to be infuriated at the notion that Ben would ask the victim's father such a thing in open court.

"Order!" Judge Freeman shouted as he pounded his gavel. "Order!" He continued slamming the gavel onto his bench. The gallery finally calmed down.

"My goodness, people," Judge Freeman said as everyone

finally started calming down. "Objection sustained. Mr. Bailey, move on from that effort you just made to humiliate the victim's father."

Ben turned to the jury. "Right there," he said as he pointed to Judge Freeman. "There lies the problem right there. The Honorable Judge Freeman just told you, right there, how he feels about gay people. To be gay must be humiliating."

"Counsel!"

Ben turned back to Dale. "Your son told his teacher, Dwight Kerry, that he was gay. He was scared to death to talk about it to anyone else, and in that conversation, my client told him that it was okay to embrace himself for who he was, and then he came home and told you. So you kept him out of school, locked in a basement to make him *fix* himself, where he stayed for at least two weeks. On Friday, May 25th, he escaped and tried to go tell Dwight, the only adult he trusted with this information, that he needed help."

"Order, Mr. Bailey!"

"And somehow, that afternoon while my client was at the concert hall preparing for the *Requiem* concert," Ben turned back to the jury, "which we will also show you in witness testimony–"

"Mr. Bailey, do you hear me?" Judge Freeman shouted.

Then Ben turned back to Dale. "Your son was killed in Dwight's classroom that afternoon and my client is being framed because he's the only guy this town thinks is queer enough to do something like this."

"Mr. Bailey! Last warning or I will hold you in contempt."

Ben stopped and simply stared at Dale, who was clearly a nervous wreck. Complete silence filled the courtroom.

"None of that is true," Dale said. "None of it."

In a softer tone, Ben continued. "So you were not a part of

an attempt to frame my client?"

"Absolutely not." Dale shook his head. "You're a sick bastard."

Dale's somber, holier-than-thou persona was withering away. Ben felt that he was unveiling the real Dale Jones.

"Then will you please tell me why you showed up at Scott Stevens' office, less than a week after the murder, and asked him to alter those DNA reports to implicate Dwight as the killer?"

"Objection, your Honor!" Scott shouted. "The defense is falsely speculating and trying to instill a conspiracy theory with no substantiation."

"Objection sustained," Judge Freeman said.

Two members of the jury dropped their jaws in apparent shock and awe. Liz and Kristen took notes on everything they saw the jury do.

"I would never have done that," Dale said.

"Why did you want to frame Dwight as the killer? Had Braxton told you that he had come out as gay to Dwight?"

"That did not happen."

"Oh you bet your ass it did," Ben said. "And I'm curious, it's standard to have a doctor's note for school if you're out that long, so did Braxton receive a note for his case of mono from the doctor, or do you plan on trying to falsify that document, too?"

"Objection!"

"Sustained," Judge Freeman answered. "Mr. Bailey, you're done with Mr. Jones."

Dale sat there, trembling with a mixture of anger and uneasiness. A prominent man in the community, he was noticeably ashamed and unable to answer for all that Ben had thrown at him. His emotional-loving-father persona had taken a dagger to its heart. Ben walked back to the defense table and looked at Kate in the back. She nodded affirmatively. He had asked her to do that if she noticed one person in the jury whose body language appeared to indicate doubt in Dale Jones's narrative.

The trumpet had rung a wondrous sound. Ben felt the tide may be changing.

16: Omnia Potens

"Your Honor, the State calls Freeden police chief Gary McDowell to the witness stand."

After a disastrous first day for Scott Stevens and the prosecution's case, Scott asked for a recess until the next day, citing the mental health of Lucy Jones, who completely lost it after Ben cross-examined Dale. Lucy was the best thing the prosecution had going for the case; as far as Ben could tell, she had nothing to do with a supposed cover-up and justly warranted sympathy from everyone. After she grew uncontrollably emotional in court when Ben called Dale out for being involved in framing Dwight, the prosecution had to regroup to ensure nothing of the sort happened again. The headline on CNN and other major national news outlets was that the defense had brought to light some serious allegations of corruption that, if proven true, should acquit Dwight Kerry.

Ben thought Scott must surely have regretted putting Dale on the stand. He was certain it was done to garner sympathy from the jury, but it had ultimately dealt a major blow to the prosecution's case. In order to win, Scott had to get as many people to the stand as possible to establish the facts of the case. No more witnesses intended to trigger emotions; Scott needed to *show* the jury Dwight was guilty. Ben believed his calling Chief McDowell to the stand would be a good play for that push, as no one would be pointed in establishing the prosecution's facts better than him. Chief McDowell was a trusted member of the community, and a man known to be comprised of integrity and a willingness to always do what's right. Scott turned to him to squander potential concerns of conspiracy, which had come to the forefront in the first day of the trial.

Chief McDowell took the stand.

"Good morning, Chief," said Scott as he paced in front of the stand. "Tell us what happened on the night of the Friday, May 25th."

In his usual stern, monotone voice, he said, "I received a call from one of my officers that an inspection of Freeden High School, resulting from a call-in concerning an open door and potential intrusion, led to the discovery of a dead body on the third floor of the main high school building."

"And whose body was that, sir?"

"It was the body of Braxton Jones."

"When you found him, had your officers moved the body?"

"Absolutely not. They didn't, nor do they ever, move anything involved in a crime scene until it is investigated. They immediately called me, and I arrived on the scene approximately eight to ten minutes later."

"What did you find when you got there?"

"Upon arrival I saw the boy lying face down on the floor, his headed pointed toward the whiteboards at the front of the classroom. About a foot or two away from him, spotted with blood, was a note that we believed to have been written by the victim just before he bled to death on the floor."

Scott shook his head. "Wait a moment. Now take me back a minute, if you will. How did he get on the floor?"

"It appears the victim was raped while pressed against Mr. Kerry's desk, and stabbed to death in the back before Mr. Kerry fled in a panic to dispose of the murder weapon. We believe Mr. Kerry thought he was dead, but the victim, still alive after

Mr. Kerry left the scene, found a pen on the desk and a small piece of paper, and proceeded to write the note. He then fell to the floor as he lost energy and fell unconscious. We believe he dropped the note when falling, which is why the note ended up on the floor a foot or two away from him."

"And if you will," Scott asked, "please remind the jury what the note says." Scott handed the bag the letter was contained in to Chief McDowell for review.

Chief grabbed it, looked at it once more, and said, "The note simply has a name written on it. Dwight Kerry."

"So I want to clear up something else. How do you know it was written by the boy?"

"The boy's father first identified it as his handwriting."

"Is that all you have to prove it was, indeed, Braxton Jones's handwriting?"

"We have something else, too."

"And what might that be?"

"The high school principal was able to give us several copies of his academic work on record. It is clear that the handwriting matches Braxton Jones's other work."

Scott walked over to the prosecution's desk and grabbed a stack of documents from a box. "Your Honor, the State would like to introduce Braxton's academic work as evidence that the handwriting on it matches the handwriting on the note left at the scene of the crime." He handed it to Judge Freeman, who inspected it carefully.

"Evidence will be admitted, Mr. Stevens," Judge Freeman said.

"Thank you, your Honor." He began pacing in front of the stand again. "So, let's talk about the murder weapon."

"Okay," said Chief McDowell.

"Where was the murder weapon found?"

"The murder weapon was found in a trash can inside the men's restroom at the main high school building."

"Was a DNA test conducted on the weapon to identify if there was a match to the victim?"

"Yes, it was."

"And did the test implicate anyone, Chief?"

"Yes, it did. The test showed only one match, and that was also Dwight Kerry."

Scott rubbed his chin with his right hand, now facing the jury, and looked directly at them. "So the DNA test that was conducted implicated the defendant, and the victim left a note with the defendant's name on it, is that correct?"

"Yes sir, it is."

"Ladies and gentlemen of the jury, you can believe all the conspiracy theories you want, but the facts remain as they are. Despite the defense's efforts to drum up ideas of corruption, the official DNA report, validated by the State Medical Examiner's office, shows you that there is a murder weapon and a note that indisputably connects Dwight Kerry to the crime." He paused for effect. "No further questions."

Scott walked back to his seat, trying to refrain from smiling. Ben knew Scott wanted to, though, as Chief McDowell's testimony proved to be a big recovery from the previous day's disaster. The story Preston Hall had released in the *Tribune* some weeks prior challenged the Chief's story, but Ben wasn't so sure Chief McDowell even knew about the alleged cover-up. It was essential for his cross-examination of every one of the prosecution's witnesses to be as effective and challenging as it was on the first day when he cross-examined Dale. All he needed was one juror to believe this was a cover-up, but he still knew it would take his absolute best effort to get even one to sway to his side.

"Counsel," Judge Freeman said, attempting to push Ben to hurry and begin his cross-examination.

"Chief McDowell," Ben said as he walked slowly toward the stand, "is the academic work the prosecution admitted just now, along with Mr. Dale Jones identifying the handwriting to be his son's, the only existing evidence to prove the note was written by the boy?"

"We believe, based on what we have seen, that it is an identical match."

"That's not what I asked," Ben fired back. "What I asked you is if the academic work now submitted as evidence and Mr. Jones identifying the handwriting to be his boy's – is that the only evidence you have?"

"Well, yes."

"I'm not trying to discount the evidence, Chief. But I'm curious. Has your office taken samples of his father's handwriting – or other members of the family, to ensure the handwriting does not match theirs?"

"What are you implying?"

"You don't worry about that, Chief, I'll do my job. I just want to know if you took samples of his father's handwriting, or anyone else in the family, to see if their handwriting was similar to that of the victim's?"

"No, we did not."

"So let me get this straight," Ben said, as he now turned to the jury. "We're talking about the man who sat right where you are yesterday and lied under oath. You're telling me–"

"Objection!" Scott yelled.

"–that you are taking his word that the handwriting matched his son's?"

"Objection sustained," Judge Freeman said. "That statement will be stricken from the record. Mr. Bailey, don't defame a witness in this case again. No one's on trial here except your client."

Ben knew it would be taken from the record, but he confidently assumed at least one juror would remember it during deliberation. "Since they're not going to let you answer that question, let's focus on something else. Can you hold the handwritten note up for the court to see, please?"

Reluctantly, Chief McDowell held the note high, facing the gallery.

"If you don't mind, point that toward the jury, please."

Chief McDowell looked at him, appearing to be in a foul mood, and finally held it facing the jury.

"This handwriting seems to be pretty solid," Ben said. "It doesn't quite look as neat as his work from school," Ben said as he looked at it, sitting on the railing of the witness stand, "but it's pretty well-written. Tell me, Chief, have you ever encountered any other victims who wrote so neatly after being raped and stabbed in the back *thirty-six times*?"

"It certainly appears like he struggled a bit to write it," Chief McDowell said.

"Struggled a bit?" Ben asked after chuckling sarcastically. "Do you really think someone could write as neat as this note is written after being raped and then stabbed in the back thirty-six times?"

"I have never encountered another case like this, so I wouldn't know."

"I can understand that, Chief, but let's try to use some common sense, here. Are you telling me that you believe someone who was just raped and stabbed in the back with a large kitchen knife thirty-six times could write *this* clearly?"

"Perhaps his adrenaline allowed him to do it, in one final moment."

"Do you really believe that?"

"It's possible, I guess."

"Objection, your Honor," Scott interrupted. "The witness has already answered the question, despite it not fitting the narrative of Mr. Bailey's preference."

"Possible?" Ben said. "That's debatable, but you don't believe it, do you?"

"Mr. Bailey, I'm about done with you ignoring my rules in this Court."

"It doesn't make sense, does it?" Ben asked Chief McDowell once more.

"Okay!" Chief McDowell shouted. Unraveled from his usual unimpassioned self, he appeared visibly shaken before the jury and court. "I will agree," he continued while stuttering a bit, "it seems somewhat difficult to believe that he could have written it in that state."

Silence filled the courtroom. Ben simply stood there, his arms crossed, looking down. "Hm," he said, then nodded once. "That'll do, your Honor, no further questions." Ben started to walk away.

"But it still could have happened, though." Chief McDowell said as Ben walked away, in an apparent attempt to retract his implication that the prosecution had it wrong. "It could have happened. It was confirmed by Mr. Jones!"

Ben did not respond. In his mind, the jury had heard exactly what he wanted them to hear. Scott's eyes looked as big as fifty-cent pieces from the shock of another witness losing it on the stand. Scott didn't know what to do. He knew Ben Bailey was winning, and realized that something had to change, or Dwight Kerry would be acquitted.

That night, the streets were still lined with protesters, growing in number each day. On the right side of the street in front of the courthouse, local townspeople dominated the crowd, chanting for Dwight to be executed and for justice to be served for Dale and Lucy Jones and the small town of Freeden. In large part, Ben believed these people felt attacked and victimized by the national media for being painted as good-for-nothing country hicks whose values didn't matter. To the left side of the courthouse stood a majority of out-of-towners, joined each day by a few locals that had begun to see the injustice shown toward Dwight. People flocked to Freeden to demand fairness for Dwight in a case that proved more biased as time progressed.

Ben knew of only three times the two groups had clashed, including two minor instances that happened a week before the trial began, but the most recent, which occurred the afternoon of Chief McDowell's testimony, left three out-of-town protesters beaten badly with one in critical condition at Freeden Memorial Hospital. Two men were arrested for the beatings, an eighteen-year-old male and recent graduate of Freeden High School, and his forty-four-year-old father.

The father was a local leader for the Boy Scouts of America, and his son had recently been named an Eagle Scout. Neither of them were charged by Freeden Police and were released hours after their arrest, as both claimed self-defense. Ben's private investigator Ken Hughes had interviewed several people who witnessed the incident, though, both locals and out-of-towners, and all of them indicated that the attack was not warranted by the actions of the victims. All accounts showed that the protesters were simply holding signs that read *EQUALITY FOR ALL* and participating in peaceful, group chanting.

Ben grew completely disheartened when he first heard about the beating. There was a young man from out-of-town in critical condition at the local hospital, but even more bothersome was the fact that an eighteen-year-old from Freeden was involved in beating the man. This indicated that the hatred and prejudice Ben had witnessed so far would likely live on in Freeden for a long time since the young adult generation was, too, participating in the madness.

Ben worried that the majority of parents here, both religious and non-religious, would continue, as he expected they always had, to teach their children that gay was evil, and that different from their own norms was wrong. Ben feared that young boys and girls were growing into men and women, and ushering this long-taught mentality into their adult life, too.

While the beating was an extreme incident, the mentality that the father and son harbored for gays and lesbians, Ben thought, was surely adopted by other young adults in the community. This did not bode well for Freeden's future, and forced Ben to realize the effects of this trial, which were already divisive in the worst sense now, would surely be felt for a long time.

Most of the team was leaving for the night, escorted to their cars by security – there was quite the protest going on near the office, and as seen earlier that day, none of them were particularly friendly. They worked from Ben's home as a result of this, but still, they knew they could never be too careful. Kate, who had continued to help with Ben and his team for no pay, was the last to leave.

"Goodbye," Ben said to Kristen as she walked out. Then he shut the door.

"Well, I better get going," Kate said as she stood near the

door.

"I wish you wouldn't," Ben replied.

"Well, it's late and I wouldn't want to intrude," she said shyly.

"Please, do stay for a bit. Perhaps we can have a beer, if you'd like?"

"Well, sure," she said, smiling.

"Have a seat and make yourself comfortable," he said. Then he went to the kitchen to fetch a couple cans of Lost Coast Tangerine Wheat beer, his beverage of choice, and returned to the formal living room in the front of the house. Kate was seated on one of his wingback chairs, so he handed her the beer and sat in the matching one next to her.

"Damn, I feel like all we have done is work on this case and try not to get hurt here lately," Ben said.

"It feels like it," she said. "You'll need a break after this."

"Kate, I don't know if I'll ever be free from what's going on right now. It's all-consuming now, but I feel like it'll always be all-consuming moving forward. No matter the verdict."

"I know what you mean."

"You know, we never finished our date. What an unbelievably abrupt ending it was."

"It was definitely an abrupt ending." She laughed. "First date I have ever had like that I can assure you."

"So it *was* a date?" Ben asked, grinning.

Kate looked surprised, but still smiled in return. "Well, I thought it was."

"I was thinking so too, you know, just wanted to be sure."

"Yes," she blushed, "it was a date."

They took another sip of their drinks. Ben tried to glance at her while he drank from his beer and noticed she did the same. The two made eye contact, set their drinks down, and gazed at one another, both of them still smiling.

"I'm not sure I ever thanked you for what you did," Ben restarted. "Telling me all you did that night is the reason Dwight has a chance."

She shook her head, her face now much more serious. "You don't have to thank me."

"But I do, though," he said. "There is no way Dwight would have a chance without you."

"I'm inclined to believe you would have still given him a chance."

"Well, I guess we'll never know, thanks to you," Ben said as he raised his can. "Cheers?" He motioned for a toast, and Kate reciprocated.

After a big gulp, he said, "What made you do it?"

She took a sip of her beer, then set it down. "It was the right thing to do."

"You risked everything. You risked your career, your reputation… everything."

"Some things are worth risking everything for."

"I never believed that, until now," he replied. "If this situation has taught me anything about how to better myself, it's that I must always do the right thing, no matter what. Because despite the fact just to live here requires security now and that we have to watch out for our safety more than ever, I feel an incredible weight lifted off of me for doing the right thing without regard to what anybody thinks. It's liberating, to say the least."

"I imagine it's a relief. And I'm glad you have found peace with that. And can I say something?"

Ben paused, not knowing what was coming. "Yeah, sure. What's up?"

"I'm so impressed with you. You're such an impressive

person."

Ben chuckled. "Well, thank you. I don't know what to–"

"Seriously Ben," she repeated, "you really are an impressive person."

"What do you mean?" he asked.

"The way you do what you do in court. The way you interact with people. The way you talk to me. The way you talk to others."

"Well, what's so impressive about all that?"

"In all of it, it's obvious you care. And I really like that about you."

"Well, thank you," he said as he took another sip of his beer, trying to hide the blush he felt creeping up his neck. "Can I tell you some things I like about you?"

She turned a bit red. "Well–"

"You know what, let me cut you off right there," he said. "If you're going to dish the compliments out you have to be willing to take some, too."

She laughed at the comment. "Being the center of attention is hard for me."

"You are the most wonderful person I've ever met."

She paused, looked down to blush, then looked at him, gazing into his eyes.

"And don't stop me, because I'm getting this out." He took a deep breath. "The minute I laid eyes on you for the first time, on the night of the concert, I knew something was special about you. And in a very short time, I've seen it firsthand. You're beautiful, both inside and out. You're a person that still considers values to be important. You're kind to people, and most importantly, I believe you have a good heart."

"You're making me blush," she said with a big smile on her face. "Thank you, that's so nice of you to say."

"Well, I mean it."

Kate squirmed a bit in her seat, seeming to be anxious about something. Ben noticed.

"Are you okay?"

"Yes, I just worry."

"Worry about what?" he asked.

"I don't know how to say it."

"You know for someone with your background in law, you're especially reserved."

"I need you to know I did this because I had to."

"Did what?"

"Switched sides. Quit my job. Gave you information to try and save Dwight. I did it because it was *right*."

"I know that, Kate," he said. "I've known that the entire time."

"I didn't do it because I like you."

Ben stopped, slowly set his beer down on the small table between them, and leaned toward her. "Wait...."

"You heard me. I really like you. But I need you to know that I haven't done any of this because of that. I did what I did to help you, and I'm continuing to help you, because it's just and right. But–"

"You're not alone, Kate. And listen, I know why you did what you did. You told me, and I trust you. But can I take this a step further?"

"Okay?"

"You may be able to relate, but I won't put words in your mouth. You see," he stumbled for a moment, trying to find the perfect words to summarize what he had to say, "my entire personal life has been a devastating disappointment. I've spent my whole life trying to impress everyone else, wanting everyone to love me, and working hard for everything I had. I have very few friends to show for it, and practically everyone hates me in this town now. But it's crazy, how lonely I was when all I wanted to do was make everyone else happy. Now, here I am, hated by most of the community, shunned away from public places in town, not even welcome without being chastised at the church I grew up in. But for some reason, I've never felt more supported than I do now. I feel less alone than I've ever felt in my life. And a lot of that is to do with you."

"With me?"

"Yes, with you. You came here, risking everything by leaving your old life to start a new one, and have inspired me to realize that doing that is okay. You've worked your hardest for justice and to save Dwight's life, but all in this very short amount of time, you've shown me that mine can be saved, too."

"Ben, I don't know what to say. Just being around you makes me feel… I just can't explain it."

"Can I tell you what being around you feels like? Though I, too, may not be able to put it into adequate words."

"Please," she said, smiling from ear to ear.

"Have you ever read *The Five Love Languages* by Gary Chapman?"

She grinned ever bigger. "I love that book."

"Well, I finally picked it up one day and decided to read it, eager to learn about myself a bit more. What my love language was, you know?"

"Yeah."

"So I read it, and my love language is undoubtedly words of affirmation."

"I figured as much," she said while laughing.

"And what would you say yours is?"

"Mine is definitely quality time."

"Exactly what I thought."

"Really?"

"Yes, really. We haven't been around each other long, but you knew mine, too." Ben was happy with how well they were bonding. It felt so natural.

"That's very true."

Ben stared into her eyes. "Well, the night we met at David's… I've thought about that night a lot. All I've wanted since then was to spend more time with you."

"I've wanted the same, I hope you know that."

"That's the thing, see," he paused and looked down at the floor, "I've never really wanted to spend time with anyone."

"What do you mean?"

"All I've thought about recently, outside of this case, is how I just want to be around you more. And no one has ever made me feel that way. Quality time is not my love language, but it's yours. And being around you just makes me want to give you more of yours."

Kate appeared to tear up. "I don't care how crazy this sounds."

"It's crazy but I feel the same way, Kate."

"I've never in my life believed in something like this."

"Me neither."

"But–"

"I love you, Kate."

Kate stopped, wide-eyed, and gasped softly. "I love you, too."

Kate stood up, and Ben followed, facing her. The two could not take their eyes off of one another. Finally, Ben took his right hand, and brushed back Kate's long brown hair behind her left ear. They kept staring at one another, and Ben caressed her left cheek as he brought his hand down to her waist. He slowly moved closer to her, and the two finally kissed.

Ben opened his eyes after the embrace, and looked at her. She giggled.

"What?" he asked. He was worried she may have suddenly come to the realization of just how crazy all this was, moving as fast as it was. But he couldn't help it; he had *never* felt this way before. She made him feel appreciated, loved, and respected. He loved her presence, and while he had felt the jitters of a new relationship on several occasions before, this was absolutely not the same thing. He hoped she wasn't regretting saying anything, or kissing him.

"You promise you don't think I'm crazy?" she asked.

"For what?"

"For telling you I love you. We just met a few weeks ago."

"I told you the same thing," he answered. "And I meant it."

"I did too."

The two kissed again, this time more passionately. Ben held her tightly against him, holding her face in his right hand and pressing her to his body with his left hand on her lower back. She slipped her hands between his arms, one hand on each side of his bearded face.

When the two finally stopped, Ben asked, "So will you do something with me that I've never asked anyone to do?"

She leaned away from him a bit, still embraced in his arms. "What's that?"

"Will you dance with me?"

"You've never asked someone to dance with you?" she said, laughing.

"Well, I mean, not in the house. I've always wanted to dance in this room. I have a record player and it's such a romantic room, yeah?"

She laughed hysterically. "You're too funny."

"Well, will you?"

She smiled. "Of course."

"Hold on for just a moment." Ben got up and walked over to his record player, situated close to the fireplace. He turned it on, set the needle, and turned back toward Kate. The music started and she instantly recognized the hit 1980 song from The Manhattans.

"Oh my God, I love this song."

"I knew you would," he said. He walked up to her, put his right hand on her lower back, and grabbed her left hand. The two just stared into one another's eyes, not saying a word, and danced.

Honey you, are my shining star,
Don't you go away.
Oh baby,
Wanna be, right here where you are,
Til my dying day.

The clock struck midnight and Scott Stevens was sat at his desk, awaiting his guests, drinking bourbon from a crystal glass given to him as a gift many years ago by Dale Jones. He was quite certain he knew what the outcome of the trial would be, but each day that passed he worried a bit more. Ben Bailey was winning, and he knew it. Scott realized the evidence didn't match up, quite like Ben described in court when he cross-examined Chief McDowell, but he persisted because he truly believed Dwight murdered Braxton Jones.

The evidence didn't add up; nothing concretely connected Dwight to the crime, but it just didn't make sense that anyone else in town would do this. He occasionally had his doubts, but his longtime friend Dale persisted that he knew it was Dwight, and so he knew he had to do whatever it took to achieve a guilty verdict. This included ensuring the DNA reports were altered to match his narrative.

In his mind, Dale would never accuse someone of doing something if they had not truly committed the act, and he could not betray his friend, nor would he. Scott believed Dwight to be an intelligent man, and believed he likely identified and strategized in every imaginable way to get away with this crime. Still, the lack of evidence made him question things. Ben had ripped the theory of Braxton being physically able to write a note after being stabbed thirty-six times in the back, and as the days went on it was becoming harder for Scott to justify it. He also knew the DNA reports were falsified, but he ordered it to protect Dale and his family; to afford them the justice they deserved, and he feared they would not get it since the investigation had been handled so poorly by the police department and medical examiners.

The DNA evidence on the note pointing only to Dale, he thought, must have resulted from when he touched it at the crime scene when evaluating it. He could not believe Dale had something to do with this as Ben had alleged. The thought was despicable, and he simply could not accept it. He knew Dale wanted Dwight to be convicted rapidly, but according to Scott, that's only because he wanted his son's killer to be punished sooner than later. And if his child had been the victim, Scott knew he would have wanted the same.

It didn't matter, though. The pressure was on him, mainly from Dale and his family, to ensure that a guilty verdict was reached. He knew the verdict would need to make sense to the community, and Dwight would need to be put away, or put to death, if the community was to return to normalcy. And so far, it did not seem to be headed in that direction. Gossip was starting to spread at church during services, at town meetings, and in restaurant scuttlebutt. Even though it was a very small number, Scott knew people were starting to ask questions about the potential of Dwight being wrongly accused. Scott recognized that he had to do something.

He invited the major players to his office for a meeting to figure out how to obtain a guilty verdict without too much repercussion from the few dissenters in the community. Two of his three invitees walked into his office, dimly lit only by a table lamp on his desk, just after midnight.

"Hello, Scott," Dale said.

"Care for something to drink?" he asked as he sat up from his leaned-back position in his plush office chair.

"No, thank you, I stopped drinking," Dale replied.

"How about you, Chief?"

Chief McDowell sat down in one of the chairs in front of his desk. "Yes, thank you."

Scott pulled a matching crystal glass from his desk, then poured bourbon into it and gently slid it over to the chief.

"What is going on right now, Scott?" Dale asked. "I don't feel like we're winning."

"We're not," Scott said. "And I think the blame can be spread all around this room."

"What is that supposed to mean?"

"You completely bombed on the stand, Dale."

"Me? You didn't prepare me for any of that!"

"I didn't know a damn thing that he was going to say. I've heard none of that. Was any of it true?"

"No, it wasn't true! Come on Scott, you've known my family your whole life. My son wasn't gay and I wasn't hiding anything!"

"I know that," Scott said. "But aside from that, you did know about the DNA reports. You asked me to do that, and he called you out in court for it. Preston Hall told that story in his article, but until your testimony two days ago it was just a media hoax."

"It still is! Nobody is going to believe that. Nor should they."

"Yeah, I disagree," Scott reiterated, taking another sip of bourbon. "You got angry when Ben brought it up, visibly angry, and you called Ben a *sick bastard* in open court. Hard to win the sympathy vote when you act like that."

"I asked you to have the DNA reports altered because the original reports were flat wrong and handled poorly. Typical government employees. Those false reports would have gotten Dwight out of this, and everyone knows Dwight did it!"

"Please don't talk about changing DNA reports in front of me," Chief McDowell said.

"Oh please, Gary," Scott said, "you know what is going on here. Stop being all high and mighty. Plus, if your team had done their job gathering evidence properly, we wouldn't be in this situation."

"My team did the best they could with what we had to work with," Chief McDowell said.

"Either way, we are in a situation now where we have to stop the bleeding," Scott said. "Every day it gets harder and harder to prove Dwight is guilty beyond a reasonable doubt, and that's the burden I'm facing. If the trial ended today, we'd be fucked."

The final guest arrived. Dale turned around in his chair. "You're late."

"There best be good reason for a meeting this late," the man said.

"Yeah, well I surely hope we didn't interrupt your schedule, Judge Freeman," Dale replied.

"Why's he here?" Chief McDowell asked.

Scott fired back. "Because we're losing this case, you dumbass."

"The reason you're losing is because Ben Bailey is making you all look like idiots," Judge Freeman said. He pulled up a chair next to Scott's desk, and took a seat. "He's poking holes in the case, which was already porous at best, if you ask me."

"But it's a fact, Judge," Dale said, "Dwight killed my son!"

"I'm not saying I don't believe you, Dale," Judge Freeman said, "but it really doesn't matter what I believe. The jury has to be convinced, and so far both yours and Chief McDowell's testimony didn't seem to resonate with the entire jury. That's just my opinion, but it's a damn good one. I've been doing this a long time."

"Well, can't you do something? Do we need a new trial? A bench trial?" Dale asked.

"I can't make that happen."

"Why not?"

"Even if I did pull strings and claim something was wrong with this jury, the national fucking media is covering this case now, Dale. We can't just do like we've always done. This is different."

"How is it different, Judge?"

"Are you not hearing me?"

"Jesus, guys, please," Scott interrupted.

"We have to do something, Judge," Dale reiterated. "We are losing control here."

"There's still time to figure this out, Dale, just calm down and let Scott and I do our jobs."

"If we have another day in court like the last two days, we

are going to lose this! Is anybody hearing me? My son is going to have died in vain and that sick bastard is going to walk. And then I'm sure they'll look for someone else, never find a perp, and end up putting Lucy and I through hell with it dragged out even further."

"We are doing just about all we can, Dale," Judge Freeman said. "I don't know what else you want us to do. We have to have substance, and this case has proven so far to have very little. I can't just tell Ben Bailey that he can't cross-examine the witnesses. If coverage got out that I was permitting shady shit like that, I'd be disbarred. And Scott would, too."

"You both need to decide if you work for the State or for *him*."

The room fell silent. Judge Freeman looked at Scott, then the both of them looked at the chief.

"What else do you want us to do?" Judge Freeman asked.

"Judge, if you think I'm going to be ticked off if Dwight walks for this crime," Dale said, "you have no idea. It pales in comparison to how Dr. Henson would feel."

"Seriously, Dale, what does he expect us to do?" Judge Freeman asked.

Dale sighed. "The verdict must be guilty. If not, a criminal walks and you make him look bad, and you do not want to make him or his church look bad. That won't be good. Now, since he is losing confidence in you all, he is going to appear in court tomorrow. And you will make him look good, both you and Judge Freeman," he said as he pointed at Scott. "Do you understand?"

"Okay, I understand," they both said, appearing to be nervous.

"Dr. Henson is going to fix this, but don't mess this up. This is turning into a shit storm. If Dwight is found guilty without us showing substantial evidence, and we leave doubt in the minds of these protesters, they will burn this town to the ground. And it'll be on your hands."

"What are you saying? That Dr. Henson is going to testify?" Judge Freeman asked.

"Yes," Dale said, "and don't get in his way."

17: Day of Retribution

Night of the *Requiem*

Terri Hathaway was especially nervous about her solo in the *Requiem*'s longest movement, "Recordare." Dwight knew she had been struggling with the piece, but had worked diligently, practicing for hours outside of normal rehearsals, to help her feel more comfortable. The other three soloists were singers hired for the night from out-of-town to fill roles simply no one else was qualified to fill, but he believed Terri was equipped to be the solo soprano for the concert. Plus, he wanted someone local to be featured as a soloist, and Terri had been a part of the community chorus since she had returned from grad school years before.

He looked at her as the piece was about to begin, nodded, and mouthed the words, "You've got this."

Something about Dwight's words always seemed to calm Terri, and most people that ever interacted with him would probably say the same. He believed in people, and he genuinely cared about them. But he was honest, and Terri knew if he said she could do this, she very well could.

She smiled back, and turned her attention to her sheet music as the orchestra began to play. The quartet began to sing:

Recordare, Jesu pie,
quod sum causa tuae viae;

ne me perdas illa die.

Quaerens me, sedisti lassus,
redemisti crucem passus;
tantus labor non sit cassus.

Juste judex ultionis,
donum fac remissionis
ante diem rationis.

Ingemisco, tamquam reus:
culpa rubet vultus meus;
supplicanti parce, Deus.

Ben and the chorus were not featured in *Recordare*, but he had studied the piece anyway prior to the concert and recalled the English translation of the longest movement in *Requiem*:

Remember, kind Jesus,
my salvation caused your suffering;
do not forsake me on that day.

Faint and weary you have sought me,
redeemed me, suffering on the cross;
may such great effort not be in vain.

Righteous judge of vengeance,
grant me the gift of absolution
before the day of retribution.

Present

The day of retribution had come. This was the metaphorical deadline for Scott Stevens and Judge Freeman to stop the bleeding. The courtroom, filled to capacity like it had been the prior two days, aired a different feel than it had before. Dwight was escorted in the room just before the trial recommenced, and even he looked different to Ben. He appeared anxious and concerned.

"What's the matter?" Ben asked him when he sat down at the defense table.

"I don't feel good about today."

"Why not? We've done all we can so far. I feel pretty good about it."

"I just don't," Dwight said.

Ben wondered if his mood was, perhaps, worsened by the weather. Rain poured down outside, beating against the big windows near the ceiling of the courtroom. The protesting hadn't ceased; if anything it had picked up, as national attention on the case continued to climb.

Judge Freeman entered the room prematurely. The bailiff stood in a panic. "All rise for the Honorable Judge Phillip Freeman presiding. The court of–"

"Thank you, bailiff," Judge Freeman interrupted. This caught the bailiff off guard, so he quickly sat down in his seat. Everyone, including the bailiff, clerk of court, and other officials of the court, could tell something was bothering Judge Freeman.

After a few moments, he took a heavy sigh and finally spoke. "We will now resume with witness testimony. Mr. Stevens, you may proceed in calling your witness."

As if he had already prepared himself to be called on

expeditiously, Scott stood up. "Thank you, your Honor. The prosecution would like to call Dr. Daniel Henson."

Dwight looked at Ben, who looked stunned. Confused and worried, he asked Ben, "What the hell does he have to do with this?"

Ben just sat there and didn't say a word. He could hear the heavy shoes of the towering Dr. Henson clicking on the wooden floor that ran down the middle of the aisle as he walked forward. Ben could not even look at the man. He knew what was going on here. Everyone knew Dr. Dan Henson, including those in the jury box, and they all knew how powerful and well-respected he was in Freeden. The previous two days had proven disastrous for the prosecution, plain and simple. Scott Stevens was bringing in Dr. Henson to save this ship from sinking. Ben felt like he couldn't move. He knew the prosecution was hell-bent on ensuring that Dwight Kerry was convicted for this crime, and irrespective of the overwhelming lack of evidence against him, Dr. Henson testifying *could* all but seal the deal.

"Ben!" Dwight whispered loudly. "Do you hear me?"

Ben came out of his daze. "What?"

"Why do you think Dr. Henson is doing this?" Dwight asked.

Ben slowly turned his head toward Dwight, and said in the most serious, somber tone, "To put you down. He's here to put you down."

Dr. Henson passed Ben on his way to the witness stand. Ben never looked at him as he walked by, and he didn't have to. He could feel the tension in the room. Ben finally looked up at Dr. Henson, who now stood in the witness stand and raised his left hand up, and placed his right hand on the King James Version of the Holy Bible.

The court official said, "Mr. Henson," then she stopped. "I meant Dr. Henson, my apologies."

"It's quite alright," he replied.

"Will you tell the truth, the whole truth, and nothing but the truth, so help you God?"

"I will."

"Thank you."

Dr. Henson took his seat.

Scott approached the stand. "Good morning, Dr. Henson."

"Good morning, Mr. Stevens," he replied.

"Sir, tell me… how do you know Dwight Kerry?"

"Mr. Kerry previously served as our Music Director at Freeden Baptist Church."

"And how long have you known him?"

"I have been the Senior Pastor at the church for several years now, but I've known Mr. Kerry through the church for over thirty years."

"That's a long time."

"Indeed it is."

"Did you ever notice anything about him that would have led you to believe he would do something like committing rape or murder?"

"Well, to be as frank as I can be, nothing ever indicated to me that he would commit murder. But committing a sexual offense, not limited to molestation or rape? Yes, that is something I warned the deacon board at the church about."

"And why did you warn them of this possibility?"

"Because he practiced homosexuality."

"Objection!" Ben stood. "The defendant's sexual identity shares no relevance with whether or not my client would rape someone. And it's absurd to think the two are naturally tied together."

"Overruled," Judge Freeman said.

"You're kidding?" Ben asked.

"Mr. Bailey, let's not go there today," Judge Freeman harshly suggested. "Mr. Stevens, make your point, please."

"Why did that make you think he would rape someone?"

"Well," he paused, "I think we must all realize that our society is permitting a slippery-slope effect when it comes to sexual immorality, which is why our world has become as valueless as it has become. Dwight practiced homosexuality, and I warned the church, in the months ahead of the crime, that he may take this a step further, if you will, and that leaving him on staff was indirectly supporting the notion that his behavior was acceptable in the eyes of God."

"So–"

"And it's *not* acceptable," he interrupted.

Scott nodded. "So what makes you believe Dwight did this?"

"Braxton Jones."

"What about him?"

"He called my cell the day he died. It must have been early that afternoon. He asked what he should do if of his superiors was coming onto him in a sexual nature. I asked him who it was, and he refused to tell me. He sounded as if he were in a panic."

"What did you do next?"

"I told him he needed to tell his mother and father who it was so they could contact the authorities."

"Did you call anyone about this?"

"I did, yes."

"Who did you call?"

"His father, Dale. He called home and couldn't reach his wife, so he rushed there. She had fallen asleep, and Braxton wasn't there despite having been home sick for the previous couple weeks. They did not know where he was."

"Why didn't Dale tell us this in court?"

"Perhaps because you didn't ask him," he said in a sharp, yet soft tone.

"I'm still trying to put the pieces together, though. How do you know this superior coming onto Braxton was, in fact, the defendant?"

"Technically, I don't, Mr. Stevens. But don't you find it strange that the boy called me and told me this, then a few hours later was found dead in Mr. Kerry's classroom?"

"Objection," Ben stood again. "Speculation is not evidence."

"Overruled," Judge Freeman said once more.

Ben stood down after throwing his arms in the air in a show of no-confidence in the judge's actions. Dwight looked at Ben and seemed very concerned.

"Do you have your cell phone with you?"

"I do."

"Can you show me the call you received from Braxton Jones that day?"

"I most certainly can." Dr. Henson pulled his phone out, flipped to the recent calls screen, and showed it to Mr. Stevens.

"Do you mind if I show this to the jury, Dr. Henson?"

He waved his right hand toward him, as if he were shewing away a dog. "Go ahead."

Scott walked it over to the jury for their examination, then said, "Sir," he pointed to one of the jurors on the front row of the jury box, then to the phone, "can you read the phone number listed right there?"

The juror did so.

"The cell phone monthly statement for Dale Jones shows

that exact phone number as the assigned number for Braxton Jones," Scott said, then walked back over to the bench. "Your Honor, I'd like to submit this cell phone statement, and a copy of Dr. Henson's call log, as evidence in the trial." He walked over to the prosecution table and grabbed the copy of the call log he had already obtained from Dr. Henson.

"Dr. Henson's call record and the monthly statement will be admitted as presented," Judge Freeman said. "Carry on."

Scott turned his attention back to the stand. "Dr. Henson, did you have a positive relationship with Braxton?"

"I did. I mentored him, and counseled him on spiritual issues."

"Would you say he was a boy who valued his faith?"

"His entire family values their faith. Perhaps the best way to put it is this that he stood out from the rest of the youth in the world today. He was a fine example for how you can grow up to be a young man and still love God and live a moral life. And that's what makes this whole thing even more heartbreaking."

"Do you believe Dwight Kerry to be a man of faith?"

"Dwight Kerry is *not* a man of faith."

"Objection," Ben stood, "even though I disagree vehemently with Dr. Henson's miscalculated interpretation of my client's faith, how is Dwight's faith relevant here?"

"Overruled."

"You can't be serious, your Honor? Dr. Henson's opinion of Dwight's faith has nothing to do with this, and is not substantiated by evidence, and–"

"Overruled, Mr. Bailey." Judge Freeman shouted. "Take your seat, now."

Ben fell back into his seat and Scott carried on. "Why do you think Mr. Kerry is not a man of faith?"

"As a leader in the church, you cannot adopt one part of the gospel and not the other. And his regular practice of homosexuality is an abomination, and not of the Christian faith."

"So how was he able to work at the church for so long if this was your opinion of him?"

"Tenure. In addition to the fact that we didn't have proof, really. But we do now."

Ben raised an eyebrow.

Dr. Henson nodded. "The DNA evidence points to one person: Dwight Kerry. The handwritten note lists only one person: Dwight Kerry. The murder happened in the classroom of, you guessed it: Dwight Kerry. It's time we realize here that it truly is just as cut and dry as it seems. And if we don't do something to stop this man, he'll surely strike again."

Scott nodded and looked at Judge Freeman. "No further questions, your Honor."

Dwight leaned over to Ben and whispered, "That son of a bitch."

"Calm down," Ben replied.

"None of that is true," Dwight whispered.

Ben nodded in affirmation. "I know, I know."

He peered over at Dr. Henson, who calmly sat in the witness stand looking at him. Most people would likely be nervous at the prospect of cross-examination; Dr. Henson did not appear shaken at all. Ben realized that the next few moments may make or break Dwight's chances.

Most of the jurors gazed over at a visibly emotional Dale and Lucy Jones, who were sitting behind the prosecution table on the front row where they had been seated the entire trial. Their faces expressed sympathy, and that emotion seemed to be guided by Dr. Henson's testimony. Scott had likely brought

Dr. Henson in for several reasons, and one of them was to simply make sense of it all to the jury. The second reason was based on his formal endorsement to convict Dwight. And Ben knew that would matter in this town.

Ben walked about halfway toward Dr. Henson, stopped, and stared at him with a confused look on his face. Dr. Henson's expression remained unchanged. He did not frown or smile; just maintained his blank, emotionless look.

"Dr. Henson, I find it odd that you were not on the original witness list. Why didn't you come forward with this information sooner?"

"I did."

"Then why are you not on the original witness list I was provided by Scott Stevens and the prosecution?"

"I cannot answer that for Mr. Stevens."

Scott rose from his seat. "Your Honor, the witness was added yesterday as a character witness for Braxton and his family and against Dwight, and as a witness who spoke to Braxton Jones on the day of his death. We overlooked the cell phone information originally, but we are providing it to the Court, including Mr. Bailey, today for examination."

"Overlooked, you say?" Ben asked before he chuckled in a disgusted manner. He kept looking at Dr. Henson. "Dr. Henson, you don't really believe they overlooked anything, do you?"

"That's what Mr. Stevens said, so I imagine that's the case."

"You really believe that a man as powerful in this town as you, *the* Dr. Daniel Henson, contacted the district attorney's office with information about the case, and they *forgot* to include what you told them as evidence?"

"That's what he said, so I can't really help you any further regarding that matter."

"Let me ask you, did Scott call you begging for you to come fix this problem he has with his case falling apart, or did you simply volunteer it?"

"Objection!" Scott shouted.

"Sustained," Judge Freeman followed, "and Mr. Bailey, who do you think you are, hurling accusations like that?"

"Your Honor, to be as frank as I can be, I wouldn't be at all surprised if *you'd* called Dr. Henson asking for him to come here today."

"Mr. Bailey, that's it. I'm holding you in contempt."

"If I may interject," Dr. Henson said, "I have no problem addressing the matter, your Honor."

Judge Freeman was visibly upset at being mocked by Ben in his own courtroom, but Dr. Henson, in his cordial way that Ben recognized from watching him interact with people so many times before, had just commanded Judge Freeman to shut the hell up and let him speak. And so, Judge Freeman calmed himself, and allowed the exchange between Ben and Dr. Henson to continue. This was now Dr. Henson's courtroom.

Dr. Henson looked at Ben unblinkingly. "Scott did call me yesterday and ask me to testify, yes. And I did agree to do it, because I believe wholeheartedly that Dwight Kerry is guilty, and I will not sit aside and do nothing when I know I can help prevent something like this from happening again. Mr. Bailey, this community is full of youths who will soon become adults, and we need more people in this world with values and morals like the ones that the families instill in their children here in Freeden. I refuse to stand aside and let a sexual deviant pick them off one-by-one and inflict harm on our children's future."

"What makes him a sexual deviant, Dr. Henson? Are you claiming that simply because Dwight is an openly gay man?"

"That coupled with his crimes. Homosexuality is wrong in the eyes of God."

"Help me understand something. How is it that no one in this community, or in your church, is looked down upon in the same light when they commit adultery?"

"Adultery is also a sin in the eyes of God."

"Is that right?"

Dr. Henson simply stared at Ben, still with his emotionless expression.

"Go ahead, Dr. Henson, you agreed to answer my questions when you called off Judge Freeman in his own courtroom and he complied like a puppet."

"Mr. Bailey," Judge Freeman interjected angrily, only for Dr. Henson to raise his hand at him so he would not say anything and let the sparring continue.

Ben went on. "So tell me, then, why haven't you been just as passionate to condemn Aaron Carroll and your daughter, my ex-wife, Rachel Henson-Bailey, who slept with him repeatedly while I was married to her? Why are they still allowed in your church when Dwight, from what you're saying, is condemned to hell for his abomination?"

"That's it Mr. Bailey," Judge Freeman said. "This conversation has no place in my courtroom!"

"Is being gay truly worse than adultery, Dr. Henson? Is the sin greater? Is that what you're saying?"

He still didn't answer.

"Answer the question, Dr. Henson. Is Dwight's simple attraction to men really worse than your daughter fucking around behind her husband's back?" he yelled.

Dr. Henson finally spoke, "I will not respond to that nonsense because it didn't happen and isn't relevant."

"You're already in contempt, Mr. Bailey, I am warning

you."

"By turning a blind eye to adultery and shaming people who are gay, you're adopting part of the gospel and not all of it, right?"

"Mr. Bailey, you're one step away from being jailed," Judge Freeman shouted.

"Ladies and gentlemen of the jury," he quickly turned to them, "Dr. Dan Henson was brought here today not by the State, but by Scott Stevens personally, to make you fear returning a not-guilty verdict. I've never known, and still don't know, how Dr. Henson obtained so much power in this town, but just because he says something does not mean it's true. I don't know if it's money or what, but you do not have to listen to this man's input on what is right and wrong in your life. He is not a prophet, he is not a man of God, and he doesn't deserve to enjoy the luxury of being in the same room as my client. Dwight Kerry is an innocent man, and a good man. This man," he pointed at Dr. Henson, "is not a good man, and is here today only to sway your vote so he can get what he wants from this."

"Objection," Scott yelled. "This is damn near libel."

"Let me respond, everyone," Dr. Henson said. He smiled slightly and then looked up at Ben. "I am deeply sorry you have such harsh feelings about me. I don't believe I warrant them, but I can't change your mind, I'm sure. But it seems you've forgotten Ben, I'm not on trial here. Dwight Kerry is."

"Oh, but you are a major player in this trial," Ben said. "This is not the State versus Dwight Kerry. This is Dan Henson versus Dwight Kerry. This is Freeden versus Dwight Kerry. You represent this town, a largely discriminatory populous that thinks they represent a culture of love, but in fact, represent a culture of hate. Over ninety percent of people in this community go to church, and most of them go to your church," he said, as he pointed at Dr. Henson, "yet thousands of them are on the streets right now holding signs that read *gays will burn*. Your church members have literally beaten people," he yelled to reiterate, "beaten people! All because of who they are and what they believe in. In the last few weeks, I've been kicked out of public places for simply defending a man in court, and chastised by members of your church for simply believing that Dwight should at least get a fair trial."

Ben turned back to the jury. "Ladies and gentlemen, you don't have to do what this man tells you. I know some of you know him well, some of you even go to Freeden Baptist Church – I've seen you there from my time as a member, but you do not have to believe everything this man says. He is not a prophet, and your faith doesn't call on you to listen to him. It calls you to listen to God, and so I ask you, do you really believe this man and God are one in the same?"

"Mr. Bailey," Judge Freeman said.

Ben calmed down, despite Judge Freeman shouting at him. He spoke directly to the jury in a softer tone. "If you believe Dwight is guilty, that is fine. But you and I both know why Dr. Henson was brought here today. You know he's here to sway your vote, and sadly, he believes he will."

"Mr. Bailey," Judge Freeman said again.

"All I ask is that you make your own decision. You know it doesn't add up. And Dr. Henson knows it, too."

"Enough!" Judge Freeman shouted. "This is your last warning before I throw you in jail for the remainder of this trial."

"If you don't mind, Ben," Dr. Henson said, "can you tell me why you are attacking me so ferociously?" In the soft, calming voice Ben had heard him use so many times to earn empathy from his followers, he said, "What have I done to you to warrant such an attack on my personal character? I'm only here for justice."

From Ben's experience, Dr. Henson had two ways of addressing problems, and it all depended on who he was dealing with and what their status was in the community. The wealthy, upper-echelon folk got treated with an unmatched abrasiveness that made them fear him as a representative of God Himself. His soft, pitiful tone he used now in court, playing the part of a verbally-beaten victim on the witness stand, was the way he convinced the commoners of Freeden to do what he wanted them to do. He played the victim because he thought so many of them could relate. Like a dirty politician, he wanted those people to believe he was just one of them. But he certainly did not view himself that way.

Ben recognized the act. He turned away from the jury, refocused on Dr. Henson, and said, "Here's my last question. When Braxton told his father he was gay, did you tell Dale to lock him up in the basement until he was *fixed*?"

For the first time, Dr. Henson, frowning from anger, said, "I would never do something like that."

"Just wondering if you told Dale to do that," Ben said as he started backpedaling slowly toward the defense table, "because one of my witnesses I'll be calling will show that Dale did just that. And I couldn't help but wonder if he got that idea from you."

Ben and Dr. Henson simply stared at one another for nearly a minute. Dale remained calm and poised behind the prosecution table, as Ben assumed he had likely been instructed to do by Scott. Ben, still looking at Dr. Henson, finally said, "No further questions, your Honor." Then he turned away.

Dr. Henson stood to his feet, infuriated at what had just occurred. Ben had done something few dared to do: he stood up to Dr. Henson in public, and the unprecedented shock and awe that filled the room left everyone's jaw dropped. Judge Freeman did nothing to restore order in the courtroom. Chatter began infiltrating the gallery, and the noise soon filled it.

Dr. Henson continued to just stand there in the witness box. Ben spoke to Dwight and his team, paying no attention to Dr. Henson. Ben worried, despite pinning Dr. Henson into a corner, if the staged, light-hearted tone Dr. Henson used would win the sympathy vote from a jury who already most likely knew and respected him. Ben had little choice, though, but to throw everything he had toward him.

After the court finally recessed and came back after lunch, Dr. Henson took his seat next to Dale, Lucy, and his family, where he would stay for the remainder of the trial. Judge Freeman brought the court back into session, "Mr. Bailey, let me start this afternoon's session by saying that this sideshow act is over. Your behavior is inexcusable. If I have to call you down one more time, I will lock you up. Do you understand me?"

"Yes, your Honor, I understand." Ben recognized he was being rebuked again in an effort to make it look as if he had done something wrong that morning by being so harsh with Dr. Henson. He knew, though, he had to maintain his composure too, or it could play out poorly for Dwight.

"Call your first witness, Counsel," Judge Freeman said.

"The defense calls Colin Johnson to the stand."

Dr. Johnson, who stood in the gallery and made his way to the witness stand, had likely just endured the most difficult few days of his medical career. Since Sunday's town forum, he had lost seventy-five percent of his patients. The inconceivable crash of his business, after being built for decades, had come in just a few days at the hands of Dr. Henson petitioning the community to stop supporting his practice, which he had done publicly by going on local television and expressing his reservations about dealing with an "immoral physician." But in Ben's eyes, Dr. Johnson, like few others, had done the right thing, and was not about to stop now.

Ben read over his notes, then approached the witness stand. "Dr. Johnson, where were you on the night of Friday, May 25th?"

"I was performing in Dwight's concert, Mozart's *Requiem*, at the concert hall."

"And what time did you arrive?"

"I always arrive early to read. It's good preparation for me. I was sitting in the balcony when Dwight got there, had been for about thirty minutes."

"And what time would you say he arrived?"

"About three-thirty in the afternoon."

"And did he leave or go missing at any point?"

"No. I saw him working around the stage to prepare for the concert literally until five-thirty p.m., when people started walking in. Then I went down to join them."

"So you never saw him leave the concert hall, and were with him after five-thirty p.m. until the concert ended?"

"That is correct."

"And what time did the concert end?"

"I'd say about eight-thirty."

"So, are you one-hundred percent certain that Dwight Kerry, after arriving at around three-thirty at the concert hall, never left the building until, at the very least, the concert ended at around eight-thirty?"

"Yes, I am one-hundred percent certain. He may have even been there longer, assuming he stayed for the reception."

Ben nodded, then walked back to his seat. "No further questions.

Scott then rose to cross-examine Dr. Johnson. "Dr. Johnson, is it fair to say you are friends with Dwight?"

"Have been as long as I can remember."

"Since there are no surveillance cameras, or any proof that Mr. Kerry was in the building that entire time, can you agree that it's just your word against the police's in relation to Dwight's whereabouts?"

"Of course. I do realize it's my word against theirs, yes."

"And can you also agree that it would be difficult to know Dwight was there the entire time when you were sitting in the balcony, looking down and reading a book?"

"Have you ever listened to music through your iPhone on, say, a set of wired headphones?" Dr. Johnson asked.

"Sure."

"If the music is playing, your phone is still connected, yes?"

"Sure."

"Dwight played music all afternoon. He does it at every concert, as a warm-up, if you will. He played for two hours, and every time I looked up he was still there. And when I looked down at my book, he continued to play, and I could still hear his music and knew he was there."

"But you're saying that you did not literally watch him every minute you were there. Is that correct?"

"No sir, I did not."

"How can you be sure, then, that Dwight was there the *entire* time?"

"Well, I'll tell you and the men and women of the jury this:

I stood up at a town forum this past Sunday night and told this story to the event's attendees, and since then my practice has lost the majority of its patients, who apparently disagree with my way of thinking, and according to letters I've received from some of them since then, think I should burn in hell." He paused, and looked at the jury. "After house calls, late nights waking up and going over to neighbors' homes to serve them in a world where doctors rarely do such anymore, I'm left to wonder what it was all for. My practice is effectively over and by year's end I'll likely have to retire as a result. Do you think I would have stood up and done that on Sunday, or came here today to testify just to watch my business of over forty years crumble in less than seventy-two hours, if what I had to say were not true?"

"I'm not sure why you told that story, Dr. Johnson," Scott said. "But it certainly seems your judgement is clouded. And it's your word against Freeden's finest. And our fine police system knows a lot more about what has happened here than you do." Scott started walking away. "No further questions, your honor."

Dr. Johnson got up, and Ben nodded at him in a show of thanks. Despite him saying that he knew he was doing the right thing, Dr. Johnson showed no emotion. He had done exactly what Ben had asked, but he wasn't satisfied; he had taken a major personal hit for this, and while he could be content with helping a man he deemed innocent, the personal pain of his practice suffering as a result was simply nothing to be satisfied with, or smile about.

Judge Freeman looked at his watch, and said, "Do you have any other witnesses, Counsel?"

Ben looked up from the desk, "Yes, your honor."

"Call them, please."

"The defense calls former assistant district attorney Kate Gregory to the stand."

Scott peered over at Ben and the two made eye contact. Ben thought that Scott had to just about know this was not going to bode well for him, because he looked uncomfortable.

Kate took to the stand, was administered the oath, and took her seat. Ben approached the stand, realizing that he must not let their personal relationship, which had strengthened in recent days, show to the jury. But he didn't fear that it would; the two of them were professional and committed to one thing while here: saving Dwight from a wrongful conviction.

"Ms. Gregory, are you from this area?"

"No, I most recently lived in Charlotte."

"And how did you get to Freeden?"

"I moved here for a job."

Scott began to shake his head. Ben peered over at him and saw that a blanket of sweat was forming on his forehead. It was clear: Scott was gravely worried about what Kate might say.

"And what job was that?"

"I was hired as an assistant district attorney back in April to work for district attorney Scott Stevens."

"This Scott Stevens?" Ben asked as he pointed to Scott.

"That is correct."

"Do you work for him anymore?"

"I do not."

"Might I ask why?"

"Because something happened in this case that made me uncomfortable and not trusting of the district attorney's office anymore."

"What was that?"

"The original DNA report was not the one submitted to the court as evidence. I have the original DNA report copy. A copy was also provided to Preston Hall at the *Freeden Tribune*, and he published it in a recent edition of the paper."

"Your Honor, I would like to submit this copy of the original DNA report to the Court as evidence."

Judge Freeman examined it, and despite his concerns of the direction the trial was swaying, he could not justify a reason to deny the request. "Evidence is admitted."

Scott looked at Judge Freeman, shocked at his move. "Your Honor, we have a DNA report from the State Medical Examiner's office. This is nothing more than going home and typing up a report on Microsoft Word and asking for it to be admitted as evidence."

"The evidence *will* be admitted, Mr. Stevens," Judge Freeman reiterated.

Scott turned around to Dr. Henson, who sat there still appearing emotionless. Ben couldn't help but wonder if Judge Freeman was going off script. He knew Dr. Henson was subtly trying to orchestrate everything happening in this courtroom.

Ben then retrieved the report and handed it back to Kate. "Ms. Gregory, can you please inform the Court what the original DNA report, dated a day before the one the State submitted as evidence, says in the summary of its results?"

"The report matches the DNA to that of Dale Jones."

The gallery erupted with noise.

"Objection!" Scott interrupted. "Dale Jones is not on trial here, but the defense continues to slander the family of the young boy. And Judge Freeman, you continue to allow it."

"Objection overruled."

Ben could sense the tension rising between Scott and Judge Freeman. Something was changing here, and he could tell it. Judge Freeman was softening his hard-nose stance toward the defense, and harshly increasing it toward Scott and the prosecution.

Scott sat back down, and turned his head back to Dr. Henson again, who had not moved a muscle.

"Order!" Judge Freeman shouted, as he slammed his gavel on the bench. "Order!" He stopped to ensure the place fell silent, then said, "Counsel, you may continue."

"When did you realize the DA office was not going to submit the original copy as evidence?" he asked Kate.

"I had seen a copy of the original report. Scott Stevens didn't know I had seen it, though. I was going for a run late one night, at around one a.m., and ran by the office when I saw Scott's vehicle there. Scott never worked at that time of day, so I walked in to see what was going on. As I got inside and closer to his office, I took soft steps to be quiet and remain unnoticed since I heard people talking inside."

"And who was talking to him in this odd, early morning meeting at the DA's office?"

"It was Dale Jones."

A few gasps came from the gallery, but not many.

"Did you hear what they said?"

"Yes, Dale told him to 'squash the preliminary test'."

More gasps followed from the gallery – and the jury.

"The next day in our meeting, he introduced the fraudulent copy to the team, which implicated only Dwight Kerry."

"Did you confront him about it?"

"Yes, I did."

"And what did he say?"

"He closed the door to his office and reminded me what he said in my initial job interview, that loyalty was important and that he didn't want me snooping around. He reminded me to trust him."

Kate was making Scott look like a complete idiot. And a

liar. And now a felon.

"What happened after that?

"The next day, the medical examiner at the local examiner's office, who I had tried to contact to verify the results, had been relieved of her duties."

Liz and Kristen, who took notes the entire trial, both documented that six of the twelve jurors seemed to be shaking their heads, their body language insinuating their disgust with Scott's actions. It was a good sign for Dwight and the defense.

"So when did you decide to quit your job as assistant district attorney?"

"After that happened, I gave the information to Preston Hall with the *Tribune* and quit my job the following Monday. Scott threatened to turn me over to the state bar if I switched sides, but I have not taken a job with you and am simply serving as a witness to ensure the wrong man is not convicted of this terrible crime."

Ben smiled. "No further questions, your Honor."

"Mr. Stevens?" Judge Freeman asked.

Scott just sat there. For the first time in his illustrious law career, he did not know what to say other than deny the allegations. Finally, he stood up, thinking of ways he could overcome the accusations that had just been hurled his way.

"Ms. Gregory, do you have any proof that the DNA report you claim is the *origina*l one was actually something conducted by the State Medical Examiner's board?"

"Yes."

"And what is that?"

"I interviewed the fired examiner and she told me she was let go and had received heavy compensation to not speak about the matter. She explained that if she talked, she would be in danger."

"Are you sure you're not confusing that with her retirement plan and an employee that was disgruntled about being asked to retire early?"

"I think you know I'm not confusing things."

"Well these are very unfair allegations you are throwing at me and my office, and they threaten the very integrity of this Court," Scott said. "So let me ask, did your new boyfriend Ben Bailey tell you to say all these things?"

"Objection!" Ben stood up. "Not only are Ms. Gregory and I not in a relationship, but–"

"Mr. Stevens, are you certain that Ms. Gregory and Mr. Bailey are in a relationship?"

"I know Mr. Bailey is still technically married to Rachel Henson-Bailey, and I also know he had Ms. Gregory over at his house last night."

"Rachel and I are separated," Ben said. "And are you watching me you son-of-a-bitch?" He was letting his temper get the best of him, but he could not help it.

"Is that an admission, Mr. Bailey, that you have asked your fired girlfriend, who also happens to be my disgruntled former employee, to come to the witness stand and share her fabricated remarks with the court?"

"I was not fired!" Kate shouted. "You are lying."

"Your personnel file says you were," Scott replied while he chuckled.

"I'm sure you tampered with that as well," she said. "You know that isn't true."

Scott turned to the jury. "Ladies and gentlemen of the jury, look at this circus. Ben Bailey has orchestrated an absolute spectacle in this courtroom for the past three days. He has dragged a good-hearted, well-respected pastor through the mud, accused a father of being knowingly involved in his son's murder, and brought his girlfriend here to testify on his behalf – who, in a resentful manner, came here today to verbally assault me since she was relieved of her job for poor performance."

"Scott, you should really be ashamed of yourself," Ben said under his breath.

Scott continued talking to the jury. "It's time you look past this circus act and realize that a murderer and rapist is sitting fifteen feet from you right now. And if you allow it, he will be back out on the streets in no time." Scott returned to his seat. "No further questions."

Ben turned to look at Dr. Henson, who sat there, smiling. He never looked at Ben, but he thought the smile was surely intended for him to see. Ben had heaved allegations at the prosecution, all of which were true, but the day of retribution had come for Dr. Henson and the players who followed his lead. While the evidence was overwhelmingly questionable, and Ben had exposed almost every gaping hole in the prosecution's case during the first three days of the trial, he still was not certain, at this point, that even one juror would vote not guilty. Ben still believed Dr. Henson had come to put Dwight down, and he wondered if his mere presence may have done just that.

Ben had brought forward Dr. Johnson, one of the few people in the community other than Ben and his team, who publicly acknowledged the belief that Dwight was innocent, and Dr. Johnson told the court that he essentially spent the afternoon with Dwight on May 25th at the concert hall. Ben wasn't sure this had convinced the jury.

He brought forward Kate Gregory, who knew for a fact the evidence had been tampered with and that both Scott Stevens and Dale Jones had been involved in the act, but Ben wasn't entirely sure that had resonated with the jury, either.

Ben sat back down at the defense table next to Dwight, deflated. Kate stepped down from the witness stand, walked over to Ben, and whispered in his left ear, "Call Marion Gonzalez. She's the examiner, and she is here."

"Being that all the witnesses on the list for today have been called, I–" Ben perked up, and looked at Kate, who smiled back at him. In a rush, he stood. "Your Honor, I'd like to call one more witness."

"There's no one else on my list for today."

"Please, your Honor."

Judge Freeman looked at him and sighed. "Okay, go ahead."

"The defense calls Marion Gonzalez to the stand."

A shorter, homely looking woman was ushered down the middle aisle by Kate. Kate had promised to keep her safe, and had done so since she'd unveiled the details of the original report to her in the weeks prior.

"Ms. Gonzalez," Ben started, "can you tell the Court who you are."

"Yes," she said. "I am the medical examiner who conducted the original DNA report."

Sounds of surprise emanated from the gallery.

"Can you show me evidence that you were employed by the State Medical Examiner's office?"

She withdrew from her purse her credentials and showed it to the jury.

Ben continued. "Thank you. Now, can you examine this report," he grabbed the report that he had submitted to evidence and handed it to her, "and tell me if this is the original report you had compiled?"

She looked it over, read most of the first page, flipped

through the others, then said, "Yes, this is the report I compiled."

"And does it implicate Dwight Kerry as the perpetrator?"

"No, Mr. Kerry's DNA did not show in our examination."

"Objection!" Scott yelled.

"Overruled," Judge Freeman rapidly fired back. "Let the woman finish talking." He paused. "Proceed, ma'am."

"I was called back early the next morning, around three a.m., on my personal cell, and asked to redo the report."

"Who called you and asked you this?"

"That man right there," she said, pointing to district attorney Scott Stevens.

A few in the gallery reacted with astonishment to the revelation.

"Did you agree to do it?"

"Absolutely not. And the next morning, when I arrived at my office, my supervisor told me I had been terminated and that I would receive a call later explaining my termination benefits."

"Did you ever receive that call?" Ben asked.

"Yes, though it wasn't a state official and I don't believe it had anything to do with my work benefits. It was someone who told me I would receive payment in a briefcase by night, but that I was to leave town and not to talk to anyone about this *or else*."

"Do you have any idea who it was?"

"No, I do not."

"Did you receive the money?"

"Yes, I did."

"How much was it?"

"One hundred thousand dollars."

"Can you prove to us you have the money?"

Marion Gonzalez signaled for her nephew, who was seated in the gallery, to come forward. He did, and set a briefcase on the defense table and opened it. Inside were stacks of cash that most certainly appeared to be in the range of one hundred thousand dollars.

"You cannot prove this is real," Scott said as he stood up. "Nobody here has this kind of money to just throw around."

"Ms. Gonzalez, why did you give up the money and tell us this?" Ben asked, as he continued examining the witness.

"Some things are more important than money, Mr. Bailey. I don't need the money, but I do need to be able to live with myself. And I know the DNA test didn't find any evidence on Braxton's body, the weapon, or the note that connected Dwight Kerry to the crime."

Ben nodded. It was more than a mere affirmation. It was a declaration: he was done for the day, and so was the credibility of Scott Stevens. He turned to Scott and smiled. "No further questions."

18: Day of Absolution

The mid-morning sunlight radiated purity. The sky was singing the blues and the clouds were listening, jiving gently back and forth above the craziness of the town and the chaos that persisted there. It was the final day of the trial; the final day of Freeden versus Dwight, of fundamentalism versus progress. It was a back and forth game of Texas Hold Em', and Ben was ready to play his ace.

"The defense would like to call Ian Christopher to the stand."

Dale Jones looked as white as a ghost when Ben uttered his name. Dr. Henson, who had yet again joined Dale in the front row behind the prosecution table, sat emotionless, not taking his eyes off the jurors, ensuring that they continued to know he was present. But Dale Jones was nowhere near as talented in hiding his emotions. From his outbursts in court to his easily readable body language, Dale Jones almost always let everyone know, in some way or another, what was on his mind.

Ian Christopher, the young boy Kate had worked hard to bring to the forefront, walked forward to take the stand. He looked nervous as he approached the witness box, as any eighteen-year-old probably would, but Ben knew he was unequivocally the best chance Dwight had at being acquitted. And while every bit of the prosecution's evidence bore gaping holes that undeniably left their case in doubt, Ben knew the trial was not over. Like a football team with an awful defense, Ben knew he had to keep scoring if he wanted to win. Ian's testimony, without question, would have to put a metaphorical nail in the prosecution's coffin, or Dwight's future would be in jeopardy.

"Young man, will you state your name for the court," Ben said.

"Ian Christopher," he said nervously.

"Are you okay, Ian?"

"Yes," he said, "just uneasy."

"Uneasy?"

"Yes, just nervous. I haven't talked about this to anyone, really."

"Well, let me tell you something, Ian. It's okay to tell the truth. So that's all you have to do, okay?"

"Yes, sir."

"So you've been recruited for basketball by the Duke Blue Devils, yeah?"

"Yes, sir."

"That's quite a big honor, to play division one basketball."

"Thank you, sir."

"I'm sure you're a pretty popular guy on campus at Freeden High, being a soon-to-be Duke Blue Devil."

His cheeks turned red when he blushed. "Not really sure. I guess people like me."

Ben chuckled. "I've heard you have a reputation on campus. I've heard everybody likes you."

"I don't know, maybe?" he said, smiling.

"I also know you lost someone very dear to you on May 25th."

Ian's smile turned to a frown, and he began to tear up. "Yes," he paused, "I did."

"Tell the court about your friendship, Ian."

"Well, it's hard for me to say this in public, but I know I

have to, for Braxton."

Ian hesitated, and Ben grew nervous. He knew that Ian would be voluntarily placing himself under a microscope, but he had to keep believing that Ian would be brave and do the right thing.

Ian took a deep breath. "We were in love."

The majority of the gallery looked astonished.

"Oh, here we go," one person said.

"Jesus Christ," Dale said. "That's a lie."

Chatter filled the gallery.

Judge Freeman leaned forward. "Order."

"It's okay, Ian," Ben said. "Don't worry about anybody out there."

Ian nodded to let Ben know he understood.

"Go on," Ben said.

"Okay." He paused. "We were friends for a long time, but our relationship grew. One day this past spring, we went to a movie together, like we always did. I wanted to be in a relationship with him. I loved him. We were both very nervous, though. He held my hand at the movie that night, and later we kissed. He told me he was scared to tell anyone. I knew he was scared to tell his parents. He loved them very much and worried about how they may react."

"Did he tell you that he talked to anyone about his sexual identity other than you?"

"Yes, he told me that he told Mr. Kerry."

"Did he give you any indication on how that conversation went?"

"Yes, he told me Mr. Kerry made him feel really good about it, and that he was very supportive. He also told Mr. Kerry about *us*."

"Did he indicate that Mr. Kerry ever made any sort of

inappropriate gesture or remarks toward him?"

"No, definitely not. Mr. Kerry wouldn't do that, and Braxton told me everything. I would have known that."

"How did your relationship with Braxton seem to affect his life? Was he depressed? Happy?"

"He was so happy. I was so happy. I really think we were meant for one another."

Ben could hear the sarcastic chatter from the gallery, kept to a lower volume this time as not to warrant suppression from Judge Freeman.

"When was the last time you saw Braxton in person?"

"May 5th."

"What did you do that day?"

"We went out with friends that evening, and I drove him home. I kissed him in the car before he got out, and then he walked inside the house. That's the last time I ever saw him."

"Did he appear sick to you that day or any days leading up to the final day you saw him?"

"No, he wasn't sick. He was never sick with mono."

"How do you know this?"

"I got worried about him because not only had I not seen him at school, but he had stopped calling and texting me. At first I thought he was mad at me, but then I started going by the house and never saw a light on in his room – on any night during that time period. So I started to think something was wrong."

"So what did you do, Ian?"

"I paid an unannounced visit to the Jones residence," he said. "Mrs. Jones came to the door, she was very nice. I pushed a little on why Braxton wasn't at school, and I told her it didn't seem like he was sick at all the last time I had seen him. That's when Mr. Jones walked up, and she disappeared. He suggested that I should leave."

"How did he do that?"

Dale looked visibly nervous to Ben.

"He told me that I should go so that nothing would get out that I wouldn't want to be made public. He implied that, whatever he was talking about, it might embarrass my family and keep me from going to Duke."

"Was he talking about your sexuality?"

"I think he was. And then I knew for sure on May 25th."

"How did you know for sure on May 25th?"

"I went by the school to talk to Mr. Kerry that afternoon and he wasn't there. Then I went to the Jones house again. Ms. Jones answered the door and she was very emotional. I asked if she was okay, and she told me Braxton had become disoriented from his medicines and left the house while she was taking a nap, so I immediately drove to our spot."

"What do you mean *your spot*?"

"We had a place we hung out in my car down by the river. A place we could talk and just be ourselves, not worrying about what people in the town think. I went there, and he had left this note." He pulled it out from his pocket. "I found it there in an envelope taped to the bench we always sat on beside the river when the weather was nice. I didn't really think I would find anything by going there, but then I did." He began crying more. "But I was too late."

"Can the court see the note?" Ben asked. He looked over at Dale and Scott, who both looked gravely concerned. It was obvious that they did not know about the note, but Ben had known about it since Sunday. Given the unfairness of the trial, he had chosen to not reveal it until today because he didn't want to give them time to prepare on how to influence the jury any further. This was the ace in the hole Ben desperately needed when it mattered most.

"Yes," Ian said, wiping the tears from his eyes with his shirt sleeves.

"Do you mind if I read this to the court, Ian?"

"No, sir."

"Okay." Ben unraveled it and read. "Ian, I love you. I would have texted you, but I can't find my phone. I hope I'll see you again, but I don't know what's going to happen to me. I've been locked in my basement for a couple weeks. I told my Dad I was gay. He beat me and threw me down the basement steps. I'm going to find Mr. Kerry this afternoon and ask for help. I'm so scared. If something happens to me, I love you with all my heart and I always will. Braxton."

Silence. Nothing but silence. No one said a word. Ben looked at Judge Freeman and said, "Your Honor, I'd like for this letter to be submitted as evidence. And I'd like to note that the handwriting matches that of the academic work the prosecution submitted as evidence."

"Very well," Judge Freeman said, after examining the letter.

"Your Honor," Ben said, "the defense rests."

Still, no one said a word. The shock from what had just been read, which correlated exactly with what Ben had said when he cross-examined Dale, fit the puzzle too well to be denied any longer. Ben had done everything he knew to do for Dwight. He walked back to the defense table, the room still silent, and patted Dwight on the back. Dwight grabbed Ben's right hand with his left, and covered his hand with his right, smiling at Ben, and realizing that Ben had done absolutely everything he could.

Scott stood up, looking as if he realized this was the biggest blow the prosecution had taken yet. In actuality, Scott worried the letter, which he was completely unaware of, may prove to be a moment the State could not overcome. He realized, at this point, the influence Dr. Henson had on this community was about the only hope they had for a conviction. He still wanted to believe Dwight committed the crime, but the thought of Dale locking his son up for weeks made him worry that, perhaps, Dale wasn't the guy he thought he was. He did not know what to think -- or what to do.

Scott approached the witness stand and examined the letter. The handwriting, he noticed, was strikingly close to Braxton's handwriting from the school work the prosecution had obtained, and it was also close to the handwritten note left at the murder scene. He didn't know what to think now.

"Um," he started, "Mr. Christopher. Uh, uh… let me ask you this question." Realizing he had to move and start saying something, he hurried along. "Do you understand that you're under oath, and are accusing Mr. Dale Jones of a pretty serious crime? You've practically said he had something to do with his son's murder! Do you realize that?"

"I'm not saying he murdered his son, but something happened and I do believe his father knew about it. It's too coincidental. But Dwight Kerry, he had nothing to do with this."

"How can you be sure of that?"

"Because I also stopped by his classroom that afternoon at around three-thirty, and he was already gone for the day."

"So when you said earlier you went to see Mr. Kerry, you meant at his classroom?"

"Yes, sir."

"So you were, in fact, at the classroom that afternoon as well?"

"Yes, sir."

"How do we know you aren't in cahoots with Mr. Kerry to

commit the crime? As far as we know, you two are the only ones that have claimed to have been there."

"Objection, your Honor," Ben said, "the witness is not on trial and there is no proof that any such thing occurred."

"Sustained."

Scott tracked back a bit. "Are you telling the court today that you are a practicing gay, Mr. Christopher?"

"I am gay, Mr. Stevens. I was born this way," he paused, looking down, working to muster the courage to say what he had to say, "and while it isn't easy being gay in a place like Freeden, I still love who I am, and neither you nor this town will change me. It's not a choice I made, it's not a choice Mr. Kerry made, and it's not a choice Braxton made. And until you and the rest of this town start to realize that, you'll keep hating who we are – merely because you don't understand."

Scott chuckled, then turned to the jury. "You see, this is exactly the problem, ladies and gentlemen of the jury. That young man right there is the epitome of what our world is coming to. Pure-T-filth." He paused for effect, then said, "You decide who you want to believe – a faith-driven man who loved his boy or," he pointed to Ian, "a condemned-to-hell homosexual who was probably paid cash to be here. Follow your conscience, ladies and gentlemen of the jury. Follow your faith." He paused again. "The State rests, your Honor."

The court recessed, and once it returned to session, Judge Freeman, whose demeanor had clearly started to change in the previous two days of the trial, sat up in his seat, adopting a more neutral posture. He turned to Scott Stevens. "Proceed with your closing statement."

Scott slowly walked over to the jury. In his typical salesman approach, he turned on the charm, seeking to pitch to the jury one last time that Dwight was the perpetrator.

"We have spent the last few days hearing from witnesses brought forward by both the prosecution and the defense. You've heard from the victim's father, and seen for yourself that the handwritten note at the murder scene, which simply read 'Dwight Kerry', matched the boy's handwriting. You have seen the real DNA report, signed by the state medical examiner, which implicates one man and one man only: Dwight Kerry. You have heard from Chief Gary McDowell, the respectable leader of Freeden's finest police force, who showed you that he is certain the evidence leads to Dwight Kerry. And you have heard Dr. Dan Henson, perhaps the most respected pastor in the area, and certainly in our town, tell you that he was worried Dwight may do something, and that on the day the boy died, Braxton called him seeking help from a superior coming onto him. Now the defense has tried to show you that it could be someone else, but let's face the facts here."

He paused, pacing in front of the jury box. "It's obvious what happened. Chief McDowell has not gone on the stand to lie to you. The world is trying to tell us the police force is corrupt nowadays, but you know how good the police here in Freeden are. And you know Chief McDowell to be a fine man, too. And Dr. Dan Henson, a pastor of the Christian faith, has also not taken the stand and lied to you. And Dale Jones, the victim's father and a prominent member of our community, would not get on the stand and lie about his son's death. Ben Bailey and the defense have pitched a ludicrous assault on your community, institutions in your community, and values that Freeden holds dear. You have to make a decision here. Ben Bailey was hired, and paid good money I'm sure, to pitch to you everything his law school trained him to do, working to convince you that the defendant is not guilty beyond a reasonable doubt. Use your heart, and remember that if you vote not guilty to Dwight Kerry, an academically gifted and intelligent boy with a bright future, a good boy who loved his community and was a faithful servant of God, will have died in vain."

Scott paused once more. "Have you heard anything here in the last several days that make you believe someone else could have done this? No, you haven't. Ben Bailey wants you to believe someone else did this, but won't tell you who it is. That's because deep down, even he knows that the man who did this," he pointed to Dwight, "is sitting right there." Scott looked at the jury for a few seconds longer, then walked back to the prosecution table.

"Counsel?" Judge Freeman said. "Your closing statement."

"Thank you, your Honor." Ben started to stand, but Dwight grabbed his shoulder with his left hand and pulled him back down.

"What are you doing?" Ben asked in a soft voice.

Dwight whispered, "I want to give my own closing statement."

"No, I don't think that's a good idea."

"Ben, you've done all you can. Let me tell these people what I have to say."

"Counsel?" Judge Freeman asked. "Is everything alright?"

"Dwight," Ben whispered back, "once you've used our time for a closing statement, that's it. You understand that, right?"

"Yes, I do. Now please, let me do what I have to do."

Ben was startled, but nodded and agreed to allow it. He hoped this would not undo anything he had worked hard to do. All he wanted was to save Dwight from a guilty verdict. This is what Dwight wanted, though, and Ben knew he must afford him the opportunity.

Ben stood up. "Your honor, my client would like to give his own closing statement."

"Wait," Judge Freeman said, "Mr. Kerry intends to speak on his own behalf?"

"Yes, your Honor," he said, "if you would allow it."

Judge Freeman sighed, then rubbed his face with his hand. He sighed again. "Go ahead, Mr. Kerry. But you're using your time to speak, and I will not allow Mr. Bailey to speak after you, no matter how this goes. Understood?"

"Understood, your Honor," Dwight said as he stood up.

Donned in his grey jail jumpsuit, Dwight walked over to the jury box. Once he was stood in front of the jurors, he interlocked his hands and held them down around his abdomen. "I'm not really sure what you all thought of me before now, or what you think of me now," he started. "I can't decide that for you, but in this brief moment, I would like to tell you about me and what I think of myself.

Dwight smiled. "I was born here in Freeden, and after college, I moved back here to take care of my ailing mother. Once she passed, I didn't really feel like I belonged here, but I stayed nonetheless and the rest is history. I've taught and directed music for Freeden Baptist Church and the Freeden concert hall for decades. I love all of it. I will miss all of it, because no matter what you decide, all that is over for me now. But I worry much less about myself than I do two much more pressing matters."

He started to break from his stiffness and return to the Dwight that Ben knew, strongly gesturing with his hands and arms as he spoke. "The most pressing matter is that a student of mine, and a friend, had his life stolen from him. Whether you think I did this or not, that's a moot point to me because I know I didn't do it, and so long as I'm at peace with that, I'll be all right. I've lived a long life, and a fairly good one I might add. Braxton won't get the opportunity to do that, unfortunately."

Dwight was fighting back the tears. "Braxton did tell me in the weeks before he died that he was gay, and that he had feelings for Ian, and I could tell he was worried about how the community he had grown up in would respond. I was, too, really. I have known for some time what it is like to be gay in a small, rural town like Freeden. It's difficult, and while none of you in the jury may know that, I assure you that for many years of my life, if I could have chosen not to be gay, I would have undoubtedly made that decision. You may believe it's a choice, but I assure you that I would never have elected to put myself through the hell of being looked down upon in this town like I have been if I could have made a choice to avoid it. But now, I am happy about who I was born to be. I'm proud that I was an example to Braxton and showed him that it's okay to be who you are. Now, I know it's hard for you all to understand this. If none of you are gay, then you wouldn't understand. But what I hope you can come to understand is that just because I'm gay, and different from most of Freeden, doesn't mean I'm a freak. It doesn't mean I don't love God, and it doesn't mean I don't have morals or values. It just means I'm different from you, and is that really such a bad thing?"

Dwight chuckled. "And for the record, Scott Stevens seems to think Ben did this for the money. Ben Bailey didn't get paid a dime for this. Everybody thinks I have money… shit, I live paycheck to paycheck just like the rest of you, okay? He hasn't charged me anything. His entire team has not gotten paid a thing to defend me. They just did it because they believe in me."

Ben and his staff had been crying since Dwight started his closing statement, but all of them along with Kate and Terri, who sat in the back of the courtroom, were weeping now.

Dwight was ready to wrap things up. "If you vote guilty, you're flat out wrong because I didn't do this. But this trial isn't about if I did it or not. You know that DNA report was falsified, and I'd bet most of you believe that Dale probably knows more than he says. And after hearing Ian speak, I'd bet most of you are truly considering what he said to be true. But this is not a trial about whether I did it or not. It's a trial on my identity. And perhaps one day, this town will learn from the mistake it made here, and become a more accepting people. If that's what all this was about, and if it will one day lead the people in the town I grew up in to be more tolerant toward people different from them, then the heartache and tragedy that resulted from this wrongful accusation, and subsequent trial, will have been worth it."

Ben couldn't believe how emotional he had become. He knew he had dispelled every bit of evidence the prosecution brought to the table, and a reasonable doubt unquestionably existed, but nothing he could have said in the closing statement could have proven more valuable than the words Dwight had just spoken.

Dale appeared genuinely upset, pointing at Judge Freeman while talking to Lucy as if he should have stopped Dwight's statement. But Ben truly believed Judge Freeman was growing sympathetic to the defense's cause.

He looked down, rubbing his forehead and trying to relieve himself of tension. "Okay," he began, as he looked up at the jurors, "the jury is now instructed to deliberate in the jury's quarters, and do so until a unanimous decision is agreed upon, that being guilty or not guilty. If all twelve jurors come to a unanimous decision, that decision will represent the verdict. If all twelve jurors do not come to a unanimous decision, then that will lead to a hung jury and the case will likely go to re-trial. It is up to you, the jury," he emphasized strongly, "to know that beyond a reasonable doubt the defendant is guilty. The State has the burden of proof upon it, meaning that they must prove, beyond a reasonable doubt, that the defendant committed the crimes he is charged with. If the jury believes there is a reasonable doubt, it should return a verdict of not guilty. Have I made everything clear?"

The jury foreman rose from his seat. "Yes, your Honor."

"Very well. The court is recessed until the jury deliberates and returns a verdict."

The day of absolution had come. After four long days of trial, and only weeks removed from the original arrest, Ben's worries of the trial not going as planned had ceased. No matter what happened now, he believed he and his team had done all they could, under adverse conditions, to exonerate Dwight in the trial. As the court recessed for jury deliberation, he realized that the fate of Dwight Kerry now rested in the hands of the jury – a body of people he hoped and prayed would, despite the influence around them to convict, do the right thing.

But Ben worried doing the right thing wasn't a given here.

19: Finis

Other than the few Freeden police officers and county deputies that stayed to ensure Dwight Kerry did not leave the room, the courtroom was practically empty. Ben and Dwight were the only people involved in the trial to occupy the room, both sitting at the defense table.

"Thanks for working it out for us to stay here while this is going on," Dwight said, referring to jury deliberation.

"Judge Freeman made it happen," Ben said. "Did you notice he grew a little softer as time progressed?"

"I did."

"Perhaps he sees it now, what's really going on."

"It's been fairly easy to see, in my opinion."

"Judge Freeman is good pals with Dale and Dr. Henson. I think his judgement was clouded."

"So what do you think will happen, Ben?"

Ben sighed. "Dwight, I can't see how they can reach a guilty verdict. I just can't. If this was taking place anywhere else, the jury would only take ten minutes to deliberate. I think it's pretty obvious you didn't do this. The jury is only tasked with determining if there is a reasonable doubt. There's that and a whole lot more here."

"I see," he said as he looked down at the table, his mind visibly wondering elsewhere.

"Are you okay?" Ben asked, noticing his behavior.

"I'm quite well, actually," Dwight said.

"Well, you don't look it," Ben answered. "I know you're

worried, Dwight. I think it's obvious that you're not guilty, and I started to see some of the jurors change their minds. All we need is one of them to go our way. My team documented every single reaction from the jury. Liz and Kristen both told me they believe at least three people on the jury were completely swayed. I think we've got this."

"Ben," Dwight said.

"Yeah?"

"I feel like I need to say a few things to you, before the jury comes back with a decision."

"Okay," Ben answered cautiously. "What do you need to say?"

"To be as straightforward as I can be, I want you to know that I truly believe they are going to return a guilty verdict."

"Dwight, that makes no sense, there's nothing about what we did, or what the prosecution did, that would warrant a guilty verdict."

"It makes no sense to you and me," he agreed. "But don't forget where we are, Ben. This is Freeden, and you've seen how people are here. Stubborn, hypocritical, judgmental. It makes no sense that I am accused of this crime, I get that. But despite the work you've done that I believe vindicates me, people are still standing in the streets calling for me to die. People are still shouting in the courtroom at me -- at you. We live in a place where people have their minds made up about what they want to believe already, and nothing you can say or do will change that."

"But I'm telling you, Dwight, all we need is one person to vote not guilty and stick with it, and we'll eventually get a not guilty verdict, or we will get a new trial, hopefully with a new jury, and maybe not here so we can get a fairer situation."

"Ben," he said. "I'm seventy-one years old. I've lived a good life. Sure, I hope they return a not guilty verdict, but damnit if they don't, then you've got to do something with this."

"We'll appeal, we'll get you vindicated, I promise."

"Ben," he said again, "that's not what I mean. Just promise me that whatever happens, you won't give up on the real problem here, okay? And you know what that is. No matter what, this is our home, too, and I've always tried to make it better. We have to keep working to make it better."

"Okay, but–"

A door swung open and Judge Freeman ascended from his chambers and into the courtroom. "Mr. Bailey," he said. "Can I see you in my office for a moment?"

Ben looked at Dwight, then at Judge Freeman. "Sure." Then he walked over to the chamber entry from the courtroom, and the door closed behind him.

"Yes, your Honor?"

Judge Freeman walked back to this desk chair and sat down. "Mr. Bailey, there's something I need to tell you."

"Okay."

"My conscience will not be clear unless I get this off my chest. And I'm not sure what kind of reaction you will have to this, but I've decided that doesn't matter. I must tell you."

Ben raised an eyebrow. "Okay. What's going on?"

Judge Freeman sighed. "I don't believe Dwight did this."

"You think? It seems pretty obvious I'd say."

"Yes, it does. But I don't know what we can do now."

"Tell me, Judge Freeman, did Dale Jones have anything to do with this?"

He shook his head. "I don't know. I know he has told me in private conversation some things that are really concerning, and it makes me wonder, especially after what you've brought to light in court. I would like to think he's not involved, but what you showed in court seems rather overwhelming to me. If that is true, then I just don't know what to think."

"Not to be too harsh, your Honor, but you and the rest of the good-'ole-boy network is the reason we are sitting here right now. They are the reason that an innocent, framed Dwight Kerry is sitting in that courtroom waiting to find out if he is going to jail for the rest of his life or not. You've got to do something about this."

"I don't know that I can, Mr. Bailey," he answered, still shaking his head. "Not now."

"What do you mean?"

"Too many people involved."

"Too many people involved?" Ben exclaimed. "Jesus Christ! Tell me, is he involved? Dr. Henson – is he in on this set-up job, too?"

"You know I don't know that."

"Bullshit! You do know."

"Mr. Bailey, I hope the jury will work this out the right way so we can move on."

"Move on? Move on you say? How the fuck is Dwight going to move on from this? Guilty, not guilty, it doesn't matter. The man will never be able to get his life back. Do the right thing and tell me, do you know if Dr. Henson is in on this?"

He stuttered. "I–I… I don't know for sure, but I think so, yes."

"Jesus Christ," Ben said as he stood up, shaking his head. "What the hell are you going to do about it?"

"You know I can't do anything."

"What do you mean?"

"Don't you know?"

"Know what?"

"How he got to be senior pastor over there at Freeden Baptist?"

"What? I don't know what you're talking about."

Judge Freeman wiped his hand across his face from his forehead to his chin, then sighed once more. "Listen, I am warning you, don't cross that man. You've already fucked up by leaving his daughter. That's extremely embarrassing to his family, and once he's done with your friend Dwight, he is coming after you. You can bet your bottom dollar. Please, just get out of town after this, for your own good. He's a dangerous man."

Ben just stood there, looking out the window onto the street where hundreds of people still stood, chanting and holding signs high above their head, calling for Dwight to be convicted and justice to be rightfully served. "Look at this," he said, pointing at them. "You and whoever else really knows what's going on, this is on *you*. The people that have been beaten, Dr. Johnson's medical career, my soon-to-be folded law practice and my staff who won't have jobs because we have been isolated so much, and most importantly, an innocent man's life… that shit is on you all. And I wouldn't be at all surprised if Braxton's death is on the hands of the same people, too."

Ben walked toward the door.

"Mr. Bailey, please."

"What?" Ben asked, as he got ready to walk out the door.

"Please don't get me disbarred for what I've told you. I wanted a clean conscience. I had to tell you something was going on here."

Ben chuckled in the most sickened way. "My God. And you people still don't care about anything but yourselves." He walked out, back into the courtroom.

Two days passed with no decision. Dwight was ushered to and from the jail to shower and eat, protesters still filling the streets and throwing food and trash at the transport truck every time he was being moved. He would look out onto the streets from his view out the front of the truck, close his eyes, and pray for them. Dwight had never felt closer to God than he did now. Coming to peace with whatever may happen was not easy for him, but after many sleepless nights in his jail cell where his mind simply wondered all over the place, he had come to peace with whatever may happen. No matter the outcome of the trial, he realized his time as a teacher, contrary to what he believed in the days following his arrest, was far from over. This moment, no matter the result, was his chance to teach the greatest lesson of his life.

I have found my purpose for coming back home all those years ago.

On the third day, the jury ascended from the deliberation room with a decision. Freeden police got the call to bring Dwight back to the courtroom. People started to trickle into the courtroom around nine-thirty a.m., and court was supposed to return to session at eleven for the announcement. Ben had stayed in the courtroom overnight; he just could not leave. All he could think about was what he would do if the jury returned a guilty verdict. To him, it seemed obvious from the beginning what was going on, and Judge Freeman, whose conscience had gotten the best of him, practically unveiled that more players were involved. And in his eyes, no one highlighted that list more than Dr. Dan Henson.

In a way, Ben saw this as Freeden's own Watergate scandal, but worse. The conspiracy, per Judge Freeman's confession, went all the way to the top of the town hierarchy and had taken the life of a young boy in the process. Ben could not wrap his head around it. *What would be Dr. Henson's motive to get involved in a cover-up that involved a boy's murder? Why would they go to great lengths to frame Dwight?*

It was obvious to Ben that Dr. Henson, Judge Freeman, and probably most law enforcement officials in the area knew something more was going on here, but he could not figure out why they would want to protect Dale if he had arranged this heinous crime. He had thought so the whole time, but now it was clear to him this undoubtedly had something to do with Braxton's sexual identity. He wondered if Dale had just snapped when his son told him he was gay and now was trying to cover the crime as well as he could, but still could not figure out why the other players involved would have worked so hard, together, to protect him.

If he did have something to do with this, Ben could not fathom how a man could show so little remorse in the public eye for what he had done. Ben didn't have children, but still couldn't imagine what it would be like to lose a child, let alone participate in the child's demise. *It takes a sick man to do something like this.*

If a guilty verdict was returned, he planned to fight it to the end of his time. He would not settle for Dwight going to prison for a crime that he indisputably did not commit.

"Ben?"

Ben didn't move. He still sat in a daydream, thinking about what he would do if this ended poorly for Dwight.

"Ben?"

He finally noticed Kate was talking to him.

"Hey… hey," he said, as he came to grips and escaped his trance.

"You okay?"

"Yes," he said. "Sorry, I was out there for a second."

"I could tell. I'm worried about you, you're wearing the same suit you had on yesterday."

"I stayed here overnight. Just couldn't sleep. And couldn't leave."

"Ben, this is going to work out, okay? I know you're worried sick."

"I really am, Kate. I hope this will work for him. We gave it everything."

"I know you did," she said. "If there's one thing I know about you, it's that you always do that. Don't let that worry you."

"Thank you for everything you've done, no matter what happens here. If they return a guilty verdict, what you've done alone should be enough to get this overturned in appellate court."

"Stop saying there will be a guilty verdict! You're worrying too much. One of the jurors will do the right thing, I pray. There's no way they've been back there for three days without returning a decision if they truly believed he was guilty. You know this."

"Yes, I know, but there's more to it now."

"You've done all you can for him, and whatever happens, I know this will work out."

"He doesn't deserve this. He's a good man."

"I know," she said, "but you've got to compose yourself, okay? I can't believe you stayed here all night."

"Yeah." He chuckled. "I will admit that it's taking its toll on me now." Ben seemed to be calming a bit now. Kate had that effect on him.

"I'll be sitting in the back," she said. "Good luck." She put her hand on his shoulder, and he covered it with his hand and looked up at her. Then she retreated to the back of the courtroom.

Reporters started filing in, and the gallery filled up with people anxiously awaiting the decision. Liz, Kristen, Ken, and the rest of Ben's team sat behind the defense table in a show of support for Dwight.

"You doing okay buddy?" Ken asked as he approached Ben from behind.

"Yes, how's everybody doing?"

"Worried, but just ready to know what's next."

"I'm worried, too."

"Don't be, you did everything you could. Look, you know we'll fight this if we have to. We're here for you."

"Let me step back there and say something to the guys," Ben said.

He stood up and walked up to the railing that separated the gallery from the defense table.

"Hey guys," he said to his team collectively.

"Hey, Ben," Brenda said, as she stood up and hugged him, joined by the rest of them.

"Brenda, you haven't ever been outside the office have you?" Ben asked sarcastically.

"Other than picking up lunch or dinner for you, which you never eat, then yeah, this might be the first time I've ever left work."

They all laughed. "I'm so glad you all are here," Ben said to his team. "And thank you so much, I'll never be able to repay you. All of you made sacrifices to be here, in more ways than one, and I'm so grateful for all you've done. We gave our best for Dwight, and I could not have done it without you."

"Wouldn't change a thing," Kristen said. "You know, at first I wondered if you were crazy, but I trusted you and you didn't let us down. I think we've done enough here to win this."

Ben smiled. "Thank you, Kristen. Thanks to all of you."

There was a brief pause, and then the room was brought to a silence. Ben looked behind him and saw why. Dwight was being ushered in through the side door by deputies. They released him from his handcuffs at the defense table, and he joined Ben.

"Hello, my friend," Dwight said as he hugged Ben.

Ben could not speak as he became emotional, fighting back the tears. The two held the embrace for a bit, then Ben pulled back, still holding onto Dwight's arms. "I love you, friend."

"I love you too, friend," Dwight said. "I'll never be able to thank you enough for all you've done for me." Then Dwight turned to Ben's team. "And I haven't been able to talk to you all as much as I have Ben, but thank you so much for believing in me, no matter what. I obviously didn't do this, but you all chose to believe me well before the evidence showed as much. Thank you, from the bottom of my heart. You are all my friends."

The team took turns hugging and exchanging remarks with Dwight. Ben returned to his seat, finally at a peace he had searched for throughout the last three days of jury deliberation; a peace he had searched for overnight as he sat in his chair in a dimly lit, unoccupied courtroom. Dwight was innocent, and now he wholeheartedly believed *enough* people knew it. Judge Freeman knew it, and he hoped others involved knew it, too. All he needed was one juror to have voted not guilty and convinced the others to do the same. The possibility that this would all end in the coming minutes suddenly felt incredibly real.

The jurors entered the jury box, and everyone began returning to their seats. Then, Judge Freeman entered through his chambers, and the bailiff stood for his introduction. "All rise for the Honorable Judge Phillip Freeman. The Freeden County Superior Court is now in session."

Judge Freeman entered and took his seat. "Thank you, bailiff. Please sit." Those in attendance complied.

Judge Freeman looked at Ben, who returned a rather unpleasant expression of dissatisfaction. Then he looked down, appearing to be disappointed that everything had gotten to this point, but Ben wondered if it was for the right reasons. Soon, he peered over behind the prosecution table. Ben turned to see what had caught his attention. Behind Scott sat Dr. Dan Henson, dressed in his typical black suit and red tie, who wore as blank a facial expression as he had in the previous few days. Ben looked at him, and Dr. Henson never moved. It was as if he were a statue, his presence as domineering as ever. He had worked throughout the trial to ensure his being in attendance made a difference, and Ben hoped that on this day Freeden would finally defy him and do the right thing.

Judge Freeman finally began talking. "Will the foreman please stand?"

The foreman complied, and slowly rose to his feet.

Judge Freeman nodded. "Has the jury reached a unanimous verdict?"

The foreman replied, "We have, your honor."

Ben was incredibly nervous.

"Counsel," Judge Freeman said as he looked at him, still featuring the uneasy expression he had harbored since he had entered the courtroom, "will you and your client please rise?"

Ben and Dwight stood together. Ben was nervous as he

could be, though Dwight looked composed and postured as usual. Dwight noticed Ben's anxiousness, and put his arm around Ben to comfort him.

"Please read the decision," Judge Freeman said.

"On the counts of first-degree murder and first-degree statutory rape, we the jury find the defendant..."

On that day, Freeden changed forever. If the verdict had been a movement in *Requiem*, then its title would have been "Reus." Reus was the Latin word for guilty.

PART 5: BENEDICTUS

20: Lux et Veritas

Daniel George Henson grew up in Freeden, the son of a modest, working-class mother and father who both worked as laborers in the textile mills of Freeden's manufacturing heyday. Recognizing that his parents lived paycheck to paycheck in the best months, he longed to live a life, like some of his friends' families did, that did not require such a frugal lifestyle. He wanted to be better than, in his words, the "poor existence" his mother and father maintained.

He was raised in the Baptist church, Southern Baptist to be specific, who in its day was even more fundamentally conservative than it was in modern-day Freeden. In the Southern Baptist church of old, the woman had a place in society and she was expected to stick to it. As far as he knew, responsibilities of the woman included submitting to her husband, serving the family by having meals ready when they should be, keeping the house in order, raising the children, and so on. His father had told him many years before that the man of the household was expected to be the provider for their family, and the unchallenged leader of the home.

His parents complied with those expectations and raised him to be this way. After graduating from Freeden High School in 1972, his excellent academic record afforded him a full academic and music scholarship at Wake Forest University, where he began his undergraduate studies in the September of that same year.

This was the first time he had ever left Freeden, because his family could not afford to travel when he was growing up.

After undergraduate school, he attended Southeastern Theological Seminary and later received his PhD in Theology. In 1980, he returned home to Freeden after being hired by the senior pastor, Robert Williams, to serve as associate pastor of Freeden Baptist Church. This was his ticket to be somebody who mattered in his hometown, a luxury he had never enjoyed.

He was soon reunited with his longtime high school friend, Grace, and two years later, married her.

After thirty-eight years of marriage, he had never felt romantically attracted to Grace. The two were merely friends and always had been. Grace, on the contrary, loved him with a passion and felt very attracted to him. Dan was attracted to her personality, which is why he was able to make it work, but he never fell in love with her or felt attracted to her like a husband should be to his wife. Besides being a friend, she was simply an object of his using to supplement his desire to gain notoriety and be somebody in Freeden. And she was a very important piece in the puzzle to his rise to power; her heavy involvement and leadership in church, covered-dish potluck suppers, women's conferences, and other church functions was exactly what he needed to integrate himself further in the community and become a serious contender for the position he had always wanted: senior pastor.

In 1984, Dan and Grace gave birth to Rachel, their first and only child. Dan wanted to have a child, but more importantly he knew a family would thrive more in Freeden than just him and Grace as a couple. As the church body fell in love with him and his family, his power continued to increase, and his influence continued to grow stronger in Freeden.

Dan Henson's parents both died in a car accident in 1990

after being hit by a drunken driver. After their funeral, Dan stood over their graves long after the crowd left, and thought to himself just before he walked away, *I am no longer the poor son of Trevor and Harriet Henson. I am Daniel George Henson, and I will be better than the peasant servants you were.*

Over the years he counseled, led worship, and often preached Sunday evening services, but he wanted to take over the church and become the metaphorical king of Freeden Baptist. After all, the majority of citizens attended Freeden Baptist. Church leadership reigned supreme in Freeden.

He waited with considerable patience, but he knew he would not be satisfied until he became *the* leader of the church. Over time, he convinced himself he was a prophet of God that had come to restore Freeden to a town that recognized and respected moral values. In his mind, Pastor Robert Williams, the man who hired him and gave him an opportunity to come back to Freeden and pastor his home church, was an obstacle to his climb to Freeden royalty. He simply had to go.

Without explanation, within weeks Robert Williams resigned as senior pastor of Freeden Baptist Church after having served there for over twenty years. He expeditiously left town, also without explanation, and never returned to Freeden again. At this point, no one even knew if the man was still alive.

A committee was formed to search for a new pastor, and in six weeks they announced to the church their decision to name Dr. Dan Henson as the new senior pastor of Freeden Baptist.

His climb to the top was complete, and for the first time in his life, he had discovered the respect that, he believed, he so rightfully deserved. On the pastor search committee that hired Dr. Henson was Dale Jones, and from that point on, the two of them forged a bond that would offer mutual benefit in the days ahead.

Dale bought into the notion that Dr. Henson was called by God to lead Freeden Baptist, and the congregation as a whole followed. A town ridden with sin and infidelity needed someone like Dr. Henson to lead it. And from that point on, things started to change in Dr. Henson's favor.

The already large attendance grew even stronger, and a crusade of sort took over Freeden. Friends and neighbors claimed they and their families had found Christ again, and unprecedented church growth led to more and more people coming to Freeden Baptist to hear what Dr. Henson had to say. His sermons were as powerful and dominating as his presence, and people began to believe every word he said as if Jesus Christ himself had spoken them.

He preached a prosperity gospel that reduced the wealthy's paranoia of losing all they had, and afforded the poor a hope that they, with no effort of their own, would possess everything they needed in life if they simply trusted in God.

Everyone listened to him. And as time progressed, his messages became more fierce. More stern. More pointed.

He staunchly opposed the growing global LGBTQ movement, and made clear in his sermons it was an abomination. He preached that abortion was flat wrong, with no exceptions. He preached that the new generation of young people around the world would, through filth and immorality, lead the world to hell. In this church that offered a place for both the "money" of Freeden and the typical, socio-economically poor residents of rural North Carolina, his fundamental, extremist ideology, and theology, found a home that grew his church, and simultaneously, a dangerous scorn toward those who disagreed with his principles.

In Freeden, Dr. Henson had developed a following that

rapidly shot him to the top of the totem pole. His rise to power and fame had culminated, so he continued to preach the message of devout intolerance toward anything not consistent with fundamental thought, and every Sunday the sermons kept getting more and more radical. As far as he could tell, the people of Freeden bought every bit of what he was selling -- and he relished it.

After a while though, rumors of church members committing adultery and sleeping around in sex parties with other members came to the forefront, but Dr. Henson did not care. His legacy and following were cemented; the religious crusade of Freeden had met a climactic point, yet the adulterers never missed a Sunday and the tithes and offerings kept pouring in. His empire never ceased when the faith movement that accompanied his rise to power ended; quite simply, people in Freeden were *not* going to miss church. He knew people saw it as a social event more than a true worship experience, but he also knew he had created a following where it was now unpopular not to attend church. He had created a following strong enough where local business owners knew if they did not attend church their sales would suffer; he had created a need for the church so strong in the community that even politicians knew they had no chance until he and his church endorsed them. Both Scott Stevens and Judge Freeman had sought the endorsement of Dr. Henson, and once he afforded it to them, they both won their first elections by landslides. He knew his power in Freeden was tremendous, and it satisfied him.

The congregation overwhelmingly believed Dr. Henson was the guide in which they should follow. And he fed their false faiths, preaching sermons in support of old, rudimentary ideals and messages that favored what his radically right-wing congregation wanted to hear. With adultery running amok in the church, though, he never uttered a word about it in his sermons. His messages were tailored, designed only to improve his status and respect in Freeden.

Dr. Henson was satisfied; his congregation collectively drank from the pool in which he led them. Except for Dwight Kerry.

Beginning with his first few days as associate pastor of the church, he and Dwight never meshed. From the beginning of his tenure, Dr. Henson could tell Dwight did not like him. He often wondered if Dwight was jealous of him, but he unequivocally knew Dwight did not care for his style or what he considered to be "Bible-based theology." Dwight was a thorn in his side, and he knew he had to watch out for him so long as he was there.

Dwight, though looked down upon for his sexuality, still found notoriety in the community in the years prior to his arrest, impressing the congregation with his music, making a name for himself as one of the best, most-respected teachers at Freeden High School, and also a cultural staple in North Carolina for his work at the concert hall. Dr. Henson, who spent years building his new empire, despised Dwight for being gay, which he viewed as completely contrary to both his and God's teachings. He hated the respect Dwight was paid in the community for his talents, and how out-of-towners came to see Dwight's musical work; he didn't think Dwight deserved such praise since he contrasted so greatly with how he thought God's followers should behave. He viewed Dwight as a demonic force against God Himself, and feared he would ultimately bring the "ideas of the world," as he often referred to them, into Freeden. *This cannot happen in my kingdom*. Every day he had to see Dwight, he hated him more.

When the time came, he planned to rid of Dwight Kerry once and for all.

One Saturday evening, Dr. Henson's phone rang, and he answered.

"Yes?"

"Pastor, this is Dale. I need to speak with you. Can you meet me at the church?"

"Dale," he replied to acknowledge he knew who it was, "yes, of course."

Dr. Henson hurried to the church, and Dale was already waiting in his office.

"Are you okay?" Dr. Henson asked as he walked in and shut the office door.

"No," Dale said in a panic. "I need your help."

Dr. Henson sat down in his chair, across from Dale. "Well, you know I'll help any way I can."

"I need to know that you will not tell anyone this. Strictly between the two of us."

"Okay, sure. I haven't forgotten your support of my pastoring this church when I became senior pastor years ago," he interjected. "You are and have always been one of my biggest supporters… you have my word that I'll do anything I can for you."

"Pastor," he said as he began to cry, "my son told me tonight that… he was gay." Dale began to sob, his face fallen into his hands.

Dr. Henson just sat there, watching Dale weep. "Okay," he said, "what did you say to him?"

"I threw him into the basement, and I told him I wouldn't let him out unless he changed his mind. I didn't know what to do."

"I see," Dr. Henson replied. "Do you think he will change?"

"I don't know," he said. "I went through his cell phone. He has been texting Lawrence's boy Ian Christopher. They hang out all the time, and apparently were in a private relationship this whole time. I'm sure Lawrence doesn't know his son is a fag, either. This is awful, Pastor, awful!"

"What kind of texts?"

"That they love each other, that kind of stuff."

"Do you think Braxton told anyone else other than you and Lawrence's boy?"

"Yes, I do. In the same text conversation, Braxton told Ian that he was going to talk to Dwight Kerry about it."

"Our Dwight?"

"Yes, *our* music director. The teacher and chorus director, Dwight."

"Do you know if he did talk to him?"

"I believe he did, yes. I found something in his room, a folder."

"What was in the folder?"

"Braxton has always been very organized... a visual person," Dale answered. "On one side of the folder in Sharpie he had written at the bottom pocket 'Yes' and the other side he had written 'No.' Nothing but blank paper was in the 'Disapprove' pocket. But in the 'Approve' pocket, he had written on an otherwise blank piece of paper the name *Dwight Kerry.*"

Like a hungry dog foaming at the mouth for its prey, Dr. Henson had just seized a tremendous opportunity to finally put the legacy of Dwight Kerry, the anti-Dan Henson, to rest for good. Homosexuality was scorned upon by his congregation, per his leadership and teachings, and this was his opportunity to end Dwight Kerry.

"Well," Dr. Henson said, "let's not jump to conclusions. Perhaps your son is confused, Dale. I think we give it a week or two. Hold him out of school, keep him where you have him, and make him feel remorse for what he has done. Make him know that God will not tolerate this type of behavior. Make him know that he shall burn eternally in hell if he makes this choice for good."

"Yes, Pastor. But what if he still defies me? What if he still wants to be this way? It will embarrass me forever, my family...."

"You must not allow your boy to be gay," he interrupted. "It is a disgrace to God and to you and Lucy, and you must make him change."

Night of the *Requiem*

Dale arrived at Dr. Henson's home around 11:30am. He knocked on the door, frantically, until Dr. Henson answered.

"Dale?"

"Pastor, is Ms. Henson home?"

"No, she won't be back for another few hours —"

"Please let me in, now."

Dr. Henson ushered Dale in and shut the door behind him. "What's wrong?"

"Braxton escaped the basement, locked Lucy in there. She's bruised from falling, and an absolute emotional wreck. This is getting out of hand, he won't give in."

"Calm down, Dale," Dr. Henson guided him to a chair in his formal living room. "Do you know where he is?"

"I have no fucking clue where he is," Dale interrupted loudly. "Excuse my language, Pastor... I don't know what to do."

Dr. Henson knew his next move may be met with dissent, but his pride and belief in his own influence had grown so much that he believed his plan could work. So he went for it.

"Dale, I think it's time to realize that a sacrifice must be made for God."

"What do you mean?"

"You must turn this ugly situation into something that can benefit God's kingdom."

"How can I do that?"

"My friend, we have someone in our midst, someone in our church, that is influencing the children of our town in an atrocious way. We must put a stop to Dwight Kerry."

"He told my son it was okay to be gay—"

"And look where that has gotten him. Look where that has gotten you."

"I'm going to kill him."

"Now, Dale, that's your heart talking and your heart is broken. In these moments we must do what is right by God, not right by our own minds."

"He made this happen. He told my son it was okay to be gay. And I should kill Lawrence's son, too."

"It's okay to be mad, Dale," Dr. Henson said, "but if you're going to react you must make a sacrifice that is just in God's eyes."

"What is that? What should I do?"

"If your son will not turn back to God, then he must die and be a sacrifice for God."

"My... my son?" Dale asked with a soft, near whisper-like voice, stuttering.

"You must protect your family name. And you must protect God's name. I know it's hard, but it's the only way that is just in God's eyes. He has given this to me, just now, in a vision. You must do this for Him -- it's your calling."

At 8:33pm that night, Braxton Jones was pronounced dead by the Freeden City Police Department, and just two hours later, Dwight Kerry was arrested for the crime.

Present

Months after the verdict was handed down, the national news had peeled away from Freeden and moved on to something else. In Ben's mind, the absurdity of the jury's unanimous decision was never properly challenged by the mainstream media once the trial ended; small-town politics didn't sell for long, and once the drama was over the media pulled away like roaches once the crumbs were devoured. Ben had no intention of appealing the decision, as requested by Dwight, and protesting had ceased in the streets of Freeden. In many ways, life had returned to normal for most people. For others, life would never be the same.

Ben Bailey closed his now valueless, fledgling firm, Bailey & Associates, and sold all its assets and split the earnings among his staff to give them a comfortable amount of time to find jobs elsewhere. He had saved enough in his life to live off of until he too found something elsewhere. His and Kate's relationship strengthened in the days following the trial, and the two decided to move as soon as everything was handled with Ben's remaining business affairs. But before he left Freeden for good, he had one last thing to do. He knew he must confront Dr. Henson.

It was a cool, fall night, and Dr. Henson was walking back home from a Wednesday night service when he was startled by a man speaking to him, who he had not seen sitting on the park bench he had just walked by.

"I wondered if you'd go back to your same routines," Ben said as he stood up from the bench. "I wondered if things would just go back to normal for you."

"Do I know you?" Dr. Henson asked, not recognizing who it was in the dark night.

"No. You never truly have. But I know you." As Ben walked forward and into the light beaming down from the street lamp, Dr. Henson recognized him.

"You son of a bitch," Dr. Henson said. "You don't know a thing about me."

"I know enough," Ben replied, "but I bet there's a lot more to know. And one day, I'm sure this town will find out all it needs to know about you."

"What is this? You confronting me in the dark of night... are you threatening me?"

"No, that would be much less satisfying."

"What is that supposed to mean?"

"Ever since I've known you, I've known how obsessed you were with being somebody. Being the *king* of this God forsaken town. Well, you got you what you wanted, but oh how the mighty shall fall."

Dr. Henson grinned. "No. That will never happen."

Ben chuckled. "Time will tell. I don't know for sure what you did, but I know damn well you were involved with Braxton's death. And the jury knew it too, at least some of them. I can't figure out if Dale paid them off, or if your prophetic influence swayed them to a guilty verdict. But I *know* you were involved."

"You don't know a damn thing."

"Let me ask you this though: did you and Dale intend for

Braxton to be raped? Murdering him because of his sexuality, now that sounds like something you'd do now that I know you. But I would imagine the raping wasn't supposed to happen. Whoever you and Dale employed to do the job, they almost screwed that up for you, didn't they?"

"You don't know a goddamn thing."

"I know this much," Ben continued. "I know that tomorrow, when they execute Dwight, there will be well over a hundred people there to support him."

"What difference does that make?"

"When all this started, nobody believed him but me. And my staff. And then Kate Gregory. And then Colin Johnson. And the lady at the town forum. And now, over a hundred people in your church have left and will be there to support a man they know is innocent. A man with a good heart, and a man that will die for good reason."

"Yes, because he is guilty."

"Oh, you know better, Danny Boy. You know better than that. And you also know that those people that will be there, many who are former members of your church now, are a sign that you are losing your grip. People are wising up."

"We can do without them. Our church has thousands of loyal members."

"Yes, but what if the rest of them start to question your theology? Your teachings? People are starting to see through you… they're starting to see through your crazy faith that claims to be Christian. Those people that will be there for Dwight tomorrow believe he was a good man who did not commit these crimes. It took them a while, but they started to see through all this. And while the rest of your congregation may be convinced, at least for the time being, of your ridiculous notion that he must have been guilty because he's gay, there's a movement of people who are mounting up against you and what you stand for."

"I will never let God's word die."

"You are not of God. Your church isn't, either. They are of themselves, and you are for you. And it's taken me a while to see that, but now I finally do." Ben started to walk away.

"Why do you want to destroy me?" Dr. Henson asked. "You must know that you will never take me down. I've made people disappear in this town… for good."

Ben stopped and turned back around to face Dr. Henson. "For a while, I did want to destroy you, Dan. I really did. But now, I just want the place I grew up loving to be better. And those people that now believe Dwight when they first believed you… it's a sign that the light and the truth will eventually be unveiled. Things can change – even here. And I believe, one day very soon, that they will."

21: Novum Cantabo in Requiem

"Please tell me you worked it out?" Dwight asked as he entered the room where he would eat his final meal.

"I did," Ben replied.

Moments later, David Ball rolled in a cart with a tray of Dwight's favorites.

"Oh my goodness," Dwight said. "You didn't forget the fried cheese, did you?"

"Damn, Dwight... needy are we?" David asked in his typical grumpy fashion. Then he broke character with a smile and uncovered the appetizer dish to reveal the fried cheese. "I would never forget."

Dwight rose from his seat and hugged David. For the first time in their long friendship, David hugged him back.

"I'm going to miss you, Dwight."

"I'll miss you too, friend. Thanks for all the memories."

Ben watched as the two old friends embraced and exchanged words. Then, Dwight kissed him on the cheek, and David left.

"Thank you, Ben," Dwight said.

"Sit down and eat before it gets cold," Ben replied with a smile.

Dwight complied. "Oh my," he said as he chewed the fried cheese, "how I have missed this."

"I hope you enjoy."

Dwight began eating. "So, you wanted to talk to me about something?"

"Yes, I did."

"Are you okay? The bitch isn't back is she?"

Ben chuckled. "Rachel, you mean? No, I haven't heard from her. She's moving on, thankfully."

"Good for you. Well then, what can I do for you?"

"It's nothing to do for me in particular, I just wanted to talk. Not surprised though, that even now you still are willing to serve others. You've been the greatest friend."

"No, *you* have been the greatest friend, Ben. You gave up everything, just for me."

"That's a matter of perspective, really."

"How so?"

"I'm leaving Freeden, Dwight. I'm starting a new life, and the prospect of it makes me happier than I can explain."

"Good for you. This place is clearly not for everybody."

"Not for us, that's for sure."

"Us? Who's us? Did you end up shacking up with that attorney lady?"

Ben laughed at the remark. "If you want to call it that. Her name is Kate, and yes, we are leaving town together. We're moving to Clearwater Beach, Florida, in the next few days. I've closed out my business affairs here. It's time to move on."

"I think so. You're so much better than this place. You'll do some real good elsewhere."

"That's funny, because I've always felt that way about you. You were more than this place ever deserved."

Dwight raised an eyebrow. "But you see, I was just what Freeden needed. A wake-up call. A stimulant to ignite a new beginning. What we went through, not just me but you as well, has gotten people thinking. Look, you remember that photo of Elizabeth Eckford from 1957 in Little Rock? The Little Rock Nine?"

A man compelled by the fairly-recent history of the civil rights era, Ben responded, "Of course, I do."

"That woman yelling behind her was named Hazel Massery. Do you remember how that photo portrayed her? Mad as hell. Adamant that Elizabeth, a black girl, would not step foot into that white high school. Do you remember?"

"Yes."

"Well, you see, that's because Hazel Massery wasn't used to the concept of a black girl being allowed into a white establishment. It was invasive to her, against societal norms. But once people saw that photo, and took a hard look at reality, it started to make less sense. Did we really run a young, minor-age girl away from the school because she was black? And as time progressed and integration occurred, the notion of black people not being allowed in public establishments became so much more outrageous. You see, Ben, this was that moment for Freeden. A guy like me, openly gay in a town that despises anything different from *their* societal norms, was never welcomed here. And then we had this moment, this moment of decision for the people of Freeden, and most of them turned against me, as expected, because I'm different from them. But some people saw the light. Some people looked at this grand picture, like the picture of Elizabeth Eckford being run off from the school building, and said, 'This doesn't seem right!' And now, more and more people will begin to see how nonsensical all this was, and ultimately, that's where you'll see real change… meaningful change, that will eventually negate these hateful feelings and lead us all, even those in Freeden, to be more accepting people."

Ben smiled, shaking his head. "No matter what you say, you are the best person I've ever known. I just wish I could still save you."

"I don't need saving from my destiny, Ben. This is my calling. I always wondered why I came back home; what my purpose was here. In fact, I even told Braxton that very thing the day he came out to me. I wondered if I would ever know for sure, and I thank God that he finally showed me before he called me home. My purpose was to come back to Freeden and be an example of love in a place that knew so little about it, and show people how to love others, and trust others, even when they're different than them. Yes, I found my purpose, Ben. And through this I've been given an opportunity to teach one more lesson to my hometown. My only hope, like all teachers, is that those watching and listening will do something with what they're taught."

"Over a hundred people will be inside today, and that's because that's all they could fit inside the building," Ben said. "So many more will be outside of the building, because they support you. Because they love you."

"I do appreciate that, Ben," Dwight said. "My hope is that they will go do something with it. Change this place."

"I feel guilty about leaving, especially after you say that."

"Don't be! When no one else stood by me, you did. Those people out there, inside the building and out, they wouldn't be here if you hadn't shown them a reason to believe me -- to believe in something different than what they're familiar with. You've made your impact. It's up to them to do the rest."

Ben began to cry. He stood up, trying to compose himself.

"When will you learn?" Dwight asked. "You don't have to bury your emotions around friends."

Dwight stood, and Ben just grabbed him. That's all he knew to do. He embraced him, all the while weeping and holding onto his friend.

"I love you Dwight," Ben said, squeezing him harder.

"I love you too, my dear friend."

Ben just held onto him. He couldn't let go. Dwight had done so much more than change Freeden's future; he had changed lives, so many lives, including Ben's. Ben attributed his new-found happiness to Dwight. He credited Dwight for giving him the courage to permanently leave an unfaithful, down-spiraling marriage. He credited Dwight for showing him what real relationships, both friendships and romantic relationships, like the one he now had with Kate, should be like. And he credited Dwight with showing him *how* to love. He had long wondered if he would ever know, but now, he knew what love was, and despite his plan to move, he promised himself to always show the love to others that Dwight had shown to him.

Minutes later, the deputy walked in the room. "Five minutes."

Dwight patted Ben on the back with his right hand as the two finally broke the hold.

Ben wiped his eyes with his sleeves, finally coming together.

"Please tell me…."

"I did." Ben reached into his bag he had brought with him and pulled out Dwight's accessories. Foundation. Eyeliner. A hairbrush. Hairspray. And his well-recognized golden cross necklace he wore when directing his church choir.

"If I'm going to do this, I'm going to look damn good, Ben Bailey."

The comment made Ben laugh. Dwight proceeded to fix himself up with his makeup, then combed his white hair back to a perfect position, spraying it down so it wouldn't move.

The deputy walked in. "It's time."

Dwight stood and hugged Ben once more. Ben began to cry

again.

"I will never forget you, Dwight Kerry."

"True friends never do," he replied.

He postured himself upright, poking out his chest as if he always did just before he directed his chorus in concert. He walked forward and the deputies guided him out of the door.

Ben waited for the door to shut, and cried once more.

Soon, he hurried into the witness room where nearly one hundred people sat. It was a large room not usually used as a witness room, but given the high demand of people who wanted to be there to support him, the maximum security prison he was housed at accommodated.

Kate met him as soon as he walked in, and the two walked to their seats on the front row.

Those in attendance included Ben's entire staff, David Ball, Dr. Colin Johnson, Terri Hathaway, Ian Christopher, and a large number of current and former student choir and community choir members. Noticeably, no one that Ben alleged had been involved in framing Dwight, or Braxton's family, were in attendance.

After an announcement from the warden that the execution was minutes from beginning, everyone took their seats, including Ben and Kate, who sat beside one another.

"I love you," Kate said.

Ben smiled. "I love you."

Within seconds, the deputies ushered Dwight into the execution room. For the first time in forever, he *looked* like Dwight. Other than not wearing the exact same clothes, he looked the same way to Ben as he had the night of the *Requiem*. Proud. Accomplished. The look that had long become associated with Dwight Kerry.

Dwight sat down on the execution table, facing the large

glass window that separated him from the witness room.

The warden approached the microphone. "For those of you in the witness room, we ask that you please remain quiet and avoid any unnecessary movements during the entire process. Thank you." Then, he said, "At this time, would you like to make a last statement, Mr. Kerry?"

Dwight stood. "Yes, may I approach the microphone?"

The warden nodded in affirmation.

Dwight stood at the microphone and blew into it, letting out a big sigh.

"I'd be lying if I told you I wasn't nervous," he said. "I don't want to die. I want to keep teaching! I want to keep playing and directing! I want to keep showing love to others, just like I've shown many of you in your lives! I see many friends out there, people I care for. I recognize each one of you. Thank you for being here for me."

Dwight choked up a bit and stopped himself for a moment. "All of this has made me shed more tears than I thought I had in me. Braxton was such a wonderful young man, and someone saw fit to take his life. Today, those same people are responsible for taking *my* life. The two of us, Braxton and I, have something very much in common. Despite the fact that I lived the life of a gay man for many years, Braxton got to experience, if just for a brief time, how it felt to be himself. And so for at least a little while, he was able to experience the same joy I did, of being the person God made him to be."

Sobs could be heard from witness room.

"And yes, I said it…God made Braxton that way. And God made me this way. I'm not a horrible person because I'm gay. I'm a decent person. I care about people, I've committed my whole life to the people of Freeden, and I don't regret a damn thing! I don't regret loving you all and making friendships with all of you, and I don't regret where I am now."

Dwight paused, and a tear dropped from his left eye when he looked down. His bottom lip quivering, he looked back up at those in the witness room and continued, "I want you to remember this day not as the day I died, but the day a new Freeden was born. It will take some time, but one day, even people here in this town will remember this as an injustice. Time will bring to light what really happened to Braxton Jones, and the veil will be lifted on how horrible people can be when they choose to shun things, and people, they simply don't understand. Yes, a new day starts now, and it's up to you all, who gave me a chance and believed in me, to change this place for good."

Ben stood up and pressed his hands against the glass as Dwight backed away from the microphone and proceeded to take his seat on the table in which the state would execute him by lethal injection. Dwight looked at Ben, now far removed from the microphone, and shouted as loud as he could so he could hear: "Ben!"

Ben looked into his eyes, and Dwight said as loud as he could, "Novum Cantabo in Requiem!"

Again, Ben began to cry and fell back into his seat as Dwight was strapped onto the table. Kate wrapped her arms around him.

Ian Christopher stood up, seated three seats from Ben, and began to sing softly, "If music be the food of love, sing on, sing on...."

Terri Hathaway, both a former student and current chorus member, joined him as she wept, "Sing on 'til I am filled with joy...."

In a moment Ben would never forget, every current and former chorus member stood to their feet, nearly the entire audience, and all of them joined in the familiar song that nearly everyone who ever served in a choir under Dwight's direction knew by heart. Dwight could hear them, and turned his head toward them and smiled. Then, he looked straight at Ben, as the audience joined together to sing:

If music be the food of love, sing on, sing on
Sing on 'til I am filled with joy,
Sing on, sing on, sing on!!!

The chorus in attendance held the last note until Dwight closed his eyes for the last time. Dwight Kerry was pronounced dead by the state at 7:22pm. But Dwight was not dead. Ben knew Dwight's memory would last forever, as a staple of the Freeden community in both his life and death.

Ben was likely the only person in the room who knew the translation for the Latin words Dwight shouted that were ultimately his final words he ever spoke: "Novum cantabo in requiem!" Ben recognized it as soon as Dwight said it: "Sing on, a new requiem."

Mozart wrote *Requiem* as an act or token of remembrance. On that day, Dwight had completed his work, a new piece that would stand out as his very own original composition that no one would ever forget. A call for the thought of old in Freeden to die, and through his sacrifice end hatred and misunderstanding once and for all.

As he faded into the afterworld, Dwight called for everyone to sing on and continue pushing the message he stood for of love, empathy, and understanding.

Ben couldn't help but smile, because on that day, a new story began. Dwight's death, unjust and uncalled for, ensured that the thought of old would one day surely die. Dwight had completed his masterpiece: A New Requiem.

CPSIA information can be obtained
at www.ICGtesting.com
Printed in the USA
LVHW090247051119
636370LV00005B/74/P

9 781925 939743